PICTURE

Fredrick D. Huebner

FAWCETT COLUMBINE · NEW YORK

POSTCARD

A Fawcett Columbine Book
Published by Ballantine Books

Copyright © 1990 by Fredrick D. Huebner

LIBRARY OF CONGRESS CATALOGING-IN-PUBLICATION DATA
Huebner, Fredrick D.
Picture postcard / Fredrick D. Huebner. — 1st ed.
p.   cm.
ISBN 0-449-90461-X
I. Title.
PS3558.U3127P5   1990
813'.54—dc20   89-91789
                                          CIP

Design by Beth Tondreau Design/Jane Treuhaft
Manufactured in the United States of America

FIRST EDITION: May 1990
10 9 8 7 6 5 4 3 2 1

PICTURE POSTCARD

ALSO BY FREDRICK D. HUEBNER
....

PUBLISHED BY FAWCETT BOOKS

The Joshua Sequence

The Black Rose

Judgment by Fire

WITH SPECIAL THANKS TO
....

Sarah A. E. McFall

and

Colleen E. Morisset

The Tao of painting is to hold the whole universe in your hand. There will be nothing before your eyes which is not replete with life, and that is why painters often become very old.

—DONG QUICHANG
Chinese "Literati" Painter
sixteenth century

PICTURE POSTCARD

....

1

I heard music spilling out of the clubs and drifting through Pioneer Square on the hot blue-lit summer night. It was the first Thursday night in August and the weather had brought scores of people out to drink and dance in the bars and restaurants lining First Avenue. They filled the sidewalks and the open doors of the cafés, caught up in the sweet delirium that summer brings to a cold northern city. Everyone was dressed for a party, the men in white slacks and open shirts, the women in bright linen dresses, their bodies tan and liquid beneath thin cloth.

At the corner of Washington Street a laughing, slightly drunken couple burst out of a music-club door, a John Coltrane blues riff trailing along behind them. The woman stumbled into me, hard enough to knock me off my stride, and I gathered her up and handed her back to her friend, accepting her laughing apology with a smile. I turned right and crossed the street to cut through Occidental Square. Here the night was darker, quieter, broken only by a sudden, muttered curse from the crowd of men gathered around the benches near the center of the brick-paved square. The men were of all races. Some of them had long braided hair and broad Indian faces. Their eyes were weary from alcohol and nights on hard pavement. They slept warily, waiting for the toe of a police boot or the sharp touch of another man's knife. Like almost everyone else who walked through the park that night, I quickened my step and turned away.

Seattle art galleries traditionally open their new shows on the first Thursday night of each month. I was on my way to the Cerebus Gallery, which had just been opened by a client of mine named Lisa Thayer. Cerebus was on Second Avenue, on the ground floor of a fine red sandstone building done in the Chicago style of the 1900's. The gallery had once been a drugstore. Lisa had designed the renovation of the space herself, and I had helped her by drafting the lease for the property and negotiating with the contractors. We had done the work as cheaply as possible, but the costs had taken all of Lisa's capital. To raise money to buy new art and stay in business, she was selling a collection of works inherited from her late grandfather, a well-known "Northwest School" painter.

By the time I arrived at the gallery the twilight had faded to blue dusk. A banner had been hung outside the gallery's double front doors. The letters were green on white silk and read, "Elton Lee Thayer: Family Paintings and Sketches, 1936–1977."

A tall man with rimless glasses and long black hair neatly pulled back with a ribbon stood outside the gallery. His face was silhouetted by the light coming from inside. He was smoking a cigarette and watching the crowd inside through the plate-glass storefront windows. He shook his head slowly as he stood there, as though suddenly ill, or somehow saddened by what he had seen. I paused in front of him, briefly concerned.

"Everything okay?" I asked.

"Fine," he said. His voice was offhand, distracted. "No. Not fine, actually. I paint. And what I've just seen in there are things I'm never going to be able to do."

"You mean Thayer?"

"What else? The man painted like God would if you gave him a brush." He dropped his cigarette on the street and crushed it with his shoe, then turned and walked slowly away, his shoulders slumped in dejection.

I shrugged. It was that sort of night, full of good and bad magic, blue lights, water smells, and carnival sounds. I smiled, embarrassed at my own superstitions. "Spirits to enforce, art to enchant," I muttered before turning to enter the gallery.

As I opened the door a wave of high-pitched conversation and warm stale air drifted out. I walked in past a group of arty college students dressed in black, eagerly sipping the usual jug white wine and talking anxiously about imagery and symbolism over-powering figuration. I nodded to a couple of lawyers I knew from some of the big downtown law firms. They were clustered to-gether, talking business while their wives roamed the outer walls, wondering whether they could afford a real Thayer, even a sketch. A couple of Iranian immigrant real-estate princes stood by the wine bar, chatting in Farsi while they eyed the women floating around the room.

Lisa's gallery had two large display rooms, with gray-painted walls and white woodwork. The front room was open to the second story, with a spiral staircase leading to a catwalk sup-ported by posts from the floor below. Lamps on ceiling tracks focused pools of light on each of the paintings and the groups of sketches mounted on the walls of both rooms. The paintings and sketches had been hung with care and balance and their arrangement gave a pleasing sense of order.

I took a glass of wine from the bar and stepped over to a group of four large black-and-white photographs that had been blown up to poster size and mounted on the far wall. Beneath the photographs was a simple printed sign that read "Elton Lee Thayer: 1917–1977."

What little I knew about Thayer had come from talks with Lisa and a few Sunday-magazine features about modern art and Northwest painting. Thirteen years after his death Thayer was finally being recognized as one of the great American painters of this century, by far the best known of the so-called Northwest School artists, along with Mark Tobey, Morris Graves, and Kenneth Callahan. I had seen some of Thayer's paintings at museums, and knew that his early work had been in the quasi-realistic style of the 1930's. In his later years, influenced by Asian art and postwar abstract expressionism, his work had become officially abstract, but I thought I could still see in his later canvases the dark waters and green rocky forms of the Pacific Northwest landscape, the pellucid oyster light of the Northwest sky.

The photographs showed Thayer at four times in his life. In the first, taken in 1937, he was a handsome but very young man of twenty, his lean sculpted face bursting with the energy of his age and the anger of the late Depression years. The second, taken in 1942, showed Thayer in a drab army uniform looking much older than twenty-five, the weariness of war etched into his features. He was leaning against the cocktail bar in a London hotel, a martini glass in one hand, a cigarette burning forgotten between two fingers of the other. In the third photograph, taken sometime in the late 1950's or early 1960's, Thayer was hunched over a worktable, brush in hand, his strong features harsh underneath a shock of graying hair. The last picture was the saddest, a frontal portrait of the artist near the end of his life. His face seemed haggard and worn, his eyes rimmed and puffy from the alcoholism that had shattered the last decade of his life. In those last years, he had been a recluse of almost paranoid intensity.

I was still lost in the photographs when Lisa Thayer burst from the crowd behind me. "Matthew!" she said, her face flushed and eyes shining with excitement as she put her hand on my shoulder and reached up to kiss me on the cheek. "I've been waiting. What took you so long?"

"Work," I said, returning the kiss. I held her for a moment, simply for the pleasure of seeing her. She wore a black wraparound cocktail dress that set off her tan skin, and her straight blond hair was up in a French twist. Her eyes were a dark gray blue, the color of water in a deep cold lake. Her face was long and her nose and jaw were too strong to be merely pretty. "You look wonderful, but everyone's probably said that already. Is it going all right?"

"All right? More than all right! We've sold over a hundred thousand dollars' worth of work since we opened! And I have to thank you for all that you've done."

"Nonsense."

"Hardly. If you hadn't bulldozed the contractors into finishing on time when they were running two weeks late, we wouldn't be here."

I acknowledged the praise with a smile. "Not necessarily true, but thank you. The show does look great. These photographs are fantastic. They give me a sense about Lee Thayer that I didn't have before."

As she turned to look at the photographs she smoothed a strand of damp blond hair from her face. "Sometimes I wonder whether I knew him at all," she said. "He died when I was a teenager, and for the last few years of his life he was remote, drinking far too much, and hardly working at all." She shook her head and turned back to look at me. "These were all family photographs. I found them just a few years ago. Which one do you like the best?"

"The World War Two picture, I think." I looked at it again, carefully. "The whole picture is impossibly romantic—London, the Blitz, the uniforms, the martini. Until you look at his eyes. Then you see that he's been in combat. Was he wounded? He has that look. The eyes look different, because he's had to confront his own mortality." I glanced back at Lisa. She looked at me oddly.

"I never thought of it that way," she said quietly. "I chose this picture for a different reason."

"Why's that?"

"The timing of it, I guess. The picture was taken around eleven in the morning. On his wedding day."

"I'm sorry," I said quickly. "I didn't mean—"

She put a hand up, palm out, to hush me. "Don't apologize, Matthew. I think I see what you do. I just hadn't made that connection. Anyway, something's come up that I need to talk to you about. Can you stay until the opening is over? It's already nine o'clock and we're scheduled to close at ten."

"That's fine. I was sort of hoping that you'd let me take you to dinner."

Lisa took my hand and held it for a moment, finally smiling again. "I was sort of hoping you'd ask," she replied. "Let's talk then. In the meantime, find a piece that you like. I want you to have something before the show sells out." She turned and worked her way back through the crowd. The life in the room seemed to follow her as she slipped away.

Lisa was something of an enigma to me. Just twenty-eight, she handled herself and her business with a control and sense of purpose that most people never developed. She had worked as an art dealer in New York and Seattle and, when it came to art, seemed to have what Hemingway used to call "a built-in shock-proof shit detector." Her goal, she said, was to avoid the trend-mongering that characterized so many other galleries and show meaningful work by new painters. But like so many strong and able women that I knew, there was something buried in that honest ambition, a core of bitterness with a cause I could not even guess at.

I moved idly around the room, pausing to study each work. Most of the Thayers Lisa had for sale from her collection were smaller pieces, sketches in pen and gouache, or egg tempera paintings on heavy paper. Many were from Thayer's youth, when he had wandered through Seattle's docks and waterfront bars: figure studies of sailors and loggers, drunks and hobos, the wandering homeless men of the late Depression years, sketched in a rough sure hand. Others were from the postwar years, when Thayer had returned from two years of living in war-shattered Japan and begun to experiment with abstract expressionism: small paintings on brown paper or hardboard that conveyed the energy of earth and water and sky. At the heart of the show were two large paintings, neither of them for sale, one an early, rep-resentational landscape of the harsh North Cascade Mountains, the other a very late expressionist oil that was heavily symbolic but not abstract, mixing mountain and human symbols. The dark green and gray tones of the painting recalled the Olympic Peninsula forests where Thayer had spent much of his time in the 1960's and 1970's. That dark country had drawn Thayer back time and again, until he found his death there in 1977.

By quarter to ten the crowd had thinned to a few hangers-on that Lisa's gallery assistant, a drawn and anxious young man who would have been at home in the world of Evelyn Waugh, finally managed to chase out. Lisa put her books and the checks that had been left on deposit into the ancient narcotics safe that had been left behind when the old drugstore had closed. When she was done, she sagged down into a straight-backed oak chair behind the polished wooden table that served as her office desk.

"Oh, God," she sighed. "I am wiped out."

"Want a rain check on dinner?" I asked.

She managed a tired smile. "Not on your life. I haven't eaten all day. Nerves. And there's something I need to talk to you about."

"Some kind of problem?"

"I don't know. Something different. And pretty strange. Can we go to the Trattoria for pasta? And a drink. I think what I have to tell you calls for one."

Lisa left her assistant to close the gallery and we walked back down First Avenue to Yesler, passing the open doors of the bars and clubs, where local bands pounded out blues and rock and roll. The warm night air had the bite of salt water. When we were away from the traffic, we could hear the low bellows of the ferries as they came into the docks. The last daylight was gone, but the night was charged with the flow of colored neon.

Trattoria Angelli was crowded with the gallery and after-theater crowd, but Lisa was a regular and got us seated quickly in a back booth. As we waited for our drinks to arrive she shook hands and accepted kisses from a stream of people congratulating her on the show. When her double vodka martini arrived, she shook off the chattering middle-aged painter who kept trying to look down the front of her dress. She drank half the glass in two quick swallows, then looked up and caught me watching her.

"I said I wanted a drink," she said archly. "I meant it."

"I could see that," I replied. "You want to tell me what this is all about?"

"It's not just opening-night jitters, and it is kind of hard to explain."

The glow of the successful opening had faded. She seemed edgy.

"Take your time," I said. "Start at the beginning." I took a sip of a cold local beer and waited.

She ran a finger around the rim of her glass. "I guess it starts with the gallery. You know that I didn't want to sell anything from my collection."

"I know, but you had to. You didn't have the capital to have the space remodeled and go out and acquire new works. This way you start out clean, no debts. And you kept the most important paintings, *Landfall* and *Shuksan Arm*. Those two paintings alone could have brought you half a million dollars."

"More, if the market keeps going the way it has been. But two weeks ago, just after the announcements for the show ran in the newspapers, I got this in the mail." She picked up a large leather notebook from the floor, opened it, and took out a manila envelope. She unwound the string closure, opened the envelope, and removed a five-by-eight-inch postal card. It was plain white, with Lisa's gallery address typed in block capital letters. There was no message written on it. She turned it over slowly in her hands.

On the other side there was a small painting. The painting showed the head and neck of a small bird joined to a brass jar or urn. The jar had legs and the image was merged together, as though the jar and the bird were the same object, set against a backdrop of thinly applied translucent amber paint.

I took the card from Lisa's hands and held it gently, by the edges, and turned it over again. The card itself had been sent through the mail: there were two stamps pasted on the back, and it had been postmarked at the Seattle Central Post Office. I turned it over again. The fusion of the bird to the brass jar was unsettling. I handled it carefully, by the edges, as I put it back into the envelope.

"Your grandfather painted birds, didn't he?"

She nodded. "He painted a whole series of birds, starting when he was in Japan, and continuing for twenty-five years," she said. "He broke them down into their basic shapes until they became quite abstract, but a lot were like this one."

"I don't understand. Is this a new painting? Do you think someone is trying to imitate Thayer's style? Fake his work?"

"It must be an imitation," she said slowly. "But this is . . . damn it, it's too good. People have been forging Thayer's stuff ever since the prices started rising after his death, and there have been rumors floating around the gallery circuit about fake Thayers, mostly of his later, abstract work. There are two ways to fake an artist's work. One is to forge it. You age the materials to match the ostensible age and style of the painting. The other is to take a similar painting from a lesser painter and paint a new signature on it. I can usually detect forgeries right away. Either the brushwork is bad or the materials are wrong or the composition is off. He was such a rigorous painter, even the abstracts have a very formal composition." She shook her head. "This would fool me. The subject is right, the paint is gouache, which was his favorite material for smaller works. And he liked to paint on this kind of stiff white cardboard. But if I had to guess, I'd say this was painted about a week before I got it. The paint smeared a little in the mail."

"So it's an excellent forgery. Why do you think you got it? Do you think it has something to do with your opening the gallery?"

Lisa shrugged. "Why would a forger want to announce his presence to me? I hate forgers, especially when they imitate my grandfather. He put his life into his work. A forger belittles that. Cheapens it."

"Then what do you want to do?" I asked.

"I don't know," she said, frustration putting an edge on her voice. "If this was forged, it's so good I'll never be able to tell the difference."

"You're saying 'if,' Lisa. I still don't understand. Your grandfather's been dead for years."

She looked at me without really seeing me, her mind focused somewhere else. "I was fifteen when he died," she said slowly. "I had dreams about him coming back to teach me to paint. I was in art school then, trying to learn how to paint. I wasn't good at it, Matthew. I had the eye but not the hands." She shook her head slowly, sadly, oblivious to the crowded, noisy restaurant. "I had those dreams so often my father put me in therapy for six months. I still have them, sometimes. Now I see this—" She gestured at the envelope in front of her on the table. "And I wonder. Could my grandfather still be alive?"

"How could you think that?"

"He was killed in a car accident on the Olympic Peninsula. By his fishing camp, all the way out near Neah Bay. His car went off the road into the ocean. They never found his body. He might have survived the accident. He could still be alive."

"I don't think there's much chance of that, Lisa. The police and the county coroners do their jobs pretty well. I don't think they would have said that Thayer was dead if there was any chance he was still alive. Besides, in nearly thirteen years you've never had any kind of contact with him."

"Until now," she said, running a finger along the edge of the envelope on the table. "Maybe. I know it sounds crazy. I just would like to know, Matthew. One way or the other. If this painting is a forgery, I'd like to know who painted it. I want to expose whoever it is and get them to stop." She paused to take a pull from her drink. "If Lee is dead, I want his work to live on without being cheapened. And if there is any chance that he is alive, I want to know that."

"The man is dead, Lisa." I tried to keep my voice even, but I knew as I spoke that I sounded patronizing.

"You don't know that," she snapped, reacting more to my tone than to what I had said. I waited a moment before speaking again.

"Lisa," I said quietly, "suppose that by some crazy chance he was still alive. He might not want to be found."

"I know. I could live with his decision, if he didn't want to be found. But this—" She touched the small painting again. "I need to find out. I'd like your help."

I shook my head. "Lisa, what do you really want? Do you want to find out who is faking Thayer's work? That I might be able to help you with. But the other thing, trying to find a dead man, that will just lead you to a lot of pain. It's pretty clear that your grandfather's death hit you hard at a vulnerable time in your life. Chasing his ghost will bring back that hurt. You'll live through it all over again."

"You don't understand, Matthew. Somebody is trying to send me a message. Why go to the trouble of painting this if it has no meaning?"

"It could be a fake. A cruel one."

"If that's what it is, so be it. I want to know."

I looked into her clear, determined eyes. I had seen that look before, on the faces of adopted children searching out their biological parents. When they came to me to file a lawsuit to open the adoption records, they had faces filled with hope. Hope that the missing parent could fill the aching empty place that lingered in a corner of the soul. Hope that the father or mother could answer the question why? Why did you leave me when I had done you no harm? After the money had been spent, the skip tracing done, the bureaucratic walls knocked down, nine out of ten had faced the pain of a second rejection.

There was so much that I liked in this woman: her walk, her laugh, the intensity she brought to solving a problem. I wanted her not to be hurt. More selfishly, I wanted time with her, in a quiet place, to find out what books she liked to read, what touches would please her, what silly things would make her smile. I was surprised at how much I wanted that time with her. And at how badly it hurt to feel the chance slipping away.

"Once you start something like this, you can't stop it," I heard myself saying. "If there is anything there, it will take on a life of its own. And it will never turn out the way you would like."

"I'll take that risk," Lisa said.

2

By the time Lisa called me on Saturday morning, two days later, I had taken the small postcard painting she had received to a friend at the Seattle Police Department and learned what I knew in advance would be true: that the mailing of the card had obliterated any fingerprints or other chemical clues that might be helpful in tracing the sender. The postmark had been applied at the Seattle Central Post Office, which told us something or nothing, depending upon how you looked at it. Lisa still had no idea why the painting had been sent to her.

When the phone rang, I was soaking up the morning sunshine on the back deck of my small shingled house on the northwest shore of Lake Washington. I juggled a bagel and the sports pages and the mug of coffee with milk for a moment before picking up the portable phone.

"Hello, Lisa," I said, before she had a chance to speak.

"How did you know it was me?" she demanded.

"Telepathy. I was just reading the reviews of your show. One paper says it was mostly minor work, but well presented. The other paper called you a reactionary."

She laughed. "That's Tricia. You remember, the skinny red-headed woman, the one wearing a .22-caliber bullet as an earring? She thinks anything painted before 1982 is boring. What did the police find out about the postcard?"

"Nothing, I'm afraid. Too much handling by too many people. What's up?"

"The Seattle Art Museum is opening its formal retrospective show on Lee's work tonight. It's the big show that I was timing the opening of my gallery to, so that I could ride on their publicity. I'm going, and I think you should come with me. I've previewed the show, and there are three paintings in it that really look doubtful to me. I'm going to run through my notes on Lee's work and see whether I can find out anything that will tell me whether they're genuine."

I noticed that whenever Lisa referred to her grandfather's work she called him Lee, as though he were an artist she knew casually, not a member of the family. "Slow down a little, Lisa." I said, "There still isn't any evidence that a forger is actually working. Someone might have painted that little bird picture as a kind of homage, or to show off, or for any reason at all. Art forgery is a felony, and you've got to be careful before you start making accusations. Who owns these paintings you think are suspect? Have you talked to them?"

"They're all listed as belonging to anonymous owners who lent them to the museum. I know there are risks in my even whispering a doubt about those paintings, Matthew, that's why I'm inviting a professional cynic to come along. Pick me up at eight o'clock. Look handsome for me; there are other aspects of my reputation I've got to consider."

I started to mutter something about that being another hopeless case, but she had already hung up before I even got a chance to ask her what the hell I should wear.

The Seattle Art Museum, known as "SAM," is in Volunteer Park, a graceful art deco structure set on the crown of Capitol Hill. It commands a view of the downtown skyline and, on fair days, the crests of the Olympic Mountains on the far side of Puget Sound. We parked near the Victorian glass conservatory at the north end of the park and walked back down the drive toward the museum, beneath the shade of Pacific maples planted a hundred years before by the park's designer, Frederick Law Olmstead. It was a warm night, still sunny at Seattle's far north latitude, and the park was full of people. The lawn to the west of the conservatory was shared uneasily between the players in a local croquet tournament, dressed in starched whites, and a Jamaican steel band that had drawn a small but enthusiastic mixed-race crowd.

I pointed toward the croquet players, who stood sipping gin and lemonade out of plastic cups between shots. "I've never understood the WASP compulsion for hitting balls with clubs," I said. "Maybe you could fill me in."

Lisa pulled her hand from my arm and turned, feigning astonishment. "It's really very simple," she said, mimicking the English accent of her mother, a once-popular actress I had seen in early 1960's movies on late-night television. "The balls substitute for the peasants we used in the good old days."

"I knew it was something like that," I said darkly. "Let's go up by the Noguchi sculpture for a minute. I want to look at the view." We stepped off the park drive and walked down to the concrete platform where the ominous black "O" of Noguchi's sculpture, *Black Sun*, had been mounted. We stepped up on the base of the sculpture and looked out at the landscape of sky and water and mountains, bathed in warm yellow light the color of old satin, a gift from the setting sun. Below us a solitary jogger, bare to the waist, ran his laps around the open reservoir with a studied intensity, oblivious to the nearby couples stretched out on blankets, picnic baskets open, toasting the sunset.

"My parents and I used to live right by the park here, over on Federal Avenue," Lisa mused, pointing with a bare tanned arm to my left. "It was the Thayer family house, a great old brick monster full of back stairways and unused dusty rooms. I loved being in this park, walking to the conservatory or the Art Museum on rainy days, running around here with my friends in the summers. The park was sometimes rough at night. I suppose that was part of the appeal. I kissed my first boy behind that pine tree over there, down by the reservoir."

"Lucky guy," I said, acutely conscious of the way the planes and curves of her body fit against mine as we stood side by side. She was elegant in a white strapless dress. Her makeup was perfect, even in the sunlight.

"I doubt that he remembers," she said. "I was twelve, I think he was thirteen. Both of us needed practice."

I smiled. "Trust me," I said. "He remembers. Do your parents still have the house?"

"No. They divorced when I was a freshman in college, at Barnard. Mother moved to New York City, ostensibly to be closer to me, if you call lunch once a week at the Plaza or the Russian Tea Room close. Dad owns a small apartment here, in one of the high rises downtown, but he's hardly ever there. He's a doctor with UNESCO now, practicing in a hospital in Uganda."

"Do you miss them?"

"Sometimes. Not often. They weren't very good parents. My father was a boarding-school child who never really had a family. And they were too young. I was an accident from a college romance, my father a UCLA student, my mother an eighteen-year-old actress living next door. I've always been surprised that they stayed married as long as they did. I was an only child and grew up fast. I was emotionally on my own by the time I was eighteen." She hesitated. "I sometimes wonder what it would be like to have a big extended family, uncles and aunts and cousins and a farmhouse to go to on Thanksgiving and Christmas. Then I think that our way was better. I guess I'll never know." She shaded her eyes with one hand and looked out at the sun setting over the mountains. She seemed about to add something, but instead she turned and said, "Come on, Riordan, there's work to do," and we walked across the drive and up the steps to the doors of the museum.

The opening of the Thayer retrospective was a fundraiser, a private showing, by ticket only at one hundred bucks a person. The high-ceilinged Garden Court at the center of the building had been set up as a reception area with a greeting desk in front, attended by a youngish red-haired matron with a serious Junior League manner and a ready pen in case anyone wanted to write a check to endow the new downtown branch of the museum. Behind the greeter a group of student volunteers waited to shepherd groups through the show. I followed Lisa past them to a bar in the back, where we ordered the obligatory glass of white wine and scouted the crowd.

I nodded to the inevitable group of lawyers, clustered in a corner drinking scotch and soda, no doubt bragging about the size of the settlements they'd managed to score from each other. Lisa smiled and chatted with a couple of customers from the gallery opening. It was an altogether typical group for a museum show in a middle-sized city with aspirations toward high culture. The older, wealthier people from the timber and shipping families were there, glad of a chance to dress up in their dinner jackets and long dresses. The younger, middle-aging group was a mixture of business types in summer suits, exchanging business cards as they always did, one more goddamned chance to convert network from a noun into a verb, and the coterie of local artists, dressed in a more dramatic style that ranged from blue jeans to a baby blue 1950's prom tuxedo. The dark-haired woman who wore that outfit matched it with black high-top sneakers, a lacy black camisole underneath the open jacket, and handmade earrings that would have set off any metal detector within a thousand yards.

I was chatting with a muscular sculptor named Terrill Hanks, who wore full biker leathers and a black T-shirt, when I heard Lisa calling my name. Lisa had the arm of a small, distinguished man, immaculate in a white dinner jacket. He was perhaps seventy-five and had a lean tan face and close-cropped white hair. "This is Morris Kuehn," she said, "the family lawyer, my friend, and a good friend of Lee's for many years."

"I've heard the name," I told him as we shook hands. "Kuehn, Laffrom and Hyde, right?"

"The usual list of criminals," he replied, smiling slightly. "Lisa tells me that you're also a lawyer, is that right?"

"Yes, in a small way. I'm a solo, doing whatever needs doing."

"That's the way I started, Mr. Riordan, and forty years later I find myself the captive of six floors in the Columbia Tower and fifty partners, some of whom I have trouble naming when I see them in the hallway. You've been representing Lisa, setting up the gallery?"

"Helping out," I corrected. "Lisa runs her own show."

"She is an extraordinary woman to succeed in that business at such a young age."

"I agree."

"Knock it off, guys," Lisa said, "or I'll begin to believe it. Matthew, Morris is a very good painter in his own right, and he knows Lee's work better than anyone. I'd like to walk with him through the exhibition. Come with us."

We left the Garden Court and walked to the special exhibition rooms. A life-size black-and-white photograph of Thayer had been mounted at the entrance to the first gallery. He was pictured leaning against the doorway of his New York studio sometime in the 1950's, wearing a workshirt and baggy jeans. A bare light bulb dangled from a wire in the background, casting haphazard light into the dark recesses of the room behind him. His long rectangular face was almost expressionless beneath a thick, Kennedy-style brush of hair. He stared at the camera with mild curiosity. It was either a perfect pose, or no pose at all.

The walls of the first gallery had been painted an oyster white color to set off the sketches and tempera paintings of Thayer's early, realistic work. As we walked into the gallery Morris Kuehn began a quiet reminiscence of the times he had lived through with Lee Thayer. "These," he said, pointing to a series of four sketches, colored with gouache, "were done after a particularly memorable night in the bars. The young lady in the short dress was a stripper at Ruby Montana's box house that Lisa's grandfather was quite taken with. The second man is a farmhand we met on the street and stood to a drink. The third man I don't remember, but the fourth fellow, in the oversized gray coat, with his ever-present fedora hat and limp cigarette, is me."

"Were you a student then?" I asked.

"No, that was about 1939, shortly after Lee came back to Seattle from Yale. I was just six months out of law school, working as a deputy King County prosecutor, a job my father, who was on the Seattle cops and up to his hips in local politics, managed to snag for me. I'd studied art at the university," he added, "but the Depression was still on and my father insisted that I get my law degree. I worked all day as a prosecutor, trying misdemeanors and garden-variety felonies. I'd go to my studio after work to paint for two hours and then go drinking half the night. And I'd get up at seven in the morning, and be shaved and dressed and in court at nine." He smiled ruefully. "Surely, if I'd known I was going to live so long, I'd have taken better care of myself."

Kuehn passed through the rest of Thayer's early work without comment. "I think the war was a pivotal force in your grandfather's life," he said to Lisa. "We both joined up in early 1941. When the war started, I got assigned to the Judge Advocate General's group in London after basic and officer training. Lee spoke good French and fair German, and the army sent him on to the Office of Strategic Services, the forerunner of the CIA. He trained stateside for nearly a year, then wound up in London in 1942. We had a week together that January during the Battle of Britain. Not much of a holiday. The outcome of the war was still very much in doubt. Then he went into France for the first time, behind German lines, moving supplies in and helping to set up the Resistance. He had a very hairy time of it, I'm afraid. He was wounded later in '42, bringing out a small group of Resistance people on a raft from a beach near Calais. A damn good thing one of them was a young doctor, otherwise he probably would have bled to death by the time the destroyer picked them up. On the other hand, he married the doctor six weeks later. Your grandmother, of course," he added, nodding to Lisa.

"He never talked about any of this," Lisa said. "I found out most of it by reading letters and looking at photographs, but I like hearing it again."

"You can't blame him for not wanting to talk about the war; Marie was killed by a V-2 rocket in January 1945. Your father was a toddler, not quite three years old. Somehow your grandmother was able to shield him with her body from the blast." Kuehn spoke with the clipped, understated assurance I had found in many World War II veterans, untroubled by the doubts that those of us who fought in Vietnam would carry with us like scars, marked for life. But I knew that his quiet tone hid strong emotions.

He paused near the archway leading into the next gallery. "Lee was never able to paint about the war, or the things he saw in it. I recall being in New York with Lee sometime in the 1950's, looking at Picasso's *Guernica*. Lee said, 'It's good, but he doesn't know a damn thing about being in a war.' I do think that the war turned his interest away from realism and toward philosophical, even spiritual subjects. I saw him when he was mustered out in 1946, in London, and he didn't have the slightest notion of what he was going to do. I was on my way to Nuremberg, the war crimes tribunal, assigned to Justice Jackson's prosecution staff. The most I could do was get roaring drunk with him at Claridge's the night before he boarded the troopship home. When I finally came back to Seattle, in 1948, I found out he was living in Japan."

"What was he doing there?" I asked.

"Studying Zen Buddhism. Trying to figure out his life. He was working as a carpenter, helping to rebuild people's homes. He was always damn good at carpentry, things like that. And painting." By this time we had moved into the next gallery, showing Thayer's early postwar work. Kuehn turned to a series of dark abstract oils and pointed at them. "This, to me, was when Lee began to paint really well. Notice how he is taking the rough Japanese landscape—mountains, rocks, rocky beaches, dark ocean water—and playing with the forms, breaking them down, making them progressively more abstract. What we end up with are fields of paint that appear to be completely nonfigurative, until you see that the forms and light are adapted from nature. Lee never did fully accept the 'thinner, flatter, what you see is all there is' theory of abstract expressionism." Kuehn sighed. "Marvelous. I can admire it but I can't do it." An old sadness had begun to color his voice. "When Lee came back to the States, he worked with Mark Rothko in San Francisco for a couple of years, then moved to New York when Rothko did. He spent a fair amount of the fifties in New York, hanging out at the Cedar Tavern with people like Guston and Rauschenberg. For a short time, there was Jack Pollock and company. That was the height of—Lisa, I'm sorry, you know all this. I'll quiet down."

"Please keep going. I want Matthew to learn this, and you're teaching it beautifully."

"Well. The fifties were the height of abstract expressionist art, and Lee became intrigued with masses of color and light. Sometimes there were references to the real world, sometimes Lee just painted to see what the paint could do. He became what some have called a 'luminist,' which means that he tried to capture the changing quality of light with fields of paint. Like these canvases here," he added, pointing to a group of three oils. He glanced at them quickly, then stopped and looked more closely at the painting on the left. It was called *Sea Study, No. 3*, and was composed of fields of blue, green, black, and gray. The effect was flat yet unsettling. I turned to Lisa, standing beside me. She was smiling as if she'd won a prize.

"I don't recall this painting," Kuehn said slowly. "I guess even Lee could have an off day."

"What's wrong with it?" I asked.

"Nothing, really," Morris Kuehn replied. "It's just that . . . well, Lee had an incredible, intuitive sense of what paint could do. 'The man has paint in his fingertips,' Clement Greenberg once said about him. "Yet this is rather lifeless. Look at the painting on the right. See how the brush strokes seem to shimmer, as if they were alive? That's what makes Lee's work so outstanding." He turned to the small, printed card on the wall next to *Sea Study, No. 3.* " 'Anonymous collector, on loan to the museum,'" he read aloud. "Well, I hope Mr. Anonymous didn't pay too much for the name. Lisa, do you know who the owner is?"

"No," she said, still trying to suppress her triumph. "I hope they didn't pay too much for it, because I don't think Lee painted it at all."

Kuehn shook his head, a vigorous no. "Surely the museum wouldn't make a mistake like that, even on a work they didn't own. Who curated this show? I've been working on those damned baseball negotiations and haven't kept track."

"Moss Taylor."

"Who provided this painting?"

"Moss told me that David Campbell lined up most of the borrowed works, including this one."

"Well, you must admit that David certainly knows your grandfather's work better than anyone. David was his local dealer for twenty years. I hardly think he could be fooled."

"I wouldn't have thought so," Lisa said stubbornly, "but look at the painting. The use of light is wrong, the brushwork is flat. The whole thing is rather murky. I don't think Lee painted this."

"Have you checked if the materials and canvas are the right age? The reference to the sea is so strong, this must be postwar, say thirty-five years old. You should be able to tell very quickly if it's a modern forgery."

"I haven't been able to turn the painting to look at the canvas. Even if it is the right age, that doesn't mean it hasn't been re-signed. Lee's signature is distinctive." She pointed to the bold brushwork "T" followed by little dots indistinguishable as letters. "But it could be imitated."

He frowned. "True. Have you spoken to Moss about this? Or David Campbell?"

"Not yet. It gets worse, I'm afraid. I think there are two others that are not Lee's work." Lisa broke off the tour and led the way directly to the other paintings, both in the third gallery. The first was an abstract work from the 1960's, called *Striations*, a playful meditation on a sea of parallel lines. The other, a gouache on paper, was untitled, but seemed to be a study for a much larger abstract oil called *Night Signs* that was also in the show. Both of them had been loaned to the museum by an anonymous owner.

"*Striations* is the one I'm not sure about," Lisa admitted. "I just have a sense that the subject matter would not have appealed to Lee. The gouache I feel sure of. There is a sketch of *Night Signs* in existence; my mother has it. It's a pencil sketch that shows the underlying organization of the painting. Why would he have made two sketches? And if he had, why would he make a sketch for an oil in gouache? It wouldn't have told him anything useful for the final painting because the paints are so different. No, this looks to me like a copy or an impression that someone else made, using gouache, as an experiment."

Kuehn had listened intently to Lisa's explanation. Now, like the good lawyer that he was, he probed the statement to see if there were weaknesses. "It's possible Lee might have tried and rejected gouache. Perhaps this was picked up by a dealer on the cheap."

"Not likely. You know Lee destroyed anything he didn't like."

Kuehn looked even more unhappy. "Are you reviewing this show for anyone?" he asked.

"No. It would be a conflict, since I'm in the family. But *Art in America* asked me to do a piece on what it feels like to sell off part of your family's own collection. I told them I would cover this show as part of that essay."

"What have you said about these paintings?"

"In the draft, I explain why I think they're fakes. I haven't submitted the article yet."

"I strongly recommend that you not say anything about these paintings in the article."

"Why? No artist should have his work adulterated by—"

Kuehn put up a hand to stop her. "I agree that there is a possibility these paintings are not authentic. But you must be very sure before you make a charge like that. You've known

David Campbell for a long time, and something like that could be very embarrassing for him. You should do as much research as you need to be sure."

"I gave David a draft of the article this afternoon," Lisa said. "If he wants to show me where I'm wrong, I'll drop that from the piece. I know he has a great reputation, but even he could be fooled."

As Lisa spoke I saw a tall, slender man, meticulously dressed in a black dinner jacket, striding across the room toward us. "I think the reply is about to arrive," I said, gesturing toward David Campbell.

Campbell was the dean of Pacific Coast art dealers, well known from television appearances and newspaper interviews. He was in his early seventies, an elegant, careful man with flowing white hair who had been a contemporary of Thayer, Callahan, Graves, and the other greats of the Northwest School. He had been a successful artistic photographer in his own right, but had built his reputation, and later his fortune, as a critic and dealer for the better-known West Coast artists. Campbell had provided artworks for the homes and office suites of the corporate elites from Vancouver to San Francisco. Like many successful people in public and competitive fields, his reputation for skill was matched by his reputation for arrogance.

A second man followed Campbell. He was about my age, closer to forty than he probably liked to admit. He was shorter than Campbell, five-ten or so, with carefully permed, possibly dyed blond hair, and a fit-looking body that bespoke a serious relationship with a health club. He wore a blousy Italian gray silk jacket with black pants, a white silk shirt, and a narrow black tie. His face lacked the style of his clothes; it was dark, heavy-boned, and full, almost jowly. He had a hand on Campbell's arm, as if to restrain him.

When they arrived, Campbell stood still for a moment, his face flushed and angry. "Lisa," he finally said, keeping his voice low and controlled. "What the hell is the meaning of this?" "This" was a typescript he held rolled into a tube in one hand.

Lisa faced him calmly. "It's a draft of an essay, David."

He grimaced, irritated even more by Lisa's quiet reply. "I know that. You say that three of the Thayers I have obtained for this show are fakes. That is a complete falsehood. I authenticated all three of those paintings myself. Don't you think I know your grandfather's work?"

"Judging by those pictures, David, I would have to say that I have doubts. When you say that you authenticated these paintings, I take it that means you sold them?" Lisa's voice was light, but carried sarcasm in its tone.

"Yes, I sold them," Campbell said, sounding exasperated. "I have been selling Thayers for thirty years. No one has ever challenged my judgment."

Lisa shook her head, as it to say that was irrelevant. "Look at the paintings, David. They just don't cut it. The brushwork is wrong, the treatment of light is different. If Lee had painted them, he would have destroyed them. He would never have let them get out of the studio."

"Nonsense. Each of them is well executed, and clearly consistent with his style at the time it was painted."

"I disagree. And I would very much like to know their provenance, David. I have never seen them in any show or catalog before."

"All three were painted in Europe, 1959 or 1960, while your grandfather was teaching in Zurich. They were sold through European dealers and I am satisfied as to their provenance. I bought them myself, in Paris this past year."

Lisa held her ground. "I said I would like to hear where you got them and who owned them before. I don't hear you offering to tell me."

Campbell's fury was growing stronger. "I am not required to satisfy some neophyte's curiosity," he said nastily. "Especially one who is out to make a reputation at my expense."

Morris Kuehn had kept his silence, but now he weighed in on Lisa's side. "David," he said quietly, "I don't think the request is out of order. I've never seen these pictures either. And I have collected Lee's work as long as you have been selling it."

Campbell turned to look at Kuehn, surprise compounding his anger. "Morris," he said haughtily, "that's nonsense. Stay out of matters where you have no expertise."

Kuehn reddened at the insult and was about to reply when the man accompanying Campbell stepped forward and partly shouldered Campbell out of the way. "I think I can cut through the crap here," he said harshly. "My name is Duane Tabor, Ms. Thayer. I'm an attorney, and I represent Mr. Campbell. If you print one word of that garbage you've written, I will sue you. When I sue people, they end up wishing to hell they'd never met me."

"Along with everybody else," I said dryly.

"Who the hell are you?" Tabor asked, disconcerted, turning to look at me.

"My name's Matthew Riordan. By happenstance, I'm Ms. Thayer's lawyer. It looks like we have a thoroughly modern kind of duel here, drawn lawyers at thirty paces."

Tabor looked scornful. "You think you're going to scare me off from a lawsuit, you're full of shit." He had both feet planted shoulder-width apart, one foot forward, as though he was ready to throw a punch. He breathed heavily.

Tabor was becoming absurd and I was getting angry. "No," I said evenly, "I think I'm too old to listen to nonsense. If Ms. Thayer prints something, it will be factual. Printing facts is not libel. It is fair comment."

He ignored me and looked back at Lisa. "I don't care what kind of facts you think you have. I'm warning you. Don't print that article, or anything else about these paintings." He took a step toward her. I stepped in front of him, blocking his path.

"I think I just heard a threat, counsel," I said coldly. "A threat that would be seen as a breach of legal ethics by any bar association, even one stupid enough to admit you. Don't do it again."

Tabor started to reply, but Morris Kuehn cut him off. With the force that had made him one of the state's most successful trial lawyers, he said, "David, this has become ridiculous. Lisa may be wrong but she has reasonable grounds for raising questions about these paintings. I suggest you respond to her questions. Because I am beginning to believe she may be right." He paused to let his words hit home, then turned to Lisa. "My dear, this old man would like to buy you a drink. Come." They turned and left. I stayed for a moment, still puzzled by the depth of Campbell's anger and the fact that he had chosen to bring his lawyer along. Campbell had been a friend of Thayer's, and Lisa had honored that friendship by giving him a copy of her draft and the chance to set her concerns to rest. Instead of taking that chance, he had chosen to escalate. I waited for an explanation, or an apology. None came. Campbell simply stared past me. Eventually he and Tabor turned and stalked away.

I started back to the bar in the Garden Court, feeling the looks from the people that had been standing nearby. I decided on a real drink instead of the acidic white wine they had served me before. They had a tolerable brand of scotch, so I took some of that. Neither Lisa nor Morris Kuehn was in the Garden Court, so I wandered off toward the museum's north wing, where the permanent collections were displayed. I looked through most of the nineteenth- and twentieth-century European art and was headed into the Asian collection before I finally saw them, talking in the Margaret Fuller Gallery, where the museum's collection of Asian jades was displayed.

The jade gallery was a long cool room with pearl gray walls and a high, barrel-vaulted ceiling. Large, steel-framed windows, rare in a museum, overlooked a sweeping expanse of green lawn, softened now by the last glow of dusk. Lisa and Morris Kuehn stood staring out the windows at the park, talking in low measured tones.

"Campbell and his lawyer have been run off," I said as I approached. "At least for now."

"Matthew, this isn't funny," Lisa said anxiously. "I really believe that those paintings aren't genuine, but a fight with Campbell is the last thing I need. He could hurt my business very badly."

"I understand that, Lisa," I replied. "Sometimes I use humor as a weapon against the pompous. Campbell and his lawyer certainly qualified." I turned to Morris Kuehn and said, "I don't know these people, Mr. Kuehn, but I thought their reaction was sort of extreme."

"I've known David for fifty years," Kuehn said slowly, "and I can't understand it. He would be upset, yes, especially since he sold the paintings through his gallery, but I can't believe he stood by silently while that lawyer made threats. Do you know him? The lawyer, I mean."

"No. I've never heard his name. I didn't like him much, obviously."

"With good reason." He paused and thought for a moment. "Lisa, it's clear to me that you will need an opportunity to examine the pictures carefully. Gus Hildebrandt is the museum director. I'll call and have him set you up a time."

"Won't Campbell object to that?" Lisa asked.

"There's no reason he has to know. Nor does Moss Taylor, for now, anyway. I've put three of my clients on Gus's board; he won't deny me a favor. Lisa, I think you ought to omit any reference to the three paintings in your current essay, but continue your research. Quietly. Let David think that he's scared you into dropping the issue. Then, if you can prove your case, you'll have him." Kuehn smiled coldly, a lawyer who relished the prospect of a good fight.

Lisa nodded. "That makes sense," she said. "I'll do it."

"Good."

The light outside had completely faded away into night. I looked at my watch and saw that it was nearly ten o'clock. "Lisa and I are going out to find some dinner," I said to Morris Kuehn, "and we'd be pleased if you'd join us."

"Thank you, Mr. Riordan," he said formally, "but no. There's still an hour left in this show, and I think I'd rather go back and lose myself in Lee's paintings. We had such extraordinary times. . . . Remembering is an old man's vice, and it really is best done alone." He walked quickly from the room, leaving the two of us behind. It was not until after dinner that night that Lisa realized she had forgotten to tell Kuehn about the picture of the bird.

I always like to know something about the people who threaten me, so at eight o'clock on the following Monday morning I was hoisting the bulky, clothbound national edition of the *Martindale-Hubbell Law Directory* from the bookshelves of Aaron Weissman, the lawyer who shared the top floor of the small Lake Union office building with me, to the library table in my own office. I didn't find Duane Tabor listed as a lawyer in Washington or Oregon. That didn't mean he wasn't admitted, since you have to pay to get into Martindale's, but almost every lawyer pays to get listed. I was cross-checking his name in the Washington State bar directory when Aaron stuck his head through my office door.

"Good morning," he said cheerfully. "You have any coffee made? Karen isn't here yet."

"Sure. In the usual place. Who's Karen?"

"Our new secretary."

"Ours? When did this happen?"

"Last week. Friday. Diane quit. You didn't know?" He came back from my kitchen area with a stoneware mug of coffee and planted his stocky frame on a wooden chair next to my desk.

Aaron was just twenty-eight, a former rock-band promoter with notions of doing entertainment law. In the year since he had moved in next door he had made a living doing tax work for restaurant owners and writing contracts for some local video companies, but he hadn't found a way to lure any California filmmakers up to the Great Gray North. Despite the size of his ambitions—and ego—he was a good tennis player and a good sounding board for my ideas about a trial strategy or an appellate brief. I even liked him well enough to have bought him a birthday present, a T-shirt that said "What I really want to do is Produce."

"I was out on Friday. Why did Diane quit?"

"She got a speaking part in a new film Tri-Star is shooting up in Vancouver. She plays a hooker. Who dies. But it's four weeks' work."

I shook my head. "Please, Aaron, please tell me that this Karen is not another actress."

"Well, she worked as a legal secretary before, so she'll need a lot less training." He smiled brightly, pleased at the way he'd dodged the question.

"At least promise me you're not dating her."

He looked uncomfortable. "I, uh, can't really promise too much there. But," he said, brightening again, "we're not living together."

"I knew there was a silver lining in there somewhere." I turned back to the state directory.

"Who're you looking for, anyway?" Aaron asked, pointing to the stack of Martindale's volumes on my library table. "I saw them all gone this morning, my first thought was to look for a very bored burglar with a hernia."

I smiled. "Cute. A lawyer named Duane Tabor. I met him here in town, but he doesn't seem to be listed."

"What's he look like?"

"Very blow-dried. Wore an Armani jacket that looked like shit but probably cost a thousand bucks."

"Got to be from California," Aaron said. He picked up his

coffee and stepped out on the deck to sniff the clear warm morning air and look at the sailboats that passed through Lake Union on their way to the Sound.

He was right, of course. I found Tabor listed there with offices on Montgomery Street in San Francisco and Sausalito in Marin County. According to Martindale's, he was the sole principal in his firm, Tabor and Associates, and employed three associate lawyers and six paralegal staff. Their listed specialties were tax, corporate business, and trusts—hardly the sort of street practice I had expected, given Tabor's crude approach to handling Lisa Thayer. The longer I thought about it, the more the dissonance intrigued me, and I ended up by calling a friend of mine, a lawyer in San Francisco named Kerry Wills.

Kerry had been one of the youngest lawyers on the New York Organized Crime Task Force in the early 1970's. She was charming, pretty, and tough, qualities that brought her an early partnership at Baker, Hardwick and Lithgow, one of the largest law firms in San Francisco. She still practiced criminal law, but now she had the kind of clientele that stole with briefcases and computers rather than sawed-off shotguns.

I got her direct office phone number from the ancient leather address book I kept in the top drawer of my desk and dialed. I was mildly surprised when she answered it herself on the second ring.

"Matthew!" she said. "It's nice to hear from you. You ready to take a job with us?" It was her standard greeting, one that had become almost a joke between us.

"Not likely, Kerry. The air in those tall buildings gets a little rare for me. Got time to give me some information?"

"Sure. I'm just sitting here reading an indictment. My guy's accused of price fixing. The government has pictures of him and the other five guys that control the asphalt industry in California meeting in a hotel every month to rig bids on highway contracts."

"Sounds like it's time for the pinochle defense."

"What?"

"The pinochle defense. What are six middle-aged white guys doing in a hotel room every month? Playing pinochle. Drinking some whiskey. Getting away from their wives. Of course their friends are in the same business; aren't everybody's?"

I could hear her humming, something she did whenever she was thinking. "You know," she said slowly, "it might work. The trial's gonna be in Bakersfield. What can I do for you, anyway?"

"Information. On a lawyer named Duane Tabor. Offices in Montgomery Street, and in Marin."

"Yeah, I know him. He was a federal public defender here for a while, then went out and started to make real money doing drug defenses."

"That's not what his Martindale's entry says. It's tax, corporate, and trusts."

"That's a new line, but it's connected. The drug defense business isn't much fun anymore. The feds are always trying to seize your client's assets as fruits of the crime and fuck up your ability to get paid, and the regular bar treats you like you're scum, even though you're just doing your job. Duane's gone into moving money. Now he's respectable."

"What kind of money? Is he running a laundry service?"

"Drug money, but nothing so crude as taking in the wash. Duane's elegant now. He gets fees from a bunch of 'Massachusetts' trusts"—a kind of statutory trust that most states had— "and closely held corporations for tax and investment advice. He sets up offshore corporations in the Caymans or Panama in the names of other corporations and twists them up so much that it takes Treasury or Justice three years just to figure where the money goes. He fronts for a lot of money and half the bankers and brokers in the city consider it an honor to buy Duane lunch."

"Are the people he's working with offshore or local?"

"I'm pretty sure they're local. From what I hear, Tabor's tight with the grass money out of the North Coast counties. In California those guys qualify as old money. But don't quote me. My information might not be current."

"Hmm. How do you know all this?"

"Duane wanted to bring a bunch of his tax work here. I screamed so loud in the partnership meeting that we finally decided not to take the work. If it had been straight criminal defense, I wouldn't have bitched. But if you start moving money for those guys, they get to know and love you all too much. I got standards. Low ones, but standards." Kerry paused and I could hear the click of her gas lighter as she lit a cigarette. "How'd you get interested in Tabor, anyway?"

"Only by accident. A client of mine was thinking about publishing something Tabor didn't like. Tabor made threats. At least they sounded like threats to me."

She paused. In my mind's eye I could see her thinking, cigarette frozen in midair, halfway to her face. "Take him seriously, Matthew," she said slowly. "He's never been tied to anything. But he's connected. The elegance is only about as thick as the silk in his suits."

That sobered me. I thanked Kerry and rang off, wondering why in hell a respected old man like David Campbell would be involved with a drug lawyer like Duane Tabor. And why in hell Tabor would care about three paintings owned by an anonymous collector.

I had promised Lisa after the museum show that I would look into the details of Lee Thayer's death, so when I finished the legal work I had to do, I called Terry Lasker, a columnist for the *Seattle Tribune*, and got permission to use the newspaper's clipping morgue. I drove up to the Tribune building on Fairview Avenue and parked on the street, near the lonely statue of Chief Sealth in Denny Park. It was late morning and the day was bright with sun. I bought and drank a cup of coffee from a street vendor and read the sports pages in the park before trudging dutifully to my labors.

The clipping morgue was a quiet room on the second floor. Blue fluorescent lights and green metal tables were scattered between the rows of filing cabinets and computer terminals. The librarian, a gaunt woman with the look of a dedicated runner, told me that all but the last five years' worth of clippings were still in paper form. She knew Thayer's name and returned quickly with two heavy manila envelopes full of clippings. I took them out and sorted them by the dates on the filing slips, then began reading in reverse chronological order, taking notes as I read. There were a number of clippings dated after Thayer's death, reviews of museum shows or retrospective stories about the Northwest School artists. I went through these quickly, working my way back to his death in October 1977.

The formal obituary piece, dated October 31, 1977, had been written by the *Tribune* art critic and covered the development of Thayer's work from the mid-1930's to the early 1970's, when Thayer had virtually stopped painting. The article mentioned his war record and the decorations he had won, including the Bronze Star and the French Croix de Guerre, but discreetly omitted Thayer's problems with alcohol and his hospitalizations for exhaustion and depression. The news story reporting his death was dated October 30, a week after the crash had actually occurred, but just after the Clallam County sheriff announced that Thayer was believed dead. Thayer, it said, had been staying for over a month at his fishing lodge in the coast hills above the Strait of Juan de Fuca on the Olympic Peninsula. He had apparently left the lodge in the late afternoon to drive into Neah Bay, the only town on the Makah Indian Reservation, at the far western edge of the peninsula. The day had been dark with a pounding coastal storm, and the road was narrow and treacherous. His black Jaguar XKE had failed to make a curve about five miles east of the reservation and had gone off the cliffs into the strait. The driver of a logging truck had seen the car as it left the road. The loggers had stopped to try to help, but they couldn't see any sign of the driver. They had radioed their base camp, which in turn had called the Clallam County sheriff's office in Port Angeles, the county seat, nearly a hundred miles to the east. The sheriff had dispatched the nearest patrol car, but the storm had gotten worse; trees were falling and blocking the road. It had taken nearly two hours for the deputy to get to the crash scene, which the loggers had marked. The young deputy had searched the area and had tried to scramble down the cliffs on a rope tied to his car, but had seen no sign of Thayer. The storm cleared by morning, but the storm tide running through the strait had pulled the car down into the deep water. No body was ever recovered.

The only follow-up to the main story was a short piece about the memorial service, coupled with a full-page color spread of some of Thayer's better-known paintings. I shuffled the clippings together, put them into the envelope, and leaned back in the hard metal chair to think. So far as Lisa or anyone else knew, Thayer had been alone at his lodge. He had been reported missing by his twice-a-week caretaker. The Clallam County sheriff's office had found the house undisturbed and the car gone. The Jaguar was distinctive, probably the only car of its type in the hardscrabble logging and fishing country of the peninsula. According to the *Tribune* story, the logging truck driver had identified the correct make and model of Thayer's Jag from a photographic montage he was shown after the accident. The drop into the water from the bluff was around thirty feet, and the shoreline was rocky. Assuming that Thayer had been in the car, it was almost certain that he had been killed, if not by the impact, then by the forty-five-degree water of the strait.

I turned back to the first envelope, sorted the clippings, and started from the beginning of the file. The first clippings about Thayer dated from the mid-1930's, small articles about local art shows sponsored by the Artists' Project of the old federal Works Progress Administration. Thayer was listed as one of the artists whose work was being exhibited. In the spring of 1938, the university gallery had sponsored the first showing of Thayer's work in a group show with paintings by more established painters like Tobey and Graves. The very old clippings were interesting but told me almost nothing about the man. I was beginning to think that I was wasting my time when I unfolded a large yellowed clipping that opened to nearly a quarter page. It was a page-one

story with an inch-high black headline that said LOCAL ART STU-
DENT MURDERED. It was dated August 9, 1939, and read:

> Cornish Art student Margaret Jura, 19, was found dead be-
> neath University Bridge this morning, after a wild party by
> local students and others on a houseboat moored in Portage
> Bay.
>
> Jura, the daughter of George and Anna Jura, 315 West
> Galer, Queen Anne, had attended a party aboard the house-
> boat of David Campbell, a University of Washington student
> on Friday night. Neighbors reported that the students had
> been drinking heavily and carousing into the small hours of
> the morning.
>
> Police sources said that the body was discovered by an early-
> morning stroller on Portage Bay lane. The body was partly
> submerged in the water, next to a steel bridge piling. The cause
> of death was said to be strangulation.
>
> Detective Howard Schwartz stated that the police have
> taken local artist and Cornish School instructor Elton Lee
> Thayer, 22, into custody for questioning. Thayer, the son of
> Seattle shipping executive John E. Thayer, was said by others
> at the party to be romantically involved with Miss Jura.
>
> Residents of the quiet North Capitol Hill neighborhood said
> they were shocked by the crime but not totally surprised. Wild
> student parties marked by public drunkenness and brawls have
> long disturbed the houseboat moorage. John Service, whose
> home overlooks the moorage, said that the students were
> "nothing but a bunch of bohemian left-wingers" and that the
> moorage should be "shut down once and for all."

There was a high-school graduation picture of Margaret Jura
printed in smeared ink beside the story. Age had faded the poorly
printed picture so badly that the girl's face was nothing but a
featureless blur.

The Sunday-morning follow-up story gave no new facts but
hinted broadly that a major sex scandal might be in the making.
The excitement was short-lived. By Monday night Thayer had
been released from jail:

> Seattle police released murder suspect Elton Lee Thayer

today. Homicide detective Howard Schwartz announced that Thayer, 22, a painter and instructor of murdered Cornish School student Margaret Jura, had been questioned and was able to demonstrate that he was at a party with friends at the time the victim was killed.

Thayer, the son of shipping company executive John E. Thayer, said nothing as he was escorted from the King County jail by prominent Seattle attorney Frank Hoffman.

The detectives of the Seattle homicide squad added nothing official, but courthouse sources say that police have another suspect and that a new arrest in the sordid case is imminent.

The article went on to repeat the facts already published in the Saturday story and quote from the family of the victim. As I read the clipping a second time I got the distinct feeling that the reporter had been disappointed. Until Thayer was released, the story had real potential to sell newspapers: depraved artist son of rich local shipping family accused in sex slaying. Pretty victim fights off advances. Community outraged. By the time the trial started the reporters would have been inventing Margaret Jura's last words.

Two days later the police made the second arrest.

Seattle police chief Edgar Markham announced an arrest today in the slaying of Cornish coed Margaret Jura.

The police arrested suspect Anton Petrov, 20, at his room in Nelson's boardinghouse on Seneca Street in the First Hill district. Petrov, a sometime art student who worked at the Federal Arts Project of the WPA, is said to have dated Margaret Jura prior to her romantic entanglement with Cornish instructor Elton Lee Thayer.

Petrov is being held without bond in the King County Jail pending indictment on a charge of murder.

The tragedy was marked by a memorial service today in Calvary Cemetery for Miss Jura. Dozens of family, friends, and fellow students of the ill-fated student attended the service conducted by Bishop James Flynn.

The stories about the murder ended as far as Thayer's file was concerned. I read quickly through the rest of the clippings in the envelope, mostly feature stories about gallery and museum exhibitions and later wire service stories about Thayer's growing national and international fame in the 1950's and 1960's. There were no interviews and few personality profiles; Thayer had had little to say to the city where he was born and had found his initial success, and to which he always returned.

I photocopied the stories about Thayer's accident and the murder of Margaret Jura and returned the clippings to the librarian. "Do you have a file under the name of Anton Petrov?" I asked.

She frowned, trying to remember. "I don't think so," she said, "but let me check the index." She turned to an IBM PC on her desk and punched a couple of keys. "P-E-T-R-O-V?" she spelled out. "Anton. Here it is. It's on microfilm, though. Sorry." She wrote a few numbers down on a slip of paper and walked to a many-drawered microfilm cabinet. She shuffled through two of the drawers and finally extracted a spool. She handed it to me and pointed to a microfilm reader-printer machine across the room. "It starts about frame one thousand, toward the middle of the spool." I thanked her, went to the microfilm reader, and after a few minutes struggle managed to get the machine going. I tried not to lose my breakfast as the frames of film whirled by at fast-forward speed.

The file began with the clipping that reported Petrov's arrest. Petrov had been a poor man, unable to make bail. There were only two stories, both concerning his indictment, between his arrest and the start of trial in late September.

The trial coverage was almost subdued in comparison to the play the *Tribune* had given the murder itself. The evidence against Petrov was straightforward, if not completely compelling. Petrov had dated Margaret Jura for a few weeks that spring and early summer. She had dropped him quickly, in favor of Lee Thayer. Petrov had been at the party on David Campbell's houseboat on the night the murder took place. He had loudly and drunkenly asked a half-dozen people where Margaret and

Lee Thayer had gone. He had left the party before Thayer had arrived, and much later that night had returned at a run, sweaty and out of breath, from the direction of University Bridge.

Petrov's statement, given under interrogation, made matters worse. He had left the party just past midnight to smoke marijuana with two university students, Marlon Lichter and Walter Gore. When they had finished smoking, Petrov had felt ill rather than high and had gone for a walk to try to clear his head. He estimated the time as 12:30 or one o'clock. He had walked past the University Bridge and up the short hill to Eastlake Avenue, thinking he would take a streetcar down to Denny Way and walk to his room from there. When he reached the car stop, he realized he had no money and decided to return to the party, planning to sleep on David Campbell's floor. On his way back he had found the body of Margaret Jura. Terrified, he had said and done nothing. When he returned to the party, he drank more and passed out until morning.

I closed my eyes for a moment. Despite the damning admissions in Petrov's statement, he consistently denied killing Margaret Jura. Petrov must have been tough, because obtaining confessions before the Miranda and Escobedo rulings were handed down in the 1960's was a pretty simple matter if the police detectives had hard fists, steel-toed shoes, rubber hoses, and sandbags for the kidneys. Petrov had lacked Lee Thayer's family connections and expensive lawyer. The Seattle cops of that day were no better than cops elsewhere and they would have spent three or four days trying to beat a confession out of Petrov.

I read on. At trial the prosecution called many people to establish that Petrov had been absent from the party at the time of the killing. The witnesses included Thayer, Campbell, and the students Lichter and Gore. Gore said he had seen Margaret Jura leave Thayer's houseboat and walk toward the University Bridge. Thayer had left a few minutes later, heading in the opposite direction, toward Campbell's houseboat. Both Lichter and Gore had denied smoking grass with Petrov. Petrov, they said, had been around early in the evening but had left by ten or eleven. Campbell testified to Petrov's repeated questions about Jura and Thayer during the course of the party.

The trial proceeded as though guided by a tragic script. Harold Jensen, the deputy prosecutor, based his case on means, motive, opportunity, and the inability of anyone at the party to account for Petrov's whereabouts in the critical hour when Margaret Jura was killed. He had also added a substantial helping of local prejudice to the mix. Petrov had been painted as a dope fiend, a left-wing threat to the fair middle-class daughters of the city. The prosecutor's strategy worked well. The jury was out less than half a day before bringing back a verdict of second-degree murder. The only mild surprise was the identity of the defense lawyer: Morris Kuehn, who resigned from the prosecutor's office to take the case.

Petrov was sentenced to a prison term of thirty years to life. A small clipping from a 1947 *Tribune* reported his conviction on another charge of manslaughter after a knife fight in prison. Petrov was sentenced to an additional eight years. He was not released until 1970.

The only other story in Petrov's file was a 1970 Sunday magazine photofeature entitled "Is This the Lost Genius of the Northwest School?" It included a picture of Petrov leaving Monroe State Penitentiary after thirty-two years inside, a short, thickset man with sallow prison skin, dark eyes, long wavy black hair, and a brushy mustache. There were color reproductions of some of his prison paintings, mostly bright expressionist pictures mixed with darker, representational paintings of prison life. The short history of the Margaret Jura case recounted in the story added nothing; Petrov's dark comment that "I know that I was innocent and I know that others know the truth" seemed nothing but prison bragging for the benefit of the young reporter who wrote the piece.

I shut off the viewer and rubbed my eyes, then looked down at the notes I had scratched on the pages of a legal pad. I couldn't give a rational reason for the time I had spent reading about Margaret Jura's sad young death. There was no possibility that it could be connected to Lee Thayer's own death nearly forty years later. Yet I wondered whether Lee Thayer would have hit that curve in the coast road at the day and time he did if Margaret Jura had not been killed in August, 1939. It might have been another day, another road, a bullet in a war or cancer or any one of the hundred banal ways that humans seem to invent to hasten their own demise. Murder is ultimate cruelty precisely because it changes the future, cutting short the promise of the victim's own life and altering the lives of those connected to the victim by ties of blood, love, longing, or even hate. I finally told myself to stop thinking nonsense. There are too many junction points in human lives to stop and say, This is it, this is the one that caused the turn to crime or success or tragedy. Still, Lee Thayer's death and Margaret Jura's murder had at least one nagging parallel. In each case it was possible that the accepted truth was wrong. No one had seen Thayer in the car that had plunged into the strait; no one had seen Petrov strangling Margaret Jura. But the accepted truth about each death had been around for many years, and no neutral observer had even suggested another possibility. I have the lawyer's dislike of possibilities. The rational solution, supported by most of the evidence, is where truth usually lies. Possibilities I leave to the people who have seen Elvis, alive and porking down yet another cheeseburger in Pocatello, Idaho, to those who know for a fact that there really was a second gun in the hotel kitchen when Bobby Kennedy was gunned down in that terrible year of 1968.

The truth here was a sad one, but it was the truth. Lee Thayer was dead. Sooner or later I would have to convince Lisa to accept that.

The next morning I had three different motions on calendar at the King County Courthouse, so I packed up my sagging black briefcase and mentally prepared myself for the exquisite pleasure of waiting half a day to spend five minutes arguing before a judge who was expected to read the lawyers' papers, find the law, and decide an issue forty times in the three hours between 9:00 A.M. and noon. It is an impossible system for everyone involved. Sometimes all the lawyer can do is smile and hope the judge had good food, fine wine, and safe sex the night before sitting on civil motions.

As it turned out, my luck was good and all three matters were heard within the first hour of the calendar. With two unexpected hours of free time I took the stairs down to the sixth floor and went into the clerk's office to read the probate file on Elton Lee Thayer.

The file was on microfilm, so I took the spool that the counter clerk gave me and found an open machine at the back of the file room, next to a window overlooking the rooftops of Pioneer Square. As I threaded the spool it occurred to me that I didn't know what I was supposed to be looking for. Lisa had asked me to look for evidence that her grandfather might still be alive; the probate file would tell me only who had benefited by his death.

I found the Thayer file on the film and scanned the first few pages quickly. The will named Lisa and her father as the primary beneficiaries. There was the usual petition for admission of the will and appointment of executor, accompanied by a death certificate from the coroner of Clallam County, a Dr. William Bledsoe.

The death certificate listed the cause of death as accidental. Morris Kuehn had been made executor and had wound up the estate without a fuss, collecting property and assets and paying bills. The only thing that seemed even slightly out of the ordinary were two payments, made shortly before the date for cutting off all claims against the estate. The two claims totaled $35,000, yet there were no receipts or other documentation in the file to back up the creditors' claims.

It seemed unlikely that a lawyer as experienced as Kuehn would pay any flimsy claims. The backup documents were probably just missing from the court file, but I made a note of the creditors' names, just to be thorough.

I returned to my office after lunch and found a message to call David Campbell, the art dealer. When I returned the call, Campbell was still out to lunch but his gallery assistant, a young-sounding woman named Jennifer Sobel, said that Campbell would like very much to see me, could I stop by around four that afternoon? She might have been young but she spoke with a strained Long Island lockjaw accent and the airy, condescending tone that was a requirement for the job. I told her that I would struggle to find the time and hung up.

Campbell's gallery, office, and home were located on the fifth and sixth floors of the Girard Building, a fine Romanesque brick structure dating from 1900. It was four blocks north of Lisa's gallery, in the no-man's-land of small office buildings, cheap retail stores, and commercial lofts that was fast disappearing beneath the twin onslaughts of gentrification and the new office towers marching down the hill from the financial district. The

Girard had had street-level stores, with loft space on the upper floors, and was mostly empty when Campbell had bought the building. According to Lisa, Campbell had renovated the entire building to create a sort of art condo, combining gallery space with residential artists' lofts. Despite the booming real-estate market, the project had not been a success. The few occupied units were mostly rented to accountants and real-estate brokers. Real artists couldn't afford the two-thousand-dollar monthly rents that went along with the marble bathrooms, Italian designer kitchens, and track lighting.

I took the elevator to the fifth floor, where the doors opened directly into Campbell's gallery. I walked into a foyer containing a couple of abstract bronzes and then into an open space of white walls and bleached oak floors. I looked around for Campbell but didn't see him. What I found instead was a defiantly unpretty young woman, fashionably dressed in white leggings and an oversized cotton sweater. She was seated behind an off-white Formica counter and was typing something into an off-white personal computer from an art-history text that lay open on her worktable. After a long and purely intentional delay she managed to wave a languid arm in the general direction of a spiral staircase that connected the gallery floor to the floor above.

Campbell's penthouse was actually a pavilion built on the roof of the original building. Like Johnson's famous glass house, the central core contained the kitchen, bathroom, and bedroom. The outer walls were almost completely made up of windows and French doors, opened on this afternoon to let the light summer winds drift through the living, dining, and office areas that surrounded the core. The furnishings were an elaborate, artificially casual mix of old art nouveau wooden pieces and modern steel, leather, and glass. Despite the overwrought decorating it was a very good space. It made me feel as though I was in an open boat floating among the city rooftops.

David Campbell emerged from the kitchen carrying a tall glass of what looked to be gin and tonic. He bore his years so lightly it seemed hard to believe that he was seventy-three. He wore wheat-colored summer boating slacks and a pale blue dress shirt with his initials monogrammed on the breast pocket. His long white hair was combed straight back and held in a short ponytail by a thin black ribbon. He had an angular slender face with deep-set, shadowed eyes and a long, narrow nose. He looked a good bit like the portraits of Thomas Jefferson as an old man. The resemblance would have been even closer if Jefferson had done his shopping at Ralph Lauren.

"Thank you for coming, Mr. Riordan. Drink? It's early but it feels like that sort of day."

"Dark rum and soda, if you've got it," I replied. If he wanted to sit around and get matey, that was fine by me. I was still curious about the vehemence of his reaction to Lisa's doubts about the authenticity of the three Thayers in the Art Museum show.

Campbell retreated to the kitchen and returned with my drink. "Cheers," he said when we were both seated in facing black leather Barcelona chairs. I took a sip of my drink and waited for him to get around to the point. "I suppose you're wondering why I wanted to see you," he began.

"Mildly," I said, "but having a drink on a warm summer day is almost enough to justify the trip."

He pondered that for a little while and said, "I don't think you'll be surprised if I say that I overreacted the other night at the museum. Nonetheless, I'm very interested in whether Lisa is going to publish that piece about the show."

I thought for a moment before answering. "Lisa is not going to say anything in this article about the three paintings she questions," I said carefully.

"That's good!" he exclaimed. He took a long pull from his drink. "But you didn't say that she'll drop the matter." His eyes were cautious, and questioning.

"That's right," I replied. "Lisa intends to satisfy herself as to the paintings. If you believe they are genuine, perhaps the best thing you could do is cooperate. Show her the evidence. You'll probably persuade her."

"I'm not usually in the habit of opening my books when a competitor comes around making unsupported accusations," he said dryly.

"Fine." I kept my voice calm and soft. "Lisa will keep looking. But don't make any more threats. It's tiresome."

Campbell shook his head slightly, as if momentarily confused. "Look," he said plaintively, "I'm sorry about that. But why is Lisa so interested in these paintings? Is it because I discouraged her from opening her gallery? Or does she just want to embarrass me to take clients away? For heaven's sake, I was a friend of her grandfather. I even gave her a job when she moved back from the East three years ago."

"You're misjudging her," I said. I hesitated, then decided there was no harm in showing Campbell the picture Lisa had received in the mail. I took the manila envelope out of my briefcase, opened it, and handed the small painting of a bird to Campbell.

He put down his drink and took the card carefully, by the edges. He held it away, at arms' length, and studied it. He frowned and put the picture on the coffee table in front of him, then with a slight air of embarrassment took wire-rimmed reading glasses out of his pocket and put them on. He looked again. The silence grew longer. When he was done looking, he picked up his glass of gin and drained it.

"Where did you get this?" he demanded.

"You first," I replied. "Tell me what you think it is."

"It looks like one of a very famous series of bird sketches that Lee Thayer did," he replied, "but I've never seen this one before. What the hell are you doing carrying it around in an envelope?"

"Now take a look at the back side," I told him. He turned the card over and read the postmark.

"I don't understand," he said slowly. "Was somebody actually crazy enough to mail this?"

"Lisa got this in the mail about three weeks ago. She says the paint is gouache, and it was only about a week old when she received it. Her first reaction was the same as yours—that the painting is genuine. She's asked me to look into whether this is a forgery, or if Lee Thayer could still be alive."

"That's crazy," he said quickly. "Absolutely crazy. Lee's been dead for over ten years. In a car wreck."

"That's what I said. But the only other possibility is that there is somebody out there who can imitate Thayer's style well enough to fool the leading authorities, including you. And that's why she thinks you could have been fooled before."

Campbell seemed troubled. He put the painted postcard on his lap and stared at it, tapping his cheekbone with a nervous finger. "Why didn't she tell me any of this at the museum?" he asked. "It would have at least made her conduct understandable."

"She probably wasn't aware of the need to have you approve her actions," I said dryly.

Campbell took that badly, which was just about what I intended. His eyes narrowed and he got up silently and walked into the kitchen to fix himself another drink. When he returned, I said, "Now that we've been honest with you, I have a few questions. First, do you know of anyone who has been or could be forging Thayer's paintings?"

"No," he said abruptly. "There were a couple of imitators back in the late seventies, right after Lee died and the prices started going up. They were pretty bad and the junk they were painting was pulled out of circulation quickly. One of them, an art student in California, even went to jail. That discouraged others from trying it."

"Okay. Second, what are you doing with Duane Tabor?"

Campbell stiffened. Four or five generations of White Anglo-Saxon Protestant rectitude surged upward. "He is my attorney," he said nasally. "Why I selected him is none of your business."

"He's a little more than that, isn't he?" Campbell didn't like being prodded by questions, which was the best reason for doing it. "Why would you need to go to San Francisco to find a lawyer?"

"Have you been investigating me, Mr. Riordan? And if so, why?"

"Of course I have. When people threaten my clients, I tend to get a little interested. Are you going to answer the question?"

"No."

"Doesn't matter. I'm told Tabor's specialty is moving money around for people who have a lot of it. You've just spent maybe ten million dollars buying this block and renovating the Girard Building. You haven't got that kind of money, so you either got it from a bank or from private sources. I'd say the latter, which makes Tabor's presence pretty logical. He represents the money people and keeps you in line."

Campbell's mouth was pinched but he made an effort to project calm. "Duane represented the investors in the Girard Building project," he said. "When we were finished, I was so impressed with his work that I asked him to represent me. As a favor, Duane agreed. That's hardly surprising."

No, it was not surprising that Tabor had a hook into Campbell. Until I knew exactly what it was and how deep it went I would have to be careful to play Campbell with a combination of misdirection and half-truths. "I simply like to know who and what I'm dealing with," I said politely. "Mr. Tabor made some very strongly worded statements the other night. I think we should all step back and calm down. I think you can see from the picture I brought that Lisa has a legitimate reason to be concerned that a forger is at work. She gave you a private chance to comment when she showed you the draft of her article. She won't say anything publicly until she has finished her research. After all, she could be wrong about the three paintings in the show and still be right about this picture." I took the painted postcard from him and slipped it back in the envelope. As I did so I looked calmly at Campbell, making myself the very picture of lawyerly moderation, the gray inside man who would smooth the waters and keep his excitable client from doing anything rash.

He bought the act because it was what he wanted to see and hear. "That's quite possible," he said. He picked up my half-finished drink and headed for the kitchen to make me a fresh one. "I'll certainly consider talking with Lisa," he said when he returned. He sipped at his own freshened gin and tonic. "You know, Thayer was really quite a remarkable painter," he added. The combination of gin and relief was making him expansive. "And he led a remarkable life. Depression, world war, the emergence of abstract art as the dominant form of painting—my god, we saw a lot."

"You know," I cut in, "the main reason I agreed to work for Lisa on this matter was because Lisa is considering doing a full-length biography of her grandfather and I really think one should be written." I was improvising but it sounded plausible to me. "There was one incident, it happened when you were all very young, that she wanted to have a lawyer's analysis of. The murder trial involving the death of that young student, Margaret, what was it, Margaret—"

"Jura," he said. "My god, I haven't thought of that in years. A terrible thing. The police accused Lee of the crime; they kept him in jail a couple of days until they found the real murderer. It was tragic for Lee. It seemed he was really stuck on the girl."

"Tell me about the murderer, Petrov. Why did he do it?"

"Jealousy. Petrov was working at the Federal Arts Project, the WPA, and he was sort of a hanger-on with our group. I never really knew him that well, he was from some farm town, in Idaho, I think. He was crude, no real education, but he was a fairly skillful painter. He did those realist murals the WPA was always producing for post offices and courthouses. No imagination, but decent skills." Campbell summed him up and dismissed him in one breath.

"Was there any doubt that Petrov killed the girl?"

"Not much. That is, I don't have any personal knowledge. I was living on a houseboat in Portage Bay, a typical graduate-student hovel, but my roommate, Harry Dexter, and I had a lot of friends, and we threw some hellacious parties. The night Margaret got killed was one of those. There could have been anywhere from thirty to a hundred people going through our place. There was wine and a lot of pretty, willing girls, and even some marijuana; we thought we were so daring." I watched the faraway look in Campbell's eyes as he spoke. It was amazing how the memory of youth was so appealing for him that even a gruesome murder could be made tolerable through the filter of nostalgia. "Anyway, I was very damned drunk and quite interested in persuading a girl named Lea—damn, I can't remember her last name—to get into bed with me. I didn't even know that Margaret had been killed until the police came to question me the next morning."

"Why did the police think that Thayer had killed her?"

"She spent the evening with him at his houseboat. They were lovers, everyone knew that. They were both strong-willed, and they had some public fights. So naturally the police suspected Thayer at first. But some people at the party had seen him when he came around later, at about the time Margaret was killed, and they cleared him."

"What was Margaret Jura like?"

"Very young, very pretty, very wild. Enormously intelligent. She could draw well but didn't have much training as an artist. She died so young. A lot of potential, but I had no real sense of what she might become." He shook his head. "I have no vision of her other than as a nineteen-year-old. I know that if she hadn't died, she would be nearly as old as I am, but I simply cannot picture her that way."

"Is there anything else you can tell me about her?"

"Not much." He hesitated, then added, "But I think I can show you what she was like. She worked as an artists' model, much to her parents' chagrin. They threw her out of the house for that. I think I hired her to pose for some photographs. I made my reputation as a photographer, you know, before I became a critic and then a dealer. Wait here. I think I might be able to find some of those old photographs."

Campbell went to a set of oak map cases that had been built into one of the inner walls. He opened and closed a number of the wide, shallow wooden drawers before finding what he wanted.

He came back with a very old photograph album, leather-covered and bound with string, and a large manila envelope with a string closure. "These are pretty old. I was still learning when I took them, so I've never cataloged or published any of them." He put the scrapbook on the glass cocktail table between us and leafed through it quickly. "These are personal pictures," he explained. "Snapshots, really." He found the page that he was looking for and turned the book to face me. "The first three were taken at Lee's studio, the rest up at a mountain cabin that belonged to someone's parents, I can't remember whose."

I looked carefully at the black-and-white snapshots. In the three studio pictures Margaret Jura was in the background, a slender, very young woman with shoulder-length hair. She was laughing, drinking beer, and posing, partially obscured by Thayer's easel as he worked. The summer cabin pictures were better, shots of Margaret alone. I saw her standing on the running board of a black Model-A Ford, her light summer dress wrapped against her by the wind. In another picture she was sitting in a swimming suit at a wooden picnic table, eating a sandwich, her eyes concentrating on a book, apparently unaware of Campbell's camera. In a third picture she was laughing, a good, wide-mouthed laugh that bunched up her features and wrinkled her nose.

I turned the book back to Campbell. "These don't tell very much, do they?" he mused. "Well, I think the posed shots I took of Margaret are in the envelope." He untwisted the string closure and handed the open envelope to me. I took it and sifted quickly through the photographs until I found the right ones.

The first picture was a head shot. Margaret Jura's face was squared off but slender, with a strong but not dominating jaw and a straight, slightly turned-up nose. Her hair was thick and flowed down to her shoulders, a light color on the black-and-white print that must have been dark blond in life. Her eyes were round and very light, a pale blue or gray that had been given shimmering intensity by the fine-grained silver film that Campbell had used.

There were two more head shots, then a reclining nude, then the best picture of all, a standing portrait in which Margaret was nude from the waist up. She stood very straight, her eyes unembarrassed, her slender strong shoulders held back easily, her small breasts high and round, with dark nipples. She had a presence in the pictures that was unforced yet strongly erotic. Perhaps it was self-knowledge.

Campbell watched me with interest as I looked at the photographs. I looked up, my throat suddenly dry, and saw something like amusement in his eyes. "She affected me the same way," he said. "Astonishing, isn't it? She has been dead for fifty years and I feel . . . drawn to her every time I see these. I never got close to her, though not for lack of trying. She was only nineteen but she could attract men without effort. She knew it and she used it. By the time I met her she was with Lee and I never stood a chance. After she was killed Lee and I never talked about her. Not even once. But I wonder if he spent the rest of his life trying to find another woman who was her equal."

I didn't answer. It was getting late and sunlight poured into the room from the west. Dust motes danced silently through the air. I had forgotten about my drink. The ice in it had melted but it was still cold. I drank half of it in two swallows.

Campbell was still talking. "She had an astonishing ability to control men, Margaret did. All sorts of rumors about her . . . that she had slept with a professor, or with another older man. Many of the women students and artists simply hated her. But I never disliked her, even though I wanted her. She simply understood her power and used it." He sat back and finished his drink, still musing.

A telephone rang with a harsh clatter that broke the spell that the photographs of Margaret Jura had created. Campbell answered it and muttered "damn it" a couple of times, followed by a reluctant yes. He put the phone down and stood up.

"I'm sorry," he said, "but I must get back to work. The executive committee of one of the downtown accounting firms is here to decide on the artwork for their new offices. This will take hours. Perhaps I can get them all drunk enough to agree on something."

"Tell me one more thing before you go. Do you ever see Petrov?"

He frowned, as though I'd said something in bad taste. "No. Not now. He came to me several times, years ago, after he'd gotten out of prison. I looked at his work. A lot of it was pretty good, but I couldn't take him on."

"Why not?"

"Because he had killed Margaret. Lee was still alive then, and he would have dropped me like a stone if I'd taken Petrov on. After Lee died, well, I still didn't think it would be right."

"Did Thayer and Petrov ever meet? After Margaret Jura was killed, I mean."

"Not that I ever heard. Petrov went straight from jail to trial to prison, and Thayer couldn't get at him. If he had, one of them would surely have killed the other. Lee hated Petrov for killing Margaret. At the trial Lee was ice cold, but every time he looked at Petrov there was unholy murder in his eyes. And Petrov, oddly enough, told me once that he suspected Lee of killing her." He started to say something else, then thought better of it. "I'm sorry, but I really must go," he said.

I stood up and we shook hands. "Would you mind if I stayed a moment? I'd like to look at these photographs again."

"Fine," he said absently, his mind apparently on the accountants, here to shop for art. "Take as long as you like. Just leave them on the table here." I nodded as he slipped on a blue blazer with some sort of indecipherable crest on the breast pocket and walked down the spiral stairs to the gallery floor.

When he was gone, I leafed through the photographs again, struck by the power that a nineteen-year-old girl had been able to generate with nothing more than her body and the light in her eyes. When I was finished, I shuffled the pictures together to put them back into the envelope, then stopped. I took the pictures of Margaret Jura and put them in my briefcase. I closed the envelope and left it on the table. I walked down the stairs and out of the gallery, utterly embarrassed by the impulse to steal the photographs, but somehow certain that they were far too important to leave behind.

CHAPTER
. . . .
5

I met Lisa for dinner later that night at her home. She lived in a small white-painted bungalow in the Mount Baker neighborhood, south of downtown, a few blocks from Lake Washington. Lisa's house was on the uphill side of the street, from which a curving stone walkway ascended to her green-enameled front door. The front windows of her house faced east, overlooking the lake. As instructed, I walked around the house to the back, where a small yard had been cut out of the slope of the hill. Lisa had turned it into a walled garden, with a brick patio in the center. There was an iron garden table on the patio that had been set with plates and wineglasses. A spray of cut flowers stood in a crystal vase in the center of the table. The garden was very like Lisa herself: graceful, understated, the result of thought and skill that ignorant people call effortless. I turned away from the garden and walked into the house through the French doors that divided the patio from the kitchen. I put the paper bag of wine bottles on the kitchen counter and said, "Lisa? It's Matt. Which wine should I open? Red or white? And where do I find a corkscrew?"

"Red," Lisa said, coming into the kitchen. "And in the drawer left of the fridge." She was dressed in a cotton sweater and faded jeans, and she gave me a quick kiss on her way to the stove. "I'm making spaghetti, the one thing I know how to cook," she explained. "Would you like a real drink? I'm going to have a martini."

"That would be fine, as long as you don't use gin."

"Coward. Okay, vodka." She mixed vodka, ice, and a half jigger of vermouth in an old-fashioned stainless-steel shaker and poured them into stemmed martini glasses that looked old. She handed me one and we went outside to sit in the garden.

"Tell me what's been going on," she said when we were sitting down.

"I've done a couple of things, mostly to get background information. I looked at the clippings file that the *Tribune* maintains on your grandfather. I read the accounts of the accident. It's physically possible that your grandfather wasn't killed, but the evidence all says he was. Neither the car nor the body was recovered, but the car was identified by an eyewitness to the crash. This morning I read the probate file on the estate, which you probably know was handled by Morris Kuehn. I read it because if your grandfather was still alive, he might have wanted to get money out of the estate to disappear on. It's possible that some money could have been diverted, but if so, it wasn't that much. One small but interesting thing was that Kuehn, who is a trial lawyer, handled the probate personally. Normally, the way big law firms work, he'd have had the work done by another lawyer."

"Is that significant?"

"Hard to tell, but I doubt it. I also got a call from David Campbell."

She held her glass in midair. "What did he want? Did he make more threats?"

"No, he was actually pretty nice, in an arrogant sort of way. He wanted us men to settle this over a couple of drinks and came on with a 'more in sorrow' kind of pitch. He seemed pretty

relieved when I told him that you weren't going to publish anything, at least not right away."

"I hope you told him to stick it. Did you say anything about
the postcard?"

"Yes, I showed it to him. I was looking for some kind of reaction that might tell us whether he knows those suspect paintings were forged. I didn't get it. He thought the damned postcard
was genuine."

She thought for a moment before answering. Her left hand
brushed the straight blond hair away from her eyes. "That makes
two of us who know the work and had the same first reaction,"
she mused. "Are you sure about the car accident? Is there any
way Lee could have escaped?"

"Like I said, it's possible but utterly unlikely. Either someone
else had to be driving the car, or he had to survive the crash. I
can look and try to find out if somebody else was identified as
missing at the time of the accident. But that suggests a very ugly
thought."

"I don't understand."

"Either your grandfather took advantage of somebody killing
himself in his car, or else he arranged for somebody to get killed
to fake his own death."

Lisa flared up. "Lee Thayer was not that kind of man," she
said angrily.

"I didn't say he was. I said only that one of the very far-out
possibilities was ugly. You've no cause to be angry."

"Sorry," she said. She poured herself another glass of martini
from the shaker and held it out to me. I shook my head no.

"There's one other thing," I said. "When I went through the
clipping file, I went all the way back to the 1930's. I found out
that your grandfather was a suspect in the murder of a young
Cornish art student he was apparently dating. She was killed
underneath the University Bridge after a pretty wild party down
at the Portage Bay houseboat dock. They held Thayer for a couple of days, and they ended up by trying and convicting another
young painter, a guy named Anton Petrov."

Lisa wasn't surprised. "I know something about that," she said. "But all I had heard was that Lee had been in love with someone when he was very young and that she had been killed. I didn't know that he was a suspect in the murder."

"I would have thought a lot of people had known," I said. "Hasn't there been a biography or something written about Thayer's early life? I've started using the prospect that you might write one as a cover for asking questions about the accident."

"There isn't one, really. There's one decent survey of his work, but that book doesn't talk much about his personal life, and there's only one short chapter on Lee's work in the 1930's. It really starts with his paintings after World War Two."

"Well, I ended up talking to David Campbell about the young woman's murder. He was working on his third or fourth gin and tonic and was talking pretty freely. He had some pictures of the woman. Her name was Margaret Jura. She seems to have been an extraordinary person. If Campbell's pictures aren't retouched, she was also very beautiful."

I took the photographs out of my briefcase and handed them to Lisa, one by one. She examined them carefully, without expression, until I gave her the last photo.

"My god," she said finally, looking at the prints spread out on the table like playing cards. "The woman should have been in Vogue." She shuffled the prints back together and stared directly at me. "Did these turn you on?"

I returned her frank look. "Does it matter?"

"It does to me."

"Why?"

"Because I try not to go into caring relationships lightly. Could you answer?"

I thought it over and nodded. "It's more than just beauty. It's an intensity, a focus. I get a sense of it even through these pictures. I don't know if I can explain it any better than that."

She sipped at her drink, musing on my answer. She seemed oddly put off by its honesty. Should I have lied and said no? Lisa had a merciless honesty in nearly everything. I thought she would want the same from me.

"I think I saw a picture of this woman once," she said. "I must have been about twelve or thirteen, an age when girls get very snoopy. I found a whole box of photos in some of Lee's things that had been stored in the attic of the Federal Avenue house. I showed them to Lee when he came to the city from his lodge. Normally he doted on me. This time he became very angry at first, then sent me away. When I sneaked back into the attic later, I found him with a bottle of whiskey sitting on the dusty attic floor and looking at the pictures. He wasn't smiling or crying or anything. Just looking." Her eyes looked into the distance of memory, then snapped back to the present. "But what does this woman have to do with finding out who is forging Lee's work? Or even whether he might still be alive?"

"I can't answer that. It was a loose thread, an extraordinary event. It might be completely unrelated. But when something like that happens in people's lives, it's like dropping a rock in a still pool. The ripples seem to go on forever."

"Meaning?" she demanded.

"Meaning that cause and effect is a very treacherous subject. The murder of Margaret Jura changed the lives of a lot of people, including your grandfather. Those lives connect to yours, right through to today. Take Petrov, the man who was convicted of killing Margaret Jura. He thought that your grandfather had actually killed her. At least he said so when he got out of prison. Petrov was a painter, supposedly a very skillful one. And he's still alive, I think."

"So?"

"So maybe nothing. But if I were looking for an artist who would know Thayer's work, who might be talented enough to fake it, and who might hate him enough to do it, Petrov wouldn't be a bad choice."

She shook her head. "Maybe. I was down at the museum today. Morris Kuehn talked Gus Hildebrandt into letting me look closely at the paintings. I examined them pretty carefully. None of the three I suspected had been painted recently, like the bird on the postcard."

"So? Are you reconsidering?"

"No, I'm not. The paintings could have been aged artificially or they could have been re-signed."

"What about the sales history of the paintings?"

"I got the same information from the museum. Moss Taylor, who curated the show, said that David Campbell sold all three to the same buyer, but he doesn't know who. He also says David bought them in Europe."

"Is that unusual?"

"No, Lee lived in Switzerland for a while, 1959 to 1961, and he was very popular over there, very heavily collected. There could be a hundred of his paintings in Europe, possibly more."

"Is there any way you could trace title to the paintings?"

She frowned, thinking. "Perhaps. It might be easier to check whether any of them have been shown anywhere before."

"Good. Do that."

"What will you do now?"

"What I've been doing. Talk to the old men who knew your grandfather, try to sift a little truth out of all that memory. Do you know how I might find Petrov? When he was released from prison, he was going to live in La Conner, but that was in 1970."

She thought for a moment, then answered. "You met Terrill Hanks at the museum show on Saturday, didn't you? He might know. He lived in La Conner for a half-dozen years or so, the first half of the seventies. The artistic community up there is small and pretty close-knit. Terrill probably knew him, anyway."

"I talked to him for just a couple of minutes at the show. Would you call him for me, to set it up? People don't like talking about their friends or even acquaintances to strangers."

She stiffened a bit, then agreed. "All right, I'll call him and tell him you're okay."

"You don't have to if you don't want to. Is something wrong?"

She shook her head. "No, not really. I'll make the call." She got up from her chair and went back into the kitchen to cook the pasta and reheat the sauce that had gone cold as we had talked. I wondered why she had stiffened at the suggestion she call Hanks. The obvious guess was that Lisa had been involved with Hanks. I wanted to ask her but was afraid to invade her personal life and drive her away. I smiled at the small irony. I wanted to be part of Lisa's life. But we both had battle scars from our lives with other people, and those remembered hurts made both of us cautious. There might still be a time when it would be right to set the cautions and hurts and fears aside. Or so I hoped, as the last of the sunlight dropped behind Mount Baker hill and left me sitting outside, alone in the gathering blue dusk.

There is a saying to the effect that old lawyers are old bastards, but it is not one that I believe to be true. Most of the old lawyers I know are men who have reached a certain understanding of themselves that shows itself as graciousness in dealing with others. There are exceptions, of course, but thankfully most of the bastards seem to die young, full of themselves and choked on their own bile.

Morris Kuehn's offices on the sixty-fourth floor of the Columbia Center suggested that he had weathered his fifty years of law practice without missing too many creature comforts. The main reception area was a sweeping expanse of hardwood floor, Oriental rugs, and leather furnishings. I gave my name to a matronly receptionist in command of a desk staff of three young women who answered the buzzing demands of a computerized telephone console large enough for a small city. While I waited for Kuehn, I wandered around the room, ignoring the exceptional view of the city through ceiling-high windows in favor of the art collection that graced the paneled mahogany walls. Kuehn himself had doubtless chosen the Thayer, Klee, Rothko, and Graves paintings that were hung with such casual elegance. I was still admiring the Thayer, a large luminist oil done in shimmering yellows and pale creamy blues, when the head receptionist came up beside me and asked me to follow her back to Kuehn's office.

Kuehn's corner office overlooked the financial district and the central waterfront, with the low green hills of Bainbridge Island rising in the distance. The islands and the peninsula were still half-hidden behind a thin fog that was burning away under the warm sun of a late-summer morning. Kuehn rose from behind an antique desk of English walnut inset with leather. He was wearing a slightly baggy summer suit in tan poplin, the kind that Brooks Brothers has sold for nearly forty years. His white hair was freshly cut and he smelled faintly of bay rum and talcum powder, like an old barbershop. He greeted me with a smile and a cheerful good morning that seemed to chase his nearly eighty years away.

We settled into facing settees upholstered in dark green wool, with a French iron and glass coffee table between us. Kuehn poured coffee from a silver service and urged me to accept a pastry from a Wedgwood platter. I did and said, "You make me wish for a moment that I had stayed with a big firm."

He shook his head and swallowed a mouthful of croissant. "Oh, no, Mr. Riordan. You should do what pleases you. I checked and am told that you handle the cases you choose to take rather well. That is the important thing. This"—he gestured loosely, taking in not just his office but the whole building—"is so much stage dressing. Sometimes I think the law firms have taken over for the Medici. We collect fine art, support the theater and the ballet, hold ourselves out as role models, and pay for it all by conspiring in quiet corners, advising our clients how to beat this law or that regulation. I started my practice in a studio apartment on Capitol Hill. When I look back, I'm simply amazed that it ended up like this." He paused to drink some coffee and said, "Lisa telephoned me after we met at the museum to tell me the extraordinary story about the painting on a postcard. I would very much like to look at it. Do you have it?"

I took it from my briefcase and removed it carefully from the envelope before handing it to him. He looked at it closely, holding it by the edges with the habitual care of a former prosecutor. His finely sculpted features arranged themselves into a frown of concentration. He stayed that way for a long time, leaning forward in his chair, oblivious to my presence. Finally he looked up and managed a quizzical sort of smile.

"I can see why Lisa was disturbed," he said, placing the small painting on the table between us. "I would have thought it was an original. It's very similar in composition to the series of bird paintings that Lee painted, although it is smaller in size. The bird series is in the collection of the Metropolitan in New York. Lisa should try to compare this painting to the ones there."

"Do you have any idea who might have the skill to forge Thayer's work like this?" I asked.

He shook his head. "Impossible to say. There might be an enormously talented student out there in desperate need of money. Or an artist who is unsuccessful at his own work, imitating another painter for eating money. So much in this business depends on luck, it's a tribute to their integrity that more struggling artists don't forge the work of others."

"But why send Lisa a postcard? If a forger is just in it for the money, he would have no rational reason for calling attention to himself. Sending a painting on a postcard, to a dealer expert in the work of the artist you're forging, is crazy."

Kuehn was nodding, but it was a polite nod that did not indicate agreement. "Not necessarily," he said. "Look at it from the forger's point of view. Assume we are dealing with an unscrupulous man or woman of considerable ego, which they would have if they can paint at all. They might very well do something like this to show off, to make a point that economic value in art is intrinsically a matter of name and promotion. They would know that the typical dealer would be paralyzed into silence. Dealers hate forgery but they do very little about it. When it becomes known that a forger is working, something like Gresham's law goes to work."

I was puzzled. "I don't understand the reference. I thought Gresham's law had something to do with money."

"It does. Bad money drives out good. Bad art—fakes—devalue the good. People are less inclined to buy the work of a particular artist, at least one who is dead and cannot testify as to which works are genuine, if that artist is being forged. They're afraid of getting stuck. The other works of the forged artist become hard to sell and decline in value. The dealer loses twice. The value of the works in inventory go down, and the dealer's reputation becomes a bit soiled, if only by association with an artist whose work is being forged. That's probably why our friend Campbell was so upset the other night. At the very least, a charge that he sold a fake would require him to refund the purchase price immediately. Indeed, I suspect that he may be talking to the person he sold those paintings to, trying to buy them back."

"So a dealer who got stuck with a forgery would try to hush the thing up, even if he weren't otherwise involved?"

"Absolutely. And forgers know this. Very, very few are ever even publicly exposed, much less charged with a crime or sent to jail. So ego might well triumph over fear of exposure. Lisa is uniquely associated with Lee Thayer, because of the blood tie and her knowledge of his work. A forger could well feel that he was going to the source to vaunt his secret triumphs."

"I'm glad," I said slowly, "that you're not the one painting the fakes, because I think you would be impossible to catch. Or are you?"

Kuehn laughed uproariously, a shockingly young sound erupting out of his small, old man's body. "Heavens no," he said, still laughing. "I'll show you some of my work sometime; all of my partners buy it and hang it in their offices, thinking I'll be flattered by it. You'll see that I'm not good enough to have painted that bird." His laugh subsided to a smile. "But I'm flattered that you thought of me. Like most lawyers, I live out my evil fantasies vicariously, just watching what my clients do." He poured more coffee into both of our cups and helped himself to another pastry, looking at me expectantly.

"I don't know if Lisa has mentioned this to you or not," I

began. "But when she first received this painting, she was half-way convinced that it was genuine."

"She did say something about that. I suppose the forger was thinking it would be taken for one of the bird series, but it is clearly too new. You can see where the paint smudged from handling in the mail."

"That's not what Lisa meant. What she's wondering is if Lee Thayer is still alive."

A sudden cold silence filled the room. Kuehn stared at me as if I were a thief. "You're not serious, are you?" he asked. His voice was low and bore a slight edge of hostility. "Are you actually charging her to conduct an investigation into whether Lee is dead or not? That's outrageous."

I replied quietly. "I'm doing this as a friend, as well as her lawyer. Lisa finds this situation disturbing and would like some answers. I've told her that the chances of her grandfather being alive are about the same as finding Jack Kennedy alive and writing his memoirs up in Vermont, but she still can't put the feeling out of her mind. What I'd like to do is prove to her that the painted postcard was forged and identify the forger."

"I understand." He sighed. "Very well. What can I do to help?"

"Help me eliminate the possibility that Thayer is still alive. You dealt with the sheriff and the coroner and handled the estate for the family. Explain the evidence to Lisa. She's upset, but not irrational. She'll understand."

"Is there anything you'll need?"

"I might want to ask you some questions about the estate."

"I imagine the probate file is in records storage somewhere. I'll have someone retrieve it for you."

"Go ahead, but let me give you a list of specific documents. I've already read most of the file from the microfilm at the court-house."

Kuehn's face gave away surprise. "What on earth for? I could have told you what you needed to look at."

"If you had, my review wouldn't have been independent. Everything seemed in perfect order," I continued. "Death certificate, will, the petition for admission to probate, a couple of court orders, final distribution. Except for two things. Just before the cutoff date, you allowed two bills to be paid. Only there weren't any bills, just notations on the closing petition. One from a contractor named Batchelder, the other from something called Peninsula Lumber."

"Obviously I can't remember them. That was more than ten years ago. I'm sure I investigated them and found them correct. They were probably a couple of small trade bills."

"They weren't small. They totaled thirty-five thousand dollars."

"So what?" he asked. "Lee was probably having some work done up at the lodge. I'll tell you what, Mr. Riordan. I'll look them up in the file and find the bills and tell you what they were for. Will that help? Even though I can't see what possible meaning they could have." He made a point of looking at his watch. "I'm afraid I'll have to wrap this up now. Is there anything else?"

Kuehn sat impatiently, watching me. I could understand his irritation but not his lack of comprehension. It must have occurred to him, as it had to me, that if Thayer had survived the crash and chosen not to resume his former life, he would have needed money. His own "estate" would have been the easiest place to find it, if the estate's lawyer would cooperate. And Kuehn was Thayer's oldest and best friend.

"There is one other thing, if you can take the time. It's completely unrelated to any of this, but Lisa was curious about it and asked me to gather some information. It has to do with the murder of a young art student, in 1939. Thayer was charged for the crime, then released. Her name was Margaret Jura. Do you recall that?"

"Of course I do," he said, "I defended Anton Petrov, the man who was convicted for the crime. I resigned from the prosecutor's office to take his case. Why does Lisa want to know about that? It feels like ancient history, even to me."

I ignored his question. "What do you remember about it?"

His impatience suddenly vanished. He looked beyond me, his

eyes focused not on the Tobey painting behind me but on his memory of fifty years past. "I remember the night it happened," he said slowly. "It was one of those hot late-summer nights when you believe anything is possible. Magic, love, anything. I often think that Shakespeare wrote *The Tempest* on a night like that. We were having a party on David Campbell's houseboat. There was a lot of drinking, dancing, couples disappearing into the night. I was in the middle of it, yet when I was trying to defend poor Petrov, I couldn't put together where people were at what time any better than the police could."

"How could you agree to defend Petrov when you were a potential fact witness?"

"The judge resolved that right at the start. The prosecution was forbidden to question me or call me as a witness. There was no conflict after that, because my testimony would have hurt Anton, not helped him. You see, I couldn't remember seeing him at the time of the murder."

"I still don't understand why you took the case. Surely you saw the conflict problem."

"You forget what things were like then," he said, his eyes flashing angrily. "Leave a friend charged with murder to the fate of an assigned counsel, typically a courthouse drunk who could barely totter into the courtroom? There was no public defender's office. I couldn't do that."

I nodded. In the 1930's criminal defense of the poor was left to the courtroom scavengers willing to work for five dollars a day. Petrov would have had no chance at all. "Tell me, though," I said, leaning forward, "did Petrov kill her?"

He shrugged, as indifferent as a lawyer should be to that question. "At the time I was certain of his innocence. Petrov had a temper, especially when he drank, which was a good deal of the time. But I knew him, had painted with him up on Fidalgo Island. I couldn't believe he had done it. At the trial it seemed that all the evidence was against him. I ended up trying the case on the lack of an eyewitness and the presumption of innocence.

The jury refused to listen. They made up their minds early that Petrov was guilty."

"So now you think he killed her?"

"I don't know what to think. It has been many years. Let me put it this way: I lost my certainty because there was never any evidence that could clear him. None." He picked up his coffee cup and sipped at it, even though the coffee must have long since gone cold.

I leaned back and tried to loosen the little knots that had formed in my shoulders. "Do you still see Petrov?" I asked.

"No. He's been very much a recluse since he was released from prison. He sees almost no one, doesn't visit galleries or attend any of the parties on the art scene. From time to time he goes out and attempts to sell his work, but that's all. I visited him in prison for a couple of months after his conviction. After a while he refused to see me. I think he blamed me and everyone else for what happened to him. I bought his paintings from prison just to give him some money, but after his release in 1970 he never asked me for anything. He should have; I would have helped him. I've never been able to put that case in perspective. We all lose lawsuits, for good clients that we believe in and care about, and we learn to put that necessary distance between our emotions and our work. But there's always one case, or two in a career, that we can't forget. You probably have yours. Petrov is mine, even fifty years later."

"I understand," I said. "I had one like that. An arson-murder case. I still dream about it."

"Then you know." He spoke absently, as if he were indifferent to whether I heard him or not. I put the small painted postcard back into its envelope and then into my briefcase. The pictures of Margaret Jura that I had stolen were in the same leather slot. I put my hand on the photographs, then hesitated.

"Tell me about Margaret Jura," I said, breaking into Kuehn's reverie.

"Very young," he said. "So very damned young. And beautiful. I remember that, even though I can't recall her face. She wasn't naive, though. She carried herself with an awareness of her beauty. She had . . . a force. About half the men in that crowd were stuck on her. Those that weren't homosexual. Petrov had a worse case than most; he had dated her, and then Lee came back and started teaching at Cornish and took her away. God, Lee really loved her, you know." He shook his head, then turned away, but not before I saw the wetness in his eyes.

I took out the full-face photographic portrait that Campbell had taken and handed it to Kuehn. "I almost forgot that I had this picture of her," I said.

He took the picture in hand as carefully as he had the painting and looked at it for a long time. His face seemed suddenly haggard, full of its years. "That's her," he said, handing it back. "A good portrait. Lee painted her twice, but he never really captured her very well. This is better." He pressed his lips tightly together, until they lost their color. "Forgive me, Mr. Riordan, but I think that you should go. I find it difficult to confront so many memories in one morning. I suspect you don't understand that, but someday, I think, you will." He went to his desk and pressed a button on his telephone. A minute later the matronly receptionist returned and waited politely in the open double doors to Kuehn's office. I had been dismissed. I closed my briefcase, stood, and walked silently out of the office.

C H A P T E R

6

I had been planning to take some vacation time in the last two weeks of August anyway, so later that week I reviewed all of my files, did enough work to keep myself in good standing with the bar association, and made arrangements with Aaron Weissman to keep watch on a couple of the active matters. Aaron didn't complain. He was on the phone trying to get Karen, our new shared secretary, a part in a Chevrolet commercial being shot down on the waterfront. Karen, all white teeth and long flashing legs, was sitting on his desk, waiting. I shook my head at them, closed the connecting door, turned out the lights, and left.

Lisa had told me at our dinner in her garden that Terrill Hanks, the burly sculptor I had met at the SAM show, might know where Anton Petrov lived. I had tried to call him a couple of times over the past two days and had to settle for leaving messages on his answering machine. Eventually he had called my machine and told me to drop by his loft anytime, casually overlooking the fact that he never seemed to be home. I supposed that if he wasn't there, I could always give his answering machine the third degree.

Hanks's loft was on the top floor of a four-story brown brick industrial building on First Avenue, south of the Kingdome. The street door opened into a poorly lit lobby created from the once-open shop floor by newly built unpainted sheetrock walls. The freight elevator was at the back. It worked on a key, so I tried the intercom box that had been mounted in the newly built wall to my left. There was no answer from Hanks's loft or from the fashion photographer on the third floor. I tried the steel fire door that had been installed in the wall. It was unlocked and opened on a staircase. It was possible that Hanks was home but not answering the buzzer. I shrugged and began trudging up the four long flights of stairs.

On the top-floor landing a second fire door opened into a workroom that seemed to be part of Hanks's studio. Hanks specialized in large metal sculptures, and this room looked like a machine shop. Light came in through northern windows and large skylights. A working platform had been built into the center of the room, underneath a large block and tackle. There was a long bench full of tools and metal junk. Propped against the bench were tanks of gas used in welding and cutting torches. A welder's full face mask had been painted to resemble an African tribal mask and hung from a hook on the wall. I opened the heavy steel doors that connected the workroom to the rest of the loft. "Anybody here?" I said loudly. There was a long silence, finally punctuated by a man's booming laugh. "Hanks?" I said again, looking around the main room of the loft. The big room took up most of the floor. It had been remodeled for living space. The floors had been sanded and coated with varnish, the walls patched and painted white. Low-slung leather furniture was grouped around bright-colored Oriental rugs. To one side an expensive kitchen had been installed, complete with a restaurant-size stove, a subzero double refrigerator and butcher-block counters. At the rear of the open loft another room, presumably a bedroom, had been walled in for privacy.

Perhaps a minute after I called his name, Hanks emerged from the bedroom, pulling on a black T-shirt over his head. He was a thickset, muscular man of about forty, with short-cropped, receding reddish hair. He walked across the room to a dining table and picked up a pack of cigarettes. As he lit up I stepped out of the doorway and called his name again.

"Hi there, Riordan," he said, exhaling a gray fog. It hung in the sunlight that streamed in from the big wood-framed windows on two sides of the room. "I heard somebody before, and I thought it might be you. You've been filling up my tape machine for two days."

"Sorry to break in like this. I tried the buzzer and I couldn't get up the freight elevator, so I took the stairs. Did I wake you up?"

He laughed again. "Sort of. Want some coffee?" He walked across to the kitchen and poured each of us a cup from a white Krupps coffeemaker. "What can I do for you? Lisa called and said I should answer some questions for you."

"I'm looking for an old man named Anton Petrov. Lisa said you might know him, maybe have an address."

"Sure, I know him. Knew him, anyway. I met him when I was up in the Skagit Valley in the early seventies. I lived in Sedro Wooley, then in La Conner, trying to paint. Anton took me on as a student. I was his only one. He taught me a lot, but it still didn't help much. My main skill is sculpture. Anyway—"

He was interrupted by a woman emerging from the bedroom. She wore a man's blue denim workshirt as a bathrobe. From twenty feet away she looked perhaps thirty, a compact woman with tangled dark hair. Up close she was over forty, with a fine web of lines around her eyes and a slight pouching under the chin. Her brown eyes looked bruised and tired. She stared at me warily. "Terrill," she said in a harsh low voice, "who the fuck is this?"

Hanks leaned down and kissed her. "He's a friend of a friend. Go back to bed."

"I can't stay too much longer." She stepped around Hanks and poked around in the refrigerator until she emerged with an opened bottle of champagne. The label said it was Dom Perignon but she poured three inches into a water glass like it was 7-Up and put the bottle down on the counter. As she left the kitchen she looked back at me as she paused to light one of Hanks's cigarettes. I had the vague feeling I had seen her somewhere before.

"You were telling me about Petrov," I said when the woman was back in the bedroom. Hanks was looking at me now, his eyes amused, searching for some sign of shock or disapproval.

"Oh, right," he replied. "Well, I don't know where he is anymore. Haven't seen him in four or five years."

"Do you have an address for him, even an old one?"

"No. Tony and I worked together, but neither of us are the Christmas-card type. What's this all about, anyway?"

"Nothing much. Lisa Thayer and I just want to ask Petrov a couple of things about her grandfather."

"This have anything to do with the fight Lisa had with David Campbell at SAM last week?"

"I wouldn't call it a fight."

He laughed harshly. "Well, Riordan, you were standing there. But so was half the town, and a lot of them were trying to get down bets between rounds. The word I have is that Lisa accused the old boy of selling a couple of phony paintings and then having the balls to slip them into the show."

When somebody already knows something, there is not much point to telling it to them again. I said, "Look, you'll have to talk to Lisa if you want to know what was said. This is her business, and she has to decide what to say. Thanks for your time."

"Yeah. Well, Lisa's plain crazy if she thinks that David would sell a painting he knew was a fake. He's the best dealer in the area, the only one with a truly national reputation. He'd never do anything to jeopardize that."

I shrugged. "I don't know enough about the paintings or about David Campbell to have any kind of opinion. Lisa would like to talk to Petrov, that's all." I put my cup down on the counter. "Thanks again for the coffee."

He came around the counter and stood facing me, not close enough to be threatening, just enough to be in my face a little.

"Look," he said, his arms folded across his chest, "don't try to push Anton around. The guy's old, his whole life has been bitched, the last thing he wants is a bunch of people bothering him. Leave him alone."

"I'm not going to push him around. Why the hell would I want to?"

"I don't know. You come in here trying to pump me about him, and you won't say what you're doing. To me that's suspicious. So just lay off him."

"Or what?"

His face darkened. He started to say something, then thought better of it. He laughed, a short laugh, almost like a grunt. "Fucking lawyers. Try to show some heart. If you've got one. The door is over there." He pointed to the elevator. I walked over and got in and pulled the door closed, then switched the elevator car on. It jolted into life and gave me a slow jerky ride. As I rode down I thought about Hanks. His conversation had been disjointed, with quicksilver shifts in subject and mood, almost as if he was coked up. I wondered why Hanks had thought that I was going to lean on Anton Petrov. I wondered who had told him that I was a lawyer. At the Art Museum I had introduced myself simply as a friend of Lisa's. And I wondered where in hell I had seen the woman in Hanks's loft before.

La Conner lies in the delta of the Skagit River, a hundred miles north of Seattle. It is an old fishing and logging village, partially built on pilings driven into the edge of Swinomish Channel, a narrow, saltwater strait dividing the marshy mainland from the harsh rocky hills of Fidalgo Island. It has, or had, a down-home sort of charm, buildings and fishing boats clustered under the soaring steel arch of the Harry Powell Bridge that ties the delta to Fidalgo Island. Several very good painters had lived and worked in La Conner since the 1940's, getting along amiably with the Indian fisherman and Dutch farmers who worked the rich delta bottomlands. In the early 1970's a new wave of artists and writers settled in. They bought old boat houses and hardware stores and converted them into shops and lofts. As the town's reputation for quaint shops and art galleries grew the inevitable crowds began to fill the local bed-and-breakfast houses and country inns. Sunday afternoons now meant a main street full of Winnebagos and gray-haired ladies in sensible shoes and shorts clustered around the espresso stand in the middle of town.

I got into La Conner around four o'clock and, after fifteen minutes spent cursing the recreational vehicles that crawled through the narrow streets at five miles an hour, managed to find a parking spot only four or five blocks from the center of town. I tried the local office of the phone company and the post office, but neither had an address or telephone number for Petrov. I walked the six streets of the residential part of town, checking names on mailboxes, with no success. At seven o'clock, tired and thirsty, I went to the place where I should have started, the La Conner Tavern.

The perverse liquor laws of Washington State don't permit bars which serve hard liquor. Instead, we have the taverns, which serve only beer and wine. Small towns and city neighborhoods all have one or two taverns that are combination living room, social club, confessional, and pool hall. In the better joints drinking is encouraged, but getting falling-down drunk isn't. There are worse places to kill a couple of hours.

The La Conner Tavern was cool and dark, in welcome contrast to the bright sunlight and late-summer heat of the day. I put my name in to use the pool table and ordered a pint of a local ale named Thomas Kemper. It was amber-colored and tasted faintly of blueberries. I drank the beer and looked around at the crowd. It was a genial mixture of local workers and business owners, clustered around the two pool tables and the dart game at the back of the room. The dart game was being scored by a famous painter in his early eighties, so famous that even I knew who he was. A reasonably well-known comic novelist sat at the other end of the bar, deep in discussion with an auto mechanic named Mingo, according to the grease on his forearms and the patch on the breast pocket of his shirt. They were talking about the cost, probability, and metaphysical rightness of finding a new rear axle for a 1965 Ford Mustang.

I thought the painter was my best source of information about Anton Petrov, so I waited at the bar, drinking beer slowly and listening to the blues that was playing on the taped sound system. On my third beer the music changed to country and I listened to Emmy Lou Harris. By quarter past nine I was on my fourth pint and giving serious thought to mugging the old man. He finally tallied up the dart scores, clapped the winner on the back, and headed for the front door of the tavern. In the doorway he paused to fit a dark green beret on his bald head. I stopped him as he entered the street.

"Excuse me," I said, touching him lightly on the arm, "I was wondering if you could help me. I would like to find Anton Petrov, but I don't know where he lives."

"Why would you want to do that, son?" he replied. He squinted up at me in the pale light from the street lamp and the glow of the tavern's neon signs. "You're big enough to be a bill collector, and it looks like your nose has been broken a time or two. No, I don't think I'll tell you where Anton lives."

"I'm not a bill collector. I'm helping a friend named Lisa Thayer, who is Lee Thayer's granddaughter, do some research involving his work, the very early paintings. Petrov was a part of the same group of painters, before he went to jail. If you want, you can call Lisa and check on me."

He looked dubious. "I knew Lee Thayer pretty well and didn't much like him. Why does his granddaughter want to talk to poor Anton?"

"History. There aren't many people left from the 1930's who were part of the Northwest School. You're one of the few. Petrov is another and he knew Thayer better." I wondered how much longer I could keep spinning this story before I got caught in my own ignorance. Still, it was better to try than to admit that I wanted to question Petrov about the forgery of Thayer's work. In La Conner the year-round people were highly protective of the artists and writers who lived there. If the word got out that I was trying to put the screws to Petrov, I could spend a month in the county and never find him, much less talk to him.

The old man was still thinking it over. "All right," he said finally, still none too sure of me or my motives. "I suppose that Tony can take care of himself. He lives outside of town, out along the highway, about three miles east. There's a big blue Victorian farmhouse with white outbuildings. Tony's studio is in one of the outbuildings. The woman that owns the farm, her name is Diekmann."

"Thanks," I said, offering him my hand. "I appreciate it."

He left my hand hanging in the air. He turned and walked away, muttering to himself as he went. I shrugged and went back into the tavern. It was too late to do anything that night. Besides, I had checked the chalkboard before I had left the tavern and my name was about to come up for the next game of pool.

In the morning the heat and sun were gone, replaced by a dense ocean fog that rolled across the Skagit delta lowlands like smoke. I did three miles of roadwork on the two-lane blacktop highway that ran south of town. The morning was silent except for the bellowing of cows waiting to be milked and the occasional rumble of a passing truck. To the west, the headlands of Fidalgo Island were scarcely visible. Now and again a breath of wind would lift the fog and the hills would appear like the shoulders of giants sunk beneath the dark waters of the Sound.

A couple of hours later I was driving east across the flat expanse of the Skagit delta. The fog had lifted enough to reveal the Cascade Mountains, harsh broken peaks that loomed over the flat misty bottomland like a landscape from a Chinese painting. The land here was rich and the farmers who grew alfalfa, grain, and flowers had grown wealthy from it. Their farms were neat and orderly, with freshly painted old farmhouses amid carefully tended fields. I found the Diekmann farm on the first pass down the highway. The house was in a style known as Dutch Colonial, a bright blue two-story with a gambrel roof and a sleeping porch on the second floor. I pulled off the highway onto a gravel driveway and stopped for a moment, trying to guess which one of the white outbuildings might be Petrov's studio.

Before I could get out of the car the front door of the house opened and a sturdy-looking middle-aged woman dressed in a green down vest and blue jeans walked out toward me. I got out to meet her but stayed by my car.

I got a better look at her as she came closer. She had a plain round face and graying brown hair swept up and back from a widow's peak. The look on her face was not hostile but didn't give away anything either. I would not have an easy time getting past her to talk to Petrov.

"Morning," I said politely. "Is this the Diekmann farm?"

"I'm Ellen Diekmann," she said, stopping a few feet away from me and looking me over. "What are you selling?"

"Not a thing. My name's Matthew Riordan. I'm looking for Anton Petrov."

"He's not here. What do you want with him?"

That was a question I still didn't have a good answer for. "I'm doing some research," I said, "for a book about painters in the 1930's. I'd like to ask him some questions. He lives here, doesn't he?"

She answered grudgingly. "He rents a building from me. He's not here now."

"Do you know where he is? I've come up from Seattle to talk to him, and I really don't want to go back empty-handed."

"He's away on business. I'll tell him you stopped when he comes back."

"Where is he? Maybe I can call him."

She looked at me with even more suspicion. "I don't think I ought to tell you that."

"I wish you would. All I want to do is talk to him. I'm willing to pay him something for his time. And I was hoping to look at some of his work. I collect paintings, and I was interested in buying some of his."

She thought that one over. I was half expecting that she'd thaw out at the prospect of money. Petrov was probably behind in his rent.

She didn't. If anything, she looked more hostile. "I'll tell him you came by," she repeated. "If you've got a card, I'll give him that."

I opened my wallet and took one out. All it had printed on it was my name and home telephone number. Not everybody likes lawyers. "Have him call me anytime," I said. "Thanks a lot." I got into my car and backed slowly out of the gravel drive. She stood in the same place, watching me go. When I reached the road, I turned east, the direction of the interstate highway. There was an elementary school about a mile away. I pulled into the nearly empty parking lot and thought.

It had looked to me like Diekmann's place was a dairy farm, mostly planted in hay and grain, with a forty-acre section lying fallow. If she had a farmhand, he had probably done the morning milking and gone. I hadn't heard dogs, and if she had them, she probably would have brought one with her when a stranger had shown up on her land. There was something in her relationship to Petrov that went beyond that of landlord and tenant. There was at least one chance in ten that she had been lying when she said that Petrov was gone. There was a fifty-fifty chance that she would leave to go into town at some point during the day. It was worth waiting around to find out.

I left the car in the school lot, parked behind a couple of buses that were idle for the summer. I took the book that I had brought on the trip, a small clothbound collection of Melville's short stories, and walked the mile back down the road to Diekmann's farm. There was a woodlot across the road from her place. I found a semidry spot underneath a stand of alder that was screened by a chest-high bunch of roadside scrub and settled in to read.

Just over an hour later I was in the middle of "Bartleby the

Scrivener" when I heard the sound of an engine and the crunching noise of tires on gravel. I looked up and saw Ellen Diekmann behind the wheel of a blue Ford pickup, stopped at the mouth of her drive. She paused to let the traffic pass and then turned left, toward La Conner. I put the book in a pocket of my jacket and ambled across the road to the farm.

Petrov's studio was the second building I checked. It was a white-painted rectangular shed of twenty by thirty feet that had probably been a toolshed or a workshop. It had big sliding wooden doors in front and a second, regular door around the back. The back door was locked but it was old and the framing around the door was loose. I grasped the doorknob and pushed the door up and in against the frame. It gave enough to slip the tongue of the lock past the catch, and I walked in.

The studio was clean and plainly furnished. A milled cedar floor had been laid over the concrete foundation. Light came in through paned wooden windows and skylights. A woodstove stood on a brick platform at one end of the room. The rough plank walls had been painted white. A wide handmade worktable had been set up in the center of the room. There were three unfinished canvases and a few butcher paper sketches tacked to the walls. Despite its plain appearance the room had been carefully thought out and conveyed a sense of order. There were touches of beauty scattered about. A half-dozen polished pebbles lay in an earthenware bowl on the worktable. A spray of summer flowers, now fading, had been arranged with greens in a hand-blown glass vase. There was no bed, nor were there cooking utensils in the room. I was willing to bet serious money that Petrov lived up in the main house. That would help explain why Ellen Diekmann had been so protective.

The worktable held the usual variety of acrylic paints in tubes and powdered pigments in jars and tins. All were clean and closed tightly. The brushes had been cleaned and were neatly laid out, the tools hung up on a rack made of hooks and masonite that was nailed to one of the end walls. A rack for holding finished canvases stood empty in the opposite corner of the room. It looked like Petrov was planning to be gone for a long time.

There was a slant-top desk, its top folded up, in one corner of the room. The desk was not locked and I lowered the top to poke through the pigeonholes. In the third pigeonhole I found a receipt from a travel agency for an airplane ticket to New York. According to the ticket voucher Petrov had left the day before. The return was set for a Saturday, two weeks in the future.

I was still poking around the studio when I heard the sound of an engine coming closer. I dropped flat, crawled across the room, and looked out the north windows. Ellen Diekmann had returned sooner than I expected. I waited until she had put the truck into the garage that stood between the studio and the main house and had disappeared into the house. When she was inside, I slipped out of the studio and walked west, to the farm next door, and crawled carefully between the strands of barbed-wire fence at the property line. I had thought to use the line of trees that ran next to the fence on her neighbor's side of the line as cover and simply walk back to the road. But I made one small error.

The neighbors had dogs. Large ones. Fast ones.

I cleared the barbed wire separating the neighbor's fields from the road with better than a foot to spare. My landing was a little less elegant. I hit the drainage ditch beyond the fence on all fours, up to my knees and elbows in Skagit County mud. Any landing you can walk away from, I thought as I walked back up the road to my car, my feet squishing in mud the rest of the way.

CHAPTER 7

I rinsed off at a gardening faucet outside the elementary school. The fog was gone and the day was growing hot. It was still a couple of hours before noon, so there would be time enough to head over to the Olympic Peninsula to see what I could find out about the accident that had taken Lee Thayer's life. I drove north, through the town of Anacortes, then south over the bridge at Deception Pass. I stopped in Oak Harbor, on Whidbey Island, to buy new jeans and running shoes at a shopping mall near the naval air station. Then I caught the noon ferry from Keystone to Port Townsend and got back on the road, headed for Port Angeles, the county seat of Clallam County, where the accident had taken place.

The sheriff's office in Port Angeles had outgrown the old brick courthouse and moved into a low-slung concrete building up in the hill top part of town, high above the log export docks that shipped old-growth cedar to Japan for a tenth of what it was worth. I stopped at the information counter and asked to see the sheriff and the accident report on Lee Thayer's death. The deputy manning the counter told me that the sheriff was out until Saturday morning and the accident report was stored among the boxes of old paper records that the county had never had the time or money to put on microfilm. She also told me that my chances of actually getting anybody to dig through all that crap were about nine decimal places to the right of zero. I smiled sweetly at her and suggested that I could probably go wake up a county judge from his postlunch snooze and have an order compelling her personally to produce the records just in time to ruin her plans for Friday night. We compromised on half-past four that afternoon and I went off to look for the county coroner who had signed Lee Thayer's death certificate.

I found a listing for two Dr. William Bledsoes, the name I had taken off the microfilmed death certificate in Seattle, on Export Street in a residential section of Port Angeles. Their clinic was a low cedar and glass office building, shared with a couple of dentists and a lawyer. The nurse at the desk told me that the older Dr. Bledsoe was with a patient, so I settled in the waiting room with my book. A couple of tired young women tending feverish-looking children eyed me cautiously as though I was invading their turf. I dug through the magazines but found nothing newer than last Christmas. My pocket Melville was only slightly wet from my all-points landing at Ellen Diekmann's farm, so I opened it carefully and read.

It was just under an hour later when a man of nearly sixty years, wearing a white coat and a stethoscope, stepped into the waiting room and called my name.

"I'm here to ask you about an old case that happened when you were county coroner," I told him after we had exchanged names and I had handed him a business card, one that identified me as a lawyer. "A car went over the edge into the strait about a hundred miles west of here. The driver was identified later as a famous painter, Lee Thayer."

"I remember it well," he said. He had a round smooth reddish face and a wide forehead under a receding hairline. His eyes were pale blue and calm. "I took the job as coroner back then because all the doctors around here each took their turn, but I never much liked it. Thayer's death was one of the real big deals during the four years I had the job."

"His granddaughter is working on a book about him," I said, retreating into my somewhat frayed cover story, "and she wanted to get the circumstances of his death correct. I looked at the death certificate in the probate file down in Seattle and found your name on it. What do you remember?"

"Well, the sheriff's office made a pretty thorough investigation, under the circumstances. The car and the driver had gone sailing off into perdition. There was a storm on and we never did recover the car or the body. The current through there is fierce, especially on a storm tide. We lose a couple people every year in there, never do get the bodies back unless they wash up before the sea gets them."

"So you signed the death certificate without a body?" I asked, trying to keep my voice even.

He answered me calmly, without any impatience. "The statute and the attorney general say I can do that, son. There was no question that the driver of the car had died," he replied. "And the sheriff's office said the driver was Thayer. Besides, even if he survived the crash, nobody could live longer than ten minutes in that water. In October it's down as low as forty-five degrees. Hypothermia would set in in minutes."

"Did the insurance companies send in an investigator? Usually they don't like paying off if the proof of death is even the slightest bit shaky."

"I did get a call from an insurance-company man. I can't remember how much was involved, but I don't think it was very large. Less than a hundred thousand. At any rate, before I could send a letter back, I got a call from a lawyer in Seattle, representing the estate. He said not to worry about it, and I never heard anything from the insurance company again."

"Do you remember the name of the lawyer?"

"No. I should; he tried a big medical malpractice case out here a couple of years after that. He came out about the Thayer accident, too, and I met him then. A short man, but very smooth. Started with a K. His name, I mean."

"Morris Kuehn?"

"That's it. Came out before I signed the death certificate, told me that the family had made very thorough inquiries, they were convinced that Thayer was dead, and there was no reason I shouldn't sign the certificate."

"Did he say anything else about Thayer's death?"

"Not much. I don't recall it, anyway. I do remember asking him about Thayer's state of mind. That road out to Neah Bay is so damned bad, it's like suicide driving it in anything but good weather. Kuehn said he didn't know anything about that."

That, I thought, was a lie but an understandable one, given Kuehn's duty as executor of the estate to try to collect the insurance money as best he could. Thayer's problems with alcohol and depression had been well-known. Any hint of suicide and the insurance company would start dragging its feet. "Do you remember anything else about the whole thing, anything at all?" I asked.

"No, I think that's it. Oh, there's a funny kind of a postscript, I guess, to the whole thing."

"What's that?"

"A couple of months later I got a letter from the lawyer. He said that Thayer would have been sorry for the time and trouble I'd been put to and would have wanted to give me something in compensation. Since Thayer wasn't around to do it, Kuehn was sending me a little sketch of Thayer's from his own collection."

"Really." It seemed like an oddly out-of-place gesture. Bledsoe had just been doing the job he was supposed to do.

"I've still got it, framed in my office. People tell me it's valuable, worth at least fifty thousand bucks now. Want to see it?"

"Sure." I got up and followed him out of the waiting room, past the nurses' station and a warren of examination rooms, back into his office.

"It's on the back wall there," he said, pointing past his diplomas.

I saw the painting, done in gouache on paper, and my heart dropped a foot into my belly.

The sketch was of an angular, slender bird, caught in a brass jar. The bird and the jar merged into one. It was the same basic picture that had been on the postcard Lisa had received in the mail.

"You all right, Mr. Riordan?" Dr. Bledsoe asked solicitously.

I slowly got my senses back and nodded. "Have you shown this picture to anybody?" I asked hoarsely. "A gallery, an appraiser, anyone like that?"

"No," he said. "The only people who see it are my staff and the occasional patient. Why?"

"It's just very similar to another painting of Thayer's I've seen," I finally replied. "It's probably not that important, but if anyone comes around asking about your painting, or offering to buy it, could you let me know? I'd be grateful."

"Of course." He looked more than a little suspicious at my reaction but offered his hand as he showed me out. As we shook hands he smiled, and a shrewd light glimmered in his blue eyes. "Come back and tell me about this, whatever it is, when you're done with it," he said. "I always like a good story and this one looks promising. Okay?"

I said that I would and left him standing in the empty waiting room of his clinic. I drove back to the sheriff's office to get the accident report, more thoroughly puzzled than ever.

At nine o'clock the following morning I was standing on the gravel shoulder of State Highway 112, on the outskirts of the town of Neah Bay, on the Makah Indian reservation. I was drinking black coffee from a one-pint plastic cup under a steel gray morning sky and waiting for Arthur Klepitts, the sheriff of Clallam County, to show me the site of Thayer's fatal crash.

The Makah reservation sits on a thumb of land that juts out

into the cold North Pacific and extends all the way to Cape Flattery, the western tip of the lower forty-eight states. At the end of August this country had already passed into autumn. Cold clouds of mist darkened the landscape and presaged the winter rains. The reservation itself was a brooding place, full of sullen anger and alcoholic pain. The Makah lived in wooden shacks or shabby tract houses along rutted streets, a tribe of skillful artists and eloquent orators brought low by a century and a way of life they neither understood nor accepted.

I shivered under the heavy wool sweater I was wearing. The mist was turning into rain. I looked out at Neah Bay and watched the storm clouds wheeling the corner of land and turning toward Vancouver Island.

I had left Port Angeles at six the previous evening, still pondering the discovery of the bird painting in Dr. Bledsoe's office. I had tried to call Lisa and gotten no answer. Back at the sheriff's office I read the accident report. When I handed it back to the deputy, she said that she had told Sheriff Klepitts of my interest in Thayer's death and that he had offered to meet me near the scene the next morning. I thanked her and drove out of Port Angeles, heading for the dark forested country of the western peninsula. The summer hot spell had broken late in the night and the storm clouds had rolled in like divisions of artillery sending rare thunder and lightning crashing through the hills. I spent the night in an old tumbledown fisherman's motel on the outskirts of Clallam Bay, drinking brandy from a pint bottle bought at the state store, trying to coax heat from a small electric baseboard, wondering how in hell the prisoners at the state penitentiary across the highway made it through a single night, much less a five-year stretch.

A white county sheriff's patrol car pulled into the parking lot beside me. "Mr. Riordan?" the driver asked. He was a big square-headed man, with white blond hair and pale eyes. When I acknowledged who I was, he slid out of the car, pushing the steering wheel up and out of the way. He shook my hand.

"Got any ID?" he said casually. "I don't mind talking, but I like to make sure I know who I'm talking with."

I handed him a driver's license and a bar association card. He looked at both of them carefully. "Hop in," he said casually, pointing to the passenger side of his patrol car.

"I appreciate your coming out here," I said when we were on the road.

"Nothing to it," he replied. "I was down in Forks last night, having a chat with a couple of restaurant and tavern owners who haven't been paying enough attention to what my deputy tells 'em about not serving drunks. Those woodchoppers like their partying, that's for sure. I don't mind that, but I don't want to have to scrape them off the road the next morning. These roads aren't good enough for drunks to drive on." He glanced at me sideways, with the detached interest of a politician who wants to know how he's playing with the crowd.

"I looked at the accident report on Thayer's death," I said. "I saw that you were the deputy that responded to the call."

"Yeah, I was just a recruit then, back home after nine years in the army. That was over ten years ago."

"And you've made sheriff since then," I said. "That's pretty good."

"Well, I saw my opening when the old man retired. I liked politics better than I thought I would. Only thing is, you put so damned much weight on eating all those lodge dinners." Klepitts grinned and took a hand from the steering wheel to pat his belly.

We drove along in silence for a few more minutes, then pulled to the side of the road beneath the branches of a wide spreading hemlock tree. "The curve is a couple of hundred yards from here, but there's no spot to pull over, so we'd better walk," Klepitts said. He pulled a rain slicker out of the back seat and got out of the car. I waited while he put it on and started off down the side of the highway.

The rain was picking up now. I stuck my cold hands into the pockets of my jeans and followed his wide back as he trudged down the road. The road hugged the line of the bluff and swung out toward the water. "Here it is," he said as he reached the bow of the curve. "I can never forget that rock," he added. I stopped and looked out toward the water, following his arm as he pointed. A jagged rock towered up from the sea at the bow of the curve. Forty feet below, the black water of the strait surged and boiled against the base of the cliff. I turned back and studied the road, visualizing the angle and direction of Thayer's car as given in the accident report. The road was badly designed and sloped down, toward the water, rather than up into the curve. With rain and wet leaves on the surface the curve would be a death trap.

"You said you read the accident report?" Klepitts asked, walking in place to keep the chill of the rain away. His breath came out in plumes of mist.

"Yes, I did. I read it pretty carefully."

"Well, then you know what the driver of the logging truck reported. The black Jag was going way too fast, as though the driver was drunk or didn't know that the curve was coming up. The car just flew right off here."

"The guy in the logging truck didn't say whether the brake lights flashed or not," I mused. "I wonder if they did."

"I'm surprised the fellow from the insurance company didn't ask that question," Klepitts replied. "But it was only a sixty-thousand-dollar policy and I guess they figured it wasn't worth the fight. I always thought it was suicide, myself."

"What did you do when you got here?"

"Well, we got the call quick enough, came over the air from the truckers' CB radio and the boys in the truck marked the spot with flares. But we didn't have a car out here and I came all the way up from Forks, where I was stationed. Took me two hours. The storm came up and it was a real bastard. I had to stop twice to drag fallen trees off the road. When I did get here, I had only my flash. I looked around but I didn't see anything, not even the car. I put a rope on my own car and went down the bluff, like I learned in the army. The car was in the water, hung up on a rock, but I didn't see any body. I went back up and radioed in and they said to stay out here overnight, so I stayed in the car until first light. The storm had blown itself out, but there wasn't anything to see. Even the car was gone. We had a Coast Guard boat take a look later but there wasn't a damn thing to find. I figure the storm current rolled the Jag out to the deep part of the strait. No way to recover anything."

"Did you send a diver?"

He looked at me the way a teacher looks at a student who asks a foolish question. "This is a poor county, friend, and that is cold, treacherous water. I wouldn't risk a man's life just to find what's left of a body when the fish have been at it for a couple of days."

"Surely the family must have asked."

"Not really. It was five or six days before we connected the Jag to the dead man, Thayer. By then we knew there wouldn't be a damned thing left. The family's lawyer, he understood that, said he'd tell them. We didn't hear anything about it, after that. We knew damn well it was Thayer."

"How?"

"Oh, for Christ's sake," he said disgustedly. "He was gone, see? It was his car. He was a drunk, and by all reports despondent. It was made to order for suicide, only the old guy probably didn't want people to think he was a weakling."

I let the nasty crack about suicides go and kept at him. "What about the death certificate? The statute implies that there should be a pretty good investigation."

"That's the coronor's decision, Mr. Riordan. Dr. Bledsoe didn't seem to have any problems. Neither did anybody else, until now." He straightened up and tugged his tight uniform pants over his hips. "What in hell is this all about, anyway? Why's some big-city lawyer so all-fired interested in a traffic death that happened over ten years ago?"

"I'm a friend of Thayer's granddaughter," I replied. "She wanted somebody who knew the business to take a look at the accident scene."

"Probably doesn't want to admit that the guy killed himself."

His voice was heavy. "Tell your friend that I've seen one hell of a lot of accidents on this road, and you can be famous or rich or an artist"—the word came out with the "r" grated, "arteest"—"and if you're drunk, the road's gonna get you."

"I'll be sure to tell her that."

"Anything else?" he asked briskly, dismissing me with his tone. "I'm sorry but I've got to get back to town. I've got a ton of paperwork to do, and my older boy's playing football this afternoon. Preseason scrimmage."

I shook my head and followed him back to his car. We rode in silence to Neah Bay. When we got there, I thanked him for his time. He replied with a nod and a curt wave. The wheels of his car threw gravel as he pulled away.

When Klepitts was gone, I got into my car and headed east toward Port Angeles, careful to stay well behind and out of sight from Klepitts's car. I wanted to take a look at Thayer's fishing lodge and didn't want to arouse Klepitts's curiosity. I drove carefully in the gathering rainstorm, looking for the private road that, according to Lisa's hand-drawn map, wound up into the low coast hills above the highway.

I found the private road about ten miles east of the crash site, marked by the fieldstone pillar that Lisa had told me to look for. The road was graveled but it hadn't been well tended in a long time, and there were minor washouts and low spots already turning to sticky mud in the early-autumn rains. The road got steeper and I was glad I had four-wheel drive as I drove through a switchback turn and crested the last rise before turning into the wet green meadow in front of the lodge.

The lodge had been built in the 1950's as a summer retreat, during the years that Thayer had lived and worked in New York. It was built of peeled cedar logs, with a stone chimney and low, wide eaves that kept the rain away from the building and the front porch. It was roofed in split cedar shingles, some of them now curling with age. Lisa had told me that no one in the family had used the place regularly since her father had left the country, but that a caretaker stopped twice a month to check on things and make whatever repairs were necessary. There was firewood, liquor, canned food, and bedding if I wanted to stay the night.

I stepped onto the wide, covered front porch and turned back to look out over the strait. The storm was passing through, following the channel, completely blocking the view of Vancouver Island with its gray-black clouds. I turned away from the view, used the key Lisa had given me on the padlock that secured the front door, and let myself into the living room. It was a big room, with massive wooden ceiling beams and a large open river-rock fireplace. Wood-framed couches with leather cushions faced the fireplace, surrounding a low wooden table made from an old hatch cover. To my left I could see a dining room with a polished oak table and sturdy matching chairs. Next to it was a kitchen with an open counter that faced into the living room.

I was still looking the place over when the smell of smoke began to register in my mind. It was faint but it was there, the acrid scent of green woodsmoke or cigarettes. I quietly closed the door behind me and moved to check out the other rooms. The bedrooms, bath, and workroom were all empty. I came back to the living room. The smell of smoke was still there.

The fireplace was swept clean and the grating was cold. There was a fine film of dust on the books in the flanking bookcases and on the stack of old *Esquires* and *Paris Reviews* on the library table behind the sofa. I checked the kitchen cabinets next. Several glasses and plates had been recently washed, but the garbage can was empty. I went out the back door, walked across the overgrown back lawn to the garage, and stopped to peer in the windows. It was empty. I walked behind it, into the scrubby wet woods, and found what I was looking for, a spot where the earth had been turned and sifted with ashes. Somebody had buried his kitchen garbage with the ashes from the fireplace to keep the animals away. It had been done within the past twelve hours, because the rain hadn't yet washed the loose dirt smooth. I kicked at the dirt with my toe and turned up a flattened unfiltered cigarette stub. I had been right about the smoke.

I went back up to the house, made coffee, and poured myself
a couple of fingers of Irish whiskey in the hope of warming my
bones and aiding my thought processes. Lisa said that she hadn't
been up to the lodge in months, and as far as she knew, nobody
was using the place. The caretaker might have stayed overnight,
but he wouldn't have buried his garbage; there were a couple of
empty raccoon-proof cans wired shut by the garage. A couple
of kids breaking in wouldn't have picked the lock; they'd have
busted in a window, gotten hammered on the liquor, and stolen
anything worth stealing. I went through all the rooms again,
carefully, but there wasn't a clue as to who had come to the
lodge or what they had done. It seemed as if whoever had been
there had wanted no one to know it.

I chewed on that thought all the way to Port Angeles but
couldn't come up with anything. By the time I got back it was
almost three o'clock. The rain and wind and the slow-moving
logging trucks had made the trip even longer than usual. I ate
lunch at a fish place near the dock for the Black Ball Ferry that
runs between Port Angeles and Victoria, British Columbia.
When I left the restaurant, the rain had slowed to a fine mist.
I wandered along the dock, stretching my legs and watching the
deckhands load cars aboard the ferry. As the last car was loaded
a crewman in a yellow slicker unwound the stern lines. I glanced
up at the passenger deck. A small elderly man wrapped in a tan
raincoat stood on the deck. He stared back at the town through
the mist.

With a sudden start I realized that the old man was Morris
Kuehn.

Before I could move, or even shout, Kuehn turned away from
the rail and walked back into the passenger cabin. I ran down
the dock for the passenger gangway. At the foot of the ramp a
young ferry worker grabbed my arm and said, "Hey! Where're
you going?"

"I've got to get on that boat," I said, breathing heavily. "I'll
pay for a ticket on deck."

"You can't," he said. "Not unless you want to swim to it. The boat's already pulling out." He pointed at the twenty-foot seam of black water separating the boat from the dock.

"Shit. Shit," I repeated as I shook off his arm and cursed into his puzzled face. I turned and walked away, fists clenched in frustration.

"Fucking tourists," I heard him say behind me. "For Chrissake, the next boat leaves in two hours." I kept walking, back down the dock and into town, where I found a quiet hotel bar.

For the next hour I fed coffee into myself and quarters into the telephone on the wall. There was still no answer at Lisa's gallery or at her home. I finally called my answering service to see if she had left a message. She hadn't, but there was a message to call Vincent Ahlberg, a Seattle Police homicide captain.

As I dialed the Seattle Police switchboard I wondered why Ahlberg would be looking for me. I wasn't doing much criminal law anymore, and he was not the kind of man who made social calls. Not to me, anyway. He and I are almost friends, as much as a lawyer and a tough cop can be. We respect each other, but we see the world in profoundly different ways.

Ahlberg was still at his office. "Where the hell are you?" he growled as he got on the line.

"Port Angeles. What's going on?"

"Do you have a client named Lisa Thayer?"

"Yes. What's this all about?" My hand gripped the phone harder.

"She asked me to find you. Her car was blown up a couple of hours ago. In a parking garage down in Pioneer Square. She was out of the car when the bomb went off. She's bruised up but okay."

"Was anybody else hurt?"

"Not seriously. A kid parking cars caught a little more of the blast, got some burns and some cuts, but he's going to be okay."

"Could it have been something wrong with the car?"

"Not a chance." His voice hardened. "The bomb was dynamite, probably on an ignition timer, mounted underneath the driver's seat. Sixty seconds after you start the car, it blows. Somebody wanted your client dead. If she'd been in the car, she wouldn't be here."

"Lisa's an art dealer, for God's sake. Why in hell would somebody want to kill her?"

"That's what you're going to tell me. Get your butt down here, Matthew. As soon as you can."

CHAPTER

8

"I always thought you had to wait seven years before somebody missing could be declared dead," Lisa Thayer said, spreading strawberry jam on a corner of toast. She ate the toast and drank coffee with hot milk.

"Not true," I replied, pouring more coffee for myself and setting the pot back down on the metal café table that I had set out on my deck. "The statutes authorize a county coroner or the county prosecutor to sign a death certificate if there is reasonable evidence that a person has died. That evidence can be circumstantial. The seven-year idea comes from English common law. Five hundred years ago it was assumed that if a man went out of England for more than seven years, without sending a message back home, he was dead."

It was noon on Sunday morning, just twenty-four hours since the bomb that had nearly taken Lisa's life exploded at the entrance to the Butler Garage in Pioneer Square. We were sitting on my deck overlooking Lake Washington, trying to make sense of what had happened. I had returned to Seattle and brought her home from the hospital at ten o'clock the night before, then sat up with her until simple exhaustion and the mild sedatives the hospital had given her finally made her sleep. Lisa was too burned out from police questioning and shock to talk about what had happened until morning. Over breakfast I began by telling her of my trip to La Conner to find Petrov, then of my drive to the peninsula. She listened without comment until I started talking about her grandfather's accident. Then she peppered me with questions.

"What did you find out about the accident?" she asked.

"Nothing you'll like, I'm afraid. I went out to the place where it happened, with the sheriff. He was the officer who actually answered the call on the crash. Did you ever go out there?"

"I've never been to the exact place where it happened," she replied.

"Well, there's a sharp curve. The road slants away from the curve, there's no guardrail, and the drop to the water is nearly forty feet. The only way your grandfather could have survived was if he wasn't in the car. There isn't any direct evidence, no eyewitness as to who was actually driving the Jag. The circumstantial evidence, your grandfather in his car at the same time as the accident, was what persuaded the coroner."

"You're saying that he could still be alive."

I shook my head. "Extremely unlikely. The evidence supports the coroner's decision."

"Did you stop at the lodge?"

"Yes, and it was damned peculiar. It looked like somebody had just been there. There were clean glasses in the cupboards, and the garbage and ashes from the fire had been buried in the back. It was almost as though somebody wanted to hide the fact that they'd been there."

She thought about that and shrugged. "I don't know about that. The lodge is remote and there are people living out on the fringes of the national park who might squat there a night or two. I'm just glad they didn't break in and trash the place." She frowned, holding her coffee cup in front of her, trying hard to make sense out of what I was telling her. "The thing that's so weird about all of this is why the doctor would have the same painting of the bird on his office wall, and why Morris would have sent it to him," she said, shifting uncomfortably on the deck chair. The explosion had pitched her forward against the wall of the garage and she was becoming stiff. "I don't understand that at all."

"I don't either. I don't believe that Kuehn could have forgotten that painting. He lied to me. He knows something that he isn't telling. I tried calling him at home this morning, then called all the hotels in Victoria, looking for him. He isn't registered anywhere. That doesn't mean much. He could be staying under another name, or in somebody's home, or he could have taken another ferry to Vancouver or back here. Wherever he is, I want to find out what this is all about. Before somebody comes after you again."

She shivered underneath her thin wool sweater. The evening storm that had blown through from the coast had taken the last of summer away with it and the air was suddenly brittle with the smell of autumn.

"Tell me what you did yesterday," I said. "Start at the beginning and don't leave anything out."

"I already told Captain Ahlberg everything."

"Tell me anyway." I knew from past experience that crime victims seldom mentioned every detail in the first interview.

She sighed. "I got up at eight and ate breakfast at home. I drove down to the gallery at nine-thirty and opened up at ten. Business was slow, just a few tourists who weren't buyers, and I had some catalogs of Lee's old exhibitions that I had gotten out of the library at the museum. I was reading them, looking for anything that might bear on the provenance of the fake paintings in the SAM show." She stopped and took two aspirins out of her purse. "Can I have something to wash these down? Like a Bloody Mary. I ache all over."

I went inside, made the drink, and returned with it. Lisa swallowed the aspirins and took a big swallow of the drink. "Ugh. I left the gallery at one o'clock. I was going to a lunch at Vickie Chan's gallery, up in the Regrade district. I decided to drive. I went to the garage. One of the teenage boys that works there got the car."

"Which one?"

"I don't know his name. Ahlberg has already talked to him, I think."

"I'll check that. Was he the one that got hurt?"

"No. He brought the car down and left it running, then went to park a car that had just come in. I went to the office to give Willis, the manager, a check for September. I had just stepped into the office doorway when the car blew up. Quentin, the boy that was hurt, had just brought down another car and was walking in front of mine. Or so they tell me. I had my back turned. When it blew up, it knocked me into the office. I lost consciousness for a couple of seconds. And my hearing is just now starting to be normal."

"Who else was going to this lunch?"

"Probably forty people. Vickie likes to give these big lunches for her new artists. She can afford it, and it's good promotion."

"Who comes to them?"

"Gallery owners, artists, art critics, media people."

"Who knew you were going?"

"Vickie. I told her I was coming. Michael, my assistant. Erin Cody, from KWAN television. She was going, too." She shook her head, irritated. "Is this really necessary?"

"Yes. I'm fond of you, I'd like to have you stay around for a while. Keep trying."

"Morris. He called me on Thursday, after you'd talked to him. He wanted to know why I was wasting money paying you to look into Lee's car accident."

"What did you say?"

"I told him that I could waste my money any damned way I chose. I didn't tell him that you keep refusing to take any money for this."

"Good. They'd throw me out of the bar association if they knew I was giving it away. Who else?"

"God, I don't know. Wait. Terrill Hanks. I told Terrill when

I called him to tell him that you'd be asking him for information about Petrov. He said he was going and asked if I was."

"That's interesting. Both Hanks and Kuehn fit into this. Kuehn knows everybody. Hanks knew Petrov, and Campbell's gallery represents Hanks."

She started to take another sip from her drink but set it down on the table. "You're joking. Morris has been my friend since I was a child. And I used to date Terrill, for God's sake. Neither one of them would hurt me."

"Lisa, somebody tried to kill you. The odds are that someone you know had that bomb planted. Ex-boyfriends make excellent suspects."

"But it wasn't like that. Terrill didn't love me and he isn't carrying a torch for me. You saw that at his loft." She said it flatly but with an edge of old bitterness.

"You don't know what goes on in other people's minds, Lisa. How much of this did you tell Ahlberg?"

"As much as I could remember yesterday. I was pretty shaken." She picked up her drink and took a long swallow. "I don't know how much this would help him, anyway. Vickie sends out a guest list to the press a couple days before parties like this; she's a real promoter. Anyone could have known I was going to that party, or even have watched me park in the garage. And a lot of people know that I've had that red Alfa for years."

I sighed. "You're probably right. In the meantime, I want you to stay here, with me. Or let me move into your place. Or let me hire a couple of decent security people. You've got to take some precautions. I'm cheaper."

"I couldn't impose on you like that."

"It would be less of an imposition than your being dead. You've got to take this very seriously, especially until we know whether or not it's connected to the paintings you think are forged."

"You have a point there," she said slowly. "Okay. But only for a couple of days, until the cops can find the creep that blew up my car. Shit." She shifted again in the chair, searching for a way to get comfortable. I had been bruised all over like that a couple of times in my life, and I knew she wouldn't find one. I sat silently, trying to think things through.

"Are you going to talk to Terrill about this? Or David Campbell?" she asked.

"Ahlberg told me last night that he's going to question Campbell and Hanks today."

"So what do we do?" Lisa said.

"A couple of things, I think. First, you have to do everything you can to find out whether those three paintings are fakes. If somebody is trying to kill you to prevent you from doing that, the sooner you find out, the sooner you'll be safe. Second, I want to talk to Morris Kuehn again. I think you should be there, too. Assuming Kuehn is not the one trying to kill you, I think he will find it hard to hold anything back from you, particularly after the bombing attempt. Third, I need to find Anton Petrov. If those paintings are faked, I think he's the most likely one to have painted them, as well as the painting on the postcard. I think you ought to ask around here in town. Find out what he's been doing, if anybody is selling his stuff. Could you identify his work by style, technique, anything like that?"

"I could if I could see enough of it. How will you find Petrov? I thought you said his studio looked like he was going to be gone for a while."

"It did, but I found a plane-ticket receipt for New York. It said that he left last Thursday."

"You'll have to go there."

"Maybe. I still have a few friends on the cops back there. They might be able to find him, but I'm not sure they'd do it if there are no charges pending."

"I think we should both go. The research facilities there are better; I can use the art reference library at the Museum of Modern Art and at the New York Public Library. They'll have a much larger collection of catalogs and listings of the paintings that went into European collections. That's where these paintings supposedly came from."

"Let's make that decision after we talk to Kuehn," I said. "He might tell us something that will take us in a completely different direction. And you need to rest. You've had a hell of a jolt that hasn't really hit home yet."

Lisa nodded and picked up the Sunday *New York Times*. She separated the arts section from the rest of the paper and began to read it, sipping at her Bloody Mary, concentrating on her reading. I picked up the book review. The sun burned the haze from the sky and the air got warmer. The stillness was broken only by the distant drone of water-ski boats out on the lake. We read without talking for an hour. Lisa was one of the few women I knew who recognized the sanctity of Sunday newspaper reading. By three o'clock I was considering proposing marriage. That was when the phone rang. I put down the paper and padded back into the cool living room to answer it.

It was Vince Ahlberg. "Matthew," he said quietly, "I need you to come downtown again."

"Why?"

"It's Morris Kuehn. He's dead."

"No." I nearly slammed down the phone in frustration. "Damn it all to hell. How did it happen?"

"He shot himself. Or that's what it looks like, anyway. In his office, down at the Columbia Center."

"Is that where you are now?"

"Yes."

"Do you want me to bring Lisa?"

"Not right now. I can send a squad car for her later, if I want her."

I sighed heavily. "I'll be there as soon as I can. Lisa's known him for years, and he's been like family. She'll be pretty upset." Ahlberg hung up before I finished talking.

I went back out to the deck. "What was that all about?" Lisa asked. She folded up a piece of the Sunday paper and dropped it on the table, then pushed her sunglasses back on her head so that she could see me better as I stood in the doorway.

I hesitated. "There isn't any easy way to say this, Lisa. Morris

Kuehn is dead. He may have shot himself. Or it could be murder. Ahlberg doesn't know yet."

She sat still for a long moment as the shock worked itself onto her face. She pressed her hands to the sides of her head.

"My god," she said hoarsely. She seemed to grow smaller under the weight of grief. "How can this be real?"

"I don't know," I said lamely, "but it is."

Lisa covered her face with her hands and began to sob, her shoulders shaking. I went to her and held her gently, then gradually raised her out of the chair. "Listen to me," I said gently. "Listen to me. Ahlberg doesn't want you there right now, but you'll have to talk to him later. I'll be back as soon as I can. You're going to have to hold it together here for another couple of hours. If Kuehn was murdered, whoever tried to hurt you may try again. Do you know how to fire a gun?"

She didn't answer. I held her standing up for a moment, then eased myself out of her arms. I picked up her chin. "Do you know how to fire a gun?" I repeated.

"Of course not," she said, looking at me as if I were mad. "Why do you—"

"Never mind. I'm going to lock all the doors and windows. I want you to stay inside. Call somebody, a friend, if you want. The phone has two lines, so if I call you while you're on the phone, you'll hear it. Just click the phone once and I'll be on the line. Can you do that?"

"I'll be all right," she said, her voice breaking. Her eyes were desolate and empty. She tried to pull away, but I wouldn't let her go.

"Don't open the door for anybody except me or a uniformed police officer. I'll get back as soon as I can."

With one arm around her waist I brought her inside and helped her to the living-room sofa. She lay down on it, turned her face to the back of the sofa, and wept. I locked all the doors and windows and returned to find her curled in the fetal position, hands over her face. I stood and watched her for a moment.

There was nothing more I could do for her now. I turned off the lights and left, closing the door quietly behind me.

I gave my name to a uniformed patrolman at the Fourth Avenue entrance to the Columbia Center and waited while he went back into the building to check with somebody up the ranks. Eventually he returned and passed me through. I took the high-speed elevators up to Kuehn's office on the sixty-fourth floor. The elevator doors opened on a lobby that was already half full of Kuehn's law partners. They stood in silence, some still dressed in tennis whites and boating clothes from their late-summer Sunday. The silence was broken only by an occasional muttered conversation or a whisper into a cupped ear.

I looked around, suddenly conscious of the stares I was drawing from the assembled members of the firm. Lawyers are a tribal bunch; two partners who can't stand each other will still introduce each other to outsiders as "my partner" or "my colleague." They were gathered there because of the death of an elder and they were in no mood to tolerate an outsider.

A uniformed sergeant, with the name Reed on a plaque pinned to his starched blue shirt, plowed through the crowd to pick me up. He verified my name and said, "Captain Ahlberg's looking for you. He's in the dead man's office." He turned and I followed him through the lobby and down the corridor.

When I reached the doorway, Vince Ahlberg turned and nodded to Reed, then came over and shook my hand. He is not a handshaker by nature and I felt, as I always did, the weight he placed on the small ceremony. Ahlberg was a man of about fifty, of average height but broad-shouldered and trim from his usual regimen of roadwork, weight lifting, and squash. He had made some money from real-estate investments and had married more. He was immaculately dressed, as usual, in a suit of rich brown tweed that bespoke English tailoring. He is a cop by choice, not by need, and had twice rejected the chief's job in order to stay with homicide. He moves, and acts, with the compact grace of a man who has learned what he is good at.

"They've taken the body out," he said, his voice raspy, "but we've kept the room intact. I'm bothered by this."

"Tell me what happened," I said.

"The body was found about one-thirty this afternoon, by one of the associates who came in because he's starting a trial tomorrow. He was the first one to sign into the office today. Normally there would be ten or fifteen people here on a Sunday, but I guess the weather was too fine today. He didn't hear or see anyone else. He was walking down the hallway to the coffee station, stuck his head in, and found the body."

"Was it suicide?"

"It looks that way. Typical contact wound in the temple. We found Kuehn in that desk chair. It was pushed a foot and a half away from the desk, a little farther than it is now. The lab boys didn't put it back into the exact same spot. The gun was a .38 caliber revolver, registered to Kuehn. It's being tested now. I'll have a print report and a test firing by tonight."

"What's troubling you?"

"I'm not sure. Something about the setup, I don't know. Take a look at the desk chair." I did and saw a high-back chair upholstered in tufted brown leather riding on round casters.

"So?"

"There's very little blood on the chair. The wound was in the temple. If he was sitting back in the chair, there should have been more blood on it. There's only a small smear, right beside his head."

I looked at the arrangement of desk and chair. "He was leaning over the desk a little," I theorized. "Maybe bracing himself on the desktop. The force of the bullet pushed him back into the chair."

"I thought of that," Ahlberg replied. "The bloodstains on the rug look a little bit out of line for that. But I'll wait for forensics to give me a read. That's not my real problem."

"What is?"

"No note. Kuehn was a guy who led a consequential life. He knew damn near everybody. He's been a Nuremberg prosecutor, a famous trial lawyer, active in politics behind the scenes, first with old Senator Maguire, then as a White House counselor to President Carter. Remember how Carter froze all the Iranians' money during the hostage crisis? Kuehn was the guy that thought that up. So now he's going to check out. No note? No explanation? I don't believe it."

"You're looking at it the wrong way," I told him. "Lawyers keep secrets for people; it's part of their job. After a while they get good at it. It becomes second nature, even in their own lives. I'd have been surprised if Kuehn had left a note."

Ahlberg looked back at the empty chair. "Maybe you're right," he said. "I haven't seen his medical records yet. Do you suppose he was ill and wanted to take himself out before whatever he had got worse?"

"He didn't seem sick when I saw him last week. For a guy in his late seventies, he seemed pretty healthy."

"What were you talking to him about, anyway? This art-forgery thing that Ms. Thayer told us about yesterday?"

"That was part of it. It's a long, complicated story, and it belongs to Lisa. I want to get her permission and have her present when we talk."

"You're not going to pull any lawyer-client privilege crap on me, are you, Matthew? I need to know what I'm dealing with here, before the lawyers in this place start deciding what they want the story to be. I don't want to start fighting the mayor and the other powers if something ugly turns up."

"It's not crap, Vince, and you know it. Send a patrol car to bring Lisa down to your office; we'll talk there. I don't want to put her through this scene. She's had more than she can handle already."

He thought it over quickly. "All right. I'll have Reed send a car." He had started for the door when he was stopped by a large florid man wearing a blue blazer and white duck slacks. The man was named Evan Anderson and he was the head of the litigation department in Kuehn's law firm. I had heard Anderson speak at legal seminars. He was said to be a very good litigator, tough and hard-nosed. He looked like the former University of Washington football hero that he was. He had curly gray blond hair and piercing blue eyes set in a bony Nordic face. He spoke to Ahlberg with the warm buttery baritone voice that caused women jurors to send him letters reporting their undying devotion and the days of the month when their husbands would be out of town.

"Mr. Ahlberg," he began, "speaking for the rest of the firm—"

"It's Captain."

"What?"

"It's Captain Ahlberg, sir. What is your name?"

Anderson's eyes glinted in the pale afternoon sunlight. His mouth worked with anger, but he controlled it. "I am Evan Anderson," he said. "As I told you, I am speaking for the firm. We need to know exactly what happened here."

Ahlberg replied with just a trace of irony. "As soon as I know what happened here, Mr. Anderson, I'll be happy to tell you and your partners, provided there's no police reason not to. Right now you'll have to excuse me, I have—"

"Look, Captain," Anderson cut in, "we have a right to know what's going on here. Our founding partner is dead. The firm is in shock."

"And I sympathize with your loss and your feelings, sir." Ahlberg kept his voice even. "But right now I have my duties to attend to. Please inform your coworkers that this office is sealed."

"That's preposterous," Anderson said. "You can't—"

"I just did. There will be an officer stationed at the door."

"Then suppose you tell me, Captain, why you have a lawyer who's got no connection with our firm standing in our offices, looking at our files, in violation of every kind of legal and ethical requirement that exists!" Anderson was winding up to a jury speech. I expected Ahlberg's temper to blow up like a grenade.

"This man is not looking at any of your files, Mr. Anderson.

He's here because he may be a material witness. Now leave the room, sir."

"I am going to leave and call the chief of police, Captain."

"Please do so. He's a most charming man. If he doesn't satisfy you, then go to the courthouse. I believe Judge Charles is the duty judge this weekend."

Ahlberg put out an arm to usher Anderson to the door. Anderson stared at him for a full five seconds, then abruptly turned and left. Ahlberg smiled a small smile at his back.

"You did that pretty well," I told him.

He grunted. "I've been up to my ass in lawyers for over twenty years. It gets so it isn't even sporting."

When we left the Columbia Center, we walked back up Fourth Avenue toward the Public Safety Building. By the time we got there Lisa had arrived with a patrol officer. She was pale and withdrawn, and she spoke only when spoken to, answering questions with a perfunctory yes or no. She gave me permission to disclose to Ahlberg what I had been doing, so the three of us went into Vince's glass-enclosed office and sat down. A patrolman brought us coffee. Ahlberg took a small cigar from a leather case and lit it with a gold Dunhill lighter. He blew a smoke ring at one of the plastic no-smoking signs that had been installed when the police chief banned smoking throughout the building.

"Okay," he said. "Tell me what the hell is going on. Slowly. Don't leave anything out on the assumption I heard it yesterday."

I started at the beginning and told him about the painting on the postcard that Lisa had received in the mail, the paintings that she thought were fakes in the museum show, my research into Thayer's and Petrov's past, the murder of Margaret Jura, my trip to find Petrov and to look at the site of Thayer's car wreck. I had to go back over things Lisa had already told him, but Ahlberg wanted to hear the whole confused mess. It took me one entire cigar to get the story out. When I finished, Ahlberg stubbed out the cigar and said, "I don't buy the idea that Thayer is still alive. You hear about people disappearing, but in ninety

· 111 ·

cases out of a hundred, the supposed missing person is dead before anybody even reports them as missing. In the other ten they come back in the next few weeks, or they eventually get caught."

"I agree. I don't see how Thayer could have been in the car and survived the drop to the water. The only way that could work is if somebody else was driving, but nobody else turned up missing." I looked at Lisa out of the corner of my eye, but she seemed so stricken that nothing I said was having an effect on her. She was staring at the floor in front of her.

"So setting that aside," Vince said, "there's four really interesting things about Kuehn, some of which connect him to these fake paintings, if they are faked. First, he's an expert on Thayer's work, and that makes him dangerous to anybody who is selling fakes. Second, he's told at least one little lie, acting like he'd never seen that painting of a bird before when in fact he had a very similar picture in his possession, that he gave to the Clallam County coroner. Third, he knows Petrov, who's a likely candidate for the role of forger. Fourth, he's on the Victoria ferry on Saturday, maybe was in Thayer's old house, why we don't know, yet he's back down here on Sunday morning, either to kill himself or get killed."

"He also defended Petrov in a murder trial over fifty years ago. God only knows what that could mean."

"You said Petrov's airplane ticket put him in New York last Thursday. Which means Petrov couldn't have been meeting Kuehn or have been down here today." Vince rubbed the bridge of his nose. "I don't see where it gets us," he said. "Assuming we have to get anyplace at all. We don't know yet whether the lab evidence will support a finding of suicide. If it does, then Kuehn's death is just an unfortunate coincidence, coming right after the attempt on Ms. Thayer's life." He looked at Lisa. "Ms. Thayer, I hope you'll take some precautions until we find out who placed the bomb in your car. I can provide you with some protection, but I can't guarantee anything unless I put you in protective custody, and I don't think you'd enjoy that."

"I'll take care of her," I said. "I'll get security people if I have to."

Vince raised an eyebrow but said nothing. "Did you talk to David Campbell?" I asked. "He's the one person with the most to lose if Lisa is right about the paintings being fake."

"Yes, I talked to him this morning. Or rather I listened while he talked down to me. A snotty old bastard, isn't he? He seemed genuinely shocked when I told him what it was about. He said he and Ms. Thayer had differences but he would never want to see her hurt. He also had a solid alibi for yesterday, all morning and in the afternoon."

"What about his lawyer? He's the one who tried to push us around at the SAM show."

"I asked Campbell if he wanted a lawyer present, and he said his lawyer was in San Francisco. That's Tabor, right?"

"Right. But that doesn't mean they're not suspects. The bombing could have been hired."

"I expect it was, and I'm having it checked out. A neat little charge like that, wired to a sixty-second delay, is very cute and not that easy to do. We're sweeping everybody we can think of who might hire out for that kind of work."

"You going to arrest them or have them in to chat?"

"Neither; my people are just working their sources. We don't have that much to go on, yet."

There was a brief silence. Suddenly Lisa began to tremble, as though suffering a seizure. "Men are such bastards," she said, her voice full of disgust. "This is my life, my family, my dear friend dead, and you talk like you're handicapping a horse race." She pressed her fists against her eyes and wept bitterly.

"Look," I said to Vince, "I've got to get her home. Can we go?"

Ahlberg had watched Lisa coldly. He was a man who had lived behind emotional walls for so long that he assumed everyone had them. He waved a hand, a frustrated gesture. "I haven't got an exit line. Sure, go ahead."

I gathered Lisa up from her chair and Ahlberg walked us to

the elevators. Along the way he cornered a patrolman to walk us to my car. When we reached the bank of elevators, he said to Lisa, very quietly, "This will seem better in a couple of days, Ms. Thayer. I know that's hard to see right now, but it will be. Get some rest."

He meant well. Lisa stared at him as if he were mad. "Right," she said finally, putting a pound of sarcasm on the single word. The elevator came and we took it down to the street.

A couple of hours later George Schulman, one of that rare breed of general-practice doctors who is medically competent, wise in the ways of people, and makes house calls, stepped out of my bedroom and closed the door behind him. "I've got her lightly tranquilized," he said. "Was she given any painkillers by the hospital yesterday?"

"Yes, but she hasn't been taking them. She's had one Bloody Mary and two aspirin today. Other than that she's toughing it out."

"Better for her in the long run if she does," he agreed. "If she has a lot of pain in the night, let her take one. Her stress level is phenomenal, not surprising with what she's been through. What about you? You maintaining?"

"I'm not the victim this time, George. I just like this woman, that's all."

He looked at me quizzically through thick rimless glasses that had slid down to the end of his nose, but he couldn't find the right words to say. "Well, call me if you need me," he said finally.

"We'll be okay, George. Thanks a lot."

He shrugged and pulled on his sport coat and left. I listened in the quiet house to the sound of his car going up the drive. I was still sitting and listening to the empty night sounds when the sound of the telephone crashed into my consciousness like glass being broken. I picked it up quickly.

It was Vince Ahlberg. "I've got the exit line," he said quietly. "Lab report came back. The bullet that killed Kuehn came from his own gun. But when they tested the gun for prints, it came back clean. Totally. Somebody wiped it after the shot was fired and I sort of doubt that Mr. Kuehn was in any condition to do that."

"This is getting even worse than I thought," I replied.

"Ain't it, though. Take care." The line went dead in my ear. I went to the desk in my living room and unlocked the right-hand drawer. I took a Walther PPK automatic out of its box and loaded it. When I went up to the spare bedroom that night, I took the Walther with me and placed it on the nightstand, within easy reach. It was the last thing I saw before I fell asleep.

C H A P T E R

9

The Tuesday-morning memorial service for Morris Kuehn at St. Mark's Cathedral on Capitol Hill was dignified and brief. The power structure of the city and the state was out in full force. The governor sat with the mayor and the two former governors whom he liked. The third former governor, an odd and reclusive university professor, sat by herself, staring moodily at the Episcopal bishop who was conducting the service. A United States senator, up for reelection that fall and looking weak in the polls, was working the crowd as though he were at a Labor Day picnic. Lawyers and corporate executives surreptitiously checked their watches and wondered whether to cancel their lunchtime squash matches.

Lisa and I sat near the back, listening quietly. Since her angry outburst on Sunday night Lisa had shown a quiet strength that surprised me. Nothing in her life had prepared her for the violence she had come close to, but she woke on Monday morning determined to carry on with her life and her work. She opened the gallery and put in a full day, watched over by a plainclothes security guard I had hired from one of the few private security agencies I really trusted. She was still too bruised up to go back to her dance class but we did go to a health club. She stretched and took a whirlpool while I worked out on the weights and one of those mechanical stair-climbing machines that always struck me as a perfect metaphor for modern life. Lisa's determination made her quiet, almost stony. She spoke only when spoken to, offering nothing. It was such a contrast from her normal personality that I began to worry, but I tried hard to keep my mouth shut and show respect for what she was trying to do.

When the service was over, we stepped outside, blinking in the sunshine, and saw Vince Ahlberg waiting for us on the walk to the parking lot. He was wearing one of the expensive dark suits he always wore, as if to be ready for the funerals that were an inevitable part of his job.

"Hello, Matthew, Ms. Thayer," he said as we approached. "Got a minute? I'd like to talk to you again."

"Sure," I said. Lisa nodded at him politely, but without warmth.

"Let's go sit down. There's a bench over here in the churchyard." We followed him to a stone bench in the small, shaded yard and sat down. Vince stayed standing, pacing a little. He is normally as nervous as igneous rock but the work load of the two investigations, the car bombing and Kuehn's murder, was beginning to wear on him. His eyes looked raw and exhaustion was embedded like grit in the lines of his leathery face.

"I was kind of surprised to see Kuehn buried from here," he said. "I thought he was Jewish." His reference, I knew, was old-fashioned, not invidious, to days when a man referred to himself as a Dutchman or Finn as a means of definition.

"He was," Lisa said, "but his second wife was Episcopalian. Morris was not religious, but he liked the ritual and attended regularly."

"I didn't know he had a wife, second or otherwise."

"She died ten years ago. Morris had no children. He had his friends and his colleagues, but no real family."

Ahlberg thought that one over. It was a line, I knew, that could be used to describe Ahlberg himself. "I have the full autopsy report," he began, "and all it does is confuse me. The wound was a contact wound, with typical gas distension, what you would expect if it was suicide. There was no struggle. None. You saw Kuehn's desk, Matthew, all those files laid out in neat orderly rows. The files were in the exact order his secretary put them in when she laid them out on Friday afternoon. I know that because she had a list in her desk of the order Kuehn wanted the files in for Monday morning, and they matched the list perfectly. Nobody could have reconstructed the desk that perfectly if there had been a struggle. The best part is the hands. Kuehn was left-handed. The ME did a nitrate test on Kuehn's hands, and the left hand tested positive. The ballistics match the gun we found down to the fatal bullet. And yet there are no goddamn prints on the gun. Somebody wiped it. We even found a linen thread caught on the edge of the grip." He shook his head as though it ached with frustration.

"Jesus, Vince," I replied, "do we have to do this now? Lisa's been through a hell of a bad time. Let me talk to you later, okay?"

Lisa turned on the bench to look at me, her eyes stony. "It's all right," she said sharply. "If this has something to do with me, I want to be part of it." She turned back to Ahlberg. "It sounds to me like someone came in, found Morris's body, and wiped the prints. The question is why?"

"That's the way it must be," Vince replied, "but why in hell would somebody want to do it? All the other physical evidence points to suicide, and wiping the prints doesn't change that. Anyway, I have to know more about Kuehn's emotional state. You both saw and talked to him recently. How did he react, what was his mood? Tell me anything that comes to mind; at this point I'm desperate."

"He seemed . . . autumnal," Lisa said. "When we were talking at the Art Museum, he told me how much he hated to see summer ending, because he couldn't be sure he'd see another one. He talked more than I can ever remember about the past, when he and my grandfather were young and trying to learn to paint.

He was a man who usually despised nostalgia, but he was immersing himself in it."

"He was much the same with me," I said. "He seemed engaged in the problem of who might be forging the paintings, and then when I brought up that old murder case, he seemed to lose control for a moment."

"Which old murder case? The murder Petrov was convicted of?"

"That's right; the woman who was killed was Thayer's girlfriend, Margaret Jura." I stopped, too embarrassed by my childish theft of the pictures from David Campbell's files to reveal how I had shown them to Kuehn.

"Why would talking about that case have that effect on him?"

"Because he lost it and maybe the way he lost it. He wouldn't come out and say it, but I think he believed that Petrov was innocent, at least at the time. Kuehn had only been practicing law for about a year, and I think he got hammered by a more experienced prosecutor. It can happen to anybody, the first time out, but losing a murder case for a friend is the most awful experience a lawyer can have. I know."

Ahlberg caught my eye and nodded. He knew the case I was talking about. "I don't know what to think," he said finally. "You're telling me about an old man who's feeling the weight of his years, perhaps lonely, but rich in money and friends, power and accomplishment. I don't see him as a suicide. But I can't tie Kuehn's death in with what happened to Ms. Thayer, or these allegedly forged paintings, or any of this. I don't even know what he was doing in Victoria last Saturday. He was definitely up there; he took the seaplane that flies from Victoria Harbor to Lake Union and flew back Saturday night. But nobody in his firm knows where he was going, or why. It just doesn't make sense." He sighed. "What are you going to do now?"

"We're going to New York," Lisa said. "On the red-eye flight, tonight. Riordan's going to look for Petrov and I'm going to try and prove that the three paintings were forged. Maybe that will tell you something about what happened to Morris and who tried to kill me. Maybe it won't. But that is what I know how to do and that is what I'm going to try." Her voice was flat and determined.

"Okay," Ahlberg said, a small note of admiration in his voice. "If you find anything, I want to know about it right away. Good luck." He shoved his hands into his jacket pockets and strode away.

Lisa handled the red-eye flight with the practiced ease of a traveling salesman. She booked us two seats near the rear of a two-aisle DC-10, away from the noise and smoke of the center cabin. Twenty minutes after takeoff she had taken two aspirin with a large glass of water and a small brandy. She removed the armrest between the seats, switched off her reading light, wrapped herself in a blanket, and snuggled down next to me. I liked the way she felt, her warmth pressed against me. I had been attracted to Lisa since I had first started to work for her, but had pushed my feelings aside, having learned the hard way not to become involved with clients. That might have changed on the night of the gallery opening when Lisa's face had been shining with pleasure at her success. Those feelings hadn't gone away with the threat to her life, but it seemed to me that Lisa needed support and friendship, not the happy confusion of a new love affair. In a deeper sense the real problem lay within us. We were two very tentative people, living in a tentative age, bearing the scars and hurts that others had inflicted on us, the guilt for wrongs we had done. We lived lives with distinct work and exercise and volunteer commitments, things that kept us busy and safe and apart. Part of the reason Lisa had been comfortable with me was that I had respected the boundaries she had put up. Sometimes I wondered if she knew just how much the fear of being rejected was keeping me in my own box. Maybe this quest we were pursuing would give us the courage to break out of our sheltered little boxes. The important thing was to try.

I put down my book and switched off my reading light. I gathered Lisa gently into my arms so that she could lean against me as she slept. She stirred once and murmured something so softly I couldn't hear what it was. I soothed her back to sleep, content to feel her breathing next to me as I stared out the window and imagined the clear bright stars streaking through the dark night sky.

A groggy fifty-dollar taxi ride took us through the industrial wastelands of northern New Jersey and into the steamy mid-morning heat of lower Manhattan. The taxi rattled up Tenth Avenue and made a left onto Seventy-first Street. Then it dropped us at the apartment Lisa's mother owned at Seventy-third and West End Avenue. I waited in the lobby, grit-eyed and grimy from the flight, while Lisa showed her mother's letter to the doorman and argued with him in a mix of English and Spanish. Lisa's negotiations for the keys were concluded with smiles and a crumpled twenty-dollar bill I had managed to find wedged in a pocket of my khaki slacks. We took the keys and loaded our bags in the elevator. Lisa traveled with surprisingly little luggage and I was able to carry both of her bags and mine down the hallway while Lisa unlocked the multiple locks and disarmed the security system at her mother's door.

The building was a condominium, a gut rehabilitation of an old hotel and men's club. The lobby was filled with green marble and ornate walnut woodwork, a reminder of the wealth New York had always had. Lisa's mother's apartment was on the southwest corner of the building, on an upper-floor set-back that provided her with both south and west terraces. The apartment consisted of a kitchen with a dining area, a high-ceilinged living room, and two bedrooms with baths at opposite ends of the apartment. It was furnished with a deft hand. The wool- and leather-covered furniture was modern, sparse, and well chosen to complement the art collection on the walls. There was a large Thayer oil over the fireplace, a major Klee in the master bedroom, and a small Matisse that the Japanese would pay several million dollars for.

"Good God," I said, dropping the bags in the living room and staring at the paintings. "She ought to have this stuff in a bank vault, not hanging in an empty apartment waiting to get burgled."

"Mother divorced very well, didn't she?" Lisa asked, a malicious grin on her face. "These were from Lee's collection. When she asked for them, my father just sat there and nodded amiably, his mind already on the next patient he'd be seeing when he left the lawyer's office. She got a Rothko, too, but she sold that for enough money to buy this apartment."

"Where is your mother, anyway?"

"She can't stand New York in the summer. She's up in Québec City, with her lover. He's a columnist for one of the French-language newspapers."

That raised a lot of interesting questions that I decided not to ask. I put my stuff away in the guest bedroom, which was fitted out as a TV/stereo room, and showered off the airplane smell. I put on white duck slacks and a lightweight shirt that I had bought in Mexico. Lisa had changed into a white loose skirt and blouse. She took me on an expedition up Broadway in search of food and other essentials. We walked up Broadway to buy deli food at Zabar's and bagels at H&H, then window-shopped with the yuppie mothers and Puerto Rican nannies along Columbus Avenue. The red brick buildings looked clean and the displays in the shop windows were rich, even sumptuous. I marveled at how gentrified the neighborhood had become.

"I left here in 1979, when the first fancy bars were going in on Columbus," I said. "I feel like I've missed an era."

"You didn't miss much," Lisa replied. "I got out of Barnard in 1982 and worked here for three more years. Expensive liquor, more expensive coke, and dating guys named Josh and Ty who worked in investment banking and whose idea of a serious relationship was shacking up for the weekend in a country inn outside of Rye. The best epitaph for the 1980's was one that I read somewhere. "'The food was good,'" she quoted. "I hope we can keep the food."

I laughed. "Maybe you're right."

We went back to the apartment, worn down by the heat of early afternoon. Lisa began working the telephone, calling old friends in the art world to make appointments for meetings and lunches. I managed to squeeze in a call to a New York homicide lieutenant named Alan Greenberg. I had known Greenberg from the early 1970's, when I worked out of the U.S. attorney's office on one of the organized-crime strike forces. Greenberg remembered me and listened patiently when I told him what I was up to. I gave him a description of Petrov and he promised to let me know if anything turned up. I settled down to read and quickly fell asleep. It was an odd, uncomfortable sleep, filled with dreams that I could remember only snatches of. Some of the dreams were about Thayer and Petrov and Margaret Jura, people I had never known but who seemed to be becoming part of my life.

When I woke, sweaty and unsettled, it was nearly eight o'clock. I found a note from Lisa next to me, saying that she was having a drink with a college friend at a bar near Lincoln Center and would meet me for dinner at 9:30. We had fought earlier in the day about how safe she would be by herself, until she pointed out that a crowded midtown street would be about the worst place in the world for someone to attack her and I was reluctantly forced to agree. I rolled out of bed, put on gym shorts and running shoes, and walked out to Riverside Park, determined to work out the kinks that remained in my back and legs from the long flight. I jogged north on the park paths, ran past the last of the evening dog walkers and soccer players, and stopped once to watch the sun go down across the Hudson. I left the park at 104th and continued up Riverside for another ten blocks before turning around. The street sloped downhill and I stretched out my stride, breathing easily. The city air was a heavy mix of humidity, soot, and ozone, but I breathed it like a tonic. At Eighty-fourth Street I turned back into the park and took the short path to the top of Mount Tom, a huge rock that jutted out over the hillside, overlooking the Hudson River. One hundred forty years ago Edgar Allan Poe had spent his summer afternoons on Mount Tom, staring at the river, dreaming of his lost love and the nightmarish things that found their way into his writing. At the top of Mount Tom I paused and looked out at the lights on the far shore of the Hudson. The lights shimmered like a magic kingdom, but even in my heart I knew it was just New Jersey, sitting there in the dark.

CHAPTER

10

On the next morning, a Thursday, Lisa began a tour of the galleries that had handled her grandfather's work. She started with the old-fashioned, silk-stocking galleries on the Upper East Side and by early afternoon worked her way down to the mid-town auction houses. She asked each owner or manager whether any Thayers of doubtful authenticity had been turning up for sale. None of the people she talked to admitted having heard even so much as a rumor. As she continued her frustrating task I drifted along behind her, checking out each gallery as she went in and then waiting in the street. I was armed with a list of every hotel in Manhattan, torn from the telephone directory, and a roll of quarters. I started telephoning hotels that were in Chelsea and Murray Hill, reasonable walking distance to the main gallery areas in SoHo. I asked for Petrov and in every case was told that nobody by that name was there. It was the longest of shots and Petrov could have screwed it simply by registering under a phony name, easy enough to do in one of the hundreds of cheaper hotels that rented rooms by the hour, day, or week, cockroaches included at no extra charge.

Lisa and I were invited to a late lunch at the Four Cats, an outpost of Woody Allen country on West Broadway in SoHo. The restaurant was a long narrow hall with exposed brick walls, a cocktail bar on one side of the room, and tables covered with starched white linen on the other. The crowd was composed of handsome men dining with each other and rich pretty children chattering in German and Italian, waving their gold lighters and Marlboro cigarettes in the air. I would have preferred a pastrami sandwich and a cold beer from any reasonably clean delicatessen, but we were the luncheon guests of a transplanted English art dealer named Claudia Warren, who had given Lisa her first job after she had graduated from Barnard. Warren was a fashionably anorexic blonde, in age somewhere between forty-five and sixty, and making enough money selling paintings to wear an original Chanel suit to work, or so Lisa had said. I listened with half an ear while they caught up on gossip and sliced up mutual friends. When Claudia left to say hello to clients at the bar, I turned to Lisa and said, "Is she always this dreadful, or is this an act for the benefit of out-of-towners?"

Lisa smiled wanly. "Always. But she knows everyone and everything, and she's got the best eyes in town. And ears. If anyone has information, it will be Claudia. Did you find anything on Petrov?"

"Not a thing. I've got about a hundred hotels to go, but my guess is he's using a phony name. Not that that helps us much. I wonder what he's doing here."

"Which we won't know until we talk to him. How much do you think I should tell Claudia about this?"

"As much as you want the world to know. Even if you swear her to secrecy, my guess is she'd spill it within two weeks. Even successful gossips have to trade for information."

Mrs. Warren returned to the table a few minutes later. "I'm sorry, my dears, but I simply had to speak to Elizabeth. She's a million-dollar-a-year client. Now," she said, taking a sip of the stingingly dry Italian wine she had ordered and lighting a cigarette, "where were we?"

"I wanted to ask you about how my grandfather's work has

been moving," Lisa said. "I've sold a fair amount in order to get myself established, and I'm wondering if prices here are holding firm."

At the mention of money Claudia changed from a slightly deranged pseudo-socialite into an intense businesswoman. "The whole postwar generation of painters is going to be very, very hot," she confided. "The Japanese and Hong Kong money has moved through impressionism like a hurricane, and it's heading into the more modern painters. I mean, good God, they paid thirty million last month for a mediocre Van Gogh. The big bucks are already out for Jackson Pollock. As for the others—Rothko, Thayer, Guston, Johns—the market is heading their way. The smart money is already buying up everything they can get their hands on. In fact, last month I bought two of your grandfather's pieces at Sotheby's. There was a lull in the bidding, one of those little price breaks that happens on off nights, and I snapped them up for thirty percent less than the estimate." She smiled the happy, nasty smile of a Renaissance courtesan. "You should hang on to your better paintings, darling, at least for now, because you'll be set for life when they start going up."

"The other reason I wanted to talk you," Lisa said slowly, "was because I have reason to believe that Thayer's work is being forged by someone currently active, and very skillful. Have you heard anything about fakes being offered for sale in New York? Usually they go through the auction houses here."

Claudia's jaw dropped so hard I thought it was going to hit the table. "No, no," she gasped. "Nothing like that. Are you sure of your facts? If you let these sorts of crazy rumors become public knowledge, they can be absolutely devastating to the value of the artist's paintings."

"But if the forger is exposed and the fake works identified, prices will firm up in the long run," Lisa replied.

"That's true, but . . ." Claudia's voice trailed off as she followed a thought. "Where did the fakes first show up?"

"In Seattle. They were included in a show at the Seattle Art Museum."

She laughed with disbelief. "Lisa," she chided in a low mocking tone, "why would anyone take such a risk of exposure, even if they could fool the curator? Surely you're imagining this."

Lisa's eyes blazed. "I didn't imagine the bomb that blew up my car after I started asking questions," she said, her voice soft but intense. "If I hadn't been delayed for a few seconds, I'd have been killed."

Claudia Warren looked stricken. I began to think there might be a human being under that rhino-tough art-dealer hide. "My god," she said softly. A look of concern flitted across her face, quickly replaced by calculation. I wondered how long it would take her to get to the telephone and resell the Thayer paintings she had just purchased. I was betting that they'd be gone by five o'clock that afternoon.

"I'm not sure if new paintings are being aged, or old paintings are being re-signed," Lisa said. "Or both. There is an old artist, a contemporary of my grandfather, who may be involved. I don't have any proof of that."

"What's his name, darling?"

"Petrov. Anton Petrov."

"He called me!" Claudia said. "Yesterday. Wanted to have me look at his work. My assistant hung up on him, but he called back and insisted that I talk to him. I finally got on and told him that I just wasn't interested in anything he had to sell."

"Did he say where he was staying, or what he wanted to sell?" I demanded.

"I'm afraid not. I didn't listen; I just told him to leave me alone."

I cursed.

When Claudia finally spoke again, her voice was subdued. "I'm sorry, Lisa, for not taking this seriously immediately. Let me go back to work and talk to one or two other people. If I learn anything, I'll call you at once." She paid the check and stood to go, bending once to offer a powdered cheek for Lisa to kiss. I still didn't like her worth a damn. I knew I was judging her harshly, but to me the sale of art was as much a matter of trust as commerce. The work of people who could take pigment and linseed oil and canvas and turn them into light and space and emotion was not something to be thrown on the block like hog bellies or oil, run up in good markets and dumped in bad. I didn't know a better way, but so far I hadn't much liked what I had seen.

When we left the restaurant it was after four and we were both too tired to keep pushing on. We strolled up West Broadway, admiring the handsome cast-iron facades of the buildings but stunned once again by the ongoing gentrification that was starting to knock even the most expensive galleries out of SoHo. Even on a day as hot as this one, the pulsing, sweating crowd was out to buy five-hundred-dollar blouses and thousand-dollar skirts. The heat made us decide on a cab rather than the subway for the ride uptown. We rode a taxi as far as Columbus Circle and walked through Central Park for a while, stopping to buy cold beer from a rangy black teenager who sold them off the back of his bicycle. We drank the beer, bottles covered in paper bags, in the quiet of the Sheep Meadow, joining about a hundred New Yorkers getting an afternoon chlorophyll fix.

"So what do you want to do now?" I asked when I had finished my beer. I looked around but the beer vendor was nowhere in sight.

"I don't know," Lisa replied. She sat on the grass with her legs crossed beneath her, gently rocking back and forth. "But I'm feeling good for the first time in a week."

"It helps to be doing something, taking a little control back."

"Even if we still don't know what's going on," she replied. She paused, then added, "Matthew? Why are you doing this?"

"Doing what?"

"The whole thing. Helping me, coming with me to New York, investigating."

"It's what I know how to do, a way I can help. And it is a way to stay close to you."

She sat quietly, thinking. "I like you," she said at last. "A lot. But you hold so much of yourself back . . . sometimes it seems like you live in some other place, a clean, well-lighted room where no one else is allowed to go. And that scares me."

"I'm not saying that's wrong," I replied. "It's been my way of staying sane for a long time. But it doesn't mean I can't change. I can share with someone else. It just doesn't come easily to me."

She didn't answer. After a while I said, "What do you want to do now?"

She paused, then smiled. "I want to get dressed up and eat some heavy French food and drink a bottle of wine. I'd very much like to do that with you."

"That salad of wild greens at lunch not enough?"

She snorted derisively. "That tasted like something collected for a survival merit badge. I want food. Meat. Béchamel sauce. Cheese. Asparagus."

"You're in the right city for it." We stood up and stretched, then walked north through the park, past Strawberry Fields and the monument to John Lennon near the Seventy-second Street entrance. Outside the park, on Central Park West, Lisa paused in front of the Dakota, the great Gothic apartment building built of black-stained stone where John Lennon lived and had been killed. We stood in the pool of shadow cast by the Dakota's bulk, and I remembered the harsh grainy news film, the bland, round face of the killer.

"I recall," Lisa said, "that I did not understand."

"A small soul," I replied. "So small that he was afraid of disappearing and leaving no trace. What he couldn't have, he grew to hate."

She nodded. "Isn't it always like that," she said, and we walked out of the shadow and into the late-afternoon light, heading home.

A short, sharp thunderstorm at six o'clock cleared the sky and cooled the air, leaving soft warmth in place of crucible heat.

The midtown business crowd had already headed out to Long Island or one of the upstate counties for the long Labor Day weekend, and the city had a lovely empty feeling. We had martinis at the Oak Room bar in the Plaza Hotel and wandered south on Fifth Avenue. By eight o'clock we had found a small French restaurant with crisp linen, shining silver, and a quiet back dining room around the corner from the Algonquin Hotel. We finished dinner around eleven and went back to the Algonquin Blue Bar for brandy and coffee in honor of the ghost of Dorothy Parker. At midnight, with no cabs at hand, we strolled back up Fifth Avenue before getting a cab at the stand by the Plaza.

When we returned to the apartment, Lisa said a quiet good night and went to bed. I felt curiously alert despite the heavy, wine-laden dinner. I tossed my suit jacket on a dining chair and went into the kitchen, where I found a bottle of decent champagne in the refrigerator and a box of Dunhill cigarettes in a drawer. I poured a glass of champagne, lit one of the cigarettes, and stepped out on the darkened living-room terrace. There was a ruddy, nearly full moon in the southern sky, hanging above the lights still shining in the apartment towers that choked the west-side blocks in the fifties and sixties. To the east, the Citicorp tower had turned off its giant light, but the angular shape of the tower could still be seen against the skyline. It had been ten years since I had lived in New York and I had no love for the endless wearing hassles that were part of its everyday life, but I missed it for nights like this. When you are young, the city is the best drug ever invented, and you could feel it rolling in your veins when you left a club at 3:00 A.M. with a new woman or watched an actor on a night when the gods were in his corner and he was giving the performance of a lifetime.

I stubbed out the cigarette and turned back to the view. A moment later I heard the French doors open behind me. Lisa stepped out onto the terrace and into my arms. She wore no clothes and her long dark blond hair streamed down her back.

"No one can see," she whispered, then kissed me. The kiss

was long and slow, and when it was over I saw that her eyes were shining.

"Come to bed," she said. I followed her inside. The curtains were open and we made love with waves of moonlight pouring over us like a warm sea.

CHAPTER 11

At ten o'clock the next morning I put Lisa in a cab over on Broadway to take her down to the New York Public Library. She planned to continue her research into the provenance of the three paintings in the SAM show. She had said nothing about what had happened to us the night before. I wanted to say something romantic and witty, but the words didn't come to me. There is something profoundly foolish about a man nearing forty who thinks he may be falling in love. Women are infinitely more practical in such matters than men.

I bought a newspaper from a stand on the corner of Seventy-second and Broadway and walked back down Seventy-third to the apartment. As I reached the front of the building a man emerged from behind a granite pillar that formed the near side of the recessed building entry.

"Matthew Riordan?" he asked.

I stopped and looked him over. He was a stocky man with long curly gray hair and a thick brushy mustache. He was dressed in a clean blue shirt and khaki work pants. A cigarette burned between the fingers of his left hand. I stared at him, puzzled for a good thirty seconds before the lights went on and I knew who the old man was.

"Anton Petrov," I replied. "I've been looking for you."

"So I've heard," he said dryly. "Shall we walk? I have not yet had breakfast and I am hungry."

"I think there's a decent delicatessen with a couple of booths over on Amsterdam." I replied. "I'll even buy. I have some questions I'd like to ask you."

"And I you." He followed me in silence to the delicatessen I remembered from the days when I had lived on the Upper West Side. I was in luck; it hadn't been gentrified out of existence. We ordered breakfast from the counterman and sat down in a booth over coffee. The deli served a local, mostly older crowd. A couple of men talking, even heatedly, would draw no attention at all.

"How did you find me?" I asked.

"It was not difficult. My Ellen told me that you visited her farm and your connection to Lisa Thayer. She called the lady's gallery and was told by the assistant that Miss Thayer was in New York and was staying at her mother's apartment. The rest was simple."

I said nothing. Irritation must have shown on my face. Lisa had left her mother's number with her assistant to be used only in an emergency, not to be handed out.

Petrov laughed, a husky rumble that subsided into a cough. "A rather naive young man, I gather," he said. "At any rate, we are here. What do you want with me?"

Petrov had the advantage of finding me before I could find him. It had built up his confidence. The ex-con in him was probably having a wonderful time. If I was to get any useful information from him, I had to take that advantage away.

"Tell me something," I said. "Why did you kill Margaret Jura?"

I half expected him to get up and walk away. If he did, it was going to be a short walk, about as far as the apartment, where I could spend a nice quiet day taking him apart piece by piece.

Petrov had to know something that could help me find out who had put the bomb in Lisa's car, and I wanted what he knew.

He stared at me, his eyes wide and uncomprehending. "Who are you?" he said, his voice rasping from years of cigarette smoke. "What do you want with me?"

"I want to have the answers to some questions," I said, putting my best ex-prosecutor's bullyboy tone into my voice. "You can start with the question I gave you."

"I did not kill Margaret Jura," he said at last. "I did not kill her."

"Who did? Lee Thayer?"

"I don't know. I have thought about it for many years. But I do not know."

"I think you've got a belief. You think Lee Thayer killed her. You always have. Thayer's dead and there's nothing you can do to him, except forge his paintings. It's an exquisite sort of revenge, really. An old man's sort of revenge. Thayer had the life you wanted for yourself. Fame, money, critical adulation. By imitating his work you're proving to the world that you're just as good. Even if only you and a couple of other people know it."

"I don't know what you're talking about."

"Of course you do," I said harshly. "You want a few people who count to know that you're faking Thayer's work. That's why you painted the bird on the postcard and mailed it to Thayer's granddaughter. It was a joke, a slap in the face. You were having a laugh at the whole damn world's expense and you wanted her to know it."

"What painting?" he asked, a confused look on his face. He looked down at the table.

I leaned across the narrow booth table and grabbed a bunch of his long gray hair in my fist. I snapped his head up to look into his eyes, then started pushing his face down toward the untouched plate of food in front of him.

"Don't fuck with me," I told him, "or you won't walk out of here. Somebody is trying to kill Thayer's granddaughter and it's got something to do with your goddamn phony paintings. You start talking or I will take you out of here and bury you."

He raised his head, fighting me. I could feel the bunched-up muscles in his neck shaking as he strained against the steady pressure. He looked at me with eyes that had looked into a hell of a lot of naked cruelty in thirty years in prison and still come out alive. I watched him for a couple of seconds longer and then let him go. He sighed once when the pain was over but he looked at me with terrible anger.

"Eat your breakfast," I said, picking up a fork. "I'm sorry, but I had to find out whether you were going to lie to me or not. Somehow I don't think you are."

His mouth worked but he said nothing. He ate for a while in silence, then pushed his plate away and lit another cigarette. His color wasn't good and surely smoking for as many years as he had was taking its toll, but his chest was wide and his arms looked as if they once had been strong, probably from years of weight lifting in prison. His hands were thick and clumsy looking, as though he could hardly hold a brush, much less wield it with delicacy. When he spoke, his voice was low and sad.

"How odd that you should ask about Margaret Jura," he began. "I had not thought of her for many years. I was—am—happy living with Ellen, and feel a sense of peace that I thought would never come when I was in prison. Yet in the past few months I have begun to dream of Margaret again. She was scarcely older than a child when she was killed, yet she seems the same age as I am, in my dreams."

I felt a sudden flash of understanding. "The dreams," I said. "They stopped when Lee Thayer died, didn't they?"

He nodded, somewhat abjectly. I pushed on.

"If you didn't kill her," I asked, "who did?"

"I will never know," Petrov said. He shrugged and added, "Perhaps one of these random rapists who attack women. They are not a new phenomenon. I knew a dozen of them in prison. Perhaps someone who lived in the neighborhood, perhaps someone who attended the party that night. You are correct in one thing. For a long time I believed that Lee Thayer had killed her. I was so drunk on that terrible night that I could scarcely remember where I was, much less anyone else. I had no facts. But I knew that Margaret had been with Thayer before she was killed. And I knew that the men who testified at my trial, the men who said they saw Lee Thayer walk away while Margaret was still alive, could not have seen what they said they did. Because I was with them."

"They lied?"

"They lied. I thought about it for thirty years, locked in prison. And when I got out of prison and finally stopped dreaming about Margaret, I let the matter rest."

"And now? You said you started dreaming about her again. Why?"

"I don't know. It is painful. In some ways love is the most terrible emotion, because it never lets you go. But trying to decide who killed her now is of no use. Everyone is dead, or nearly so." He fell silent, then asked, "Why are you asking me about the forgery of Thayer's works? I have painted in a similar style, we all did during the 1930's, and even after the war. But I have never forged his works."

"Lisa Thayer believes that someone did. She saw three paintings in that retrospective show at SAM that she believed were not genuine. A few weeks before that someone sent her a postcard in the mail. It was a plain piece of white cardboard, with a painting of a bird on one side. It was such a good imitation that at first it even fooled her. But the paint was less than a week old. The painting is very similar to one that Thayer had done years ago and that I saw hanging in the office of a doctor in Port Angeles. To me that could mean the forger is someone local, who knows about that Port Angeles painting."

"And someone has tried to kill Miss Thayer, because of these forgeries?"

"Someone put a bomb in her car, in Seattle. She was lucky and wasn't in the car when it went off. Otherwise she'd be dead."

"I see." He seemed to shudder inwardly, as though the death

of another young woman was a thought he found difficult to bear.

"The bombing has to be connected to those paintings in the SAM show. They aren't new paintings. Lisa estimated that they were at least twenty years old, given the condition of the canvas and the paint. Your style has always been similar to Thayer's. She thinks the paintings might be yours."

"What do the paintings look like?"

"One of them was called *Striations*. It's an abstract, in white writing. Sort of an experiment with parallel lines. Another is a gouache on paper. The third is a large oil, abstract, but the colors, blues, grays, and greens—recall the sea."

Petrov hesitated, then nodded. "The third one sounds familiar. I painted something like that in prison nearly thirty years ago. I was experimenting with the New York School style called abstract expressionism. It sounds like it could be my painting."

"What happened to it? Do you know?"

"I had it when I left prison and moved to La Conner. When I was broke, I sold it for a few dollars that I owed to a young man who studied with me for a while."

"Who?"

"His name was Hanks. Terrill Hanks. He is a sculptor now, I see him occasionally."

Lights went on, at least a little. I thought back to Hanks's handsome loft studio, the recently built kitchen, and elegant furnishings. "What did Hanks do with it? Did he keep it?"

"I have no idea. I haven't seen the painting in a long time."

"Did you sign it?"

"Yes, in the lower right-hand corner. I use a small 'p' as a signature, nothing more."

"Didn't you see the painting in the Thayer show? Why didn't you say something?"

He shook his head. "I have not seen that show, or any of the paintings you mentioned, in at least ten years. If someone is re-signing my work as Thayer's, with his name, I do not know about it." He laughed bitterly. "Most people who know a little about my work think I am dead. Those who know me better know that I have no desire to leave Ellen's farm, to go out in a world that thinks of me as a murderer, if it thinks of me at all."

"What about the postcard?" I asked, pressing him again. "It's a small painting, egg tempura on a plain white five-by-eight-inch card, of a bird joined to a brass jar."

Petrov looked puzzled again. "I have never painted such a thing."

"Are you sure you didn't see something like that and copy it, even for an exercise? Thayer painted a whole series of birds."

"I know that, but I've never painted anything like them."

I sat back in the booth, laced my fingers behind my head, and stared at Petrov. He met my stare, then shifted his eyes to the table and fumbled for another cigarette. He lit it, then looked up at me over the cloud of smoke.

"There's something about this you're not telling me," I finally said. "Like why you went to such trouble to find me in New York. Like what you're doing in New York. Why in hell are you here?"

"It's very simple. None of the Seattle galleries will handle my work. I came here to try to find someone who will represent me."

"I think there's a little more to it than that. You found out that someone was re-signing your paintings, didn't you? Why in hell don't you just come forward and put a stop to it? A woman I care about is risking her life trying to figure out what is going on. Damn it, tell us what you know."

He closed his eyes to think. A ruined life had made trust almost impossible for him. I waited. There was nothing else I could do to him. He would have to make his own decision.

When he spoke again, his voice was low and halting. "All right. About five months ago I was in San Francisco. I went to galleries there, trying to find a representative. I despise trying to sell myself, but I have no choice. I saw two of my paintings, very old ones, just sketches, really. Tempera on paper, waterfront scenes that I had done in the 1930's. They were re-signed as Thayers.

I spoke to the gallery owner, a young man who knew very little about painting, really. I told him that I had painted those sketches, not Thayer. Even after I explained who I was, my background, and my involvement in the Seattle group at that time, he refused to believe me. I understood why; he probably had paid ten or twenty thousand dollars for those two sketches. I persisted. He threatened to have me arrested if I did not leave. He threatened to sue me if I ever told anyone about the paintings. I realized that it was not enough to give testimony about my work. I had no money for lawyers or experts to prove my claim. And even if I could, it would mean nothing to me. An artist has no legal rights once a painting has been sold. I was powerless."

He spoke with a cold anger so intense that it left him out of breath. I waited while he paused, gasping a little for air. He went on. "I tried harder to find a Seattle dealer. If the world knew of my work, I thought, my other paintings wouldn't be taken away from me. But no one would take me. The newer dealers want the things being done now—collages, semisculptural pieces. I work only with paint. The dealers of my generation won't touch me. David Campbell wouldn't even speak to me. He regards me as a murderer."

He stopped and drew another ragged breath, glaring at me. Few things anger a man like revealing his own weakness. "A month later Terrill Hanks called me. He said he knew of someone who wanted to buy several of my paintings. At first I was delighted. I met Terrill and another man at my studio. The second man didn't want to give me his name. They bought two paintings. Later Terrill came back and said the man wanted to buy more. I remembered what had happened in San Francisco, so I asked for the name of the collector; I asked what he intended to do with the paintings. Terrill became angry. He said I was a fool to question a collector who would preserve my work. I refused to sell them any more paintings."

"What did the second man look like?"

"He was about your age. Shorter. An unfriendly man."

"Can you draw him?"

"I can try." He took a paper place mat, smoothed it on the table, and began to sketch with a stub of a pencil he found in a pocket of his jacket. He worked intently for a few minutes. I watched him and drank my coffee.

When he was finished, he took the sketch and held it up to show me. "I can't say it is accurate, because the meeting only lasted an hour and my mind was on other things."

It was accurate enough. He had caught Duane Tabor's heavy jowls and bristly, blow-dried hair.

I nodded. "I want you to sign the sketch, and date it."

"Is it important?"

"It may be." He signed the sketch and dated it. I took it from him and folded it, then put it in my breast pocket. "I'm beginning to understand a few other things," I told him. "When I drove out to Ellen Diekmann's farm, she practically ran me off the place. She must have thought I was tied up with Terrill Hanks, making another approach to buy your work."

"That is what she told me, that is what we thought. That is why I came looking for you."

I was silent for a moment, trying to figure out how much else the old man knew. I felt as if I was coming up against another barrier of some kind. I decided to take a different approach. "Morris Kuehn is dead," I said, watching for a reaction. I didn't get one.

"Yes, I know," Petrov said flatly. "Ellen told me. A suicide, I understand."

"How did she know? It just happened a few days ago."

"I assume she heard it on the radio."

His voice was still quiet and his features expressionless. The police hadn't issued any finding of suicide as far as I knew. Why did Petrov think it was a suicide?

"No reaction?" I asked rhetorically. "The man gave up his job to defend you. He bought your paintings and supported you while you were in prison."

"It turned out all right for him," Petrov snapped. "He became rich and powerful. What he did for me happened long ago. He needs no sympathy from me." His voice had taken on a harsh sarcastic edge. He was steeped in his bitterness, cured in it until he was as tough and scarred as old leather.

The morning had passed and the lunchtime rush was beginning to fill the deli. I wondered how much else I could get out of him. I kept trying.

"Tell me about Margaret," I said.

"I don't know where to begin," he replied. "It was so long ago. I can no longer distinguish truth from memory, or the memory of memory."

"But you still dream."

He nodded. "When I came to Seattle, I was very poor. But lucky. I found work at the Arts Project, the WPA, and I worked at Cornish School, stretching canvas and cleaning up, in return for paints and instruction. I met Margaret there in the spring of 1939. She was older than I was, perhaps twenty, and she seemed so much more sure of herself. She lived on her own. She liked my work, liked me. I fell in love with her right away. But she saw many men, and I . . . felt very anxious, about my poverty, my lack of schooling. When she made love to me, I sensed that she . . . Not pity, but something close to that." He was stumbling over his words now, almost stammering as he forced them out. I wondered if he had ever said this to anyone.

"You said Margaret lived on her own. Did she have her own apartment?"

"Yes, near Cornish, on Capitol Hill. It was a studio, but very nice." He looked pained. "I think someone else paid for it. A man. She would never say who it was."

"Why didn't any of this come out at your trial? The other man would have been a suspect."

"Morris tried to find out who it was. But he couldn't. The rent was paid in cash. With no proof, he said not to bring it up."

"Did you ever find out?"

"No."

"Was it Thayer?"

"No, because he did not come back to Seattle until that summer. He didn't meet Margaret until then."

"Is there anything else you know about this man who may have been supporting Margaret?"

"No."

I sat back in the booth and took a deep breath, then blew it out slowly. The possibility that Margaret Jura had been involved with a third man was interesting, and, if true, lent a little credibility to Petrov's claims of innocence. But it was as much a dead end now as it had been fifty years before. The important thing was to expose the people passing off Petrov's paintings as Thayer's. I turned my attention back to Petrov. "What will you do now?" I asked.

"What I am doing. Trying to find a representative so that my work will be known as mine, not Thayer's."

"I might be able to help you," I replied. "Lisa might be willing to represent you. She's an expert in Thayer's work. She spotted the differences in the paintings in the SAM show. If she represents you, there would be no doubt as to your work."

He looked dubious. "She is young, without any reputation. Her word would have no weight against the word of others."

"It would go a long way, combined with yours. Come with me; I'll take you to her. Then you can decide."

He looked uncomfortable. "I don't know if I can trust you," he said at last. "For all I know you may be one of those trying to resell my work as Thayer's." He added a tired, wary smile. "I don't often work well with people who threaten me."

I nodded. "Fair enough. But you're not going to find out whether you can trust me sitting here."

"All right," he said finally, "but I cannot meet with you today. I have an appointment this afternoon. I must think about this and discuss it with someone. Then I will know if it's safe to deal with you."

"Who? Who would know?"

He smiled enigmatically. "All things may come in time, Mr. Riordan. But not today." He stood up to go.

I followed him out of the restaurant and into the crowded sidewalk on Amsterdam. "Where are you staying?" I asked.

He shook his head. "I think I would be safer not telling you."

"I think you'd be safer telling me. If the people who tried to buy your paintings are the ones who bombed Lisa's car and they find out what you're doing, you're not safe."

"I may have already run that risk, telling you what I have. I won't compound it by giving you an address. In any event, I think the people who want my paintings would have to find them before they would try to hurt me. And they won't."

"Then you'd better send Ellen Diekmann away from the farm. If she knows, or even if Hanks thinks she knows where the paintings are, they may try to force her to tell them."

His face clouded with concern. "Perhaps you're right. I will do that. I will call your apartment building tomorrow morning and leave a message at the doorman's desk, no later than ten o'clock. It will tell you where I want us to meet." He turned and started to walk away, then thought better of it. He came back and we stood in the center of the busy sidewalk, the crowd swirling around us. The din of traffic, horns, and engine noises seemed to fade away in the intensity of the old man's stare. Finally he said, "Why did you ask me about Margaret Jura?"

I thought very hard. I wanted to answer his question honestly. "I saw a picture of her about a week ago." I replied. "There was a . . . force, a sense of overwhelming spirit, even in an old photograph. When I started to investigate the forgery, I learned of Margaret Jura almost by accident. I saw her murder as peripheral, an old sad story that didn't mean anything. Now I'm not sure of that. If she had not died, none of you would be what you are, perhaps none of this would be happening. But even more than that, I would like to know what happened to her. I want to know who could destroy such a promising life."

I thought I saw a hint of understanding form in his aged black eyes. "Perhaps I can trust you," he said. He turned to go.

"Then tell me one more thing," I called out to him. "Is Lee Thayer still alive?"

He offered me a twisted, sad smile. "Of course he is, in his paintings," he replied. He headed away, toward the Seventy-second Street subway station. I had a brief thought of following him, then realized that if I did, he could simply get off at the bus terminal at Forty-second Street, board a bus for anywhere, and wait me out. I had to believe him, and I had to wait.

Two things I'm not very good at.

12

I made my way up the broad Fifth Avenue steps of the New York Public Library surrounded by the usual groups of sad exiles protesting murderous regimes in their home countries and the T-shirted, sweating tourists who ignored them in favor of the mimes and street magicians performing on the sidewalk. I dodged a pair of crying children being mocked by one of the mimes and minded not at all that I had to collide with the mime to miss the children. I am one of that irascible minority who believes that mimes should be given a choice between honest work and capital punishment.

Once inside the building I slowed to a stroll, absorbed in the luxury of the wide cool marble corridors. I walked up the steps from Astor Hall to the catalog room, with its chest-high, carved oak research tables. The late-afternoon sun streamed through the high arched windows and shone on the brass balustrades and reading lamps. I paused to study the ornately painted and gilded ceiling, as culture-struck on that afternoon as the day when I first saw the library, over twenty years before. I remembered my father, an unhappy college professor turned hard-bitten rancher, explaining how the wealth of a continent had been poured into the creation of places like these. He was a man who hated the East, hated the way that places like Montana had been stripped by unbridled, robber-baron capitalism, yet also a man who loved learning for its own sake and reveled in the sheer presence of so much art and science and history collected in a single place. It was, I thought, only one of the many contradictions he had never learned to resolve.

When my reverie was over, I walked past the catalog desk and into the main reading room. With the Labor Day weekend at hand it was nearly deserted, and the absence of people enhanced the almost religious silence of the place. I looked over the long rows of polished wood tables and finally saw Lisa at the far west end of the room, bent over the table, her long intelligent face intent on the document she was reading. She twisted a strand of blond hair around a finger as she read. When she was through, she put the document on a six-inch stack of catalogs and what looked like photographic prints at her side.

I went over to the table where she worked and slipped quietly into a chair beside her. She looked up and I stroked her cheek and kissed her lightly on the mouth. She rewarded me with a brief but distracted smile.

"How's it going?" I asked. "Anything?"

"Something," she acknowledged. "Not conclusive, but look at this." She handed me a color photograph of the dark abstract oil called *Sea Study, No. 3.* I glanced at it and handed it back.

"I'm not following. It's the painting you think is a fake."

"No, it's not. See the way the paler colors, the grays and blues, are focused on the edges of the work? Almost like reality fading away. The picture in Seattle has those dark masses of greens and blues all the way out to the edge of the canvas. The light's handled differently, too." She took the photograph from my hand and put it back in a separate, much smaller pile to her left. "Moss Taylor, the curator at SAM, finally gave me the full provenance that Campbell claimed for *Sea Study* before we left. According to Campbell, that painting was done in the late 1950's, when Thayer had moved to Switzerland for a year, and was sold through Thayer's gallery in Basel to an unnamed French collector. Campbell said he bought the painting in Paris last year and brought it home."

"Go on."

"*Sea Study* isn't anything like the stuff that Thayer painted in Switzerland. Now, this painting"—she pointed back to the photograph—"was also called *Sea Study, No. 3*. It was painted at the Lodge, on the Olympic Peninsula, in the summer of 1956, according to the gallery catalog. That makes some sense, the work fits where it was painted. It was shown in a European show in Zurich, in 1959, and sold to a French collector. But this"— she held up a copy of a faded French arts magazine dated from the 1960's—"says that *Sea Study, No. 3* was one of the paintings lost in a fire at the home of the French banker who bought the painting."

"So the one in the SAM show was a fake. And you can prove it."

"Maybe." She brushed a strand of hair out of her eyes and leaned back in her chair, obviously exhausted from her hours of intense study. "This report could be wrong about what was destroyed in the fire, but it makes sense to me. The painting at SAM isn't an exact copy; it's more like a painting from another artist who heard about the original, maybe saw a bad reproduction in a magazine. It's the perfect painting to re-sign and sell as an original, because the original was destroyed. Yet anybody who checks on the first sale will find out that yes, there was such a painting, and yes, it was sold."

"It fits together, Lisa. Congratulations."

"I don't know how much good it will do. It's the kind of evidence that will lead to a nasty little spat in the art press. It's not gonna nail the creep who blew up my car."

"But what you're saying more or less fits with what I've got. I saw Petrov today. The son of a bitch came walking right up to the building, looking for us. I described the paintings in the SAM show to him. He said *Sea Study* sounded like something he painted in prison. He could tell us whether he painted it." I went on and told her what Petrov had said about himself and the sudden interest that Terrill Hanks and Duane Tabor had shown in buying his paintings.

"My god," Lisa said when I was finished. "Is there any way I can take a look at his work? If he's here talking to galleries, he should have a set of slides with him. Where is he staying? Can we go see him now?"

"He doesn't really trust us," I replied. "He said he wanted to talk to someone, then meet us tomorrow. Maybe we can get slides from him then."

"We need those slides if we're going to stop this thing," she said, frowning. "You see what they're doing, don't you? If they can get their hands on twenty or thirty of Petrov's paintings that are similar in style to Thayer's, they can sit tight, perhaps pay Petrov some money to stay silent. If they wait until Petrov is dead, that's even better. They can send one or two paintings into the market every year. If Campbell authenticates them, no one will suspect they weren't painted by Thayer. Re-signed paintings attributed to Tobey and Rothko get sold all the time. Eventually, they could be looking at fifteen or twenty million dollars, if prices keep going up."

The rich silence of the reading room filled the air. After a long time I said, "That explains why they're willing to kill you, Lisa. For that much money, they're willing to take the risk."

"I still can't believe Terrill would be part of this," Lisa whispered. "For God sake, he was a friend."

"He may not have known about the bomb," I replied, "but he's part of this. Hanks has known Petrov since the early seventies. He studied under him, so he knows Petrov's work. Petrov says Hanks bought *Sea Study* ten years ago. Hanks brought Duane Tabor out to La Conner to buy up Petrov's paintings. For all we know, Hanks may have thought it up after noticing the similarities between Thayer's works and some of Petrov's. What I can't figure out is who Petrov's talking to. He said he had to talk to someone before he would know if he could trust us. Is there anyone here in New York, a dealer perhaps, he could be talking to?"

She shook her head. "Not that I can think of. I've already talked to most of the dealers who would handle this type of painting."

I felt frustrated, but there was nothing to be done. "We'll just have to wait, I guess. Are you done here?"

She nodded. "For now, anyway. I have to turn these things in and arrange to have photocopies made. I want to see if they'll make a copy of this picture, too."

We went to the reference desk. I waited while Lisa made arrangements for copies to be made and sent to a spare post office box that I maintained in Seattle for things I didn't want sent to my home or office. Paranoia sometimes has its uses.

When we were finished, we walked up Fifth Avenue and west on Forty-ninth Street to an uptown IRT station. The day itself wasn't that bad but the subway remained furnace hot. We crushed our way into an uptown local train and rode to Seventy-second Street with a trainful of weary, sweating office workers who hadn't been able to leave early for the weekend. When we finally got back to the apartment, Lisa cracked open a beer and sprawled on a sofa, worn down by heat, work, and the sad knowledge that someone she considered a friend might have tried to kill her.

I poured myself some mineral water and went to the combination answering machine and telephone that sat on the kitchen counter. I rewound the tape, listened to the short, impersonal message left on the machine by Lisa's mother, and waited for what I hoped would be a message with something useful from Vince Ahlberg.

His was the third call. "It's Vince," he said in his raspy voice. "Call me when you get back. Have the dispatcher track me down if you have to. It's important." I cut off the machine and hurriedly dialed the nonemergency number of the Seattle Police Department.

It was three o'clock on the West Coast and Ahlberg was still at his desk. "About time," he said as he picked up the phone. "I talked to your friend on the New York City Police, Lieutenant Greenberg. He's going to cooperate with me on a search for Petrov." I started to interrupt, but Vince talked past me. "Listen, you fucked up when you did your checking on him. The airplane ticket, I mean. He was booked out of Seattle last Thursday, but he changed his flight. He didn't leave here until Monday morning."

"So what?" I started to say in reply. "He—"

"Let me finish. There are some other things about him I found out. I had his records pulled up at the slammer in Monroe. Petrov did work assignments in the machine, auto and electrical shops. He was good at it. In fact, he was regarded as some kind of mechanical genius. That got my interest going, so I did a little more checking. It turns out that Ellen Diekmann, the woman whose farm he lives on, has a dynamite permit from Skagit County."

"I'm not getting this," I said slowly, feeling a sudden ache in the pit of my stomach. "I talked to Petrov today. He walked right up here, to the building, looking for me. What are you saying?"

"Petrov was here in Seattle last weekend, not there in New York. He has the means and the skill to have tampered with Thayer's car. He could put together the kind of timed dynamite bomb that took out Lisa's car. He was here on Sunday when Kuehn got killed. He's the only guy connected to this Thayer business whose whereabouts I haven't been able to pin down. You said he might be the guy painting these fakes. Well, my money says he tried to kill the only two people who could prove he was doing it."

I swore, loudly and with conviction. "Goddamn it all to hell. I saw him, I talked to him. He told me—"

"Screw what he told you," Vince said with sudden urgency. "If the man made one bomb, he might have made two. Get Lisa out of there and get on the phone to the doorman. Find out if anybody was in the apartment today. Now move."

I slammed down the phone. "Lisa," I shouted, "Get out of here. Go down the hall to the elevators and wait for me."

"What is it?" she asked. "What's wrong?"

"Just do it. Now! Please." She ran to the front door, fumbled with the three locks, but finally got it open and ran down the hall. I picked up the house phone and looked around the room for packages or bags, any sort of container that hadn't been there when we had left that morning. I saw nothing. After a long minute the doorman answered.

"This is 17-B," I said. "Has anyone been let into the apartment today?"

"I don't think so," the doorman replied in a soft Puerto Rican accent.

"Check, please. It's important." He put the phone down. It clattered on his desk. I circled around again, suddenly conscious of my heart beating in my chest.

The doorman came back on the line. "No one in today. I don't think we had any maintenance people come, except Carlos, the manager, fixed some plumbing next door to you. Is something wrong? Something missing?"

"No," I replied. "Were there any packages for 17-B today? If you find one, don't pick it up. Just leave it until I get there."

He put the phone down again. I waited. When he came back on the line, he said, "No packages. Is everything okay, sir? Should I come up?"

"No, I think everything's okay. I'll call back if there's a problem." I hung up, leaving the poor man confused. I walked through the apartment, taking my time, looking for anything out of place. I checked all the rooms for packages or hiding places where a bomb could have been put. When I was done, I felt foolish but relieved.

I went back to the door and called Lisa in. When she returned, I closed and locked the door behind her.

"What was that all about?" she asked nervously. "I thought you had gone crazy for a minute."

"Not crazy," I said grimly. "Just stupid. Exceptionally stupid.

When I called Ahlberg, he told me that Petrov didn't leave for New York until Monday of this week, not last Thursday, like I assumed from looking at his ticket voucher. He also said that Petrov learned auto mechanics and electrical work in prison, and that he has access to dynamite. In other words, he's a prime suspect for the bombing of your car and the murder of Morris Kuehn."

"But why? I thought you said he was trying to find somebody to represent his work so that it wouldn't be re-signed as Thayer's."

"That's what he told me, and I bought a big piece of it. But it makes just as much sense the other way: he's here peddling his old paintings as your grandfather's work, trying to make as much money as he can and getting a little revenge at the same time. We've got to find him. He knows where we are, and he might try to kill you again."

I went back to the phone and called Vince Ahlberg again. "We're okay," I said when he picked up the phone. "No little packages. But the hell of it is I don't know where Petrov's staying. He wouldn't tell me. Said he had to check me out with somebody, to know whether I could be trusted."

"I'll call Greenberg back," he said grimly, "and put out a warrant, make it official. I don't know what they can do, though. If Petrov has his head down, he's going to be awfully hard to find." He hung up.

I put the receiver back on the counter and pulled one of the Breuer chairs out from the dining table. I slumped on the chair and looked up at Lisa. "I don't know what to think," I said. "Petrov had me convinced that he might have painted those three paintings in the SAM show, but that he didn't know they were being passed off and wanted to put a stop to it. If Ahlberg's right, that was a wagon load of shit. And you're at risk even here." I could feel myself tightening up. "Damn. I thought we were so close to getting this thing out in the open."

"What can we do now?" Lisa asked. She came up behind me and rested her arms on my shoulders, her face close to mine.

"We wait, I guess. If the old man shows up tomorrow, we find out what he has to say." I looked at my watch. "It's nearly seven. Do you want something to eat?"

"In a while. I don't want to go out. We can order Chinese food and beer from that place on Seventy-first." She grinned and added, "Cheer up. You've had worse offers lately."

"I just feel so damned stupid. I should have back-checked Petrov's plane ticket to make sure that it was used. I wonder where the hell he was last weekend."

"Ask him tomorrow. Anyway, what would you have done differently? We'd still be here, trying to figure this thing out."

"Maybe you're right." I stretched and felt the stiffness in my legs and back. "If you can wait for a half hour on the food, I'd like to go for a run. I'm pretty stiff."

She frowned. "Is that a good idea, after what Ahlberg said?"

"Nobody's interested in me," I replied. "You stay in with the door locked until I come back. I'll leave some money with the doorman to pay for the food. Tell them to bring extra beer." I changed my clothes and left the apartment a few minutes later.

I ran up West End Avenue in the twilight, passing the proud old prewar apartment buildings that lined the sides of the avenue, as stately as a line of ships at anchor. I had lived on the Upper West Side in the early 1970's, on the corner of West End and Ninety-second Street, before the great gentrifying wave had washed over this side of the island. The neighborhood had been louder, funnier, and much cheaper; I had practiced my poor Spanish in the bodegas on upper Broadway and had two cars stolen before I finally gave it the hell up and walked everywhere I needed to go. As a brand-new federal prosecutor I had made the whopping salary of $16,000 a year, but the neighborhood bars were cheap and sometimes filled with women from Barnard or some of the upstate schools who had come down to the city for the weekend. Those years had been good to me, a breathing space between the madness of Vietnam and the pressures of really trying to make a career.

I turned west at 100th Street and south again on Riverside

Drive. The air was again heavy with heat and the haze made the street lamps on Riverside glow softly like old moons. I ran down the paved sidewalk, my feet kicking through the dusty leaves that had already fallen. I was breathing hard now and stopped to rest and stretch at the Soldiers' and Sailors' Monument at the foot of Eighty-ninth Street. I walked slowly around the monument, a white stone rotunda supported by fluted columns, trying to catch my breath without stiffening up. As I came around the back side I saw that a car had stopped on Riverside. I glanced at it idly. It was dark, but I thought I could make out two men inside.

I heard the muffled cough of the silenced machine pistol too late. A bullet chipped the marble pedestal beside me and went screaming off into the park. I dove over the low stone railing at the back of the monument and rolled through the bramble bushes, down a steep slope. The brambles tore at my skin and I covered my eyes with my hands as I rolled on my side. Up above me I could hear the metallic sound of the car doors slamming shut as the men came after me. Heavy footsteps clattered on the stone stairs.

One of the men grunted. "He's down the fucking hill somewhere," he shouted. "Go after him."

I heard the man crashing through the brush as he came after me. I rolled onto my feet and ran down the hill, desperately trying to shove the thick brambles aside. I was heading for the flat part of the park, thinking I would outrun them on the trail, then beat my way back to the apartment and call the cops.

I broke out of the bushes a couple of blocks south of the monument and ran south on the deserted promenade. The man pursuing me came down the hill about forty seconds later. In the dark his silhouette looked heavy and slow. He ran clumsily, losing ground. I sprinted for a hundred yards and put distance on him, but it was too late. The second man had outguessed me by taking the car ten blocks down Riverside, driving into the park from Seventy-ninth Street and coming up from the south. He bounced the car up the pedestrian path to the promenade, dodging the trees. He kept coming, and caught me in his headlights as I slowed. The man on foot to my rear gained on me, his footsteps pounding heavily. Sour bile and fear rose from my stomach. I was caught between them with nowhere to go.

I broke to my right and vaulted over the cast-iron picket fence at the edge of the promenade. When I landed, I lost my footing and rolled down the hill toward the West Side Highway. By the time I reached the bottom the men had made it to the park fence. I saw the small flash from the gun's suppressor as they opened up, wide left and too high, the bullets ramming into the surface of the highway in front of me. When the shooting stopped, I broke from the cover of the brush and sprinted across the highway. A big panel truck in the southbound lane barely missed me. On the far side of the highway I ran down the hill and tried to think. In a way I had done them a favor by going the way I had. All they had to do now was get back in their car, go under the highway, and drive along the riverside walkway until they saw me. The night had gone to full dark and the only people in the park would be muggers and homeless people trying to bed down for the night. Neither group was likely to be much help. If I ran north, the highway would be like a fence all the way to Ninety-sixth Street. They would either catch me running or catch me trying to scramble back up the hill. My best chance was to head straight for them and try to slip past them in the dark.

I got to my feet and sprinted south, gasping, my chest burning for lack of air. Ahead I saw the same dark-colored sedan come under the bridge and turn onto the walkway. I stayed close to the highway, away from the scattered streetlights, and kept running until they passed me on the right. Just after they passed I broke right, across the strip of green and the walkway, heading for the fence outside the Seventy-ninth Street boat basin. Somehow they saw me behind them. As I climbed the fence I heard the car squeal into reverse. I got hung up at the top in the barbed wire. In desperation I shoved the wire down, slashing my hands on the barbs. A car door flew open as I cleared the top of the fence and shots streaked past me as I pounded down the dock. When I reached the end of the dock, I dove headfirst into the narrow gap between two old houseboats and knifed forward into the cold black water of the Hudson.

The sudden plunge into the cold river shocked the breath out of me. I rose toward the surface, trying to emerge beyond the end of the last boat. I didn't swim far enough and my head banged against a slimy wooden hull. Gripped by panic, I fought my way along the hull, heart pounding against my ribs, chest burning with pain. When my lungs would hold no longer, I finally grasped the motor shaft and pulled myself into the clear and up to the surface. I floated free, gulping great drafts of air and trying to clear my head.

I was drifting about fifteen feet off the stern of an old wooden hulled cabin cruiser tied up at the end of the pier. The lights on the pier cast small yellow circles among the boats. I couldn't see the dock or the riverside esplanade very well, but I heard no car sounds, only the muffled roar of the city. The river current began to pull me downstream, so I swam north, keeping the old cabin cruiser between me and the pier. I kept swimming until I had reached the north side of the pier, then circled in toward shore, swimming silently, hands and legs beneath the surface of the water. I passed by old houseboats and cabin cruisers, none of them showing any great signs of wealth. Most of the people tied up to this dock were live-aboards, more interested in avoiding Manhattan apartment rents than in sailing on Long Island Sound. Some of the boats looked like cheaply built summer cabins, with plywood walls and woodstove chimneys, built on top of ancient double pontoon hulls. I paused at the stern of an empty old ChrisCraft, and hidden in a pool of shadow from the yellow glow of the dock lights, I peered in toward shore.

The car on the embankment was gone. I waited, treading water, listening, trying to guess whether one of the shooters had stayed behind. After ten minutes or so the chill of the river was becoming painful. I decided to take a chance on one of the well-lighted houseboats tied up at the side of the dock. I swam toward it and slipped onto the rear deck, where I lay on my stomach while I listened and watched the shore. Still nothing. I was about to get up when a door on the boat opened and a stocky, bearded man wearing boxer shorts and no shirt stepped onto the deck, cradling a nifty little sixteen-gauge shotgun in his arms. He looked me over carefully. I tried to look sodden but harmless.

"I assume it's a good story," he said, holding the shotgun casually.

I smiled. "I don't suppose you'd believe me if I said I fell off the Circle Line tour boat."

"Probably not. Why were they shooting at you, anyway?"

"Beats the hell out of me. I never saw them before. Have you got a phone down here? I'd like to call the cops. Walking home through the park at night always makes me nervous."

He nodded, grinning, and held the door open for me. I tried to manage another smile as I went into the cabin.

Lieutenant Alan Greenberg had the grim but sympathetic face of a professional mourner. It was, I knew, a professional face, created out of twenty years on the New York City police force, acceptable to the public and his superiors. A face that took nothing as certain and gave nothing away. He studied me intently as I sat in a detective's workroom on one of the lower floors of the police tower in lower Manhattan, dressed in a borrowed gray sweatsuit two sizes too large even for me. Ever since the patrolman had brought me down to Centre Street, Greenberg had treated me more like a suspect than an old friend. His continued silence wore heavily on my already-jangled nerves.

"Who does this sweatsuit belong to, anyway?" I asked irritably, holding up a sleeve that extended six inches past the end of my hand. "The Incredible Hulk?"

Greenberg ignored me. He was a slight, graying man in his early forties, with short-cropped hair and a spade-shaped beard. I had gotten to know him in the early 1970's, when he was a new detective and the paperwork liaison between the New York City police and the federal Organized Crime Strike Force. I had become pretty good friends with Al and his wife Debra, to the point where we would spend one or more nights a month exploring restaurants in Little Italy or Chinatown, then take the subway back to Brooklyn Heights, drink coffee with rum, and talk until dawn.

Finally Greenberg said, "Aren't you getting a little old to be out cowboying around, Riordan?" He spoke with the cultivated accent that native New Yorkers had before they all started to talk like Jersey City mobsters. "First I get a call from your Seattle police captain, asking me to do him a nice easy favor like finding an old man hiding in New York. Never mind that we've got several hundred thousand old men hiding here, he wants it done pronto. Next I find you swimming in the Hudson with people shooting at you. Now tell me just what in hell is going on."

"It's a very long story, Al. I'm not sure how any of it fits together."

He glanced at his watch. It was after nine. "Plenty of time," he said. "You won't start ruining my weekend for at least another hour."

I sighed and gave him an edited version of everything that had happened since Lisa had received the painting on a postcard. Wanting to be taken seriously, I left out Lisa's stubborn hope that her grandfather might still be alive. Greenberg was that rare thing, an experienced cop who was also completely rational. He had none of the cop superstitions that most guys get after twenty years on the force. When I was done, he was shaking his head, half in amusement, half in disbelief.

"That story," he said, "has more inconsistencies than a grade-Z detective movie. You going soft in your middle age? Something your client is telling you isn't right."

"She didn't make this up, Al, she's just trying to live through it. Did you have any luck finding Petrov?"

"Nothing, as I expected. What makes you think that he had anything to do with what happened to you tonight? Poor old artists seldom know how to hire any kind of muscle, much less the kind that tried to whack you out."

"I don't know that he hired anybody, I'm not saying that. But you could be underestimating him. He was in the joint for thirty years on a murder conviction. He might have made friends. And there's kind of a nasty pattern here. Petrov worked in the electrical and auto shops in prison. He gets out of prison, and a few years later Thayer dies in a car wreck, maybe with his brake lines slit and his tie rods filed. Ten years after that a bomb gets put in his granddaughter's car. The lawyer who knows everybody involved dies in his office, maybe a suicide, maybe not. Petrov may have had nothing to do with that. But he's got to know something that he hasn't told me that can help me figure out what's going on."

Greenberg was staring off at a blank wall. "You're involved with this woman, the granddaughter, aren't you?"

"Yes." There was no reason to hold that back.

He sighed. "You don't change, do you? You should grow up, get stalled in your career, find your children incomprehensible, wonder if your wife still really loves you or if she's just comfortable where she is. All those normal things." He shook his head. "Okay. The clinic down on the third floor will give you a gamma globulin shot for all those nasty viruses that live in the river. If I find your old man, I'll tell you. But if you want some advice, I think you should get on an airplane in the morning.

You're out of your league here. If somebody wants to whack you out, they can do it. At home maybe you'll have a better chance." He nodded good night to the uniformed officer who had brought me in and left without another word.

After he was gone the uniformed officer took me down to the clinic for my shot and then gave me a ride uptown to Lisa's apartment. On the way back I didn't think about Petrov or Thayer or any of that. I thought about three very young and slightly crazy but hardworking people who stayed up too late and sometimes drank too much. They sat on a brownstone roof on summer nights and talked too much about how they were going to change the world. It saddened me that the friendship that once had belonged to those other, younger, people was gone.

Saturday morning passed without a call from Petrov. Lisa sat at the kitchen counter, rereading the morning *Times* and trying not to show how worried she was. The attack on the previous night had shaken both of us nearly as badly as the bombing of her car had. Whoever was behind this had the power to move people three thousand miles from where this thing had started. That was more power than I liked to think about going up against.

When the phone rang at a few minutes after noon, we looked at each other. She started to reach for the handset, but I stopped her with a glance and waited for the answering machine to respond to the call. When the tape had stopped playing, I heard Alan Greenberg's voice.

"Riordan, if you're there, please pick up the phone," he said.

I cut off the tape and started talking. "I'm here, Alan. What's going on?"

"I may have a little more information for you," he replied. "Can you get down here within the hour? I'm going to get some lunch, and I'll look for you in Foley Square."

"I'll take a cab and be there in twenty minutes. Find a good hot-dog cart." I hung up.

"I want to come along," Lisa said. Something must have shown in my face, because she added, "Don't be so goddamned paternal, Matthew. You keep forgetting that this is my problem."

"I'm not being paternal. I'm only ten years older than you are." I smiled. "And much less emotionally mature."

"*Exactly* my point," she snapped, already looking around for her purse. By the time we went out the door we were laughing together again. It was nervous laughter, but you learn to take what you can get.

Foley Square, a triangular plot of dusty trees and dying patches of brown grass, stood across from Cass Gilbert's wonderful limestone and terra-cotta United States courthouse in lower Manhattan. A few hot, tired tourists sagged on the benches, grateful for the fitful shade and a place to rest on the walk from Wall Street to Chinatown. Their children clustered around them, some staring in blank amazement at one of the homeless, mentally ill people swaying and holding elaborate conversations with the demons only they could see.

We were early and stopped to buy Italian sausage from a street vendor on Broadway. Lisa watched in amazement as I relished mine, tearing my mouth on the crusty Italian roll and savoring the sweet peppers that covered the sausage. She silently passed her sandwich over after taking only a couple of bites. I ate hers, too.

"You eat too much weird food," I said when I was finished. "So you don't know what's good." I sipped through a straw from a can of cream soda. She rolled her eyes and drank her Tab silently.

When Greenberg finally showed up, he had another man with him, a short man with a weight lifter's build and one of those blue J. C. Penney three-piece suits that screams "cop" at you from thirty yards away. They sat down beside us on the park bench. "This is Michael Reese," Greenberg said. "He's DEA. He'd like to talk to both of you."

"If this is professional," I said quietly, "I'd like to see some ID. Nothing personal."

Reese shrugged, pulled out his leather-cased credentials, and passed them over. I looked at them and passed them back. I offered my hand, and Reese mangled my knuckles. I had the feeling we were not going to get along.

"So, what can we do for you?" I asked.

"I was telling my friend Reese about this screwball story of yours, and he got interested in one of the names. Tabor. Duane Tabor."

"I used to work out of San Francisco," Reese began. "My hometown, actually. Tabor's a guy we've been interested in for a long time, ever since he left the federal defender's office and started handling drug cases."

"Being a defense lawyer isn't a crime."

"He got too close to them. He became one of the boys."

"I'd heard that about him," I said, "but I never got any farther with it. Things have been happening too fast."

"Well, Tabor's big time now. He's the finance guy for most of the Northern California grass money. He moves cash and sets up fake companies and invests for a half-dozen guys, most of the Mendocino County dope growers. We know he's doing it, but he's damn good at it. I spent almost a year trying to put together a racketeering case against him and never got it in good enough shape to prosecute."

"What's the connection with us? We're trying to find out who's forging some paintings. Tabor turned up as a lawyer for an art dealer in Seattle who sold a couple of those paintings."

"That's what interests me. Tabor buys a lot of art, mostly paintings, mostly good stuff by well-known artists. His clients love it. Paintings are portable. There's no import duties on them in most countries. You can take one out of the frame and ship it in a small package, even mule it on board an airplane. Unlike cash, there aren't any laws that require someone to report when they take a painting out of the country. You can buy a painting, carry it to Bermuda or Switzerland, consign it to a gallery, or sell it at auction. When it sells, you get a nice clean cashier's check in whatever currency you like that goes to whatever bank you want and nobody asks any questions. If you're facing a bust and our people have got seizure orders, you can hide millions of dollars in economic value in a warehouse space the size of a closet."

"I know all that's true," Lisa said, breaking into the conversation. "But why would Tabor be involved in selling fakes? He's got nothing to gain from it. If a dealer questions the painting later, somebody is going to lose a lot of money."

Lights came on in my head. "Of course they would, if they had to sell the paintings. But a lot of the drug people are investing for the long run. They like tangible assets, real estate, gold, gems, things they can see and touch. Look at it from Tabor's point of view. He's buying expensive pieces, spending hundreds of thousands of dollars, for people who don't know a damn thing about art. Suppose he connects with a dealer to sell them forgeries or re-signed paintings. Tabor gets a hell of a lot more than a commission, he gets a big chunk of the money that goes into the painting. And if somebody does find out they've bought a fake, they're not the kind of people that are going to go running to the cops or making a public stink."

Greenberg turned to Reese with a slight smile. "See, I told you he could probably still think."

"And along you come," I said to Lisa, still thinking out loud, "and you threaten to tell the world that a couple of the paintings Tabor has bought for his clients are fakes. Tabor's probably safe from the cops, but if the people he's buying the paintings for ever find out, they won't be too happy. He might wind up as fertilizer somewhere around Bakersfield." I turned back to Reese. "Could you find out who he sold the three paintings to, the ones that Lisa thinks were re-signed?"

"Maybe, if I could get a search warrant for the records of the Seattle art gallery they were sold through. Right now I doubt if I've got probable cause for a warrant. And the records would probably show a sale through at least three or four dummies, individuals or corporations."

"Maybe we can go about it backward. Can you tell me the names of the growers you think Tabor represents?"

Reese looked at Greenberg dubiously, his black eyebrows rising until they nearly met the shock of black hair on his head. Reese appeared to be black Irish. He had that unusual combination of Celtic and Spanish blood, green eyes, and dark skin.

Greenberg said, "Don't look at me. But I think you'd better ask him what he'd do with that information."

"It's pretty simple," I cut in. "I'd find out who Tabor sold these fakes to. And then I'd tell him about it."

"They might kill Tabor," Reese said.

"Yeah, that's possible. And I'd grieve. For about ten seconds. You'd do even less."

He shook his head. "I can't let you have it. Not like this."

"Why in hell not?" I said angrily. "If you're right, Tabor's almost certainly tried to kill both Lisa and me. I'm getting sick of having us take all the risk. You've got a way for us to get out of it, and I want it."

"I can't let you have it. Not without getting something for it. You do that to Tabor and there will be somebody taking over his business within hours. The dope will get sold and the money will get laundered, same as always."

"And if I don't do it, we might get dead. Us citizens really appreciate the government's efforts to help." I turned back to Greenberg. "Maybe I can do it another way. Have you gotten any information on where Petrov is? He didn't call us this morning. I'd like to know whose side he's really on."

Greenberg looked uncomfortable. "Yes," he said. "We found him. This morning. He's dead."

I stared at him. My anger was so intense that the world seemed to turn cold.

"You shit," I said when I was composed enough to speak. "What are you trying to do to us? Why didn't you tell me that before? I've got to deal with people who don't play by any rules and you're sitting there quiet as a cat, holding out on me." I was breathing hard and my hands were clenched so hard that the nails were biting into the skin.

He sat quietly, a faintly bored expression on his face. Then he said, "Feeling better? I didn't tell you because I wanted you to talk straight to Reese, not try to figure out some angle. You haven't done criminal justice work in ten years. It's not our job to coddle you when you step into it."

"Who killed him? When? Where?"

"He was found in his hotel this morning, shot. We don't know much yet."

I was thinking about slugging him when Lisa said, "Do you have his things? Petrov's, I mean. He might have something in them that could help me prove that his work is being passed off as my grandfather's."

"Why should I care about that?" Greenberg said coldly. "I want to know who killed him."

"Because it might be evidence of why he was killed," I said. "Listen to her. Petrov told us that Tabor was trying to buy up a lot of his paintings. Tabor wanted them because they could be re-signed with Thayer's name. He could pull the scam twenty, thirty times. Depending on the price they could get, Tabor would be looking at millions of dollars."

Reese said, "They're right, you know. It's proof of Tabor's motive, the proof you're going to need to connect him to the people who did the shooting."

"All right," Greenberg said tiredly. "Everything is still in his hotel room, under seal. I'll take you there."

The hotel where Petrov had stayed was in Chelsea, on a mixed street of tenements in various states of disrepair, welfare hotels, and a new apartment tower under construction on the corner of Eighth Avenue. The hotel itself was a four-floor walk-up, with the usual cluster of hookers on the afternoon shift who scattered like deer when Reese and Greenberg flashed their shields at a bored desk clerk who scarcely glanced up from his magazine. The desk clerk pulled a key from the wall of pigeonholes behind him and went back to his magazine, which appeared to have something to do with bondage. Greenberg took the key and we walked up two flights and down a grungy, ill-lit hallway that smelled of Lysol and human pain.

The room itself was small, with a metal bed, a painted wooden dresser, and a porcelain washstand in one corner that had been acquiring chips and stains since World War II. The plaster on the walls was cracked, and flakes of paint and plaster littered the corners of the room. Petrov had been killed as he lay in bed. The body had been removed, but the bedding was soaked with blood and the death smell was strong. Reese lit a cigarette and offered me one. I lit it and dragged on it, then handed it to Lisa.

"I haven't smoked since college," she said.

"Start," I said. "It kills the smell." She took it and smoked nervously. I turned to Greenberg.

"What time did it happen?"

"The medical examiner thinks about five this morning. The desk clerk on duty said two guys came in with a hooker around four A.M. and took the room next door. The hooker was a regular here, but when she went past time, the clerk went to roust them. The clerk found her dead. The cops knocked on Petrov's door to see if he'd heard anything, and found him."

"Could the desk clerk describe them?"

"Are you kidding? When they came in with a hooker, he paid no attention. Best he could do was say one was white, the other black."

"Where's Petrov's stuff?"

"In the two suitcases there. He kept everything in them, didn't hang anything in the closet or use the bureau."

"We'll need to check them."

"Okay, let me go through them first. I'll lay everything out on the floor." Greenberg rifled through the bags, piling the dirty laundry to one side, laying out books and notes and the rest of Petrov's things on the other. When he found a cheap Instamatic camera, he smiled sadly. Petrov had gone to New York to try to write a proper finish to his life, but he must have been excited as a child at the thought of seeing the city. Thirty years in prison and his subsequent poverty had been emotional starvation for him.

Lisa was reading through the notes and a typed, bound résumé that listed Petrov's paintings and few exhibitions. "He wasn't lying," she said. "This was prepared just this past month, probably for this trip. Listen." She began reading from it. " 'I ask that you judge me for my work, not on the basis of my age or my lack of public acclaim. What you see is work from a life half-lived, broken apart by thirty years in jail for a crime I did not commit.' " She closed the résumé, a deep sadness on her face.

Greenberg pulled a black plastic case from the smaller of the two cheap suitcases. "Is this what you're looking for?" he asked.

Lisa bent over and snatched the case from his grasp. "That's it. His slides." She pried the case open and held the first slide up to the dusty afternoon sunlight coming in from the room's single window. "It's a painting. I'll need to look at the rest of these carefully."

"Wait a minute," Greenberg said, gesturing for the return of the slides. "These are evidence. I've got to maintain the chain of custody on them."

"Then get them copied," I told him. "One of your photographic people can do it. Lisa will need time with them, and there's nothing more that we can do here. We're leaving tomorrow. She'll be safer at home."

"It's Labor Day weekend, for God's sake. There won't be anybody around to make them."

"You'll find a way." I took Lisa's arm and walked her out of the hotel and down into the sunlight of the street. We stayed there for a moment, mentally trying to scrub off the stench of the hotel. We drew a stare or two from some of the younger people, too poor to leave town for the weekend, who passed by us on the sidewalk. The air on the street was dirty and sharp with traffic fumes, but it helped.

We were still standing there when Greenberg and Reese

walked out of the hotel. Reese went straight to the car, but Greenberg came over to talk.

Before he could say anything I said, "I'd like to know what's going on, Al. Maybe it's been too long a time for me to come back here, asking you for favors. But you've been treating me like a suspect, not a friend. We were friends once, Al. Good friends."

He looked at me stubbornly. "I told you when you quit in 1976," he said. "You were doing some good, working on the strike force, taking the bad people down. And you walked away from it."

I shook my head. "I was just one of the guys, Al, like you, like anybody else. I wasn't making any big decisions, setting any courts on their ear. We were all just doing our jobs."

"And some of us kept doing them," he said angrily. "You walked out, first for money down on Wall Street, later to go to the coast. I didn't. I stayed and did my job, scraping what was left of people off the floors of shitty hotels like that one. I try to give them their due: an understanding of what happened to them and punishment for the people who did it."

"Al," I said softly, "it's a job. It's important, and more people should do their share, but nobody can do this forever. When your time comes, you move on."

He stood silently, his eyes locked on mine. I was filled with a sudden enormous sadness, seeing what a hard and honorable life had done to him, leaving a humorless neurotic shell.

"I'm so sorry, Al," I told him. "Truly. You are such a fine man. But whatever it was that has caused this to happen to you, I'm glad that I was not part of it."

I took Lisa's hand and we walked over to the corner of Eighth Avenue to find a cab and go home.

Lisa selected the last of the slides from the plastic box and fitted it into the portable viewer. She held the viewer to the light coming in through the rounded airplane window and gave a low gasp of recognition. "My god," she said. "No wonder they wanted to buy Petrov's paintings. Some of these look just like Thayer's work from the late fifties and early sixties, the height of his abstract expressionist period."

"Was he copying Thayer's pictures?" I asked around a mouthful of lox and bagel. I sipped at my coffee and made a face. Lisa had had the foresight to have our taxi stop at a delicatessen on the way to the airport, but we didn't have a coffee thermos and so we were drinking vile airline brew.

"Maybe. Painters aren't recluses; they look at each other's work, trying to find new ideas, just like people in any other vocation. But Petrov was in prison, getting whatever information he could from the outside, and most of what he saw was about Thayer. It reinforced the similarities in their styles that had existed since the 1930's. Petrov never really developed a style of his own, at least not until the past few years. About twenty of these slides are newer pictures and they are interesting. Petrov became more figurative, more representational, but the figures are warped and almost brutal looking. It's not surrealism; it's something cruder and more powerful."

"Petrov was obsessed with your grandfather for a long time," I said, thinking aloud. "Perhaps he mimicked Thayer without even knowing it consciously. Can you link these older paintings to the three in the Seattle show?"

"Oh, yes. Petrov and Thayer didn't follow the same exact style or technique. Thayer tended to leave a border around the canvas, not take his paintings all the way to the edge. Petrov doesn't do that as much; he tends to go right to the edge. Petrov's brush stroke is flatter. Thayer's stroke was much sharper." She held her thumb and forefinger together, holding an imaginary brush, and flicked her wrist forward and back. "Like that."

"Could you give an opinion in court?"

"Sure. I don't have any doubts, after what I've seen."

"What about the bird on the postcard?"

Her face clouded over. She hesitated before speaking. "I think Petrov could have done that. But if he did, he was consciously imitating Thayer's style. He was painting a fake."

I frowned. "It doesn't fit. Assume that he told us the truth, and that was what got him killed. Why would he have painted the bird now? After looking at his paintings, you think he was trying to develop his own style. Why would he copy a painting of Thayer's? And there are other things that don't fit. Why did Kuehn send that painting to the doctor in Port Angeles? What was Kuehn doing out on the peninsula, on the ferry? Who did he see? Was he the one at your grandfather's lodge? If he committed suicide, who wiped the prints off the gun?"

Lisa didn't answer.

"I don't know either," I said quietly. "But this thing about Tabor, it has to be right. So that's what we have to go to work on, eliminating that threat."

"But how? We can't do any more than we could two weeks ago. We have my word against Campbell's that those three paintings aren't authentic."

"We've got a couple of things. We've figured out what they're doing, and why. We can start trying to document the links between Petrov, Hanks, Campbell, and Tabor. We'll have the cops helping us. Vince Ahlberg knows that this won't end with Petrov's death."

"Did you find out from Petrov where he kept his paintings? I thought I remembered you saying Petrov's studio had been cleaned out."

"It was, but he didn't tell me where the paintings are. When I called Ahlberg yesterday, he promised to break the news to Ellen Diekmann and ask her about the paintings."

"I feel so awful for her. She was so protective of Petrov. She must have loved him very much."

I nodded. There had been too many violent deaths among this small group of people. Margaret Jura's murder, Thayer's probable suicide, and now Kuehn and Petrov. I tried to put the thought in words. "It's almost as if there's a cycle of tragedy that runs through the lives of these people," I began. "A cycle, or a chain."

"What are you talking about?" Lisa said.

"It sounds crazy," I replied. "But somehow this all starts with the death of your grandfather's lover, Margaret Jura. If she hadn't died in the way she did, none of this would have happened, at least not the way it has happened. There's something at the center of this we're not seeing."

Lisa shifted uncomfortably in the narrow airplane seat. "Maybe Lee really is still alive."

I shook my head. "Petrov said he wasn't. And I don't think Petrov would lie about a thing like that. He envied Thayer, blamed him for killing Margaret Jura, and hated him. I can't shake the feeling that Petrov was telling the truth, or some of it, anyway. He wanted to be recognized for his work, to be known as something other than a murderer. He wanted his identity and his dignity. So if we believe that Petrov was trying to prevent people from re-signing his pictures, we have to conclude Thayer is dead. After all, the one sure way to prevent anybody from passing off Petrov's work as Thayer's would be to have Thayer identify his own paintings."

Lisa said nothing. She carefully put the slides she had been looking at back into their case and placed the case in the overnight bag at her feet. I said, "When we get back, I don't think we should go back to your house, or mine. I'll rent a car at the airport and leave mine in storage. Then I think we should probably get a room somewhere. We'll need to keep moving around for a couple of days, until we can figure out how to expose Tabor and Campbell."

She made a face. "I hate hotels. I feel like I've been living out of a bag for too long already."

"I know. I hope it won't be too much longer."

"What can we do?"

"The first thing will be to talk to Ahlberg, but after that I think we go to Hanks. He's probably the weakest link. He doesn't have Tabor's toughness or Campbell's pull and social standing. How successful is he? Financially, I mean."

"He works steadily and gets commissions, which in a sculpture market as small as Seattle's means a lot. I doubt if he's ever cleared more than twenty thousand dollars in a year after paying his expenses."

"That's interesting. I saw his loft when I went to talk to him. He's really fixed the place up. Hell, the kitchen alone probably cost more than thirty thousand. If he's spending the money, there will be all kinds of records he won't find easy to explain. There's always the tax angle, too. When people are getting hot money, the tax violation is almost always the easiest to prove."

"What will you do to him?"

"Put on pressure. Show that he's been getting money, threaten him with that, try to turn him and get him to rat on the others. If Ahlberg can show that he tipped the people who put the bomb in your car, he'll bust him for attempted murder."

"I still can't believe Terrill would be involved." She looked worried. "When you confront him, I want to be there. I want to hear his explanation."

"Why?"

She hesitated, pursing her lips, then said, "Terrill and I were together, a few years ago, shortly after I moved back to Seattle from New York. It lasted a year. He was important to me. Very important."

"I understand," I replied. "But why didn't you tell me that before?"

"Because I was starting to have feelings about you, and I thought you might feel the same way. I didn't want to hurt that."

"It wouldn't have," I told her, "and it doesn't." I took her face between my hands. "But I am not going to stand by and watch you get hurt."

The plane was delayed in Denver and it was five o'clock Pacific time when we finally landed. I rented a brown Chevrolet Camaro after making sure that it was a V-8 model with enough punch to get us out of trouble if trouble came. We checked into a motel room along the airport strip. I paid cash and signed us in under a phony Mr. and Mrs. Lisa was amused. "You're pretty good with motel clerks, Riordan," she said as we walked around to our room. "Is there something in your past you're not telling me?"

"Nothing you'd want to hear. It's sordid. Very sordid. The scoutmaster's wife. Then—" She hit me with her travel bag. Hard.

"You're right," she said. "You can boast when all this is over."

When we reached the room, I stretched out and took a shower while Lisa worked the phone, trying to locate Terrill Hanks.

"He's not home and not at the wrecking yard where he cuts the metal for his sculptures," Lisa reported as I came out of the shower. "Are you going to call Ahlberg?"

"Not if you want a chance to talk to Hanks first," I replied. "Ahlberg is probably going to pick him up and sweat him as soon as we go in to make our statements. Is there anyplace he hangs out that we could try?"

"He likes to take the papers on Sunday afternoons and go to a bar and read, or at least he used to. He gave up drinking for a while, because if he went to a bar, it was for four or five hours and ten beers. I don't know if he's started again."

I thought back to Hanks's loft, to the dark-haired woman who drank from the open champagne bottle at eleven in the morning. "I think he has. There was a woman with him when I saw him at his loft. She was about forty, slender, dark hair and eyes. She looked familiar to me, but I couldn't place her. She was drinking in the morning, and Hanks looked like he had been the night before."

"She doesn't sound familiar," Lisa said. "But if Terrill's drinking, he'll be at one of the taverns around the Market or up in the Denny Regrade."

"If we don't find him, I still wouldn't mind a drink. Let me get dressed and we'll go."

The night was foggy and cool and the downtown streets were quiet at the end of the holiday weekend. We crawled the art bars and clubs from Gravity's Rainbow to the Oxford to Free Mars and back to the Virginia Inn. At the Virginia Inn we stopped for a pint of beer ourselves. We took a couple of stools at the bar, next to the open can of Top tobacco that was once a fixture in every sailor's bar in Seattle. I amused myself by trying to see if I still could roll a cigarette one-handed, the way I'd learned as a teenager at Cathedral High School in Great Falls, Montana. I couldn't; the tobacco grains kept falling from the paper. Lisa stared at me with the look of suffering patience that seems to be genetically programmed into women. I suspect it is the biological relief mechanism they have for putting up with men.

"This isn't getting us anywhere," she said. She looked up at the artwork displayed on the VI's exposed brick walls. The show was of torn paper collages, precious little assemblies below glass. "Even the art's no good tonight."

"Can you think of anyplace else we can try?"

"Only the Two Bells, over on Fourth Avenue. But I think it's closed on Sundays."

"I don't know whether it is or not. Let's go by on the way back."

The Two Bells was open and the small barroom was packed to the rafters with people. The crowd was an uneasy mix of artists, television people from the nearby stations, and a few retired workingmen who still lived in the last crumbling residential hotels of the Denny Regrade district. The old men drank quietly, a little sullenly. The Two Bells had recently become excruciatingly hip, and most of the people who worked there wore black clothes and sardonic smiles, and could tell you all that you never wanted to know about performance art and video life. It had become the sort of place people hung out in to practice for their big move to New York.

As we walked in, a wave of Robert Cray blues and warm smoky air greeted us at the door.

"There he is," Lisa said, gesturing toward a back table. I looked and saw Hanks, dressed in his usual motorcycle leathers, a black cigar clamped between his teeth. He was listening to a man across the table from him and not liking whatever he was hearing. As we walked to the back of the tavern he looked up and saw us coming. He stared at us for a moment in apparent confusion, then looked back to his companions, determined to ignore us.

We stood by the table and waited. From the wreckage of empty beer pitchers and glasses it looked as though Hanks had been there most of the afternoon and night. We waited. Finally he looked up, his eyes slightly glassy from alcohol. "You want something?" His voice was harsh and threatening.

"We want to talk to you. Alone," I told him.

"I'm busy."

"Not busy enough, man. Tell your friends good night."

He got to his feet, wavering a little. I put up a hand.

"Don't be silly," I said. "We're going to talk to you one way or another. It might as well be now."

He tried to throw a punch. It was weak and slow and I stepped back and caught his fist in my hands. "Terrill!" Lisa said sharply. "We have to talk. Damn you, you owe me that."

He looked at the anger written on Lisa's face and sat down abruptly. "So talk," he snarled.

"Alone." I turned to his friends, a burly man in his late fifties, dressed in army fatigues, and a skinny, mean-looking woman of twenty-five or so with a pinched face and tangled brown hair. "It's been swell," I told them. "Terrill's going to pick up the tab. Good night." They both started to object at once, but I waited until they fell silent, unsure of themselves and what was happening. When they gathered up their jackets and walked away, Lisa and I sat down where they had been. Hanks looked at us warily.

"We want to ask you about three paintings," I said. "You've seen them, they were in the Thayer retrospective at SAM. Lisa thinks they were painted by somebody else and signed with Thayer's name."

"I don't know what you're talking about." Hank's voice was thick and surly.

"Of course you do. One of the paintings was a large oil, an abstract, color-field piece in dark greens, grays, and blues. *Sea Study, No. 3.* You used to own it."

He laughed, his voice rasping. He reached into the ashtray, picked up his cigar, and reignited it in a cloud of oily blue smoke. "I've never owned a Thayer in my life. I'm not exactly rich, in case you haven't noticed." He laughed again, choking his words through the laughter. "I don't know what drug you're using, man, but I want some of it."

I smiled at him coldly. "I wasn't finished. When you owned the painting, it wasn't a Thayer. Petrov painted it and gave it to you to settle some money he owed you."

The laughter stopped, and Hanks's eyes were suddenly bright and sober. He turned to Lisa. "What the fuck does this guy want, Lisa? He's crazy."

She ignored him. "I talked to Petrov three days ago, in New York City," I said. "He described the painting in the SAM show. He says he gave it to you ten years ago. Petrov also says that you showed up at his studio, on the Diekmann farm outside La

Conner, and tried to buy up a bunch of his older work. You had a lawyer with you, a man named Duane Tabor. Tabor works with David Campbell. Tabor was the man who threatened Lisa at the SAM show."

Hanks looked again at Lisa, with something close to hatred in his eyes. "Did this creep put you up to this?" he demanded.

"No," she said coolly. "I put him up to this. He'd rather hang you by your heels from a tall building and drop you on your head if you don't talk. I'm starting to think that's the only way you'll ever tell the truth."

"This is bullshit," he said quietly. He started to get up, but I shoved him back down.

"She is trying to do you a favor, shithead. She's giving you the chance to tell us what you know. If you're not involved, no problem. If you are, and you talk, then maybe the cops will give you immunity for your testimony. But you haven't got much time. Tomorrow I'm going to start checking you out so thoroughly you'll think you're walking naked down Main Street. I'm going to find out what you own and where you've got it. From the looks of your loft I suspect you're the kind of dumb shit who spends everything you've got. Fine. I'm going to get the tax people interested in where you got the money for that fancy remodeling, and the sixty-dollar champagne you keep in the fridge, and your other toys. I'm going to put somebody on your tail twenty-four hours a day and wait and watch until they see you panic and try to make contact with somebody. When that happens, you're going to be on your way to Walla Walla or Clallam Bay. You think you're tough. The guys there will think you're cute. They'll punk you. They'll get you a cotton apron and a subscription to *Better Homes and Gardens*."

I had to give Hanks credit. He sat through the best prosecutor rap I could lay down and toughed it out. When I was through, he said, "You hassle me with cops and I'll sue your ass. Petrov will tell the cops that you're making all this shit up. Sure, I tried to buy a couple paintings. I wanted to help the old guy out. So what. You can't prove anything."

"Maybe I won't have to," I replied. "Petrov's dead. Somebody walked into his hotel room in New York and shot the old man through the heart. The same somebody might do you next."

The expression of drunken disdain slid from Hanks's face. He stood up without a word and stalked on uncertain legs toward the front door. The bartender yelled at him about his tab and then shrugged, as though he knew Hanks would be good for it. I looked at Lisa. "Go after him," she said.

I dodged through the tavern crowd and ran out the front door. Hanks was disappearing around the corner of a building and heading toward the alley that bisected the blocks between Third and Fourth. I caught him there and grabbed his arm before he could get on his motorcycle.

"We're not done," I told him. "You know you're going to spill it. Do it now and get it over with."

He didn't answer. Instead he suddenly wrapped his arms around my chest and shoved me back against the rough brick wall of the building. My head snapped on the brick and for a moment I was stunned. He tried to get me with a knee to the groin, but I turned and caught it on my thigh. I spun out of his grasp and stepped away.

There are two things to remember when fighting a drunk: their grip is very strong and their tolerance for pain is high. You have to stay out of their grasp and try to finish things quickly.

"Come on," I taunted him. "You can't do it, man. You haven't got the stones."

He lowered his head and charged at me, growling deep in his throat. I took a half step sideways and sent a straight right hand crashing into his face. That slowed him down. I straightened him with a couple of jabs. While he was still weaving, I put a foot in the pit of his stomach and stepped out of the way as he fell.

He fell forward, onto his hands and knees. He gasped for air and then vomited sour beer on the ground. As I waited, heart pounding with adrenaline, I noticed that Lisa was standing beside me with an expression of utter sorrow on her face.

Hanks groaned and tried to get up. I put a foot into his rib cage and shoved him back down on the ground. Lisa stepped forward.

"Terrill," she said firmly, tears running down her face, "you knew they were going to try to kill me, didn't you? You told them what kind of car I had and where I parked and when I was going to leave so that they could attach the bomb." Her voice was filled with a reluctant, awful certainty.

He didn't answer her. He stayed on the ground and turned his face away, toward the brick wall.

"Terrill," Lisa said, her voice breaking, "how could you help them? Didn't the fact that I loved you once mean anything to you?"

There was no answer. I stayed where I was, hearing the pain that Lisa was feeling in the way she spoke in broken little gasps. She fought to keep her voice under control.

"Damn you!" she hissed. Her rage turned suddenly cold, her voice grew menacing. "When you die, Terrill," she said slowly, "there will be no one, *no one*, who will grieve for you."

Lisa's terrible curse hung in the empty alley. I listened to Hanks's ragged breathing and the sporadic night sounds, cars and sirens and the meaningless chatter of televisions through open windows. There was nothing more that we could do. If Hanks was involved, he feared his partners more than us. I wrapped my arms around Lisa and pulled her away. Hanks lay on the pavement until we were gone.

15

In the morning we slept like death, tangled in each other's arms. Lisa had stayed awake until nearly 4:00 A.M., made sad and silent by her suspicion that Hanks had tried to have her killed. She stared at the walls of our room as though searching for the knowledge of good and evil. I stayed at her side and said very little, even though I had spent much time looking for answers on motel-room walls and had never found any.

The insistent drill of the motel phone dragged me from sleep. I groped for the receiver, momentarily confused as to which end was which. I finally got the right part to my mouth. "Hello?" I asked sleepily.

"Riordan?" Vince Ahlberg growled. "Where the hell are you? What is this number you left last night?"

"Motel," I said, trying to talk through what felt like a bucket of sand. "What's on your mind?"

"Answers, that's what. You've been back for a day and haven't come in. What are you up to?"

"Hiding out. People have been trying to kill us, remember?"

"So Greenberg told me. He also said that Petrov got himself killed."

"That's true." I sat up in bed and put the phone in my lap. Lisa stirred and then burrowed deeper into the covers on the far side of the bed. "But Lisa says he definitely painted the pictures in the Thayer show. Terrill Hanks, the sculptor, was apparently the guy who saw the resemblance to Thayer's painting and arranged for Campbell to sell them. You should pick him up."

"We did. Last night. A patrol unit found him in an alley, pretty thoroughly beat up."

"Street crime is terrible this year," I said sympathetically. "Did he give you anything?"

"Not word one. I questioned him this morning. He had a lawyer and refused to talk. I had to kick him."

"Then we've still got nothing. Only what Petrov told me about him, and that's inadmissible hearsay. Shit." I thought for a moment. "So we'll have to do it another way. You got anybody down there who can read and write and knows his or her way around the courthouse?"

He sighed. "We manage, Riordan, even when you're not here. What are you looking for?"

"Hanks lives far too well. He's got a fancy loft in a building on First Avenue South. He probably owns the building. Where'd he get the money? And did he declare any of it on his taxes? You start asking questions like that, you're going to rattle him, anyway."

"That sounds reasonable. What are you going to do?"

"Try to figure out who's behind Tabor and Campbell, find out if he's part of the deal or if he's the anonymous collector who got stuck with the fake Thayers."

"Why?"

"So I know who and what I'm dealing with."

"And then what?"

"If there's somebody they've screwed, I'll sell him Campbell and Tabor."

"We'll get them. We're getting closer."

"With what? You can't even get a search warrant for Campbell's records. You've got no probable cause, no evidence that ties Campbell to anything. I can invade his privacy a little easier than you can."

He grunted in frustration. "What's the sales price going to be?"

"Only that he leave me and mine alone. Look, this thing could go one of two ways. If Campbell and Tabor sold paintings re-signed as Thayer's to a rich drug grower, then maybe I can let him know he's been taken. If there's some grower that's behind Campbell and Tabor, part of the scheme, then I want to know that, too. Because somebody involved here was able to reach all the way to New York to kill Petrov and force me to break the world record in the run-crawl-dive-swim competition, live-ammunition division. I am much too old to be playing with such people."

"Your hypothetical drug grower might just kill Campbell and Tabor if he finds out he's been cheated."

"And I'd grieve. You going to help me on this? There's a DEA agent named Michael Reese in New York. He used to work in San Francisco. DEA's got a big intelligence file on Tabor and they know who he works for. Reese won't tell me anything. Maybe he'll tell you."

"If he did, I couldn't tell you. If you're right and you used the information, you'd be an accessory to a pair of murders. So would I."

"Nonsense. The most I could do would be to let the victim know there's been a crime. What he does about it is not my business."

Ahlberg's voice was sarcastic. "You're back to making fine legal distinctions. Sometimes I wish you'd stick to that."

"Sometimes I wish that, too. But I'm going to do this one way or another, Vince."

"For Christ's sake, I can put both of you in protective cus-tody."

"For how long? You're not going to make a bust anytime soon, pal. I'll call in, Vince, or you can call my office. We're going to keep moving around." I hung up and put the phone back on the nightstand.

"So where are we off to today?" Lisa asked sleepily. She sat up, clutching the covers around her. Her blond hair was tangled and her tan skin looked rich against the white sheets.

"To work," I said regretfully, running a finger along the curve of her bare shoulder. "To work."

By five o'clock that afternoon Lisa and I had moved into a rental condominium in the Silicon Forest area of Redmond along the Sammamish River. We were posing as a couple relocating from San Jose to work for one of the local software companies. I rented a portable personal computer and a telephone modem, and after a couple of false starts I actually managed to make it work. Using my office billing code and password, I logged on to one of the many business data bases that are commercially available. This particular data base contained the corporate record filings that are customarily made in each state. I had hopes that if I pursued the paper trail far enough, I might turn up the name of the man or woman who was behind Duane Tabor.

I had gone to the county courthouse earlier that day and learned that Campbell's art gallery/loft building was owned by a company named Artform, Inc., and that there was a deed of trust on the building in favor of an entity called the Methow Investment Trust. I checked the Washington secretary of state's filings and found that Artform had been incorporated by Campbell, with Tabor and a local lawyer named as officers for the purpose of creating the company. The Methow Trust was named for one of the high mountain valleys in eastern Washington, but I couldn't locate any offices or listings for it in any Washington State directory. It had filed its trust declaration with the state and I read it carefully, my eyes straining as I scrolled the text up on the screen. The sole beneficiary of the trust was another corporation, Klamath Investments, Inc., a California company. I sighed. Whoever had structured the financing for Campbell's building changed corporate entities like other people changed clothes.

I was still at the computer at three o'clock the following morning. I had traced the chains of corporate ownership back as far as I could. The Methow Trust had dead-ended in an offshore Panamanian corporation that was a complete blind. Panama was not exactly forthcoming about the financial affairs of the drug dealers and deposed dictators who found its bank secrecy laws so congenial. The other chain of ownership, which had started with Artform, Inc., twisted its way around to an Oregon corporation, Big Bend Properties, that appeared to be the controlling entity. A man named Joseph Wheeler was listed as the president and holder of 997 out of 1,000 original shares. That didn't necessarily mean much; Wheeler could be a puppet who had served as original incorporator and held his shares for the benefit of the real controlling power. But I thought I had seen the name before, and I cross-checked it against a file of all of the names I had taken from the corporate documents I had checked.

Joseph Wheeler's name appeared four separate times.

I believe in coincidences about as much as I do television evangelism. Wheeler was either the head cheese or he was tied in, and either way I wanted to find him. I went into the kitchen of the condominium and bought myself a beer and thought. I still needed information; maybe this time I could trade for it. I took out Michael Reese's business card and turned it over in my hands. The small blue seal of the Drug Enforcement Administration had been printed on a corner of the card. Reese's interest in Tabor had always bothered me a little. He might be what he seemed, a man who hated Tabor's blow-dried greed to the point where it had gotten personal. Or he might have been bought, put on retainer to pass any bad news back to Tabor. If he was straight, the worst that Reese could do was turn me down. If he wasn't, I could get dead without even knowing it was coming.

I looked at my watch. It was quarter to four in the morning, a damned poor time for walking through a hall of mirrors, trying to decide which images were distorted, which real. The real tragedy of the drug wars, like Prohibition before it, was that it made both laws and law enforcers suspect.

I picked up the phone and dialed. Reese answered on the second ring.

"It's Riordan," I said. "I think I've got the name. I want you to tell me if it's the right one."

"What do I get for it?" he replied, pausing to take an audible sip of his morning coffee. It was seven o'clock in New York.

"Maybe a ringside seat," I said. "Maybe not. It depends on how it goes down."

"Give me your name, then."

"Wheeler. Joseph Wheeler."

There was a long pause.

"Bingo. But this is a prize you don't ever want to meet, Riordan. I'm on my way. Don't do anything stupid until I get there."

Lisa had insisted that we do with David Campbell as we had done with Hanks: go back and provide him with one last chance to come clean and avoid a confrontation with the man he had cheated.

"This man Wheeler will kill him if he finds out that Campbell defrauded him," she said. "I can't just go along with that."

"Lisa, we are running out of time and choices," I said. "They've tried to kill us twice. I don't see anything wrong with stopping them. We don't know much about Wheeler, or what he'll do. But if he kills them, they'll have gotten no more than they deserve."

"I can't be that bloody-minded about it," she replied. "David Campbell was my grandfather's friend. He gave me a job when I needed one. He isn't all bad."

"We are taking one hell of a risk going in there," I said stubbornly. "Talking to Hanks was bad enough. Campbell is probably scared now, and if he is, he might have people waiting there for us. We could pick up a tail. I can't promise that if we do this I can get us out of it."

"I know all that, Matthew," she said. She came across the bedroom, knelt behind me on the bed, and rubbed the muscles in my neck. They burned with tension and lack of sleep. "But I can't live with myself any other way."

I reached back, pulled her hands down, and drew her close. "Okay," I said, "but we do this my way. I'm going to call someone to watch over us. If he's free, we'll go today."

The someone I had in mind was a man named Mick Grogan. He had played football for twelve years, as a linebacker for two junior colleges, three army bases, Oregon State University, the USFL, and, briefly, as a scab San Francisco Forty-Niner during the strike. Grogan is roughly the size and shape of a three-quarter-ton pickup, and he looks a little like one that's been through a couple of head-on collisions. He's retired from the game and makes a living as free-lance muscle. He is reliable, and honest in his own way. He will guard your body or deliver your goods or bounce the unruly from your premises. He is very good at doing unto others what they are planning to do unto you.

I found him at the third of the three numbers I had for him, the home of a reasonably well-known women's advice columnist and talk-show host who had once been a university professor. She wrote soft fuzzy books about interpersonal relationships and the need to find a caring man who would provide space and comfort and nurturing and get in touch with his female side. Mick lived with her from time to time, doubtless getting in touch with his female side. I tried to visualize their domestic evenings at home, the lady tapping out her delicate prose on a word processor while Mick watched arena football on ESPN and scattered crushed Foster's Lager cans all over the living-room floor.

"Mick," I said when he picked up the phone. "Riordan."

"Hey," he replied. "Been a while. Where you been?"

"In a hospital, recovering from all the beer we drank."

"Hell," he said, chuckling, "I had a bit of a headache myself. What's up?"

"You free this afternoon? I've got a job for you."

"Doing what?"

"Check out a building, let me know if it's clear, then walk in with me and a friend of mine while we do some business."

"Sounds too simple."

"It is. It'll get hard only if somebody tries to shoot us."

"Not necessarily."

"That's the spirit. I'll pay two bills for two hours' work. Wear a suit and a gun, okay? I'll pick you up at noon." I heard him grunt affirmatively and rang off.

I showered and changed into a pair of khaki slacks and a dark green cotton turtleneck. I put my arms through a woven leather shoulder harness and holstered a Walther PPK automatic. Karen the actress/secretary had delivered it to me the day before at a Stop-'n'-Shop off Interstate 405 in Bothell. I hadn't told Lisa about the errand. When she returned to the room, her eyes widened and then were sad.

"It's like that?" she asked.

"I'm afraid so, Lisa." I covered the holstered gun with a short leather jacket, and we turned out the lights and left.

The days had turned gray with the coming of early fall. A light rain fell and settled the construction dust that had afflicted downtown all summer long. I watched the lunchtime crowds, most of whom hadn't yet bought new umbrellas to replace those lost over the summer. Mostly I watched the entrance to the Girard Building, across Third Avenue from the parked car where Lisa and I waited for Grogan to come back.

He returned, shaking his head. "Nothing," he said. "I checked all the floors except the penthouse. You sure you got a problem?"

"No," I replied, "but you know I've always been the nervous type. Let's go, then."

We got out of the car, crossed the street, and went into the building. Lisa was quiet on the elevator to David Campbell's fifth-floor gallery. The ride seemed very long. When the doors opened, we walked past the sculptures and over to the reception desk. David Campbell was standing behind it, staring down at the screen of a computer. As he looked up I saw his eyes widen with surprise.

"Hello, David," Lisa said firmly.

He looked from her to me and then to Grogan, looming like a bear behind me. "Who's that?" he asked thickly.

"A savant, a critic of the arts," I replied. "If he doesn't like the stuff you're showing, he might just compel you to eat it. Are you alone?"

"Yes," he said. "Jennifer has gone to lunch."

"Go check the upstairs," I told Grogan, nodding toward the spiral staircase that joined the gallery and Campbell's apartment. I waited to speak until Grogan returned.

"It's clear," he said.

"Suitably dramatic," Campbell said scornfully. He stood straight, his back stiff. "I suppose I should ask you what this is about. Then I will call the police."

"If that's the way you want it," I told him. "Lisa wanted the opportunity to talk to you privately."

"About what?"

"Forgery. Fraud. Facilitating the commission of a narcotics felony. Violations of the Travel Act and the Controlled Substances Act. Investment and laundering of drug proceeds, which are subject to forfeiture. Attempted murder. Murder. I think that's about all."

He laughed derisively. "This is lunacy."

"David," Lisa pleaded, "this is going to destroy you. I know that the paintings you sold were fakes. Anton Petrov painted them, and someone else re-signed them as Thayers. Petrov is dead, David. He was killed in New York, shot in a hotel room. The bomb in my car, the attempt on Matthew's life, they were trying to silence us about those three paintings."

"Lisa, I don't know what you're talking about." He busied himself straightening papers on the desk in front of him.

"Of course you do," I told him. "You and Tabor are in this

up to your heads. You're looking at selling fifteen, twenty pictures of Petrov's over the next couple of years, passing them off as Thayer's. With the way prices are rising you might net ten million dollars, maybe more. That would bail you out of your financial difficulties, wouldn't it?"

Campbell fixed me with a cold eye. "If I had any financial difficulties, Mr. Riordan—which I don't—I could solve them with a phone call to any one of a half-dozen friends. The notion that I would resort to crime is utter garbage."

I shook my head. If Campbell was going to fall back on his goddamn upper-class snottiness, this was going to be a mighty short conversation. "Don't hand me that crap," I said. "Anyone with eyes can see that you lost your ass on this building. Half the apartments still aren't rented, and the storefronts on the street level are still empty. You needed financing in the worst way, and that's how you got it—from Tabor, who is a front for drug money out of California. You know you've got to pay them off, because those people really know how to foreclose on a mortgage. So you decided to sell a couple of fakes as a quick fix."

"David," Lisa added, "please listen. I am here because I honor the friendship that you had with my grandfather. And I can't bear to think of what will happen to you if you don't go to the police now."

"What on earth makes you think something is going to happen to me, Lisa? Really, this is foolishness. Take your friends"—he paused scornfully over the word—"and go. You'll be hearing from my lawyers."

"David, wait. You don't know what's going to—"

"Enough," I said, taking Lisa by the arm. "You've done all you can. Your conscience is clear. We have to go."

"But," she said, "I can make him see."

"No, you can't," I replied. As I pulled Lisa away her eyes were still pleading, but Campbell wasn't bothering to look. He busied himself at the desk, ignoring her. I nodded to Grogan, and we walked to the elevator. The cool beauty of the sculpture in the clean white gallery seemed to mock us as we left.

16

The death of Terrill Hanks was reported on the morning news by one of the local talking heads, a man with styled hair and a hip ironic style that could make pestilence and war sound like mundane social activities. I snapped off the television and put in a phone call to Ahlberg. He was already at Hanks's loft, where the body had been found, but his desk officer promised that he would call in soon. I broke the news to Lisa over cups of very black coffee. She seemed unsurprised. An empty stillness came over her for a moment before she spoke.

"I want to go into my gallery," she said. "I want to work."

"I understand," I replied. "But keep the gallery closed. And let me get Grogan there, just to keep a weather eye. These people are getting desperate."

She nodded listlessly. I began to wonder how much more stress she could handle. We were living like two people in a war zone, surviving on adrenaline and instinct. I could feel the weariness and the fear building up in myself. For Lisa it must have been ten times as bad, not because she was a woman, but because she had never been put under this kind of stress before.

She could walk and talk and even laugh, but I knew the damage would go on inside, until this was over.

Within the hour I had called the cops back and learned that Ahlberg wanted to see me at Hanks's loft. Lisa and I drove into Bellevue and met Grogan at a suburban park-and-ride lot near I-405. Lisa went with Grogan to her gallery. I followed them out onto the freeway into downtown Seattle, hanging back to see whether we had picked up any kind of a tail. If we had, it was so well done I couldn't spot it, and that made me nervous. I was going to have to dump the car today and move us to a new location if something didn't break soon.

The industrial district south of the Kingdome bustled with freight trucks splashing through a desultory rain. I checked in with the uniformed officer covering the door and rode the grimy, clanking freight elevator to the top floor of Hanks's building.

Ahlberg met me on the landing outside of Hanks's loft. He peeled off a black leather glove, shook my hand grimly, then put the glove back on. "No touch," he said. "The lab's not even close to finished."

"How bad is it?"

"Pretty bad. They beat him to death with a piece of steel rod, probably one he had here in the metal junk he used in his sculptures."

I nodded. I took out a pack of Marlboros, shook one loose, and lit it.

"I thought you gave those up years ago," Ahlberg said.

"I did."

We went into the loft. There was blood damn near everywhere. Hanks had been a strong man and they had been forced to work at it.

"You got an opinion?" Ahlberg asked, snapping me out of my staring reverie.

"Yeah," I said. "Somebody beat him to death. It looks down and nasty and completely personal. Which probably means it isn't."

"I agree. It's a good thing for you that it happened this way."

"Meaning what?"

"Meaning I don't think you've got the stomach for something like this. Even though you beat him up pretty good in the alley behind the Two Bells Tavern the other night."

"He started it." The words came out like a schoolboy's. I could feel myself flush with embarrassment.

"Don't they always."

"It's true. Lisa and I went to see him, to try to warn him off or get him to come in and talk to you. Lisa felt she owed him that. She used to live with him. She was serious about him for a long time."

He nodded. "She okay?"

"Yes and no. When she saw him that night, it seemed to burn off whatever feelings she had left for him. But today she's a sleepwalker."

"What about you?" He looked at me intently.

I looked around the room. The medical examiner's crew was lifting the body onto a gurney. I took a drag on my cigarette and crushed it out in an ashtray on a nearby table. I said, "I didn't like him. And he tried to have Lisa killed, I think. I don't feel much of anything at all."

I needed space, so I walked out of the loft, back to the small, roughed-in lobby by the elevators. A small dark-haired woman sat on the floor, staring straight ahead, smoking. She looked up at me with a blank expression on her face, and I suddenly remembered her. She was the woman I had seen come out of Hanks's bedroom on the day I had gone to question him. I had also seen her at the Thayer retrospective show at the Art Museum, and at another gallery before that, a painter who was meeting the prospective buyers of her work.

I knelt down beside her. "I don't know your name," I said slowly, "but I know you're a painter and I know you were Hanks's lover. Are you the one who painted Thayer's signature on those paintings? I promise I won't tell the police, or anyone else. This is just between you and me. Because if I don't stop this thing, other people are going to get killed. Maybe even you."

She turned and stared at me, her dark eyes mournful. "Yes," she whispered. "Terrill had me sign them." She smiled a painful, ghostly smile. "Terrill couldn't paint very well. So I had to do them." She turned away, crushed out her cigarette, and immediately lit another.

I took the new cigarette from her and stubbed it on the rough wooden floor. "Listen to me," I said quietly. "The people who did this may be back. Do you have someplace to go, someone to stay with?"

"No. I was living here." She could not raise her voice above a whisper.

I stood up. As I turned to go back into the loft I saw Ahlberg looking curiously at us from the doorway.

"I just wanted to make sure she was okay," I told him, following him back into the apartment. "She was involved with Hanks. She's a casualty, too."

"I know that, I questioned her. She says that she had a fight with Hanks last night, then came back early this morning to try to patch things up. She found the body. I couldn't get any more than that. Is she involved with the paintings?"

"She'll have to tell you that herself. She was living here and she's got no place to go. I think you'd better put her in protective custody, but for God's sake, keep it quiet. Sooner or later somebody is going to make the connections between Kuehn and Petrov and Hanks, and I want to have Lisa clear before that happens."

When I was back inside the loft for the second time, I made a careful tour, looking for anything else that might tie Hanks to the faked paintings. It was a foolish task but it kept me busy while Ahlberg did his job. Later I waited patiently in the kitchen area while Ahlberg called his office for a matron to take Hanks's lover into custody. When he got off the phone, he had a bemused look on his face.

"My desk sergeant says that Campbell is waiting at headquarters for me. He's got a lawyer in tow and looks like hell," he added, a trace of satisfaction coloring his voice. "I think he's ready to break. But there's more. Your friend from DEA in New York just joined the party. He's at a hotel down by the airport, keeping a low profile. He wants a meeting."

"I don't get it," I said slowly. "The last time I heard, you and the DEA were on the same side. Why doesn't he meet you here in town?"

"DEA's been fucked up for a while now," Vince replied. "They keep all their information in compartments, they work in separate groups, they fly guys in and out. They don't trust anybody on the outside, and they don't trust each other."

"Politics?"

"Worse. Nobody knows who's been co-opted and who's still honest. Miami got that way five years ago, and the problem has spread across the country. There's just too damn much money from drugs flowing through the system." His voice mixed anger and sadness. "You take somebody, detective level, a good guy, three kids, wife stays home, and they can't make it. The house payment or the cars or just taking a damn vacation, and suddenly they're so far behind they aren't ever going to get out of debt. And then somebody talks to them, sometimes it's a lawyer, sometimes it's another cop, and all they ask is that a certain corner not get patrolled for fifteen minutes, or a certain piece of paper get lost from a certain file. In return they offer ten, twenty grand, more loose money than some of these guys have seen their whole life." He sighed. "Maybe they don't bite the first time, maybe not the second, but sometime the family car is going to be on the edge of getting repossessed and they take it. And when they do, they're gone forever. We've had a couple guys this year resign the force. Nothing we could prove and nothing they would admit. But we know what happened and so do they. The thing is, the system's not set up to handle it. DEA can't handle its own counterintelligence, much less a department like mine, with three officers working internal affairs. Reese wants these guys bad, so he's not taking any risks. He's going to keep this deal small, just a couple of people he trusts. I can't say I blame him."

"How do you think we ought to play it?"

His eyes narrowed. "Did you figure out who was behind Campbell and that lawyer, Tabor?"

"I think so. Reese confirmed the name I gave him." I hesitated, wondering how much farther Vince was willing to go on this. As it turned out, not very far.

"You're going to have to work with us now, you know."

"I know. The question is, how much risk are we going to have to take? You're going to love Reese, by the way. He thinks us civilians are a nuisance. If we get burned, well, that's just too bad. It's not serious as long as Reese gets the bust he wants."

"Back off," he said sharply. "You start this kind of thing, you've got to accept the risk. Let's go hear what the man has to say."

"What about Campbell?"

"If he's got a lawyer, he's shopping for immunity. I might as well get the prosecutor's office to send over a deputy. We should cut a deal all at once, both federal and state. But Campbell won't be able to give us the people who did this. We've got to get Tabor. And the guy behind him."

We left Hanks's loft. The woman who had been his lover was gone from the vestibule. I spent the better part of an hour parking my ass in Ahlberg's office, waiting for the where and when of the meeting. When it finally came, I drove down to Pioneer Square to pick up Lisa and then went south on Highway 509, toward the airport.

Reese had set up shop in an anonymous chain motel that was one of a dozen scattered along Pacific Highway in the airport strip. He had taken two adjoining rooms that had been lovingly decorated with green shag carpet and Naugahyde furniture that had been bolted to the floors. Even the ashtrays were glued to the tops of the tables. The motel didn't think much of its usual customers.

When we came in, Reese was standing in the middle of the

room talking to an assistant United States attorney I knew by
the name of Eric Rosenthal. Reese was hitting on a cup of coffee
and a cigarette, his big sloping shoulders encased in another one
of his cheap blue suits. He looked like a man who was working
in his element, sure of himself and his job.

Ahlberg and I shook hands with Rosenthal. Reese didn't move.
When the formalities were over, he said, "I don't want Ms.
Thayer involved in this."

"I don't much care what you want," Lisa replied. "Tell me
what's going on."

"Campbell and his lawyer are in the next room," Rosenthal
said. "He's ready to cooperate, but the question of immunity is
still on the table."

"He's got to plead to something," I said. "For Christ's sake,
he tried to have Lisa killed. Or knew about it, anyway."

"We'll never be able to prove it," Rosenthal said. "Not without
another witness putting him in the deal. Tell me how you think
it went down, Riordan. I'm on the spot; I've got to make the
immunity call." He turned to Ahlberg. "By the way, Captain,
can you get somebody from the King County prosecutor down
here to sign off on any state charges? If I give him immunity,
it will bind the state, but I'd just as soon work with you guys."

"He's supposed to be here already," Ahlberg replied. He went
to the phone.

"Not that one," Reese cut in sharply. "Use the pay phone in
the lobby. I don't want security breached on my location."

"Oh, for Chrissake," Ahlberg said, "you think they won't notice a Seattle Police captain making a phone call? In this dump?
Vice is down here five, six nights a week. Use your head." He
picked up the handset and started to punch numbers into the
phone.

I turned back to Rosenthal. "How much do you know?"

"Probably not that much. Start from the beginning."

"Campbell's an art dealer," I began. "He went into real-estate
development, bought the Girard Building downtown, renovated
it, and lost his ass on the deal. He needed money to complete

the project, and he brought in Tabor, who's a lawyer in San Francisco and a front for a lot of the grass money out of Northern California. That got Campbell further in the hole, with some people who don't take it kindly when they don't get paid. Either Campbell or the dead sculptor, Hanks, knew that an artist up in La Conner, Anton Petrov, had done a lot of paintings in a style very similar to that of Lee Thayer. Petrov's an unknown; his paintings sell for a couple of hundred bucks, maybe a grand. Thayer's big paintings sell for up to half a million dollars, and the market is heading straight up. Hanks, I think, found another painter to forge Thayer's signature on the paintings, and Tabor, who buys artworks as investments for the drug dealers, unloaded them on his main client, a man named Joseph Wheeler. Campbell arranged for the paintings to be put in a major show of Thayer's paintings, probably to show Wheeler that he was getting good value. That's when Lisa spotted them. She confronted Campbell about it, and then all kinds of shit started to happen. A bomb was put in Lisa's car. We went to New York to do some research, and a couple of players tried to shoot me in Riverside Park. We had one chance to talk to Petrov, the old guy who really painted the stuff, and he confirmed some of what we guessed. The day after I talked to him, somebody killed him."

"What can you prove?"

"Just that the paintings were fakes, that Campbell did sell them, and that Tabor was involved somehow."

"That's not much," Rosenthal said. "What we really have working is the threat you'll tell the buyer. Okay. You and the woman, take off for a while." He tossed me a room key on a wide plastic holder. I caught it and took one step toward him, with the intention of making him eat it. I was sick of other people making decisions that could haunt Lisa's life, and mine. Ahlberg took my arm.

"You're going to be witnesses," he said. "You know you can't stay in here. Go and order some lunch. We'll be ready for you again in about an hour."

I gripped the room key and said nothing. I turned and took Lisa by the arm and we left the room.

It was more like three hours than one. We sent out for hamburgers and ate them without really tasting them. We talked about what Reese and Ahlberg might be doing. Finally I went out and got the newspapers and we hid behind them, neither of us wanting to talk. Lisa and I had been living so closely, under so much stress, that we each wanted nothing more than to be in our own homes, alone, if only for a day.

When the room phone finally rang, it was Reese. "Come on down here," he rasped. "I think we've got something that's going to play."

When we returned, the motel room was stuffy with the heat of a half-dozen people. David Campbell sat in a low vinyl chair, answering questions in a soft bitter monotone voice. His attorney, a locally well-known criminal lawyer named Donald Henry, sat next to him, guiding him with the occasional word or gesture. One of the men Reese had brought with him was a court reporter. He sat across from Campbell, his thick neck and sausage-fat fingers working as he took down Campbell's words on a portable stenotype machine.

When they were finished, Eric Rosenthal, who had been asking the questions, wiped his perspiring face with a white handkerchief. He sipped from a cup of cold coffee and said, "Riordan, I think we've got a plan."

I nodded toward Campbell. "How little is he going to get?"

"Riordan, I don't think that's any of your business," Donald Henry cut in.

"Go fuck yourself, Donald," I said evenly. To Rosenthal I repeated, "How little?"

"Campbell's going to plead to two counts of Section 843(b). Using a telephone to assist the investment of narcotics proceeds."

"What's that going to buy him? Eighteen months?"

"We've agreed to ask the court to suspend all but six months

on account of age and health. He's also going to forfeit the building to us."

I could feel myself getting angrier. Campbell was going to walk
with something like two months' jail time. The forfeiture would
hurt him, put him out of business, but not put him into poverty.
Federal judges had been known to give stiffer sentences for con-
tempt of court.

I turned to Reese. "Did he confirm what we thought?"

Reese nodded. "Pretty much. He says Hanks spotted the similarity in the pictures and got another painter to re-sign them.
Tabor came up with the idea of selling the fake paintings to
Wheeler. They got just over one-point-two-five million for
them."

"Who ordered the bombing of Lisa's car?"

"Campbell says that was Tabor. Tabor went nuts at the
thought that Wheeler might find out, because Wheeler would
come after them. Campbell says he didn't know what Tabor was
doing until after it happened."

I looked at Campbell. He was still sitting in the chair, his lean,
aristocratic frame slumped over, hands folded in his lap. He
didn't look up.

"My ass he didn't," I said slowly. I was still struggling to control
my anger when Lisa broke the silence.

"Where do we go from here?" she asked sharply. "I'm glad to
know that I've been right, but there's a man out there who's still
trying to kill me and I would sort of like that stopped."

"Fair enough," Reese said. He gestured at Campbell. "Take
him out of the room, please. You too, counselor," he added,
pointing at Donald Henry. Henry shook his head.

"If this has something to do with my client, I'm staying," he
said firmly. Henry was a small man who dressed in expensive
dark suits and cowboy boots. He had a reedy tenor voice and
affected the sort of Texas druggie-hipster drawl that was popular
during the 1970's. "I'm not going to tell anybody your thinking,
if that's what y'all are worried about."

"Counselor," Reese said, his raspy voice turning cold, "that suit you're wearing got paid for by what children put in their veins. If you think I'm going to tell you the time by your own clock, you got another thing coming. Get out."

Henry thought it over and shrugged, then walked out of the room, slowly, to let Reese know that he wasn't intimidated. Reese looked at him with something close to hatred in his eyes. Reese, I thought suddenly, was another cop whose sense of balance was wearing thin.

"All right," he said when Henry was gone. "Campbell confirmed that Wheeler was the pigeon. The best way to get Tabor and Wheeler is put them in conflict. So we use a variation of what Riordan suggested earlier. Campbell gave us three numbers that he has used to reach Wheeler in the past. Riordan, you should call Wheeler and set up a meet. Tell him you're representing Campbell, and that Campbell wants to return the money, make it good to Wheeler, and get Tabor. We'll get Campbell to get in touch with Tabor. When we bring the two of them together, we might get enough to take them both down." He smiled sourly.

"How do you figure?" I asked skeptically. "All you'll have is two guys standing together. That's not criminal."

"Yeah, but when Tabor and Wheeler get popped together, Tabor will be under maximum pressure. Wheeler will think Tabor set him up, in addition to the scam with the paintings. Tabor will have just two choices—cooperate with us or go back on the street and wait for Wheeler to kill him."

I paused to think. Reese's plan made some sense. If they busted Tabor and Wheeler together, quickly, the risk to bystanders ought to be minimal, but the setup would be tricky. "I suppose you'll want me to be wired for any meetings with Wheeler," I said.

"Sure."

I shook my head. "Not a prayer," I said. "I may have to be the goat, but I'm not going to be tied to the stake. Wheeler's not stupid."

"How're we going to get Tabor in?" Eric Rosenthal asked. "We've got to give him some incentive."

"Tell him I'll give him affidavits of authenticity for the three paintings," Lisa said. "That's what he really wants, protection against having the paintings exposed as fakes."

"But you want some money, too," I added. "Tabor won't believe it unless we make him think you've had it, you're running scared, and you're selling out."

"How much?" Reese asked.

I glanced at Lisa. "Say thirty thousand. That's cheap enough to make it worth his while, expensive enough to be credible. If he balks, Campbell can say he'll repay the money."

Vince Ahlberg had been standing silently in the back of the room, plainly unhappy about what was going on. Unless by some miracle Tabor confessed, Vince was about to lose any chance of getting a conviction in the attempt on Lisa's life or the death of Terrill Hanks. Nothing that was said by Campbell, or any evidence found because of something Campbell said, could be used against Campbell because of the grant of immunity. I started to say something to him but then thought better of it and shut up. Vince was making it very plain that he didn't trust the DEA. If he would talk to me at all, it would be privately.

I turned back to Reese. "Let's take it one step farther. I should get in touch with Wheeler, try to get him up here to Seattle. I don't want any cops or wires or surveillance at the first meeting. I'm going to have to sell him, and if he sees one thing wrong, it's no sale."

Reese shook his head. "It's totally contrary to procedure. I can't let a civilian go out and meet the target without any backup."

"Stuff your procedures. From what you've said it's clear that Wheeler has survived in the dope business for a very long time. That means he's not stupid. The minute he sees a bunch of guys climbing in and out of repair vans wearing coveralls that are too clean and black shoes with thick soles I'm likely to get dead. Do it my way or no way."

Reese scowled. He looked at Rosenthal, who shrugged. "Okay," Reese said. "Campbell gave us three telephone numbers for Wheeler. Our intelligence turned up one more that we think is still good. Take them and see what you can do." He paused and wrote them out for me, using a gold-cased pencil and a small leather pad. When he was finished, he added, "But if you run a line on me, Riordan, I'm going to see that you get squashed."

I took the paper from his outstretched hand and laughed at him. "Ah, fuck it, Reese," I said cheerfully. "If that temptation comes over you, Just Say No."

Much later that night, with ten dollars in quarters and the list of numbers in hand, I started telephoning from a gas-station phone booth on a northern stretch of Sand Point Way in Seattle. All the numbers Reese had given me were in Northern California, one in San Francisco, one in Marin, and two in the Mendocino area. The first two numbers I tried had been disconnected. The third one started to ring. I let it ring a dozen times while rain fell on the roof of the phone booth and the drip of cold leaking water fell on my neck. I shifted away from the water, trying to keep dry. The phone continued to ring.

When it rang twenty times, I was ready to give up. On the twenty-first ring it was answered.

"Yes," a voice said. It was a short, impatient voice, deep and clear.

"Is this Mr. Wheeler?" I asked.

"No, it's not. Who is this?"

"My name is Matthew Riordan. I'm a lawyer in Seattle. I have some information that Mr. Wheeler would want to know."

"What kind of information?"

"Nothing that concerns you, friend. Only for Wheeler."

"Mr. Wheeler doesn't talk to cranks."

"I'm not a crank. I'll tell you this much. Wheeler's got somebody in his organization who's turned. And if you don't pass this message along to him, you're going to be attending the Artichoke Festival in Castroville next year. As fertilizer."

He laughed. "Hold the line."

I waited a long time. When the man on the other end of the line came back, he said, "There's a pay phone in the lobby of the Medical-Dental Building on Olive Way in Seattle. The building is open at night with a security guard. The phone's in the back of the lobby. You've got fifteen minutes to get there."

"Wait a minute," I said, "That's ten miles from here, and it's raining."

"You're wasting time." The phone clicked dead in my ear.

Every light I had was red and I ran every one of them. As I walked into the Medical-Dental Building I heard the phone ringing. The security guard was an old man with sparse gray hair. He was slumped back in his chair.

I picked up the phone. "This is Riordan."

"This is Wheeler," a soft voice said.

"I have some information for you. It's important."

"So you said. Who's my bad apple?"

"Not over the phone, Wheeler. In person. And don't check me out with your people, or I'll be blown and so will you. I'll meet you wherever you say."

"What's in it for you, Riordan?"

"I'm being paid at my end. Of course, I also accept gratuities."

He chuckled. "You probably are a lawyer. I'll meet you at the beach across the street from Ghirardelli Square in San Francisco, tomorrow. At noon."

"All right," I replied. "I'll be on foot. I'm about six-three—"

"Never mind that. By tomorrow I'll know damn near everything about you. Don't worry about how I'll get the information. I'll go outside my usual people." He hung up.

I put the phone back on the cradle and leaned against the wall. The old marble lobby was silent, save for the snores of the security guard, who was getting more sleep than I would that night.

I left the Powell and Hyde Street cable car at the turnaround near Ghirardelli Square. The day was bright and warm as only San Francisco can be in September, when the summer fogs are gone and the Marin County hills rise in impossible golden splendor across the Bay. The cable car had been jammed with tourists who pushed their way on like it was the Tokyo subway, reducing the conductor and the grip to cursing frustration. According to the new president it was still supposed to be morning in America, and California was learning to say "How do you like your eggs?" in Japanese.

I was just over an hour early for the meeting, so I walked through the area around The Cannery, then once through the shops of Ghirardelli Square, and down along the beach to the grassy border of Fort Mason. I knew they were there, they had to be there. Wheeler was a cautious man who had survived a long time in the drug trade. But I couldn't see them.

I bought an espresso from a bakery shop in The Cannery and waited on a park bench near the Hyde Street pier. I still couldn't see whether I was being watched. In a way I was safer if I was, because they could see that I had no tail and no backup.

The minutes went by on crutches. The street vendors hawked cheap jewelry and fake netsuke to the tourist mob. A German woman accompanied by her elderly and obviously distraught mother asked me whether there was a taxi stand nearby. I went and found her a taxi, then came back to the same bench. I said no to two ice cream vendors, a newsboy, and a dour-looking teenager who wanted to sell me marijuana.

At ten minutes to twelve I left the pier and walked down the concrete steps to the half-moon crescent of beach. The tide was going out and the beach was good walking, wet firm sand. At the far end of the beach, beneath the screen provided by the tall fir trees growing around Fort Mason, a heavy man with a brushy brown mustache and a look of well-fed vigor walked down the hill toward me.

"Mr. Riordan?" he asked. He had the polite but firm manner of a beat cop, which is probably what he once was.

I stopped and nodded.

"Could I ask you to step over here, please?" He gestured up the hill, toward a stand of three pines planted in a triangle. They would screen us from the pier and from the office building up the hill, outside the park. I joined him by the pines and endured a brisk but efficient pat-down search. When that was over, he took out a small electronic gadget with an antenna loop. It looked like a cross between a transistor radio and a padlock. I waited patiently while he swept me for a body wire.

When he was satisfied, he led me uphill to a bench on the path that wound through the park above the beach. I sat down and waited. Five minutes later Joseph Wheeler came down the path from the nearby parking lot and sat down beside me.

He took his time looking me over. He was a slender man of about six feet, with a finely boned, almost delicate face. He had light brown hair and hazel eyes that seemed flat and somewhat lifeless. Wheeler wore corduroys, a straw-colored cotton sweater, and boat shoes. He had an expensive tweed jacket draped loosely over one arm. Under other circumstances I would have thought him a literature professor with family money. His slight build was deceiving. The sleeves of the sweater were pushed back and I could see that his wrists and forearms were very thick and strong and that his hands were callused like those of a martial-arts instructor.

When Wheeler spoke, his voice was both mocking and cold. "So you're Riordan," he said. "The guy who's got the goods on my organization. The man who finds the moles."

"The thing that always gets me about you drug guys," I replied, "is your sense of self-drama. You're always setting up meets on windswept beaches, or in lonely industrial districts where street lamps shine on wet streets, or aboard racing yachts in tropical harbors. It's boring. And I'm getting hungry. There's a little saloon over on Greenwich and Buchanan that makes excellent corned beef sandwiches and has Bass Ale on draft. What do you say?"

He stared at me in amazement, a small smile playing on the corners of his mouth. "You're either a lunatic," he said at last, "or you're the genuine article. Either way I'll buy you lunch. Let's go."

He led me to the parking lot on the edge of Fort Mason. The stocky bodyguard followed us, three paces behind like a proper retainer. He unlocked the front doors of a gunmetal 750 Series BMW and held the driver's door for Wheeler. I got in on the passenger side. The Beamer rumbled into a soft throaty roar, four thousand pounds and $50,000 of steel and black leather, as pure a form of automotive fascism as you are ever likely to find.

As we drove out of the parking lot and down Van Ness I was both bemused and horrified by the kind of man that Wheeler was. The intelligence file that Reese had given me portrayed a onetime street dealer who had risen to the niche of gentleman farmer in the drug trade, growing potent smoke on remote valley farms and in the national forests of Northern California. According to the DEA, he had made his fortune through intimidation, sharp dealing, and murder. Yet the man sitting beside me, cutting through traffic with precision, had an obvious intelligence and a cold grace about him that would have been prized in any San Francisco bank or Wall Street investment firm. What did that say about him? I asked myself. Or more importantly, about all of us?

Wheeler found a parking garage on Filbert and we walked the block north to the Greenwich Street Inn. It remained the quiet neighborhood joint I remembered, almost untouched by the gentrification of the Union Street shopping and restaurant district two blocks to the south. The bar had low ceilings and thick wood beams above rough plaster walls. The whole effect was pleasantly like being aboard a wooden ship. Wheeler and I took a back table and ordered lunch while his bodyguard nursed a slow beer at the bar, his eyes on the door.

"Well, this has been fun," Wheeler said, slicing a corner off a Reuben sandwich with his knife. He ate the corner and washed it down with brown English beer. "But just about now I think we ought to be getting down to business, don't you?"

"It's bad for the digestion," I replied. "But talking about politics would be even worse." I paused to drink more beer. "You've been buying a lot of art lately, haven't you, Wheeler?"

"Some. Not that it's any of your business."

"No reason it should be. Art has a lot of advantages for you. It's portable, it holds a lot of value in a small space, and you don't have to report it when you take it out of the country. Hell, you don't even have to pay duty on it." I was being a good deal more obtuse than I normally am for a reason. One of the best times to watch another person without being observed doing it is when you are talking.

"But you ought to be more careful about what you buy," I continued. "Take the three paintings by Elton Lee Thayer that you bought this year. Duane Tabor bought them for you through the Campbell Gallery in Seattle. He told you that you were getting a discount, as well you should, since you hold the mortgage on Campbell's building and you've put a lot of other money into it. The only problem is, the paintings are fakes."

I had his attention now. He stopped eating and carefully placed his knife and fork across his plate, in European fashion.

He took a small sip of his beer and waited. "The paintings," I went on, "were actually painted by a minor but rather skillful painter named Anton Petrov. He knew Thayer, worked with him when they were young, and often painted in the same style. Tabor and a man named Hanks, a sculptor, saw the similarity in some of Petrov's paintings and had the paintings re-signed with Thayer's name by another painter. They sold them to you for what, one and a quarter million? That was a decent price if the paintings were genuine. But they weren't."

"How," he asked carefully, "do you know all this?"

"I'll get to that. To allay any doubts you might have had, since you don't know paintings very well, Tabor and Campbell arranged to have the paintings placed in a retrospective show of Thayer's work. That kind of public display would show you that you had gotten quality and hadn't been stiffed. Worked, too."

"Why are you here, Riordan? Who do you represent?"

"Campbell. He knows he cheated you, he wants to make it right. He's willing to repay you the one and a quarter million, with interest. If you want to take the money back in the form of other artworks, you'll get them at Campbell's cost."

"Why is Campbell confessing this?"

"That's pretty obvious, isn't it? He's scared to death. Of you. Of Tabor. Especially Tabor. You see, when the paintings were shown publicly, a couple of people thought they didn't look quite right. One of them, another art dealer, pushed the issue. Tabor panicked. In the four weeks since that show Tabor's killed Petrov, the artist who really painted the pictures you bought, and Hanks, the sculptor who helped set it up. Campbell's afraid he's next. He probably is, too."

"What does Campbell want from me?"

"Peace. He wants to pay you off and, eventually, buy you out. But the main thing is, he wants Tabor stopped before Campbell himself gets killed."

"How is Duane doing the killings?"

"He's having them done by hire. He's probably using your contacts. But he's not doing them very smart. One of the first things he did was put a bomb into the car of the young Seattle art dealer who asked a few questions about the paintings. She was lucky and didn't get killed. The Seattle cops are taking it seriously. They know a professional hit when they see one, and that's not something they can ignore. They're getting closer to figuring out who was behind it. If they get Tabor, you know he's going to try to bail himself out. You're his bail ticket."

"Do you know where Tabor is?"

"He's somewhere in the Seattle area. We can find him if we have to. There's a message drop Campbell can use."

"What about his office?"

"It's not through his office. He's been out of touch with them for over a week. They keep saying he's gone to Europe, on vacation."

Wheeler thought for a moment, hands folded, eyes examining the middle distance. "I can't corroborate this. Not easily and not in time."

"Probably not," I agreed. "But look at it from my point of view. I may be foolish enough to be a messenger boy, but I'm not crazy enough to come down here and try to set you up. On the whole I enjoy living and don't care to have the experience cut short." And I am sure as hell mixing lies and truth in that one, I thought.

Wheeler was coming to some sort of decision. He pushed his plate away and put his hands flat on the table. "All right," he said. "I'll bite. Tell Campbell to put together a settlement package, half cash over time, half paintings now, all major, easily salable stuff. I'll take care of Tabor."

"How?" I asked.

"That doesn't concern you."

"The hell it doesn't. Tabor's gone bad and he's got at least half a million dollars in cash to defend himself with. You don't know who he's bought. If you try to call him on the carpet, he'll know he's been blown and he'll go to war. He's got nothing to lose."

"I can take care of him."

"You can if you take him by surprise. Let me set up a meeting with him and Campbell. I've made a deal to buy off the art dealer who spotted the fakes, and I'll draw Tabor in with that. I'll set it for a place and time so that you can sneak in unobserved. You take him on the spot and we've got both our problems solved."

"When will I know what's been set up?"

"As soon as it happens, if you give me a reliable telephone or message drop."

"I don't like having somebody else choose the ground. It violates fundamental principles of strategy."

I nodded. "I don't blame you. I'll do the best I can but I've got to have some flexibility. If I insist on a particular spot, one that you give me, Tabor's going to figure something's going on."

"I'm not disagreeing," he said, "I just don't like it." He paused and sipped at his beer. When he looked up again, he locked his eyes on mine. I returned his stare.

"You ever been shot, Riordan?" he asked.

I nodded. "I was in Vietnam."

"That's good," he said slowly, getting up from the table to leave. "I don't like dealing with a man who thinks he's bulletproof. Keep that in mind."

When he was gone, I pushed away my half-eaten sandwich. I went to telephone a taxi, then to the bar, where I sipped slowly at a very large glass of scotch and waited for the taxi to arrive. By the time it pulled up and honked outside the front door, my hands had almost stopped trembling.

I stepped into a phone booth near the United Airlines gates at Sea-Tac airport and telephoned the number that Reese had given me. It connected to a switching exchange and I listened to the clicking sounds of a new number being dialed. It finally connected and Reese picked up the phone.

"Reese," he said.

"You ought to call yourself Captain Midnight," I replied. "You're using a switching exchange now? Where the hell are you?"

"Same place," he answered. "Why?"

"Never mind." I sighed. "I'll take a cab over there."

The motel room seemed tighter than it had the day before. There were magazines and sandwich wrappers scattered on the beds and desks. Open briefcases lay with piles of paper spilling out. Reese was sitting at the narrow desk, jacket off, tie loosened, working over what looked like a legal pleading. His white shirt was stained under the arms by dark half-moons of sweat. The two agents he had brought out with him waited silently, one standing, the other sitting on one of the twin beds, squeezing a tennis ball in his left hand. I never did learn their names.

"You're either getting the government rate," I said sourly, "or you're learning to like orange velour bedspreads."

"You know, Riordan," Reese said, fixing me with a cold eye, "you're getting to be a real pain in the ass."

"I was hoping you'd notice. Shall we continue to trade weak wisecracks, or do you want to know what's happening?"

"If it had gone sour, you'd have told me that from the airport," he replied. "So give."

"He bought. I'm to set up a meet with Tabor. Wheeler will crash the party. I get to pick when and where."

"What do you think?"

"I don't know yet. Where's Campbell?"

"At his gallery. There's a woman from our Seattle office guarding him."

"Then let's get in touch with Tabor from there. I've got to talk to Campbell, find a place that works and that sounds reasonable."

"Fine." He took his jacket from the back of the chair and slipped it on. He reached into the desk drawer and took out his piece, a .38 police special in a belt-clip holster. He clipped it to the back of his pants and shook the suit coat down over it. "I'm ready."

"Wait. Is Campbell's place being watched?"

"Only by us."

"We hope," I said to myself as I followed him out of the room.

CHAPTER
18

"I'm not going to permit you to expose my client like that," Donald Henry said stubbornly. "No fucking way."

"The grant of immunity calls for cooperation, Mr. Henry," Michael Reese said stubbornly. "Cooperation means doing whatever I say. The government paid a good price and it's going to get what it paid for. Or else we walk away from the deal and let Ahlberg use the information to make a state court case against your guy for attempted murder. I understand you've got determinate sentencing out here. He'll get a minimum of ten years. Nice way to grow old." He turned to David Campbell, who waited in one of his fancy leather Barcelona chairs. Campbell sat like a man suddenly afflicted with arthritis. I felt no sympathy for him.

The argument had been going on for over two hours and showed no signs of letting up. It was past seven o'clock and the sun was setting through the west windows of Campbell's art gallery. Streaks of orange and red light shone through breaks in the clouds. Ordinarily I would have wandered over to the windows and shut the bickering out of my mind with the play of light and form, city and water and green islands rising in the distance. Today it would have been no good. My gut burned from too many cups of coffee. The strain of the long day had taken up residence inside my skin.

I got out of my chair and walked around the room, stretching a little, trying to drain my mind and keep my temper under control. It didn't work.

"You've been awfully quiet, Riordan," Donald Henry drawled. "You losing interest here?" he added sarcastically.

"You forget, Donald, that I'm the civilian here. I got non-negotiable demands. The first one is, we do it my way or no way at all. And my way says Campbell gets to go to the party and have a front-row seat. It won't work without him."

"Sure it will. All you have to do is—"

"Donald," I said sharply, cutting him off, "you are a piss ant. That's a word I think they know down there in Texas, where you pretend to be from. And if you don't shut the fuck up, I am going to telephone Wheeler and tell him the deal's off, that Campbell has reconsidered and has decided to go to the cops and tell them everything. I'll even tell Wheeler it was your idea."

His eyes widened behind the darkened steel-rim glasses that he wore. "You wouldn't dare."

I shook my head. "The old man goes."

Henry turned and whispered to David Campbell, still hunched over in his chair. "I don't really have any choice," Campbell said distinctly, his voice shaking slightly. "No choice."

"That's right," Reese said. "And now, it's time to send your lawyer on home to his dinner, if he's got anybody who'll cook one for him."

He stared pointedly at Henry, who shrugged once and said, "You can play any kind of games you want to, Reese, but my client can tell me anything he wants to about what you're going to do."

"That's right," Reese said. "And if I find out you've leaked it, counselor, I promise you one hell of a lot of law. Not a lot of due process, just one hell of a lot of law."

Henry looked at him scornfully, then walked carefully out of the room, his new cowboy boots squeaking on the polished hardwood floors.

When he was gone, I said, "We have to figure out a good place to stage this. Turf is going to be important." I turned to Campbell. "You live and work here, but where else do you go, on a regular basis?"

"To friends, the theater, the opera, shops, most of them near here. The Public Market. My summerhouse."

"Where's that located?"

"On South Whidbey Island, the west shore, opposite Langley."

"What's the terrain like?"

"It's densely wooded on the land side, open, of course, on the waterfront side."

"No good," I told him. "I want to be able to see Tabor coming and verify how many people he's got. And we'll need to get Wheeler into place, or have a way for him to come in unseen, except by us." I thought hard for a moment. "But we could use the ferry," I said slowly, to no one in particular.

"I don't get it," Reese said.

"The Mukliteo Ferry connects the mainland north of Seattle to Whidbey Island. Tabor has to walk on or drive on. You can control the access by putting one man in the ticket taker's booth, another with the deckhands loading the cars. The meeting with Tabor can be on the passenger deck. It takes about thirty minutes to sail over to the island. Plenty of time."

"What about Wheeler?"

"He can come in from the Whidbey Island side, stay in a car down on the auto deck until Tabor boards at Mukliteo and the boat sails."

"What if Tabor decides to do that, too?"

"Oh, for Chrissake, Reese, you can't control everything. Sure, he could do that. But if you post people at each loading dock, you can try to spot him. If he comes on early, we improvise."

"There's going to be a lot of people on board this boat," Reese said stubbornly. "If you've got too many bystanders, you've got all kinds of problems. Somebody could get taken hostage, or shot."

"Not if your people are controlling the boat. Put agents in every corner of the main cabin. If things turn to shit, control the zone." I sighed. "And we'll do it on the last run of the night. It'll be less crowded. I mean, we're not talking about the Staten Island Ferry here."

Reese looked doubtful. "I'll need at least a day to set up, get people into position."

"You'll have that." I turned to Campbell. "When is Tabor going to call you back?"

"In about another hour," he said quietly. "If he got the message."

"So we wait," I said aimlessly. "We wait."

When Campbell's private phone line rang at nine o'clock that night, it cut into a silence that was thick with anxiety and dread. Campbell looked at the telephone as though it were a coiled snake. Reese clapped his hands once for attention, then counted silently with his fingers, three seconds to make sure that the electronic team from the local FBI office had time to intercept the call before the receiver was lifted. I went to an extension phone ten feet away and waited. When Reese closed his fist, Campbell picked up the line.

"Duane? Yes, I know, but this is important. Listen to me." A flash of Campbell's arrogance emerged through his fear. Good touch, I thought, keep it up.

"Duane," Campbell said, "Riordan is here. That's right, the lawyer for Lisa Thayer. He wants to make a deal. I think it's a good one. It will solve our problems. I'm going to put him on the extension now."

I picked up the extension. "Tabor, this is Riordan."

"This had better be good," Tabor said, his voice low and heavy.

"We want to make a deal. Lisa will stop asking questions about the paintings. She'll give you affidavits of authenticity for all three of them."

"What's the price?"

"Ten thousand per painting, cash. And you stop trying to have us killed."

"I don't know what you're talking about."

"That's okay," I said quickly. "I understand. Just meet with us, and we'll get it done."

"Where?"

"Where are you?"

He snorted. "Just tell me where."

"The ferry boat from Mukliteo to Clinton, on Whidbey Island. Saturday night, the last boat. It leaves Mukliteo at twelve-fifteen, gets into Clinton at twelve-forty-five."

There was silence. "Not Saturday," he said. "Tomorrow. And I pick the spot."

"Then it's no deal. I want it on the boat, nice and public. I've got no interest in being blown away in some vacant lot somewhere."

He hesitated. "All right. I want Campbell there. And bring the woman."

"No."

"Bring the woman. Or it's no deal."

I looked across the room at Lisa. She stared back, unaware of what was being said. "Okay," I said thickly. "She'll be there. When it's done, we all drive off the boat and never see each other again. Agreed?"

"Just be there, Riordan. And don't cross me." The phone went dead in my ear. I put it down slowly and found myself hunched over the telephone. The muscles in my lower back ached from tension. I straightened slowly, taking shallow breaths.

I turned to Reese. He had already turned away and was huddling with one of his agents. "Some place called Bellingham," he said, reporting the results of the phone trace. "A telephone booth on Interstate Five. Shit."

"It's on," I said quietly.

. . . .

I had traded the Camaro in for a Nissan sports coupe that handled quickly and surely on the rain-slick streets. We were moving again, this time to any motel north of the city that had a room for the night. I pulled into a deserted parking lot outside a strip mall on Evergreen Way in Snohomish County and stopped for a moment, listening to the heat ticks from the engine and the soft rush of traffic on the arterial behind me. Lisa sat silently in the car's other seat, staring straight ahead, her face in profile, silhouetted by the blue light from an overhead street lamp.

"It will be over tomorrow," I said. "Life will go on."

She nodded. Her hands tapped restlessly on the dashboard. Her manicured nails had been bitten back to the quicks. "I want to do this right," she said. "I want to be quiet and brave. But I'm—I feel like Alice, falling down the hole, turning over and over in the air. I don't have any control. I don't like it."

"You've never been through anything like this," I told her. "Nobody expected this to happen. It's not something to be ashamed of. The people who've gotten used to things like this, the people who aren't frightened, are people who have lost a piece of their humanity."

"But how are we different?" she asked plaintively, turning to face me for the first time. "Anton Petrov and Terrill are dead, David Campbell is ruined, and others may get killed tomorrow. Is it worth it? I don't even know why I started this. What was I trying to prove?"

"You were trying to protect a truth," I replied. "Maybe some people would call it a small truth. But your grandfather's paintings are part of the culture, part of history. It's worth doing." I stopped and thought for a moment, then went on. "The price is high this time, because you brushed up against the drug people. I sometimes think the corruption that comes from the drug trade is worse than the drugs themselves. In ten years we've come very close to ruining half of Latin America, because we're rich and sometimes decadent, and we leave them to deal with the murders and the greed of crooked cops and lawyers and politicians. Now it's come home, it's come here. And here is where you have to fight it."

She shuddered with the sudden chill that had come over the car and drew back into herself again. I knew there was something more to say but I couldn't find the right words. I got out of the car and walked to the phone booth on the sidewalk in front of the shopping mall.

I let the phone ring ten times, then ten more, in a way hoping there would be no answer. It was not a night for answered prayers. After twenty rings Wheeler himself answered.

"Riordan," I said. "It's on."

"Where and when?"

"Tomorrow night. Tabor will be getting onto a ferry boat at Mukliteo, Washington, about twenty miles north of Seattle. The ferry goes to a town called Clinton, on Whidbey Island. You need to get on the boat in Clinton, when it sails at eleven-forty-five. Campbell and I and the art dealer will get on in Mukliteo at twelve-fifteen. Tabor should be getting on at the same time. He may come in by car or on foot. The meeting is going to be in the forward cabin. Wait at least five minutes after the boat leaves the dock."

"Don't worry about that, I'll be in place," Wheeler said. "How many people does Tabor have with him?"

"How the hell should I know?"

"No reason. You're getting nervous, aren't you?"

"Wheeler," I said testily, "go fuck yourself. And when you're done, fuck yourself again."

He laughed. He was still laughing when I slammed down the phone.

It was past midnight when Lisa and I found a motel, on the south side of Everett, near the interstate. We dragged ourselves wearily from the car and were checked in by a bored night clerk. Lisa was silent as we padded down a hallway carpeted in brown shag. When we reached the room, another vinyl-and-Naugahyde nightmare, Lisa stood in the doorway, surveying it sadly. The room smelled of Lysol and cigar smoke and sleepless nights.

She was in bed when I got out of the shower. I padded in quietly, not wanting to wake her, and slipped between the cold sheets.

She was not asleep. I listened to her breathing in the still darkness, trying somehow to hear her thoughts. When I reached out to stroke her cheek, my hand came away wet, from tears. She shuddered with the touch and reached for me. We made love with a fierceness born of fear and anger, but there was no tenderness in it. Lisa cried out once, then rolled away from me and huddled at one side of the bed. I reached a hand out to her, but she pushed it away. We stayed like that for the rest of the night, together but apart, separate, and alone.

I stood on the rear passenger deck of the Clinton Ferry, anxiously scanning the cars being loaded from the Mukliteo dock. A light autumn rain dappled the quiet waters of the cove. It was about quarter to one in the morning and the ferry was less crowded than I had feared it would be, with only a few islanders who had come to the mainland for dinner or a movie. Lisa and I held hands like any other couple headed for an impulsive weekend in one of the country inns around Langley or Coupeville. David Campbell stood beside us, his hands clutched together, shivering under his heavy green loden coat. He whistled tunelessly.

"That might be him," I said, pointing to a windowless Ford Aerostar van. "If I were coming in, that's the way I'd want to do it, as few windows as possible."

"Is Reese checking the cars?" Lisa asked.

"He's already on board, but one of the two car loaders is supposed to be his," I replied. "If they spot Tabor, it's going to be pure dumb luck."

"What about Wheeler?" Campbell queried.

"He'd better be on the boat, or it's going to be a real short party."

Campbell nodded. The tuneless whistling resumed. "Will you please stop that?" Lisa said sharply. "It's driving me crazy."

I glanced at her in the low half-light coming from the cabin. Her expression showed simple irritation, without much sign of nervousness. I relaxed and allowed myself to admire the way she was handling herself. She had been withdrawn for the last twenty-four hours, but now that it was time to go through with it, she looked calm and ready to face whatever happened.

"Take Campbell back inside," I said to her. "Stay with him. I'm going to watch the rest of the loading. I don't think Tabor will have come up on deck yet, but if he has, don't do anything. Just wait for me and say nothing."

Lisa nodded and took Campbell inside. I went back to watching the cars, increasingly worried. Reese was to supply four men to control the main forward cabin of the ferry. They were to come aboard in a food truck from the Mukliteo side. The truck had not yet appeared.

The loaders on the dock below lowered the gates and untied the lines. The ferry blew two blasts on its horn and pulled out, the diesel-electric engines giving a momentary surge to clear the dock. I swallowed a string of curses and turned away from the rear deck.

Reese was at the bulkhead door to the rear stairs. A crease of worry had appeared around his eyes. I grabbed him by the shoulder of his woolen jacket and pulled him back into a dark corner of the rear deck.

"Where the hell are they, Reese?" I growled. "They're supposed to be in a truck."

"I don't know, damn it," he replied. "They were supposed to come down at the last minute to avoid being spotted." He looked past me toward the Mulkliteo dock, an island of light that was rapidly shrinking behind us. "Oh, shit," he muttered, pointing. A panel truck was parked at the end of the dock.

"How many men have you got on board?" I demanded.

"Just me and the loader."

"Is he armed?"

"Yes."

"Go get him. Keep him on the open passenger deck up forward. Have him circulate through every once in a while like he's got boat duties to attend to. Hurry."

I turned away and went forward, forcing myself to slow down, to stay at a walk, to draw as little attention as possible.

Lisa and David Campbell sat in the second row of seats, facing back toward the center of the cabin. The forward cabin was harshly lighted by blue fluorescent lights. It was less than a quarter full. Most of the passengers were folded into the booths that lined each side of the cabin, away from the glare of the lights. I circled the cabin once and then took a seat beside Lisa. We waited. There was no point in telling them what had happened. I watched the two entrances at the rear of the cabin.

Reese appeared at the rear of the cabin and busied himself at the tourist bulletin board, picking up leaflets from the wall racks and watching the cabin. His eyes caught mine once and I looked away. There was no sign of the loader.

A bearded fat man with a curious hitching step wandered into the cabin from the front deck, shaking the rain from his waterproof nylon jacket and casually glancing around the cabin. He moved smoothly except for his walk, like he was coming off a knee operation, or maybe a slightly sprained ankle. He steadied himself with a hand on the corner of the bolted-down row of chairs where we sat.

"Showtime," I said to Lisa. I stood and tried to look as though I was stretching out my back. The heavy man turned slightly toward me.

"Sit down, man, and stay there," he said softly. I sat. The man gave a nod and Duane Tabor walked into the cabin.

Tabor wore blue jeans and a fancy canvas coat, a modernized version of a cattleman's linen duster sold by catalog companies with fake WASP names like J. Crew or Barnwell's. Underneath the coat he wore a black turtleneck sweater. I caught the flash of a black leather holster underneath the coat. His jowly face was lined and his eyes looked strained and tired.

"Let's see the papers," he said as he sat down in the next row of chairs, facing us. Lisa took a slim leather portfolio from the bag at her feet and handed it to him. He opened the portfolio and read the affidavits of authenticity that I had prepared and Lisa had signed, checking the signatures and notary seals.

"The money," I said when he had finished reading.

"Get it from Campbell," he replied, closing the portfolio and putting it on the seat in front of him. "You've been a hell of a lot of trouble. Be glad you're still alive."

"Then it's no deal," I said. "The man you sold the paintings to isn't going to care about those papers. Those are good to you only if we stay silent."

"You aren't going to say anything, public or private," he said. "Or I'll be back." He nodded to the man he had brought with him. "Check the stairs back down to the car deck," he said to him. "I'll follow along."

The man grunted and headed toward the rear of the cabin. As he turned into the passenger stairs the lights in the cabin abruptly went out.

I jumped to my right, pulled Lisa down on the deck, and covered her with my body, trying at the same time to roll up and get at the Walther automatic I was carrying in a shoulder holster.

"Easy," said a soft commanding voice. "Easy. Or things will turn messy."

Joseph Wheeler stood in the space between the rows of chairs to my right, dimly visible by the emergency lights in the cabin. A second man stood behind Duane Tabor, the same gray-haired man I had seen in San Francisco. He was wearing a blue nylon jacket to keep off the rain. His right hand was shoved into a small red nylon gym bag. His left hand steadied the other at the wrist, which meant that the gun was heavy, probably an Ingram or some other type of silenced machine pistol. The fat man who had been protecting Tabor was gone.

I moved slowly to my feet and helped Lisa back into her chair. I had knocked the wind out of her when I pulled her to the floor, and her breath came painfully, in short ragged gasps.

Tabor stood where he was, his face frozen. "Hand me the gun, Duane," Wheeler commanded. "Butt first, and slow."

Tabor took the .38 police special he was holding and reversed it. He took a step forward and handed the piece to Wheeler.

Wheeler nodded. "That's good, Duane." His voice remained soft. It had happened so quietly that the passengers sitting in the benches along the sides of the cabin had done nothing more than mutter to themselves when the lights had gone out. The cabin remained dark. Without Reese's men in place, Wheeler controlled the cabin.

"Sit with our friends," Wheeler said to the gray-haired man. He walked very slowly around the row of chairs and sat down where Tabor had been. "The lights will be back on in a second," Wheeler added. "Come with me, Duane. Outside." Tabor walked forward and Wheeler followed. "You too, Riordan. Give your gun to my friend. Do it quickly." I did.

The lights came back on as I followed Tabor and Wheeler out to the deck. I saw out of the corner of my eye that Reese had taken a position at the front of the cabin. He was watching carefully but made no effort to interfere.

Wheeler took Tabor to a corner of the front deck, out of the sight lines from the ferry's bridge. Tabor stood with his back to the rail, waiting. Wheeler tucked Tabor's gun into the back of his jeans and rested his hands on his hips. He stared at Tabor impassively.

"None of this was necessary, Duane," he said. "You've been paid well. You just got greedy."

"I don't know what you're talking about," Tabor said. His face was half-lighted by the small lights on the cabin bulkhead. His eyes were frightened and his voice was pleading. "This is my business. It doesn't involve you."

"Don't lie to me, Duane." Wheeler took a step forward. "You've got no time for that. Buddy isn't going to come to your rescue. He's down on the car deck. He's going to have one hell of a headache when he wakes up."

"This is a private matter, Mr. Wheeler," Tabor said. "I don't know what you're doing here."

"I paid you a million and a quarter for the pictures, Duane. Riordan here tells me they weren't the genuine article."

"He's lying. The pictures are Thayers, good ones. They're going to be worth a lot more pretty soon. The market's still going up."

"Duane, what made you think you could cheat me? You're a clerk, Duane, a money mover. You haven't got the guts or the brains to play games with me." A patronizing edge had come into Wheeler's voice.

"I'm just trying to protect your investment, Mr. Wheeler."

Wheeler shook his head. "Duane, we haven't got that much time." His hands flashed in the half-light from the cabin. There was a quick solid sound, like meat being cut, and a muffled cry. Tabor suddenly slumped against the railing, his face spilling blood. When Wheeler stepped back again, I could see that he had nearly flattened Tabor's nose. Tabor sobbed once and choked. He turned his head and spat blood over the railing into the water. When he turned to face us again, I could hear the whistled, reedy sound of his breathing.

"You stupid shit," Wheeler said. "If you needed more money, I'd have given it to you. How much more of this do you want to take? If you come clean, I might still be able to use you."

Tabor shook his head, trying to clear it. "Please," he said. "I'll pay the money back. I didn't know the pictures were fakes until after I bought them for you."

"Making progress," Wheeler said. "How much for you, how much for Campbell?"

"I just got a commission on the purchase. A hundred thousand. Campbell got the rest."

"Riordan?"

"Nope," I said. "More like five or six hundred thousand. Campbell says he kept five hundred."

"Try again, Duane." The hands flashed and Tabor's head rocked back under the blow.

Tabor turned and spat blood again. "We each took five hundred," he said. "We gave the sculptor two-fifty."

"And he's dead, isn't he? Because you were afraid he'd talk. Who'd you use for that, Duane? Buddy? You'd better tell me now because the cops are getting close."

"Buddy did the sculptor. The Spanish guy set the bomb. Everything else came out of New York."

Wheeler shook his head. "You fool. If any one of them gets tied to a job, they'll turn on you, and you'll turn on me."

Wheeler started to turn away, as if in disgust, but his anger got the better of him. His hands flashed again and Tabor fell back against the rail, clutching his throat. In the half-light from the bulkhead it looked like a movie. Or a nightmare. After a long time Tabor stumbled back to his feet, wheezing.

"Don't kill him here," I said sharply. "I don't want to have to explain what I'm doing with this."

"No, you wouldn't, would you?" Wheeler said with his back to me, still watching Tabor. "So what do you think I should do with him, Riordan?" He glanced back at me.

"Get him out of the country. Get him a job. And tell him if he ever shows up here, he's dead."

Wheeler slapped Tabor again. He was toying with him now, a torturer who enjoyed his work. The cruelty was beginning to make me sick. "You've got what you need from him," I told Wheeler. "You broke him. He's no threat to you now. Take him out of here and let us go."

"A merciful approach. And one that I would use if I didn't think Duane was as stupid as he is. No. I have to keep an eye on him, or kill him."

He turned back to Tabor. Tabor was leaning against the rail for support, but there was something different in his face. Before it had shown fear and pleading and pain. Now there was something new, a hate that looked like it had been growing for a long time, a hate born of the memory of a thousand small humiliations swallowed, a thousand angry words choked back. Anger, not money, must have been Tabor's motive for defrauding Wheeler. Tabor had wanted the secret pleasure of cheating Wheeler. The sudden appearance of the old anger frightened me.

Wheeler saw it, too. He whirled and kicked out. The kick caught Tabor in the belly and he crumpled to the deck. His head touched the steel deck plate. He gasped, as if about to vomit. But his hands went back, toward his legs, not forward to support himself.

When he stumbled to his feet, he was holding the hideout gun, a little nickel-plated .22 that had come from an ankle holster. He pushed the gun straight at Wheeler's head and shot twice, point-blank. The shots struck Wheeler in the face and snapped his head back. He rocked a half step backward, then crashed down on the deck, already dead.

Tabor dropped his arms and leaned forward, like an exhausted runner trying to catch his breath. I stood frozen in the half-light of the deck. Before I could move, Tabor had pulled himself back. He was sick and bloodied but his eyes were alive with purpose and triumph. He looked at me and steadied himself. He started to raise the gun.

I slammed into him with all the desperate force I could muster, driving my legs like a fullback going through the line. My shoulder caught him straight in the chest and I drove him back and knocked him over the rail. I had to grab at the rail to keep from going over with him. His body wheeled over once in the air in the terrible second before he struck the steel edge of the ferry's hull and dropped into the cold black water.

The sound of the waves slapping against the ferry's hull and the sting of the rain in my face brought me back to reality. I leaned over the rail, afraid I might be sick, then I gradually straightened up. I turned to face Wheeler's bodyguard. The machine pistol was out of the bag now. It was pointed at my gut.

"They're both dead," I shouted, raising my hands in the air. "Tabor pulled a hideout gun and shot him. He was going to shoot me and I knocked him over the rail and into the water."

He nodded. Wheeler's bodyguard was a pragmatist. He put the machine pistol back in the red bag and knelt to check Wheeler for a pulse. There wasn't one. A trickle of blood ran from the back of his head and flowed down the deck.

Reese stepped onto the deck. He leveled his revolver at the bodyguard. He made the usual announcements about dropping weapons and going down on the deck. The bodyguard handed me the machine pistol and the red bag and complied. Reese searched him and cuffed him, then handed him over to the agent who had been loading cars, to be locked in the purser's cabin until the ferry docked in Clinton, now only a mile or two away. When he was done, he came back to me and looked down at Wheeler. He didn't bother to cover the body.

"Nice work," he said, a grin on his face.

"You didn't bust them," I said woodenly. "You were supposed to take them, right at the beginning."

Reese turned away from me, cupped his hands from the wind and rain, and lit a cigarette. He said nothing.

"You wanted this," I continued. "You wanted them dead. What did you do, have somebody delay your team at the dock so they'd miss the ferry? You could have gotten half the people in that cabin killed."

Reese turned back to face me, the grin still in place. He looked obscene. "It worked," he said defiantly.

I stared at him as though he was mad. I remember thinking that maybe they all were mad in the world where Reese lived.

20

They let us go around four o'clock in the morning. I watched as the court reporter, a lean elderly man whose name I had already forgotten, shuffled his long accordion pads of stenography paper into neat piles and bound them with a rubber band. He placed the pads and his stenotype machine into a black plastic case and stood to go. All around the room the swarm of DEA agents, Seattle cops, and Island County sheriff's deputies finished the last dregs of coffee from their white plastic cups and also began to wander out, probably to look for scrambled eggs and bacon and decent coffee topped up with a little rum. I yawned. The stress and sleeplessness of the past five days had left me with a bellyful of nervous tension that was only now starting to fade away.

Lisa had fallen asleep in a detective's swivel chair, her head cradled in her arms on a desktop. I reached out and stroked her temple, smoothing the dark blond hair. She stirred and muttered something I could not hear, then fell again into sleep. I wished that I could take her home and put her to bed, give her the twenty-four hours of deep sleep that would make life seem worth living again when she woke. But there was one more thing to do.

When Reese and Ahlberg came out of the sheriff's private office, the crowd in the detective's workroom had nearly cleared out. Ahlberg looked as unhappy as I had expected; with Tabor dead he was going to have to close the books on the bombing of Lisa's car and the beating death of Terrill Hanks. Campbell had steadfastly maintained that Tabor had hired the bombing and the killing without his knowledge. Tabor's identification of Buddy the fat man as the killer of Terrill Hanks was inadmissible, unverified hearsay. Ahlberg would hold Buddy for a while but probably couldn't get the evidence to make a case. The unnamed "Spanish guy" who had placed the bomb in Lisa's car was probably asleep somewhere in Riverside or Yuma or Sacramento, with nothing to tie him to the bombing in Seattle.

Reese paused as he passed me and gave me a strange look. "What are you still doing here?" he demanded. He stuck a cigarette in his mouth, lit it, and exhaled the smoke as he spoke. "It's all over and done with. Take yourself and the woman home." Ahlberg stopped and waited to hear my answer.

"I'm going to. Where's the old man? Are they going to hold him tonight?"

"No. He's not going to be arraigned until Monday. He won't run. If he does, his plea agreement is terminated and we can use his confession against him when we catch him."

"Where's he headed now?"

"Out to his summerhouse, I guess. He and his lawyer left a couple of minutes ago."

"Thanks." I started to pull on my jacket.

"Riordan," Ahlberg said sharply, "what are you up to?"

"Nothing that would interest you. There's a couple of pieces missing from Campbell's story that have nothing to do with his connections to Tabor and Wheeler. I have to get them before I can let this thing go."

"Does this have anything to do with Kuehn's death?" Ahlberg demanded.

"I don't think so. If it does and I find anything out, I'll tell you. But you heard what Campbell said already. One of Tabor's men probably killed Kuehn and made it look like a suicide."

"I'm going with you."

"No. If you do, it won't work. Lisa's the only one who can ask these questions. She might be the only person he'll answer."

Ahlberg looked at me, his lips pressed tight together. "All right," he finally said. "I'll let you slide on this. If you find something, tell me." He strode out of the room with only a slight slump in his broad shoulders to betray his exhaustion.

Reese hesitated before going, a smirk playing on the edges of his mouth. "If I had a cop working for me who could be bull-shitted like that, I'd fire his ass."

I stood up and took two very careful steps toward Reese, until I was standing six inches away from him. He twitched a little as he fought the natural tendency to step away. "A cop like that," I said slowly, "wouldn't work for you, Reese. You got the death you came for. Go home."

I turned to wake Lisa. I got down on one knee beside her and patted her arm, trying to wake her gently. I could feel Reese standing behind me, waiting to get in the last word. I kept my back to him. Eventually he turned and walked away, his footsteps clattering on the hard tile floor as he went.

When Lisa was finally awake, we left the sheriff's office and made our way slowly to the parking lot and the rented Nissan. The rain had slowed to a fine mist and Lisa stopped for a moment and turned her face toward the sky to feel the mist on her face. She shook herself, still half-asleep, and then returned to my outstretched arm. She reached around me and pulled me into an embrace, her head pushed up against my chest.

"I know what you're going to say," she muttered.

"What's that?"

"That it's almost over." She laughed softly, with a tinge of bitterness in her voice. She was still punchy from exhaustion.

I laughed, too. "Yes, but this time I mean it. I think."

"Don't you always," she replied. She pushed me away and opened the car door for herself. "Don't you always."

The drive to Campbell's summerhouse was only ten miles, but it took nearly thirty minutes on the narrow blacktop highway. There were no lights and the rows of evergreens seemed to close in on the road. When we turned off onto the gravel drive that led to Campbell's place, I slowed and said, "There's a couple of things that still don't make sense. We still don't know who painted the postcard that you got when all this started. We still don't really know who killed Morris Kuehn, or why. And we don't know if your grandfather might still be alive."

"I thought you decided there wasn't any chance of that," Lisa said. I glanced over and saw her face barely outlined in the darkness by the dim lights of the dashboard.

"There's not much of a chance," I conceded. "But a lot of Petrov's actions haven't been explained. And I believed him when he said he didn't kill Margaret Jura. The murder happened fifty years ago, but Petrov acted like the wound was still new."

"He was in prison for a long time. He probably had a tremendous sense of injustice. Perhaps he even blocked the murder out of his mind and thought he was innocent."

"Perhaps. But I don't buy the idea that Tabor killed Morris Kuehn. Kuehn was smart, but he wasn't an expert who could detect and prove that those paintings weren't Thayers. Why would Tabor want to kill him? When you leave out Kuehn, Tabor's moves make a kind of desperate sense. He missed you, then he missed me in New York. But he was in the process of getting rid of everyone who could tell the world that the pictures that Wheeler bought were fakes: Petrov, Hanks, then probably Campbell. Kuehn just doesn't fit. If Tabor didn't kill him, or have him killed, who did?"

"But Morris was a very smart and very powerful man. If I had been killed in the bomb blast, and you had been killed a short time later, Morris could have investigated very thoroughly. David Campbell would have known that. And David might have told Tabor that Morris would have to be killed, too."

"That's good reasoning," I said grudgingly, "and you might be right. Which is one of the reasons we're going to talk to Campbell tonight. Whether he wants us to or not."

The gravel road sloped down now as the ridge dropped away toward the waterfront. I slowed down again as the road turned rougher. The trees were thick and blocked our view of the shore. Within a quarter mile I saw a wooden sign that read "Campbell" and turned off onto a narrow gravel driveway. The driveway dropped downhill and then widened into a parking area in front of Campbell's house.

Campbell had a summerhouse that any preppie would approve of. It was a big shingled cottage with a wide veranda and a sloping shed roof. Dormer windows stuck out from the roofline. The upstairs windows were dark, but light came from the downstairs windows and smoke drifted lazily out of the fieldstone chimney. In the distance I could hear the light swell of water lapping at the shore.

Lisa and I got out of the car and walked toward the house. There was a silver Mercedes 560 SL parked off to one side. The car had vanity plates that said "defender." Only Donald Henry would be enough of an asshole to drive a car with plates like that.

"The lawyer's still here," I said to Lisa, pointing to the car, "but let's do it anyway. We'll never have a better chance."

We went to the red-enameled front door and knocked. It was opened by a wide-eyed Donald Henry.

"Riordan," he said, slumping against the doorframe. "What the hell do you want? It's five o'clock in the morning."

"I want to talk to Campbell," I said. "Now. Or I'll raise every variety of hell I know of when he comes up for sentencing. I'll flood the court and the federal probation service with paper."

"No deal. We're not buying." Henry started to close the door. I stuck my shoulder through it and pushed it open. Henry tried to lean against the door and hold it closed. His shoes made squeaking noises on the polished hardwood floor as I shoved it open.

"I forgot to add something, Donald," I said when we were inside. "We talk to Campbell now or I'll clean the floor with you."

"I'll have you arrested."

"Fine. But we're going to ask these questions first."

By that time Campbell had come out to the entry hall. "Let them in, Donald," he said. He looked every one of his seventy-three years. "I don't think there's anything else they can do to me now."

"More's the pity," I said. Campbell led us all down a white-painted hallway, through a pair of leaded French doors, and into the living room. The room was tall and wide, dominated by a massive rock fireplace. Campbell and Henry sat down on the pair of matching leather sofas that framed the fireplace. There were empty plates and snifters of brandy on the cocktail table in front of them. A warm smell of eggs and toast and burning applewood filled the air.

"There's a couple of questions that never got asked," I began when Lisa and I were seated on the sofa opposite the two men. "They're not about your deal with Tabor, or the paintings. First, who painted that bird on the postcard that was sent to Lisa?"

"I don't know," Campbell said mildly. His features looked haggard in the play of firelight and shadow. "I never saw it until you showed it to me. Neither Hanks nor Tabor found anything like it in any of the paintings by Petrov that they looked at."

"Is there anyone else out there, any other painter, who is forging Thayer's works or painting in his style?"

"Not that I know of. I didn't go looking to make this happen, Riordan. I was desperate. I owed Wheeler so much money that I was going to lose my gallery, maybe my life, if I didn't find some way to pay him off. Tabor talked me into this." His voice mixed bitterness and self-pity.

"What about Kuehn?" I asked. "He had the skill to forge Thayer's work, and he used to own a very similar picture."

Campbell shook his head and looked scornful. "Morris

couldn't paint like that on the best day of his life. He was strictly an amateur, albeit a talented one."

"If he had no connection to this, why did Tabor have him killed?"

"I told the police everything I know. I told Tabor that Morris was a smart and powerful man; if he allied himself with Lisa, we were in trouble. I don't know if Tabor did have Morris killed. I didn't know in advance what he was planning. He panicked when Lisa attacked the authenticity of the paintings. He might have thought Morris was an expert, or . . . damn it, I don't know! The man took leave of his senses. I know he would have killed me next. I was paralyzed by fright. That's no excuse, I know. I should have gone to the police the moment I heard that Lisa's car had been bombed. I will never be able to forgive myself." As he finished talking he was looking at Lisa, searching for some sign of forgiveness in her eyes. She looked away.

"I don't mind you practicing the little speech you're going to give the sentencing judge," I told him, "but I wish you wouldn't do it on my time."

I paused to think. Either Campbell was telling the truth or it was hopeless. I had no leverage on him, none at all.

"When I saw Anton Petrov in New York," I said softly, almost as if beginning a story, "I tried to anger him by asking questions about the murder of Margaret Jura. It worked. Petrov denied killing her, denied it like it had happened yesterday, not fifty years ago. He did it so well that even though I didn't believe him at first, it haunts me now. You testified at his trial and helped convict him. Your accomplice had him killed. If there is anything you know, anything at all, about what happened on the night that Margaret Jura was killed, I wish you would tell me. I think you owe Petrov that much."

Campbell stared straight into the fire. He picked up his brandy glass and drained it. The cognac must have had bite; he coughed as he put the glass back down.

"Anton killed her," he said finally. "It had to be him. He had been asking for her and threatening to beat up whoever she was

with. He was insanely jealous. What we did made no difference."
I could feel him looking back into his memories. If he were ever
going to tell the truth, it would be now.

"What?" I asked, trying not to sound too eager. I leaned forward and stared into Campbell's eyes. "What did you do?"

"I told you before that there was marijuana at that party. It
sounds silly now, almost childish, but that was a major crime
back then, even if you just were caught holding the stuff. Two
of my classmates, Lichter and Gore, had bought some marijuana
from me that night. They smoked some of it with Anton. When
the police came around in the morning and took everybody who
had stayed overnight or who lived nearby in the moorage out to
be questioned, they panicked. They came to me. I told them to
say nothing about smoking grass with Anton. They still had a
couple of cigarettes of the stuff left, and I had them throw them
away. I know Petrov told the police about it, but we all denied
it. No one believed Anton."

"Did you tell Kuehn about this?"

"I didn't. He was going to represent Petrov, and I was scared
to death that Morris would use that fact in court. We didn't say
anything."

"But if you'd told the truth, you might have cleared Petrov."

"No, he killed her. He came back later from the bridge, out
of breath, like he'd been running. He must have killed her."

"But that was later," I said, more to myself than anyone else.
"At least an hour, more likely two hours, after Margaret Jura
had left Thayer's houseboat. She had a car; it was found where
her body was. She wouldn't have just waited there for an hour,
under the bridge. She'd have driven home. Someone had to be
waiting for her, or followed her to her car."

"I still don't believe it," Campbell said. "Petrov was crazy. It
had to be him."

"Perhaps. But the timing might have given a jury pause. If
Petrov didn't kill Margaret Jura, who else could have? Did anyone else leave the party?"

"I don't know," Campbell said. "How could I? I was high, trying to seduce a girl, not paying attention."

"Do you think Lee Thayer killed her?" I demanded. "Lichter testified that he saw Margaret Jura leave Thayer's boat, then Thayer left and went the other way, toward your party." I heard Lisa's sharp intake of breath beside me.

"No, of course Lee didn't kill her. He loved her. Lichter saw him leave the boat and come to the party—"

"But that was another one of the lies, wasn't it? Petrov told me he didn't see Thayer, and Petrov was with them. Did Lichter and Gore have a reason to lie about having seen Thayer? You rich boys seem to have pretty protective instincts for each other."

"I don't know." Campbell pressed his hands to his face, as if he could rub off the fatigue of another questioning.

"That's enough," Donald Henry cut in sharply. "He's an old man, Riordan, you're killing him with this."

"Shut up, Donald." I looked back at Campbell. "Did you ever admit any of this to Petrov? That you told Lichter and Gore to perjure themselves to save your skin?"

"No. Petrov would have killed me. He hated all of us, as it was. He hated me even more after he got out of prison, when I wouldn't sell his pictures."

"What about Thayer? Did you ever tell him that you lied about Petrov, that Petrov could have been innocent?"

"No. Lee would have felt the same way about me that Petrov did. I couldn't afford that. Lee was the first major artist who gave me pictures to sell. I'd have been cutting my own throat."

"Would that you had," I said harshly. "So tell me just one more thing, Campbell. Is Lee Thayer still alive?"

Campbell was taken aback. "No. Why would you think that?"

"Because nobody else could have painted that small bird on the postcard."

Campbell stared at me. "You bloody fool," he said, suddenly calm again. "Thayer couldn't have painted that picture. I know he's dead."

"How do you know?"

"Because Petrov killed him. He as much as told me so. He tried again to get me to represent him after Lee died. He gloated that Thayer was dead. Literally gloated. And then I remembered Petrov had worked in the prison automobile shop. Thayer died in his car. Petrov must have fixed the car so that it would go off the road. He cut the brakes out or something. Because he was very pleased that Thayer was dead."

"Did you tell anyone about that?"

"What could I tell? That Petrov had gloated? That wouldn't be evidence in court. And they never found Lee's body, or the car." He looked at Lisa, a sudden understanding evident on his face. "You thought he was alive, didn't you, Lisa? That's why you started to investigate the paintings in the SAM show. I am so sorry. If only I had known how you felt."

The fire was burning down, and Campbell's face reflected the red glow from the embers. Lisa was staring at the old man with something close to hatred. "Take me out of here, Matthew, please," she said. "I just want to go."

I nodded and stood up. "I won't thank you," I told Campbell. "I don't know whether you're telling the truth about any of this or not, and there's probably no way I can find out."

"Then take your pleasure in my ruin," he replied, rising to his feet. His voice whined in renewed self-pity.

I looked slowly around the elegant room, furnished with antiques and paintings that could have kept ten working families going for a year. I looked at Campbell, in his perfect country clothes, his elegant face stricken with sorrow, and all of it for himself. He would be all right, I knew. He might forfeit his business, might even spend a few months in jail. But when it was over, his rich friends would rally around him; there would be contrition features in the press. He might, like Claus von Bülow and Richard Nixon, even make the cover of *Vanity Fair*.

It was suddenly too much. I stepped forward and slapped David Campbell across the face. The blow dropped him onto the sofa. There was a small trickle of blood from the corner of his mouth. His eyes were shocked by the small violence.

"Pig," I said.

Dawn was breaking by the time we caught the ferry back to the mainland. Lisa was silent on the return trip, absorbing the things that Campbell had said about her grandfather's death. It meant the end of her hopes, and the knowledge that Thayer might have died as a murder victim disturbed her even more. It would take time for her to distance her memory of her grandfather from the shock of the past few weeks.

The clouds had scattered and morning sunshine had begun to dry the streets in the Mount Baker neighborhood where Lisa lived. It was still early on Saturday morning and the traffic was light. Lisa ran up the stairs to the front door of her small white house like she was going to greet an old friend. I trudged along behind her, weighed down by the bags and the disturbing confession that David Campbell had made. The accepted version of events had been wrong, and the odds were that Petrov had not killed Margaret Jura. Was Thayer the killer after all, protected by the tight network of wealthy friends and parents who could afford small lies and expensive lawyers? And what did this have to do with the death, by suicide or murder, of Morris Kuehn?

I placed Lisa's bags inside the front door. She was standing in the middle of her living room, surveying the house. Dust had gathered on the polished hardwood floors. The flowers in the vases were dead, leaves and stems brittle, and the water had evaporated, leaving a sweetish musty smell. A cascade of mail was scattered across the coffee table where Lisa's gallery assistant had left it. The ashes of a fire in the tile fireplace had soured and their smell carried throughout the house.

Lisa shook her head, as if to ignore the interruption of her life, and went into the kitchen. "I know you're not supposed to drink in the morning, but I figure it's all right when you're approaching it from this end. You want something?"

"Just a beer," I replied, following her there. Tired as I was, anything stronger would take my head off.

I found her cracking ice cubes over the sink. I put my arms around here from behind and held her. She sagged back against my chest.

"That feels so good," she said. "So good." She sighed. "But would you mind if I was alone for a day or two? My house is a mess and so am I and I just need some time to make sense out of what happened."

"I understand. In fact I'm glad you asked. I want to go home, too. I have cases that are probably out of control and right now I just want to stand under a hot shower for about a hundred years."

She turned and reached up and kissed me. "Thanks. For understanding." She slipped out of my grasp, went to the cabinet that she kept liquor in, and poured herself a hefty slug of Tanqueray over ice. She put the bottle back and then looked in the refrigerator.

"All I've got is light beer," she said, her head still in the refrigerator. "I know you regard that as a criminal offense."

"Yeah, but this is an emergency." She pulled out a bottle of Amstel and dug in a silverware drawer for a bottle opener. She was wrestling with the beer bottle and the opener when I spoke again.

"I'm going to try and find the transcript of Petrov's trial," I said quietly. "From what Campbell said I think it's almost certain that Petrov did not kill Margaret Jura."

She turned to face me and froze, the beer bottle still clenched in her hand.

"What?" she asked.

"I'm going to take a look at the trial transcript, talk to any remaining witnesses, and try to figure out what really happened. I'm not eager to do it, but it is something I think should be finished."

Lisa's face twisted. "Why? Why do you want to find out if Petrov is innocent? He's dead. And he's guilty enough; he killed my grandfather." Her voice broke once but she went on, a tone of something like threat in her voice. "Isn't what we've been through enough? Are you a junkie, hooked on other people's pain, while you stay removed, dancing on the edges?"

"I hope not," I said quietly, answering the last question first. "There's a kind of collective memory, Lisa, that makes it important to know what really happened to these people. They were all extraordinary, in their own way. Your grandfather was a great man, perhaps one of the great artists of his century. You should know the truth of why he died."

She shook her head. "You are insane," she said bitterly. "Didn't you learn anything from this? Look at the people who are dead, the risks we took. There is a time when you have to stop."

"I don't think it's that time yet."

"You want to know if Lee killed her," she said, her voice low.

"I want to know who killed her."

"You think Lee killed her."

I said nothing.

She closed her eyes, as though struggling for control. When she opened them again, she had it.

"Get out," she said.

"Lisa, I—" She threw up her hands and silently commanded me to stop. But I went ahead and finished what I wanted to say. "Lisa, I love you."

"Get out."

I stopped and stared at her for a long moment, trying to memorize every plane and angle and curve of her lovely face, trying to steel myself to do what I had to do.

I nodded. And I got out.

A gull spiraled down out of the sky and took the fish in the near part of Portage Bay, just past the first row of houseboats moored to the east of the University Bridge. The sun was barely over the horizon, and the morning light streaked through broken clouds. Above me, on the shoulder of Capitol Hill, the old Tudor and Craftsman houses were barely visible behind a dense growth of alder and maple that was burning yellow and red with the first cool days of autumn.

I tossed the rock I had been rolling over in one hand into the channel. The girders of University Bridge above me began to shudder and move, a sign that an early-rising sailor wanted to maneuver his boat into Lake Washington. As the bridge rose to let the sailboat pass I got slowly off the log stump where I had been sitting and stretched to shake off the morning chill.

Fifty years ago the body of Margaret Jura had been dumped onto the gravel banks of the channel that connected Lake Union to Portage Bay about fifteen feet from where I had been sitting. I had been at my office all night, reading the transcript of Anton Petrov's trial for the murder of Margaret Jura. According to the marked-up volume of transcript at my feet, the body had been discovered half in, half out of the water. That, and the heavy rain that had fallen in the small hours of the morning after her death, had prevented the coroner from estimating a time of death on the basis of body temperature. Thayer's houseboat had been about a five-minute walk away on Portage Bay Lane, the narrow track that wound beneath the hill and connected the moorages. David Campbell's boat, the location of the party, had been no more than ten minutes' walk away.

A barge containing sawed lumber from one of the few remaining Lake Washington mills passed through Portage Bay, creating small waves that lapped at the gravel bank. I sat down and picked up the trial transcript again.

Most of the testimony from the people attending the party was confused as to where anyone was at a particular time, which is what you would expect, given the large number of people present and the amount of alcohol being consumed. The only witnesses who had placed the actors in their locations had been Marion Lichter and Walter Gore, the students I remembered from the newspaper accounts of the crime. Gore and Lichter had both claimed to be drinking in a stand of small trees across Portage Bay Lane from Lee Thayer's moorage when they had seen first Margaret Jura, and then Thayer, leave his boat and walk in separate directions. They had followed Thayer back to the party. Both denied that Petrov had been with them.

The problem in analyzing that testimony, after all these years, was in figuring out which part of it was truth, which falsity. If Petrov had been with them in the same spot, smoking marijuana, he might have seen Margaret Jura leaving Thayer's boat. Given his jealous feelings, he might well have followed her, argued with her, and killed her under the bridge. On the other hand, if Lichter and Gore were protecting Thayer, they would only have had to change the direction in which Thayer had walked in order to deflect suspicion from him.

The trial transcript did show one lapse: somehow, Morris Kuehn had failed to cross-examine either Lichter or Gore about the crucial testimony. Perhaps he had been afraid of highlighting their testimony, or of having no evidence with which to impeach them, and had preferred to turn it into a swearing contest between them and Petrov. Perhaps it had been an inexperienced lawyer's bonehead mistake. Perhaps, worst of all, Kuehn had been shielding Thayer from suspicion.

I stared again at the spot where the woman's body had been found. The scene had changed remarkably little in fifty years: the bridge, the channel, the gravel bank, the tangled underbrush shielding this spot from the adjacent houseboat moorage, all were still there. It held no more answers for me than it did for the police in 1939. After a long while I picked up the book of transcript and walked the two miles back to my office along the north shore of Lake Union, passing the boat-repair docks and small manufacturers, the last of their kind on the rapidly gentrifying lake shore.

That Saturday morning under the University Bridge was one week after Lisa had told me to get the hell out of her life. In that week I had combed the trial transcript and the newspaper accounts for the names of the people who had been at the party on the night Margaret Jura died. Eventually I came up with a list of about twenty names and called in Paul Schaeffer to check them out. Paul is a free-lance researcher, the best in the business, but dealing with him has its price, and not just in dollars.

"I'm telling you, you've got to cut that shit out," he said, pointing to the ham-and-cheese-filled croissant I was eating for breakfast when we met in my office. He rested his lean, muscled arms on the edge of my desk. Aside from his balding head Schaeffer looked ten years younger than the forty-four I knew he was.

"Paul," I said tiredly, "when I met you, you were still a reporter. You smoked two packs of Camel straights a day and your notion of breakfast was Jack Daniel's and a carryout from Dunkin' Donuts. Lay off."

"Yeah, and look where it got me. Hooked up to the monitor, listening to myself under the oxygen mask. I'm telling you, diet is the key to prevention. Look at this."

He handed me a magazine from his briefcase, folded open to an article about the pleasures of eating raw grains and the miracles that did for reducing serum cholesterol. I closed the magazine to the cover. It was a new health-and-life-style publication that had been started locally and was poised to go national. In keeping with the spirit of our times it had been named *Me, Myself, and I*. I handed it back to him. "Paul," I said slowly, "I have a message I want you to give these people."

He looked confused. "What?"

"Tell them that they're going to die. Every last one of them. No matter how much raw alfalfa they eat. Now, can we get down to business here?"

He took the magazine and shrugged. Like a street-corner preacher whose mark has walked away without taking the religious tract or dropping a dollar in the bucket, Paul was disappointed but ready for the next potential convert.

I handed him my list of twenty names. "I want you to find addresses and telephone numbers for each of these people. Past occupation or business would be helpful, too. Some of them are likely to be dead, many will probably be retired."

"Are any of the people on the list more important than the others?"

"Yes. Two of them. Marion Lichter and Walter Gore."

"What's the common denominator here?"

"They're all old. Many of them were probably students at Cornish, the University of Washington, or the old federal Arts Project of the WPA. They all attended a party at the houseboat of a man named David Campbell, the local art dealer who got indicted last week. The party was in August 1939."

"I don't get it," he said. "What's this got to do with any of your court cases?"

"Nothing. Call it a debt. A woman got murdered at the party. I think the wrong man got convicted for it. Later the man got killed himself."

Schaeffer nodded. He took the list of names and squinted at it, then folded it and put it in his canvas briefcase. As he stood up to go he said, "Riordan? Mind if I say you're the weirdest lawyer I have ever worked with?"

"Not at all. Provided you give me a discount."

He smiled. "Not a prayer. I'll be in touch." He bounded out of the office, his running shoes squeaking on the hardwood floor. I thought about taking a drink from the office bottle in his honor, but it was still morning and I had too much to do. Schaeffer was eccentric but he knew his stuff, and I had some hope.

It took him a week to nail down all of the names on the list. I spent most of the time trying to bury myself with work. Lisa never called. Once a day I looked at the telephone and thought about calling her, then put the thought away. She had been within her rights to call a halt to the pursuit of knowledge that might only bring her pain. Masochism is a personal hobby, not one I could expect her to share. But her absence hurt like an old wound that was cut open once a night.

When Schaeffer caught up with me again, I was ass-deep in lawyers at a bar and fish house called McCormick's, on Fourth Avenue, near the courthouse. It was quarter to five in the afternoon, fifteen minutes after the courts had closed for the day. I listened with half an ear to the usual war stories about who did what to somebody else's witness and gave most of my attention to the shot of scotch I was nursing at the bar. When Paul touched my arm in greeting, I was so surprised I nearly decked him.

"What the hell's wrong with you?" he asked.

"Nothing. I just feel like a walking toothache. Want a drink?"

He named a nonalcoholic beer. I shrugged and ordered him one. "Got anything for me?" I asked.

"Yup." He took a swig of his nonbeer and made a face. "Not quite the same, is it?"

"That's the price of being perfect, Paul. Let's have it."

He took out his list. "Thirteen of them are dead," he said.

"Only two of the survivors still live in the Puget Sound area. The rest are all retired someplace else."

"What about Lichter and Gore?"

"Lichter lives outside Chicago with his daughter. He used to be a writer for the *Chicago Sun-Times*. Gore was a professor of art history at a small college in St. Paul, Minnesota. Macalester College. He's listed as a professor emeritus. He lives near the campus, I think. I'd try the college first."

"Did you talk to any of them?"

"Not directly. I figured you'd want to make your own approach."

"You figured right. Thanks, Paul. Send me the bill."

"It's in the mail already." He took another swig of imitation beer. "Matthew? Why are you getting all twisted up about a murder that happened over fifty years ago? Even if you clear the name of the guy that got convicted, nobody's going to know, much less care."

"I'll know," I told him. "Thanks again."

By the time I got home a storm had come in from the west and rain had begun to knock the leaves off the Pacific maple trees in my yard. I took a load of split alder from the wood box and kindled a fire, the first of the year. The wood was dry and caught right away. I poured myself a drink and sat down on the living-room sofa with the telephone and Paul Schaeffer's information.

I got rid of the locals first. Sean Rattigan was a lawyer who had worked as counsel to the Boeing Company for many years. In retirement he had served on a number of civic boards and commissions and was known for taking on some of the dirty jobs on the fringes of local politics. He had a bluff, friendly voice that turned guarded when I told him who I was and what I wanted.

"I'm afraid I can't help you, Riordan," he said. "I was there, but I was inside David's boat, playing a bunch of records. I got a subpoena to testify at the trial but then never got called to the stand. I suppose they wanted me to say that I hadn't seen Anton around midnight. The fact is, I only saw him once, around ten o'clock, and he was already drunk as a skunk. Sorry." He hung up even before I could thank him for his time.

William Kroger was a retired high-school principal, living in a nursing home. The head nurse refused to put him on the telephone. "He's at dinner, sir," she insisted. "Come tomorrow, between ten and two." I said I would and hung up.

Peggy Wong Taylor lived in Sedona, Arizona, and had acquired a Southwestern accent somewhere in her travels through life. "I sure remember that night," she drawled. "I was seventeen, raised in a proper Chinese family, and I'd never seen such carrying-on. I thought it was wonderful. Until that poor girl got killed. I didn't know either of them, her or that fellow Petrov. I got such hell from my family after that party, they didn't let me out again for another year." She was still talking as I drew a line through her name and rang off.

Barbara Branch White lived near Rock Creek Park in Washington, D.C. The name had struck something in my memory when I first saw it, but I couldn't remember what. Schaeffer listed her occupation as lawyer. I closed my eyes and thought until I remembered: it was Ambassador Barbara White, a salty-tongued Republican power broker who had resigned as a deputy secretary of the treasury several years back in protest over Reagan's budget deficits. To my taste, her politics were Neanderthal but she had a reputation for honesty, and had never engaged in the public Bible-thumping of recent years. I looked at my watch. It was only ten o'clock in Washington. The worst she could do was hang up on me. If she took the call at all.

Barbara White answered the telephone herself on the third ring. When I told her who I was and what I wanted, she laughed. She had a public voice that sounded a little like Katharine Hepburn's, with more gravel in it.

"The thing I want to know first," she said, "is how in hell you got this number? This is my private unlisted line."

"I use an investigator who is much loved by someone at the

phone company," I replied. I explained what I was doing. "Do you remember any of this?"

"Of course I do," she answered. "I went to Cornish with Margaret Jura. I was trying to decide between becoming an actress and a lawyer, which I later found out was a distinction without a difference, except lawyers eat regularly. I was immensely jealous of poor Margaret, of course. Every woman in the school was."

"Why?"

"Have you ever seen a picture of her? A good one?"

"Yes. I saw some that David Campbell took."

"Then you know. She had an intense sexuality that was considered fairly shocking in those days. Made the rest of us look quite dull in comparison. But I liked her."

"What else can you tell me about her?"

"Not that much," she replied. "Wait a minute." I could hear clicking on the line while she thought. "You're the lawyer that got David Campbell busted. And you killed the drug lawyer that David was connected to. I saw a story about it in the *New York Times*."

"That's right. My client spotted the fake Thayer paintings he had sold, the ones that were really painted by Petrov."

"Good for you. And her. Lee Thayer's granddaughter, isn't she? I'll be damned. Why this sudden interest in Margaret Jura? And Petrov. I liked him, too. He had big black eyes and was very sweet and very tough, in his own way."

"I met him once while I was investigating the fake pictures. Petrov had painted them years ago, and they had been re-signed with Thayer's name. His life had been destroyed, and he was trying to salvage what he could, trying to sell his work. I talked to Petrov about Margaret Jura's death. He denied killing her. Before I could talk to him a second time Campbell's partner, the drug lawyer, had him killed. When it was all over, Campbell told me that two of the people at the party, Marion Lichter and Walter Gore, had lied about not having been with Petrov when

Margaret Jura was killed. Now I'm just trying to find out what really happened."

"Have you talked to Lichter or Gore?"

"Not yet. I want to have all the facts I can before I question them, and I'm going to do it in person."

"That's a sound approach, but I don't think I can help you. I saw Petrov that night, at around ten or eleven. He was very drunk. And very angry that Margaret Jura was nowhere to be found. I was very sad about what happened, but I thought he killed her."

"Did you see him any later than that? Jura left Thayer's houseboat around midnight and apparently was killed shortly afterward."

"No. I had left. I didn't come back to the party until around one or one-thirty."

"Where did you go?"

"I don't think that's something you need to know."

"I'd like to. I'm trying to run down every possibility."

She hesitated. "Have you spoken with James Tyler?"

"No. He lives in Paris. I planned to get up early and try to put a call through."

"Perhaps I can save you some sleep. I was with Mr. Tyler. Neither of us saw anything relevant."

"Are you sure? If you could even describe what you did see, maybe I can learn something."

Barbara White laughed, a throaty chuckle. "All right, Mr. Riordan, I'll confess. When I say I was with Jamie, I meant *with* him. Or more specifically, in bed with him. At a nearby houseboat that Jamie rented."

It was my turn to laugh. "I understand, Ambassador. And thank you for being so honest."

She laughed again. "After all these years it can hardly matter. And if you do talk to Jamie, as I'm sure you will, tell him that this old woman still thinks about him from time to time. Good night, sir. And good luck."

22

I took a morning flight from Seattle to the Minneapolis/St. Paul airport and had myself in a rental car and lost by twelve noon. Macalester College was located in the western section of St. Paul, an old city that reminded me of Boston, with its river hills and brown brick houses beneath tall shade trees starting to turn gold. The college campus was handsome, with Georgian and Victorian brick buildings settled amid the trees and broad lawns. The students were well dressed and improbably polite. I felt no less than one hundred years old.

The art departments were located in a modern building at the southern end of the campus, not far from the football stadium. The receptionist in the work-study office was a pretty, intelligent-looking student dressed in clean blue jeans and a Scandinavian knitted sweater. I thought back to the way I had looked in my less than successful two years at Yale, in 1968 and 1969, and marveled at how the world had changed.

"I've met Professor Gore," the student said politely, "but I don't know what his schedule is or whether he'll be in today. He teaches a seminar once in a while, but that's all."

"Is there anyone else here who might know?"

"Well, it's lunchtime, but I think Tom Loftgren might be here. He's the department chair. The third door on your left."

I thanked her and headed down the hall. Dr. Loftgren was in his office as promised, eating a brown-bag lunch and scribbling on a long yellow pad. He was a short, trim man with sandy hair and a graying mustache. He offered me a seat and listened patiently to an edited version of my mission.

"Walter's not been well, Mr. Riordan. His wife died a year ago and it was damned hard on him. His health is failing, and I've reduced his teaching schedule to a very occasional seminar. Frankly, I've wondered if he might be in the early stages of Alzheimer's or something. He's been very forgetful lately. Is it really that important?"

"Important enough that I came out here myself to talk to him," I replied. "I have his home address. I came here first as a courtesy, to avoid disturbing him at home if I can avoid it."

"I understand. Well, he lives in Tangletown, just west of the campus. That's what we call the neighborhood. Do you want me to call him first?"

"Under the circumstances, that might just excite him. But tell me honestly, do you think he would be able to undertake an interview? I've no desire to cause him any difficulty." But I am sure as hell going to question him, I added mentally.

"I think he'll be all right," Loftgren said, clearly impatient to get back to his work. "Just take it easy."

I thanked him and found my way out of the building and back to my rental car, plausibly established as that nice lawyer so concerned about not upsetting Professor Gore. It might not be necessary, but if Gore had witnessed something that could identify Margaret Jura's killer, and if the killer was still alive, I wanted to be careful about accusations of tampering with an elderly witness. I had learned early, and the hard way, that you always have to preserve the integrity of your evidence, no matter how remote the prospect that you might use it.

Tangletown lived up to its name. It was the remnant of what must have once been, before the turn of the century, a Victorian streetcar suburb of St. Paul. The curving streets didn't follow the gridiron plan of the rest of the city. The shingle and Queen Anne–style houses had been painstakingly restored in gaudy cream and blue and yellow paints.

The street addresses made no particular sense and it took me nearly half an hour to find Walter Gore's house. Age had been no kinder to his home than it had been to him: the grayish paint was peeling in long strips, the spade-shaped shingles were cracked and splitting, the porch and roof sagged beneath the weight of too many years, too many harsh winters.

I parked and walked through the weed-choked front yard to the door. The buzzer had long since stopped working. I pounded on the oak door. It was grimy from a dozen coats of yellowing shellac, but it had aged as hard as iron. My fist was getting sore, but I kept pounding anyway.

Finally the door opened. A big-framed man stood in the door-way. His wide shoulders were stooped; he seemed to be col-lapsing in on himself, going hollow from the inside. He had a few strands of graying hair that swept across his bald head. His chin had three or four days' white stubble. Food and what might have been old beer stained the front of his plaid woolen robe, worn over a dirty white shirt and black wool pants that were shiny with grease. His eyes were hidden by thick gray eyebrows and heavy black glasses, but even so he blinked in the autumn sunlight.

"Professor Gore?"

The old man nodded uncertainly.

"My name is Matthew Riordan. I'm a lawyer. I came out here from Seattle to ask you a few questions. May I come in?"

"My house . . ." he said. "I—what did you say your name was?"

"It's Riordan, Matthew Riordan. Please don't be frightened. I just want to ask you a few questions about something that happened a long time ago."

His voice quavered. "Come in."

I followed Gore into a living room that was a dark gloomy

cave. I had to stop for a moment to let my eyes adjust. Heavy shades were drawn across the windows, and the walls were covered with wooden bookshelves and ancient dusty books. The beamed wooden ceiling was almost black from varnish that was probably a hundred years old. The heavy furniture dated from the 1930's or 1940's. The smell was of dust and wet wool, old food, and dogs. I pushed aside a pile of papers and clothes to clear a space on one of the sofas. I found a lamp on a side table and switched it on. Only one of its two bulbs worked. In the half-light from the lamp I could see old photographs on the mantelpiece, black-and-white portraits of a younger man and woman, probably Gore and his wife. There was a black-bordered color photograph of a young man, perhaps seventeen, in an army uniform. It was the kind of photo the Army gives to the families of soldiers killed in war. There were other photographs, of a middle-aged woman, probably a daughter, and her children. Gore must have taken no comfort from his pictures: they were scattered at odd angles and coated with dust.

There was a wooden cocktail table between the sofas, piled with dusty books and magazines. Two half-eaten plates of food, of indeterminate age, were flanked by a nearly empty half-gallon bottle of Jim Beam.

"I'm sorry," he said when we were seated. "My wife died."

"I understand. I'm sorry, too. The reason I came here, Professor Gore, is because of a man named Anton Petrov. He was murdered last month in New York City. Before he died, he told me about the night that Margaret Jura was killed, a hot summer night in August 1939. You were there at a party. You were a graduate student at the University of Washington then. You testified at Anton Petrov's trial. Your testimony probably sent him to prison."

The old man stared at me, his eyes wide with something like fright. "Petrov? Dead?" he asked.

"Very," I said dryly. "Shot through the heart." I took out a volume of the trial transcript from my briefcase and opened it to a dog-eared page. "This is your testimony from the trial. You told the court that Petrov had walked out of the party with you and Marion Lichter around eleven or eleven-thirty on the night Margaret Jura died. You said that Petrov kept going, toward the University Bridge, while you and Lichter stopped to have a drink. You said you saw Thayer leave his houseboat and walk toward the party. Petrov says that the three of you went across Portage Bay Lane and found a quiet spot under the trees on the hill where you all smoked some marijuana."

"I didn't smoke any marijuana."

"Of course you did. I talked to David Campbell a week ago; he says that the police knew that there was grass at the party. They were asking a lot of questions about that, typical 1930's reefer madness hysteria. Campbell said he told you to deny you'd even been with Petrov, much less smoked marijuana with him. And that you did just that."

Gore looked away from me and stared into the dark corners of the room. He had gotten used to the dark, and took comfort from it. "All this happened so long ago," he began, "and I can't remember these things. Being young seems like a dream to me."

"Of course you can remember," I said sharply. "You don't want to. You're afraid you'll die with it on your conscience if you remember."

He turned back to me. His eyes seemed to be trying to focus. "Who are you?" he asked desperately. "Why does this matter?"

"The quality of memory matters," I said quietly. "It mattered to Petrov. He was killed because he wanted people to remember that his paintings were his. If he was innocent, if he didn't kill Margaret Jura, that should be known. You caused him to spend thirty-two years of his life in prison. Honor him now."

The single light in the room cast shadows onto Gore's face, so that I could not read his expression, but his voice was full of pain. "I was young," he said hollowly. "I had a life. Do you know what a drug conviction would have done to me? I could never have taught, never have done the work I wanted to do."

"I know you were afraid then. I can understand that. But why are you afraid now? No one can prosecute you for what you did. Tell me what you saw."

His attention seemed to drift. His big hands, gnarled with age, worked for a moment. He rubbed his face with them, hard. I leaned forward.

He slowly pulled himself together, willing himself back to life. When he took his hands away, his eyes were focused and his face had hardened into a mask. "I saw exactly what I said I saw in the trial," he said harshly. "Now get out."

"Please," I said. "If not for Petrov, then for the woman who was killed so young. Let the truth come out."

He shook his head. "She was a slut," he mumbled. "Worthless. She could draw a little. So what." He lapsed into silence. I fought back a sudden surge of anger. Why do some men think they can judge and pronounce sentence on women who don't conform to the roles men set?

Gore trembled. His voice emerged at a high whining pitch. "Get out, get out of my house!" He lurched forward, his body loose and uncoordinated, as though he were drunk. He seized my arm with both of his hands and tried to pull me up. I broke his grip and shoved him, as gently as I could, back down on the sofa.

"I'm going," I said quietly. I picked up my briefcase and walked toward to the door. "But let me say this much. I do hope there's a hell, Professor. It would be the only proper place for the likes of you."

I left him and the house and paused in the front yard. The clear prairie sky was the same cheerful blue, the leaves on the birches and elms were still bright gold and rust. And none of it seemed to matter at all.

Later that day I waited for over three hours in the passenger lounge at O'Hare Airport in Chicago, getting up every twenty minutes to telephone the home of Marion Lichter's daughter. Paul Schaeffer had said that he was living there, in retirement.

At eight o'clock I gave it up and checked myself into the O'Hare Airport Hilton, an enormous concrete box conceived for the sole purpose of collecting travelers who had missed airplanes and converting them into dollars. I spent what was left of the evening in an ersatz London pub located in the basement concourse that connected the hotel to the airport, morosely drinking a little scotch that had come out of a steel barrel and tasted like it. I watched a videotape of last Sunday's Chicago Bears game and tried not to think about what I was doing, or why.

In the morning I reached Lichter's daughter and got directions to their house, in the leafy suburban town of Elmhurst. I rented a car and fought my way through O'Hare traffic to the tollway. The tollway cut through a corner of Chicago itself. At the city limits a sign read, "Welcome to Chicago, A Nuclear Weapons Free City." Go and check, the sign is there. They're proud of it. Probably because nuclear weapons are the only kind they don't use in Chicago.

Lichter's daughter lived in a 1920's vintage brown brick Tudor house on a quiet side street called Kankakee Avenue. I pressed the bell in front of the arched oak front door and waited, then pressed again.

She answered the door on the second ring, a handsome woman in her early forties. Her hair was dark and she looked haggard.

"Come in," she said. "I'm Mary Breitenbach, Marion Lichter's daughter." I followed her into a sparsely furnished but spotlessly clean living room. As soon as I was seated she hurried into the kitchen to get coffee. There were framed modern-art posters hung on the living-room walls. There were pictures of healthy teenagers on the mantelpiece, but none of a husband or family group. She was, I guessed, divorced recently enough for the pain to have stayed fresh while she lost herself in a world of dating and weekends with new men when the children could be farmed out to the other, reluctant spouse.

"Are you all right?" I asked when she had returned with a tray containing English coffee cups and a small porcelain pitcher that she placed on a low wooden coffee table. "I can come back if you like."

"I don't know if there will be a better time, Mr. Riordan," she replied, pulling a wooden chair over from the corner of the room so that she could sit across the table from me. "Dad went into a nursing home a couple of weeks ago after a mild stroke. I thought he'd be better off with a trained staff nearby in case his condition didn't improve."

"How is he now? You said over the phone that he was ill."

"Much worse, I'm afraid. He had a second stroke last night. This one was somewhat more severe. He's quiet now and not in any immediate danger. But I don't know how much his condition will improve." She got up, took a cigarette from a box on the fireplace mantel, and lit it. She waved away the smoke like someone who had not smoked in a very long time and was embarrassed by it. "I don't know if he's going to be able to talk with you. The doctors said his speech center was affected."

"I'd like to try," I said, "even if it's for only a few minutes. Your father was a witness in a murder case that happened nearly fifty years ago. His testimony provided the alibi for the grandfather of a client of mine and sent another man to prison. If he can tell me what he saw, I might be able to reassure my client that her grandfather was in fact innocent."

"Why does it matter to your client? This case is so old."

She needed reassurance about what I was doing, and I tried to look properly lawyerlike. "My client's grandfather was a very famous man," I explained. "She doesn't want his memory called into question without proof."

Mary Breitenbach stubbed out her cigarette in a small dish. "I suppose we can try," she said. "The doctors said I could see him about noon. Could you drive me? My son has the car today, he has to go to work this afternoon."

"Of course."

I waited while she cleared away the coffee things and got herself ready to leave. My stomach knotted and refused to let go, reacting either to the bad scotch I'd drunk the night before or to the tension I was feeling. Lichter was the last possible witness.

The hospital and nursing home was on the other side of Elmhurst, close to the interstate. It was a flat-roofed one-story building of painted concrete block, as undistinguished as a warehouse. Which is precisely what it was, a warehouse for the old and the ill.

The inside was no better. Harsh fluorescent lights glared off linoleum floors. The cleaning crews were working that morning and old people lay strapped into their beds in the hallways while their rooms were being swabbed out. The omnipresent nursing-home smells, disinfectant and denatured alcohol, bad cooking and urine, filled the air.

Lichter was in a room in the hospital wing, hooked up to the usual monitoring equipment. The sheets had been turned down and he was lying with an IV in his arm. A catheter tube snaked under the sheets. He was a runty man with steel gray hair and a stubborn chin. He had been a police reporter and a sportswriter. I had no problem imagining him reporting on a hockey game, a drink in his hand and a cigar in mouth, hitting a typewriter, working on deadline. But his eyes were wrong, too wide, too impossibly blue.

"Daddy," Lichter's daughter said, drawing a chair close to the bed. "Can you hear me?"

Lichter nodded. His throat worked and he swallowed. "Daddy," she continued, "this is Mr. Riordan. He's come all the way out from Seattle to see you. He wants to ask you some questions about something that happened a long time ago."

I leaned in close to Lichter's face. His daughter edged away and took his hand, pressing and stroking it. "Mr. Lichter, I'm Matthew Riordan. I want to ask you about the death of Margaret Jura. It happened during a party at the Portage Bay houseboat moorage, in Seattle, in August 1939. You were there. Do you remember what happened?"

His throat worked again and his head moved slightly. I wasn't sure if it was a nod or not. I kept trying.

"You told the police that you hadn't seen Anton Petrov that night, but that you did see Lee Thayer and Margaret Jura leave Thayer's houseboat. You said that you saw Thayer go toward the party and Margaret Jura walk the other way, toward the bridge. Do you remember?"

No response.

"Please try to remember," I said, surprised at the urgency in my own voice. "Please."

No response.

I picked up my briefcase and rummaged through it, searching for the photo of Margaret Jura. When I found it, I helped his daughter raise the bed so that Lichter was propped up to see. "Here she is," I said, holding the picture in front of him. "This is the woman who was killed. Do you remember her?"

His eyes seemed to focus. He stared at the photograph of Margaret Jura, almost as if he were looking into her wide clear eyes.

Lichter's mouth worked. His blue eyes suddenly filled with tears.

"Please," I begged him. "Do you remember?"

He nodded once. The tears ran down his stubbled cheeks. Then the eyes lost their focus and became as innocent and un-knowing as a child's. I pleaded with him again, then once more, but his eyes remained fixed on the ceiling.

I sighed. Lichter's daughter said, "I'm sorry."

"It's all right," I told her.

We left the room. I waited while she talked with the doctors. I drove her home and thanked her for her time.

An hour later I was back at O'Hare Airport, waiting to board a Northwest 767 for home. For lack of anything better to do I sorted through the work I had brought in my briefcase, dictated letters, and read a deposition in another case that would come to trial soon. I wanted a drink. I felt numb.

It was over. I had run out of questions, and of old men to put them to.

23

Lisa Thayer called me in the third week of October, on a dark Friday afternoon of hard rain.

"It's me," she said quietly. "How are you?"

"Neither bad nor good," I replied. "You?"

"All right."

"I'm glad you called," I said. "Even though I'm not sure that I have anything to say."

"I don't blame you for being angry."

"I'm not. I'm hurting some. No, that's not right. I just feel . . . burned out, I guess."

"I understand. Can you come down here?"

"Lisa, I don't think that would do any good. I don't question the way you feel or your right to feel the way you do about me. You don't owe me anything. I still don't think that I was wrong. We each did what we thought was right. Let's leave it at that."

"Matthew," she said urgently, "please. I need you to look at something with me. And to tell me what to do."

"What's this about?"

"I don't think I should talk about it over the phone. After all that's happened—Shit, I'm scared."

"I'll come," I said quickly. "But I'm not going to try to tell you what to do. I don't have that right."

I hung up. I took my raincoat from its peg on the office wall and went down the outside stairs to the parking lot. The rain had stopped and the clouds were breaking up, but the afternoon was still dark. Across Lake Union dense pillows of fog rolled over the lower part of Queen Anne Hill to cover the lighted office towers downtown.

I had to force myself to get in my car. I did not want to see Lisa Thayer. I wanted to prescribe myself a tall beer and a sandwich in a quiet bar and then home to read in front of the fire. But Lisa had said she was frightened.

I found a parking place on Second Avenue, across from Lisa's gallery, and splashed across the street. It was almost six o'clock and the other stores and galleries had gone dark.

When I walked in the front door, Lisa was standing beside her desk in the back, talking on the telephone. She wore a simple dark suit, but her long legs gleamed in the bright lighting of the gallery. She waved once and turned back to her telephone conversation. With her free hand she made a pushing gesture, palm out and fingers up, that I knew meant that she was trying to end the call. Sometimes what hurts the worst are the small things you remember about a lover.

I turned to the pictures on the walls. Lisa was showing the work of a woman from L.A. who painted in a style reminiscent of David Hockney: outsize swimming pools and pink houses, the sprinklers hissing on summer lawns. They were big bright ironic pictures and I liked them, but not well enough to hang one in my home.

Lisa dropped the phone in its cradle and walked out to meet me. She put a hand on my arm and kissed me on the mouth, halfway between a lover and a friend. I stiffened. She pulled back. "Sorry," she said. "Not such a good idea."

I took a deep breath. "No," I said. "Not such a good idea. Not now, anyway."

She nodded. "Did you find out anything?" she asked. I didn't need to ask her what she meant.

"There were only the two witnesses," I replied. "Gore and Lichter. Gore is a bitter old man, living behind drawn shades in a dark old house filled with trash. He's lost his wife and his son and the last thing he wanted to do was talk about the killing of Margaret Jura. The other one, Lichter, had a stroke. I showed him a picture of Margaret Jura. He broke into tears but he couldn't talk. He died three days after I saw him."

She was silent. I said, "You asked me down here. Why?"

She gestured toward the back of the gallery. "Let me show you something."

We walked through the archway into the back room. She opened a drawer of her desk, took out a glassine slide folder, and handed it to me.

It held a plain white five-by-eight-inch postcard. On the front there was a painting in ink and gouache of a bird and a brass jar or urn. The bird had broken free of the urn and stood beside it. The painting had been done in a quick, sure hand and washed with color.

I looked up. Lisa met my eyes and said, "Turn it over. There's an address on the back."

I did. The address was a rural free-delivery route number and the name of a road, written in ink in square block printing. It had been postmarked in Prosser, Washington, at 11:00 A.M., two days before. The word "Harlan" had been hand printed at the bottom of the card.

I put the postcard back in the glassine envelope and placed it carefully on Lisa's desk. "What can you tell me about the painting?" I asked.

"It was painted less than a week ago," Lisa replied. "And it's good."

"I'll take you there," I heard myself saying. "We should leave very early tomorrow morning."

24

We drove over Snoqualmie Pass a little after seven in the morning. The sun had just risen over the Columbia basin, streaking the heavy mountain fog with bands of salmon and gold. As we rode down the eastern slope of the Cascades the fog flowed like streams of water and settled into pools in the pinewood and alder canyons, where the trees were ablaze with the colors of autumn. The sun rose higher as we passed through the green irrigated valley lands around Ellensberg, then skirted the desert ridges of the Saddle Mountains. At Yakima we turned south and followed the Yakima River between golden hillsides of cheat and bunch-grass interspersed with the dark green vineyards that had been planted in the rich volcanic soil.

We stopped for breakfast at 9:30 in the old farming town of Prosser. Prosser was shaded streets and old houses filled with the children of Hispanic farm workers. Their influence and hard work showed in the newly painted stores on Main Street. The signs in shop windows promised low prices in both English and Spanish.

Beside me in a café booth, Lisa fiddled anxiously with a plate of scrambled eggs and ate almost nothing. She feigned interest in a copy of the morning Yakima paper for a few minutes, then tossed it angrily on the table.

"Look," I said gently. "We don't know who is going to be there or what they are going to say. We don't even know if it is your grandfather. So I think we had better not rush things."

"I know," she said miserably, the pain of waiting showing plainly on her face. "But I am just so damned afraid. What if this is another fraud? Or somebody playing a joke? I don't think I could take that." Her blond hair was pulled straight back into a simple ponytail, but she kept patting it nervously, as though it were out of place.

"It's almost ten o'clock. We'll leave in about fifteen minutes. From the post office delivery number I'd say the place is about a half hour west of town, on the side roads across the river. So hang in there. It won't be too much longer."

A short time later we were back in my car, wandering along the dirt roads that connected the farms and vineyards on the south side of the river. The sun was overhead now, bringing down the prickly heat of a late Indian summer on the edge of the inland desert. Late-season flies buzzed angrily alongside the car. We drove slowly, leaving a cloud of dust behind us.

Lisa was the first to spot the mailbox. The name "Harlan" had been carefully lettered in a fine draftsman's hand on both sides of the box. A side road led us toward the river through a shaded tunnel of cottonwood trees.

We stopped and walked the last hundred yards along the gravel road. At the end of the road a plain, turn-of-the-century farmhouse, painted blue with white trim, stood beneath a grove of oaks and alder trees that shaded it from the fierce valley heat. The Yakima River flowed behind the house, low in its course, waiting to be replenished by late-autumn rains and winter snow.

A small vineyard had been planted in front of the house. We saw a tall man with wide strong shoulders and white hair setting fence posts at the far side of the vineyard. He was working with a two-gripped post hole digger. He looked to be in his seventies, but his flat, slablike muscles worked smoothly beneath his sunburned skin. He drove the post hole digger into the ground, grunting with effort as he pulled the plug of earth out of the hole. He looked up as he turned to put the plug of dirt to one side. It was Elton Lee Thayer.

Lisa stood rock still beside me. She made a sharp rushing gasp as she looked at her grandfather for the first time in more than ten years. The old man looked calmly back at us. He raised a hand as if to wave, then thought better of it and reached down for a towel that hung from the barbed wire of the new fence. When he had dried the sweat from his chest and neck, he took a blue denim workshirt, put it on, and began to walk toward us.

When Thayer reached us, he stood in front of Lisa and looked at her carefully. "Hello," he said huskily. "I . . . Lisa, I am so very glad to be seeing you again at last. I hope you believe that."

Lisa stood mute, staring at him. Tears rushed down her face. She made no effort to brush them away. Finally she took one of his big, work-hardened hands in both of her own. "Why?" she whispered brokenly. Then she stood straighter and spoke firmly as she looked the old man in the eye. "Why?" she demanded.

"I'm afraid that is going to take some explaining," Lee Thayer said dryly. He squinted up into the hot cloudless sky. "Come," he said. "Let's get out of this heat. Explanations take a lot of time."

Thayer took us to a garden table beside his farmhouse, beneath the shade of an ancient, dusty oak tree. He called out in Spanish and a small, elderly dark-skinned woman brought out a bowl of ice and pitchers of water, lemonade, and beer. Thayer put ice in a glass, filled it with water, and handed it to Lisa. I poured myself a small glass of beer and caught Thayer watching me. I returned the old man's stare. He looked much like Lisa, allowing for the bluntness of male features and the ravages of age. His face was long and narrow and his eyes were the same intense gray blue. "You're Riordan, aren't you?" he finally asked. His manner was neither hostile nor friendly. I nodded.

"I understand you killed that man who put the bomb in Lisa's car," he said slowly. "I want to thank you for that. If you're the kind of man I think you are, it would not have been an easy thing."

"I did what I had to do. I was trying to find out what had happened to you. I was trying to keep your granddaughter from getting killed." I looked into his eyes, so very much like Lisa's. I was looking for something, but I wasn't quite sure what.

"You did a good job of that," Thayer was saying. "I think that means you've got a right to hear me spill my guts."

He turned back to Lisa. "I can't tell you the why of anything, Lisa. I can only tell you what I did, and what my reasons were. Then you have to judge." He took the water pitcher and poured himself a glass, drank enough to wet his throat, and began to speak.

"In 1977," he said, "I was sixty years old. I wasn't able to paint, I was estranged from my son and his family, and I was an alcoholic. I did a fair amount of thinking and decided to end my life. I did not wish to live as the useless person that I had become. I made my decision at my fishing lodge, out on the Olympic Peninsula. I took my time about it. I've always been melodramatic, and having decided to kill myself, I began to enjoy myself, in a perverse way. I did a fair amount of drinking, and very late in the afternoon I drove out to Neah Bay to buy some more bourbon from the bootlegger on the Indian reservation. I lost control of that black Jaguar I had and slid into a skid, somewhere around seventy miles an hour. I pulled out of the skid but ran out of road. And the car and I went sailing out thirty or forty feet into the Strait of Juan de Fuca."

"Had somebody tampered with your brakes?" I asked.

"I don't know, I didn't use them. I had suicide in mind and that time was as good as any other. Anyway, when I went over, the car door flew open and I went with it. It seemed like I fell for hours before hitting the water. And the damndest thing happened. I studied Zen, you know, for many years. In all that time I never reached the state of self-knowledge, enlightment, that Zen teachers call satori. But in the split second between the car and the water, I found it."

Thayer paused and took another sip of water. "I blacked out in the sea, but somehow I got tossed up onto the rocks at the edge of the strait. I had a broken foot and a broken arm and couldn't climb all the way back up to the road. Somebody must have seen me go off the edge because an hour later a deputy sheriff came scrambling down the rocks, looking for the wreckage of the Jag. It was dark as hell, pure accident that he found me. But he did and he took me to the little clinic at the coastal radar station the navy used to have at La Push. While I was in the squad car, riding to the doctor's, I did some hard thinking. I was glad I was alive and felt at peace with myself for the first time in years. But I was afraid that what I had felt was created by my own near death. And I decided in that moment that I would stay dead."

He looked up at Lisa expectantly, searching her face for any sign of scorn, or understanding. "I expect that sounds crazy. But that was how I felt. I just had no interest in going back to the life I had led as Elton Lee Thayer."

"How did you manage to get the sheriff's office and the navy medical people to go along with you?" I asked.

"That was easy. I cut a deal with the deputy right in his patrol car. I gave him a thousand dollars, most of the cash money I had, and promised him two small paintings that Morris Graves had done years ago—I had them in the lodge—worth probably five thousand each back then. I claimed amnesia with the navy people. A year later that base got closed down, so I figured the deputy was the only one who knew."

"He's sheriff now," I said dryly, "but he stayed bought."

Thayer laughed. "My kind of honest cop," he said. "The navy clinic transferred me to a hospital down in Aberdeen, where I recovered from exposure and a mild case of pneumonia. I couldn't go back to my fishing camp because my death had already been reported. I holed up in a motel down in Copalis Beach and got in touch with Morris Kuehn. When he got over his surprise—which was considerable—he agreed to let me stay dead. He arranged for the Clallam County coroner to sign a death certificate and he lent me what I needed until he could divert some money from my 'estate.' Morris got me a phony set of papers, driver's license and social security card, all made out in the name of Harlan. I took about thirty thousand, enough to travel for a time and do some thinking. I bought a truck and wandered down the coast to California, then as far south as Mexico. After a while the money started running low and I drifted back north again. Somehow I wound up in Yakima. I started out there as a housepainter, which struck me as appropriate somehow. After a year or so at that I started designing and building houses, making pretty decent money. I worked for ten years, long enough to buy this little place."

Lisa shook her head. "I don't understand."

"I think I do," I said, turning to Thayer. "A little, anyway. The beam fell, and you got used to that, and then no more beams fell, and you got used to that, too."

Thayer grinned. "It's nice to know that people still read *The Maltese Falcon*," he said. "Pretty close, Mr. Riordan. Pretty close. With one exception. Even when I stopped drifting, I didn't want to go back to living the same life, because I couldn't seem to paint anymore. So I had to do something else, or lose my mind the way I had before."

"Like I have had to," Lisa said, her voice low. "I understand—some, anyway. But if you felt you couldn't work, why did you paint those two postcards and send them to me?"

"That came much later. A few months after I moved to this farm, about two years ago, I was talking to a friend of mine and wanted to describe how a certain hawk had looked at me one morning. Words just couldn't convey that and out of frustration I took a napkin—we were in town, having coffee—and drew the bird in pencil in about half a minute. Both of us sat there, stunned by the drawing. It was simple, just a few lines, but it seemed to capture exactly the things that I wanted to say. And that was when I thought that I might be able to paint again."

"But why send the first painting to Lisa?" I said, an edge of anger creeping into my voice. "You had your own life here—

fine, it's yours. You can work again—that's fine, too. But why push yourself back into Lisa's life, especially like that?"

"I'll concede that it wasn't the best way," he said stiffly, "but I had my reasons. I knew that my work was being faked—I get most of the gallery and some of the auction catalogs, and I'd seen over the years a couple of paintings attributed to me that were forgeries. One of them was lousy, but the other one was quite good—so good I was certain that Petrov had painted it. It was a joke among us, years ago, about how Petrov could imitate Tobey or Graves or me. Even though I thought Petrov had painted it, I believed that he hadn't been the one to take the painting and sign my name to it. That would have to have been a dealer. I knew I could expose the forgery just by showing up and tearing it off the wall, the way Graves did once, but as angry as I was, it wasn't worth it to me to come back into my former life. Then in the summer of this year, I saw the catalog for the SAM show, with three more paintings I thought had to be Petrov's, attributed to me. At that point I thought Petrov had to be in on it. So I painted the small bird and sent it to Lisa. I hoped that she would see that it was a message, and that she would understand it. If she didn't, if she thought it was a fake, then I thought she would consult Morris about it, and that Morris would tell her the truth." He sighed a little, tired from the long explanation. He took a long pull at his glass of ice water.

"I didn't understand the message, not right away," Lisa said, "but in hindsight it's pretty obvious. The bird emerging from a funeral urn. Birth. Or rebirth."

Thayer nodded.

"Kuehn sent the original version of that painting to the coroner in Port Angeles who signed your death certificate," I said, sarcasm in my voice. "The two of you must have thought it a wonderful joke."

"It was a bribe to that doctor." Thayer said, "He was very cooperative, when Morris got done with him. But Morris always appreciated the irony. I saw no harm in it. At the time I couldn't have predicted that all this was going to happen."

"There's still a lot of things that I don't understand," I said stubbornly. "Why didn't Morris Kuehn tell Lisa what was going on? And why in hell didn't you let Lisa know the truth sooner? She was damn near killed trying to find out who was forging your work."

"I know that. But I was afraid," he said, looking calmly at Lisa. "I was afraid of my old life, afraid that I would be forced to give up the serenity I had found here. It was purely selfish, and there's no excuse for it. Lisa, I can only beg your forgiveness."

Lisa stared at the old man. There was a curiously brittle expression on her face. "I think that was part of your reasoning," she said quietly, "but not all of it. You went to see Petrov, didn't you? You confronted him about the paintings."

Thayer was silent.

"Damn you," Lisa said suddenly. "I know you. You wouldn't have been able to resist. What happened between the two of you, anyway?"

"He knew the paintings were his, not mine," Thayer replied. "And it bothered him. He wanted his work recognized as his own. After I found him in La Conner and saw him the first time, he told me that the sculptor Hanks and that lawyer, Tabor, had come to him wanting to buy up all of his work, and Petrov was suspicious that it would all be sold under my name, eventually." He shook his head. "But I did make a mistake. I should have told Petrov to tell you everything."

"But that wasn't all that happened," I said.

Thayer turned and looked at me, a sarcastic smile on his face. "If you know all this, why are you here?"

"Don't evade me. You talked to him about Margaret Jura."

"Margaret has been dead for fifty years," he said, pain in his voice. "There wasn't anything to talk about."

I shook my head. "I don't believe you. Margaret Jura wasn't dead for Petrov, or for you. Each of you thought the other had killed her. Petrov told me that he dreamed about Margaret Jura for nearly forty years, until the day your 'death' was announced.

Then the dreams stopped. He wanted you dead. You probably felt the same way about him."

Thayer looked at me with rising anger. "We talked," he finally said. "I had very little choice, because Petrov sat me down in his studio the first time I saw him and pointed a shotgun at my chest and tried to force me to admit that I had killed Margaret. Eventually I was able to persuade him that I had not killed her. But his behavior made me start to think that perhaps he was not guilty either."

"And the two of you kept talking about it," I continued. "You kept meeting with Petrov. The last time you met out at your lodge, out on the Olympic Peninsula. I know because I came by a couple of hours after you left. You had cleaned up pretty thoroughly, but I could still smell the smoke from Petrov's cigarettes, and I found the place in the woods where you buried your kitchen garbage. What did you do? Go back over everything, put your memories together, try to reconstruct what had happened on the night she was killed?"

"Something like that," the old man conceded. "We tried. We couldn't find the answer."

He was still lying and I knew it. So did Lisa. She sat quietly, something like fear in her sidelong glance. Did she not want me to go forward? I looked hard at her, searching for guidance. I didn't find any. She was still afraid of knowing the truth.

"The police are still wondering," I said, "whether Morris Kuehn committed suicide or not. I don't know how much you know of what happened to him, but when they found him dead, it looked like a suicide. But the gun had been wiped clean of prints. Petrov didn't leave for New York until Monday morning, the day after Kuehn's death. Did Petrov want to kill Kuehn? A grudge, because he was wrongly convicted?"

"I don't think so," Thayer said carefully. "I think that Morris was killed by Tabor or one of his hired thugs, perhaps the same ones who tried to kill Lisa with the bomb in her car. In that respect, it's too bad that you killed that man Tabor. He could probably have provided that answer. I suppose there's little chance that the police will be able to find the hired killers."

"Very little," I agreed. I looked again at Lisa. She took a deep breath and nodded, telling me to go on.

"Let me tell it another way," I said. "You've been talking to Petrov, the two of you struggling to find out what really happened on the night Margaret Jura was killed. You made lists of the people you could remember at the party, compared your recollections. Petrov was drunk that night, he couldn't remember much, but you were reasonably sober. Both of you attended the entire trial, though, and heard the witnesses testify. You worked it over, again and again. It took a long time. Most of the people who were at that party are dead now, and even if they weren't, they had reasons not to talk. I know, because I went back through the trial transcript and talked to them and I couldn't figure it out. But then you came up with the one person who hadn't been asked to testify, who had never explained where he was that night. There was one piece of information that Petrov or you had in your mind but never thought was important. I don't know what it was. You'll have to tell me. But when you had it, you confronted Morris Kuehn with it on board the Black Ball Ferry to Victoria on the day before he was killed. I happened to be in Port Angeles on the same Saturday afternoon. I saw Kuehn get on the boat. Did Kuehn confess? Is that when the two of you decided to kill him?"

Thayer sat silently, his long, weathered hands placed flat on the table in front of him. He poured more water from the pitcher into his glass, then sipped at it. He was composing his answer. For Lisa's sake I hoped it would be the truth.

"It was the smallest thing," he said. "So obvious. Like the purloined letter, if you want to hide something, you put it in plain sight. Morris told me at the trial, told everybody, that he'd stayed at the party until around two o'clock in the morning. I never questioned that, even though I hadn't seen Morris at the party, because I remembered seeing Morris's Plymouth parked about fifty yards past the dock when I went over to David's around twelve-fifteen, just after Margaret left me. I didn't stay long at the party, maybe half an hour, and the damn thing went on until dawn. I went back to my boat and tried to sleep. I woke up in the night and listened to a storm rolling through, the kind of big summer busting thunderstorm you hardly ever get on the west side of the mountains." He paused and looked off into the middle distance, then shook himself slightly and resumed his story. "The night that Petrov and I talked for the last time, out at the lodge, we had the same kind of storm. We both couldn't sleep, so we stayed up, talking, and Petrov told me that one of the few things he remembered, drunk as he was on the night when Margaret died, was being woken up around three or four o'clock in the morning by that storm. And he remembered seeing Morris Kuehn's car parked near David's place, the top still down, filling up with water."

"I don't understand," I said. "Maybe Kuehn had taken a cab or a streetcar home, if he'd been drinking."

Thayer laughed hollowly. "People didn't worry about driving drunk in those years," he said. "Five bucks to the cop who pulled you over and you could sleep it off. Morris was fussy about his clothes, his cars, things like that. He would never have left his brand-new car sitting out all night, top down, in the rain. Not unless he was running from something, scared out of his mind." Thayer paused, his gray eyes full of sadness. "So Petrov and I went through it all, one more time. Morris was the only person at the party we couldn't account for at the time Margaret was killed. Morris hid it brilliantly, of course, but that was Morris. The judge ruled that Morris didn't have to testify because he was Anton's lawyer. And who would think to question the accused man's own lawyer, who had given up his job, maybe his career, to defend his friend?"

"What did you say to him when you saw him on the ferry?" I asked. "That's hardly the kind of evidence you could make stick, not with half the witnesses dead and the physical evidence long gone."

"We confronted him. He denied it for a time, but I think he

found it hard to lie to us after all the years. I told him that it was his choice. He could do the honorable thing, pay the price, or I would expose him. He knew there wasn't a thing the courts could do, but I could draw plenty of press. Resurrections, especially connected with a tale of murder, tend to make news. He knew that his whole life would be shown up as a lie. Old men care about their reputations, Mr. Riordan. They have very little else. I gave Morris twenty-four hours. By Sunday morning he had made his choice."

Lisa was sitting quietly at the garden table, tears running from her eyes. She wanted to believe him, wanted to believe that things could end with Kuehn's gentlemen's departure, no note, no scandal, the sacrifice made, the stolen life given back. I wondered whether she could ever forgive the next words I said.

"You're still lying," I said harshly. "Your story has two holes in it, gaping ones. First, it doesn't explain why there aren't any fingerprints on the gun that killed Kuehn. You shot him and then wiped off the gun. Second, you still haven't explained why you stayed hidden away here while Lisa was out risking her life to protect your reputation. You could have put a stop to the forgery scheme simply by walking into David Campbell's gallery and denouncing him. That would have ended any threat to Lisa, but it would have taken away the cover story about the forgery of your paintings. You wanted to stretch it out as long as possible because that way the police wouldn't even think of questioning you, even if they decided it was murder. They wouldn't know you were still alive. The murder would be blamed on Tabor or Hanks or Campbell, and when you made your return to your old life, you would be safe."

Thayer smiled sadly, his long weathered face finally showing its age. "Anton and I agreed that I would see that Morris kept his bargain. I flew back to the Seattle with Morris from Victoria late Saturday night. We talked a lot that night. Morris told me why he had killed Margaret. He had been her lover. He was supporting her; he was the only one of us who had any money." Thayer's voice took on a distant, sorrowful tone. "When I fell in love with Margaret Jura, it was the most sudden, powerful thing I'd ever felt. I didn't keep it secret from anyone, much less Morris. Yet he never said a word to me, the perfect friend. He was obsessed with the woman himself and he never said anything, just kept his emotion behind walls until he finally lost control. He lived much of his life that way. And I never knew it.

"Morris asked that Anton and I forgive him. I couldn't forgive him, but in an odd sort of way I tried to comfort him. I talked with him as one does with a dear friend who is in the presence of death. Perhaps it was the fact that Morris had loved her, too. In a way it made a bond among the three of us, loving the same woman."

Thayer paused. He took a deep breath, as if steeling himself for what he would say next. "In the morning, on Sunday, Morris and I went to his office. He took us in through the garage, avoiding the security guards. We had an arrangement: I was to wait outside his office and simply walk away when I had heard the shot. Instead I heard Morris calling me. He was sitting at his desk, in tears, the weapon in his hand, brutally ashamed. He could not pull the trigger. He asked for my help."

Tears suddenly ran from Thayer's eyes; he cried easily, as old men do. He looked at Lisa and spoke to her as if I were no longer there. "I went to my old friend and helped him up from his chair. I steadied him, one arm around his waist, and together we held the gun. I don't know whether it was the pressure of Morris's finger, or mine, that pulled the trigger."

It was over, the last piece fallen into place. I felt numb, used up. Lisa was stiff and silent with shock and dismay. Thayer was nervous. "Come," he said urgently, breaking the stillness. "Come with me, Lisa, please." He seized her hand, pulled her up from the table, and walked her down the path that wound through the center of the small vineyard, toward the low building at its far edge. I followed, blinking in the light, wondering what he wanted her to see.

The building he took us to was made of brown-stained planks, with large windows on the north side, facing the river. It had a steep red-painted metal roof. Thayer marched to the double doors and threw them open, then he stood to one side so that Lisa could go in.

The building was his studio. It was filled with paintings, done in a style I had never seen Thayer use before. The paintings were full of the arid light of the high desert country, rich yellows and sere browns and the silver of foothill rivers. There were powerful figures and symbols of horses and men, reduced and spare but still knowable. Lisa was stunned, then as excited as a child. She took her grandfather's hand and they walked back and forth, their eyes devouring the paintings that filled every wall and surface of the room.

I left them and stepped outside. I was still standing there, looking in, when Thayer gently disengaged himself from Lisa and came out to me. We walked together, away from the studio, to a gentle rise that overlooked the studio, the vineyard, and the river beyond.

"What will you do now?" I asked.

"That depends a great deal on you, I think," he replied. "After Morris was dead I knew that someday I would have to show my work again, under my own name. And you're right, Mr. Riordan, Anton and I put you and Lisa at risk to give ourselves the time and the cover to deal with Morris. I hope that you will both understand, and someday forgive me. If not, I'm willing to make a confession."

I thought for a moment. What he had said at the last, about how Morris Kuehn had died, could never be proven, one way or the other. But it had the feel of truth. I knew Lisa wanted to believe him, and now I wanted to believe, too.

"When I talked to Petrov in New York," I said, "he told me that he needed to check with someone, to confirm that I could be trusted. Why didn't you tell him to talk to us then? A lot of this could have been avoided. And it might have saved Petrov's life."

"I did tell him that," Thayer replied. "I told him to tell you everything. But they killed him before he could see you the next day. After that I knew things had gotten out of control. I was afraid that if I came forward, it would increase the risk to Lisa. I had to trust and hope that you could do the right thing. And you did." He turned to look at Lisa, who stood at the door of the studio, watching us. Thayer turned back and saw me looking at Lisa. "You do love her," he said gently.

I smiled, trying to hide the sadness. "But she does not love me," I replied. I put out my hand. "Welcome back to the world, Mr. Thayer," I said. He took my hand and we stood together, for just a moment, under the clear autumn sky. He went back to the studio, and I started to walk away. When I looked back, I saw them, standing together. I felt a small part of what a painter must feel. I had fumbled and failed and started over again, but I had at least a small part in creating this scene. That knowledge eased the pain that came with knowing other truths.

I turned away and walked slowly through the vineyard, heading home.

ABOUT THE AUTHOR

FREDERICK D. HUEBNER is an attorney and the author of three other mystery novels featuring Matt Riordan. He lives in Seattle.